Richard Stuart Wood,
Monken Hadley in H
than thirty years in the
in Cornwall.

A lifelong country-lover and active participant in a wide
variety of sports, he now divides his time between writing
historical novels, painting in water colours, playing golf, and
walking the Cornish coastal footpath.

The Rose of St Keverne is the sequel to his first novel, *The Riding
Officer*, which is also available in Bantam.

THE ROSE OF
ST KEVERNE

Richard Stuart Wood

BANTAM BOOKS
TORONTO · NEW YORK · LONDON · SYDNEY · AUCKLAND

THE ROSE OF ST. KEVERNE

A BANTAM BOOK   0 553 17453 3

First publication in Great Britain

PRINTING HISTORY

Bantam edition published 1988

This book is set in 10/11pt Baskerville

Bantam Books are published by Transworld Publishers Ltd.,
61-63 Uxbridge Road, Ealing, London W5 5SA, in Australia by
Transworld Publishers (Australia) Pty. Ltd., 15-23 Helles
Avenue, Moorebank, NSW 2170, and in New Zealand by Transworld
Publishers (N.Z.) Ltd., Cnr. Moselle and Waipareira Avenues,
Henderson, Auckland.

Printed and bound in Great Britain by
Cox & Wyman Ltd, Reading

AUTHOR'S NOTE

Once again I would like to acknowledge the help so readily given by the Librarians at the Falmouth Library in producing appropriate background reading.

In seeking to achieve historical accuracy, the following books have been consulted:

Memoirs of the Bastille by Latude and Linguet
The Cambridge Modern History
The Chouans by Balzac
The French Revolution by Georges Lefebre
The Thermidorean Regime and the Directory 1794-1799
  by Denis Wronoff
The French Revolution, Napoleonic Era
  by Owen Connelly
Quatre-vingt treize by Victor Hugo
The Naval History of Great Britain by W. James
The Memoirs of Madame de la Tour du Pin
The Spencer Papers 1794-1801, Vol I

THE ROSE OF ST KEVERNE

Prologue

'I can't help that,' she hears him roar. 'I can't *possibly* leave without Rose!'

Words engraved on her mind as though cut with a diamond.

Other voices raised in protest. Zeph Curnow's urgent warning about the falling tide. A Scottish voice declaring, 'Then we're all as good as dead! Caught like rats in a trap.'

Plaintive cries of, 'Certain death for all of us . . .' 'They'll torture us for trying to escape!'

But then Ashley's voice again . . . strong, determined, inflexible . . . and to Rose sounding sweeter than a taste of her own St Keverne honey . . .

'I'm sorry . . . *but I cannot leave without Rose!*'

Gnarled, vice-like fingers grip the back of her neck. They are hurting. She is being frog-marched back to the imprisoning Château Fontanelle from which, only moments before, she was leading the escaping party to their freedom.

But even now, struggling furiously to get free, she distinctly hears the encouraging sound of running footsteps on the far side of the high château wall.

Ashley's voice again; commanding Zeph to 'sail without me if I'm not back in time . . .' and concluding with that final shout, 'D'you hear me, Zeph! . . . That's an *order*!'

The sound of running footsteps again! Is he coming for her?

More footsteps – different ones. Two people running; three people running! Sounds of confusion within the château walls. Muttered oaths; shouted orders – down there by the gate with the ironwork monogram on the top.

Still footsteps running. He *must* be coming for her!

Then, suddenly, flaring into the shadowy darkness of the night, the flash of an exploding flintlock . . . followed instantly by the sickening, heart-stopping *crack* of a musket shot.

'ASHLEY!' she screams, struggling afresh to get free. 'Oh, Ashley! . . . NO!'

In reply, a hand . . . seemingly the size of a deck-swab . . . brutishly clapped across her mouth. Impossible to scream; useless to struggle.

Goaded forward now – traversing the once immaculately kept parterre, up the flight of stone steps which half-circle that lily pond with its marble statuette of the Madonna and Child – that lily pond which held such recent and vivid memories of the patrolling, urinating soldiers. Forced along the broad, gravelled terrace until at last she is roughly impelled through the massive, porticoed entrance of the Château Fontanelle.

Flung down, finally, on the floor of the once elegantly furnished salon, now occupied only by the still-captive prisoners and their pathetic little bundles of straw bedding, it is little comfort to be immediately surrounded by a group of sympathizing Carmelite sisters. Among them she recognizes at once the girl she has come to regard as her rival for Ashley's love – the beautiful Alethea MacKenzie; she who possesses almost everything which Rose herself so singularly lacks: charm, poise, and an impeccable social background. Younger daughter of Sir Andrew MacKenzie, squire of Trevadne, that imposing manor house overlooking the tree-lined waters of the Helford River, Alethea MacKenzie knows exactly who she is and where she comes from – a knowledge and a truth which has been denied to Rose throughout her young life.

Now, faced with the grisly prospect of imprisonment in revolutionary, guillotine-overshadowed France – and as on countless former occasions of doubt or despair – Rose fingers the heart-shaped locket and fine gold chain which always adorns her neck. It brings her comfort; it gives her hope.

''It is a Toutin locket,'' he had said. He had said it while they lazed together on the sun-kissed, sea-washed turf above the cove at Porthoustock in Cornwall. Henri Toutin, master goldsmith, had workshops at Blois and Paris in the early part of the seventeenth century, he had told her, and the locket is probably quite valuable.

It is gold-enamelled, bearing in very distinct letters the monogram 'L de V'. It is hinged, so that it can be opened, and inside are two exquisitely painted miniatures – a man and a woman dressed, Ashley had thought, in the style of the seventeenth-century French aristocrats.

It is the only adornment of any value which she, Rose Roskruge of St Keverne in the county of Cornwall, has ever possessed. She cherishes it exceedingly. Many, many times she has fingered it, caressed it, clung to it . . . and wondered.

*   *   *

On the highest point of Rosemullion Head the lonely figure of a horseman sits astride his patient mount. For the thousandth time – whether it be in reality or in his mind – the horseman gazes out across the blue-grey waters of the English Channel.

The timeless tranquillity of his surroundings – the herring gulls gracefully wheeling and dipping beyond the cliff edge, the gentle wavelets caressing the rock-strewn shore below – is in bitter contrast to the anguish in his soul.

Out there, beyond the limits of that misty, early-morning horizon, and languishing in some disease-riddled, rat-infested French prison, lies the girl he loves.

But he is married to another.

With a suddenness suggesting a firm decision made – as one who can withstand a constantly recurring sense of shame no longer – he gathers the reins into his powerful hands, swivels his horse on its hocks, and then gallops off, back down the track along which he has just come . . .

*   *   *

11

CHAPTER ONE

To stake one's all on a single toss

Thrown to the ground, a tree-trunk of a knee in the small of her back, and an evil-smelling gag thrust into her mouth, Rose could do little further to resist. Forlornly she reflected that perhaps it was just as well. Had she been able to yell for help, it would inevitably have placed Ashley under an obligation to come to her assistance. And for his sake, most emphatically that was what she did *not* want. Almost certainly he, too, would have been captured. Yet another English head would drop into the gory basket . . .

Moreover, such an attempted rescue could only mean delay for the fugitives. And delay now at that little quayside, as Rose knew only too well, would certainly spell disaster. An overloaded lugger caught on a falling tide! There could be only one result; a boatload of pathetic fugitives, caught like sitting ducks and brought back to the château for the certain penalty of execution. Shot while trying to escape – or worse, their necks beneath the descending guillotine.

She was being frog-marched back towards the château when she heard the heart-stopping sound of footsteps running along the gravel path on the far side of the wall. Could it be Ashley! Was he, after all, coming for her? Oh, dear God! let it be him – despite all her unselfish thoughts for his safety – *let it be him!* – It could mean only one thing! *That he loved her.* And even if it meant they both must die, at least they would die together, sure in the knowledge of each other's love.

Then, more footsteps! – running along the same gravel path beyond the wall. Was it soldiers chasing Ashley – or was it someone else? Zeph Curnow, perhaps – and another; there seemed more than one. Were all three of them coming to her rescue?

Some kind of altercation was going on down by those ironwork gates, the ones with the indecipherable monogram above them. Angry voices shouting, 'Ah, Mon Dieu! Ouvrez! Vite! Vite!' – Noisy jangling of keys. Fumblings, cursings, swearings – and, seemingly, threats!

Then came the shot! A single musket shot – ringing out into the night above the general sounds of confusion – and seeming like a dagger in Rose's heart. Then an oath! – a full-blooded English oath! – cleaving the darkness. Ashley's voice! Oh, dear Heaven! let it not be Ashley's voice. Someone else's – but not Ashley's. Immediately, a scuffing, grating sound – like somebody stumbling, slithering to the ground. Footsteps still running . . . coming to an abrupt halt. Then the noise of something – like a sack of corn – being dragged over the gravel. A body! Oh, Lord, dear Heavenly Lord! *Let it not be Ashley!*

Mutterings, groanings . . . heavy breathing. Then the sound of that 'sack' being hurriedly hauled over the side of the lugger? Dare she hope! Or was she just imagining.

No time to speculate further. The commotion down at those huge iron gates was reaching a crescendo. Tempers fraying; threats mounting. Obscene oaths befouled the purity of the night. Was that lodge-keeper, Rose wondered, one of Zeph's friends also; was he deliberately feigning stupidity, fumbling with his keys and thereby delaying the soldiers from bursting forth on to that gravel path and capturing the lugger and its occupants. Was he, in fact, buying time – at his own peril – to give the fugitives a chance to get away?

Whether or not he was, it soon became clear that, for the sake of his own skin, he could play the idiot no longer. Within the next few seconds Rose heard the creak of the gates being swung open and the unmistakable sounds of soldiers running along the path and clambering over rocks. Even as they ran, sporadic musket firing reverberated around the sheltered inlet.

13

She could picture the scene very clearly. The lugger, probably overloaded but under way at last, and with every stitch of canvas hoisted to obtain maximum speed, making for the mouth of the inlet and then the comparative safety of the Baie de Morlaix. Zeph would be at the helm; yes, Zeph would have to take the helm because only he knew the navigation of this rock-strewn coast. But where would Ashley be? Would he be taking command of the fugitives, making them keep their heads down, out of the soldiers' line of fire, while he and Sir Andrew MacKenzie, and Sir Andrew's brother as well, made ready to fire a little retaliatory broadside as the lugger slipped through the mouth of the inlet.

Or was he even now lying mortally wounded on the lugger's deck!

Dear God! Let it not be so, she prayed. And when a tear began to trickle down her cheek she quickly brushed it aside. This was no time to show weakness – especially in front of this inhuman concierge-woman who was holding her so roughly by the scruff of the neck and twisting one arm painfully behind her back.

Resolutely she refused to feel sorry for herself. She had got into this dangerous situation entirely of her own free will. No one had persuaded her; she could blame nobody.

But, when a sudden blaze of musketry from the rocky promontory conjured in Rose's mind the vision of 'Heather-belle II', close-hauled and running the gauntlet of fire as she made her dash for the open sea and ultimately the safety of her beloved Cornwall, then Rose could contain her feelings no longer. She sank to her knees, covered her face with her one free hand, and wept.

Immediately a brawny arm was hauling her to her feet again, propelling her forwards once more. In the new sacred order of 'Liberté, Egalité et Fraternité' there was no room for self-pity. All feelings must be subordinate to the needs of France. Enemies of the Republic could expect no mercy. 'Vive la Révolution!'

Dishevelled and tear-stained, Rose was unceremoniously

flung into the long room in which the Carmelite sisters and the other remaining prisoners lived and had their daily being. She would be dealt with later, the woman concierge implied.

That she presented a pathetic picture – sprawled there on the bare boards, her brown and white home-made habit torn and in disarray, her dark hair fallen over her eyes, her cheeks streaked with the marks of dashed-away tears – no one, not even the most antipathetic, could deny.

Certainly not Alethea MacKenzie. As soon as Rose was cast among her fellow prisoners, Alethea was at her side – kneeling down, cradling the prostrate figure in her arms, soothing her, and murmuring words of comfort.

How strange, Rose thought, that this lovely, high-born girl who had posed such an insuperable threat – as she had imagined – to her own love for Ashley should now be regarding her so tenderly. And tenderness it most certainly was that now filled those beautiful cornflower-blue eyes.

'What happened?' she asked, her voice suffused with sympathy. 'Tell me.'

'The man-like woman overtook me . . . grabbed me from behind,' Rose explained. 'I had no chance. But nearly all the others got away, I think.'

'My father . . . my cousins . . . and Ashley,' Alethea queried, 'do you think they are safe?'

Rose nodded. 'I think so . . . Indeed I hope so . . .' The sudden catch in her voice betrayed her uncertainty.

'There is some doubt?' Alethea asked.

'Only that there was a shot . . .' Rose faltered. 'And then there was a thud . . . a sort of scuffing sound . . . as though someone had been hit . . . had fallen to the ground . . .'

'And then what?' Alethea coaxed gently, sensing Rose's distress.

'Well, then there were footsteps . . . running. More than one person, I think,' Rose recollected. 'They stopped. And then it sounded as though they were dragging the injured person back where they'd come from . . . back to the lugger, I think. At least, that's what it sounded like.'

Again, that sudden catch in Rose's voice.

Alethea regarded the girl in her arms with compassion. 'Ashley, you think,' she suggested quietly.

Rose could do no more than nod. It was enough. Without another word, Alethea drew her closer; pressed the head of dark curls against her slender but compassionate breast; remained for several minutes gently stroking the back of the girl's head.

After a while she murmured softly, 'And you love him, don't you?'

Again, Rose could only nod. Again, it was enough. Without altering the soothing motion of her hand, Alethea went on, 'I can understand so well. Yes, I can understand.'

Drawing away and looking straight into Alethea's eyes, Rose asked, 'And you love him, too?'

Alethea, her eyes now veiled by the mists of nostalgic recollection, answered, 'Yes, I've loved him for as long as I can remember – ever since as a small boy he came to Trevadne to share a governess with me and my sister, Jeannie. He was such a lovely, sturdy little boy – even then. I fell in love with him on sight; his curly hair, his blob of a nose looking then as though it had been put on as an afterthought. It's grown into a fine nose now, of course,' she smiled, 'but then it used to fascinate me – tip-tilted and with such a cheeky 'insouciance', and yet such an air of expectancy. Oh, yes, – I loved him – as we all did – from the very first.'

'But not enough?' Rose asked.

Alethea's expression clouded, momentarily. Rose wondered why. But then it cleared again; the warm, forgiving smile returned, as she said, 'More than enough. I loved him then, and I shall love him always – but I know what you mean. Did I not love him well enough to become his bride? That's what you mean, isn't it?'

Without waiting for a reply, Alethea went on, 'Yes, there was a time when I believed we were meant for each other . . . childhood sweethearts grown to be mature, passionate lovers . . . you know what I mean. But then I came to realize . . .' She broke off; frowned, as though looking into herself. And then, gently patting Rose's hand, she added in a more cheerful tone, 'But there'll be more than enough time to talk of such things in the future, it seems.'

She got to her feet, drawing Rose with her. 'And now,' she said encouragingly, 'I must introduce you to Mother Eugénie and all these other good sisters of the Carmelite order . . .' She began speaking in French, fluently yet deferentially, to the rotund, smiling figure who had earlier been conducting the singing.

Then she broke off suddenly, and in some confusion turned to Rose, saying, 'My dear, do you know I don't even know your name. All I know is that you very bravely came with Ashley to try and save us.'

She turned once more to the Reverend Mother, explaining how it was that Rose came to be usurping the habit of a Carmelite sister, and although the Superior had difficulty in preventing her amusement from being too apparent, Sisters Cecile, Aloicius and Madeleine were quite unable to contain their mirth. They laughed merrily. 'Très amusante! Si drôle!'

The followers of St John of the Cross and of Saint Teresa of Avila could not have been kinder. They took the bereft Rose to their hearts straightaway, and although few only could converse in English, the language barrier quickly melted before the radiant warmth of their friendship.

And friendship was literally all they could offer; for the room in which they all dwelt contained no comforts beyond straw-filled sacks for bedding and such scraps of tasteless food as their hostile gaolers grudgingly offered.

But they were not dismayed. Had not the prophet of Mount Carmel himself, hiding by the brook of Cherith at the Lord's command, been fed both in the morning and in the evening with the bread and flesh brought by those compliant ravens? And when the brook had dried up, had not the good Lord sent his prophet, Elijah the Tishbite, to the woman who had nothing more than a handful of meal in a barrel and a little oil in a cruse which she was keeping for herself and her son so that they might at least eat something before they died?

And what had happened to that impoverished widow and her son? What had become of that barrel containing no more than a handful of meal and that cruse with such a modest supply of oil? Had not the Lord God of Israel, speaking through the mouth of his prophet, Elijah, promised that the barrel of meal should not waste nor the cruse of oil fail? And they had not.

Why then, if the Lord had taken such care of Elijah the Tishbite, why should He not care equally for the Sisters now following the Carmelite tradition? Through trial and adversity – as well as through mendicancy – their faith would sustain them.

And so, except during moments of contemplative devotion, they were merry company – singing often with the purity and sweetness of angels, yet never too serious to play practical jokes on each other. And that, of course, included both Rose and Alethea.

Even amid the squalor of their imprisonment – forced out of their convent at Morlaix, as they had been, to make room for a Jacobin club – they were never dispirited, never revengeful, always secure in the knowledge that the Lord would provide.

Rose wished she, too, could feel as inwardly fulfilled as did Alethea. Together, in those moments of blissful freedom when, under the watchful gaze of the guards and turnkeys, they were allowed to perambulate around the parterre in front of the château, they would talk with increasing intimacy of their cherished hopes for the future. For Alethea, it seemed, the height of her ambition was to become a novice of the Carmelite order.

'You may understand,' she said one day as they walked, arms linked, up and down the length of the herbaceous border at the foot of the terrace, 'when I tell you that I never knew a mother's love. My mother died soon after I was born, and although it may be difficult for you to comprehend, perhaps, I have felt all my life a deep emotional longing for a mother's love. And then, just when I seemed to be emotionally adrift and drowning in a whirlpool of uncertainty, I found the most extraordinary inner peace and tranquillity amongst these lovable Carmelites.' She turned her cool, clear blue eyes on Rose as she concluded half-apologetically, 'But then I can hardly expect anyone else to understand. My father certainly couldn't.'

After a pause, Rose said quietly, 'I can.'

Alethea gazed at her with renewed interest. 'You can?' she queried.

Rose nodded, staring at the gravel path beneath their feet. 'You see, I too lost my mother in childhood. In fact, like you, I never knew her – never even saw her. At least, that is, not so that I can remember her. The ship in which she and I were passengers was wrecked on the Manacles.'

The mutual loss of a mother in early childhood cemented the growing friendship between Alethea, daughter of the wealthy squire of Trevadne on the one hand, and Rose, child of unknown parentage and brought up in the cottage home of Sampson and Amia Roskruge, on the other. They became almost inseparable. Sister Aloicius, formerly sleeping next to Alethea, gladly made room so that Rose could lay her palliasse between the two of them.

Sometimes the two girls would talk long into the night – albeit in subdued tones but disturbing enough to cause Mother Eugénie every now and then to take Alethea to task for thoughtlessness towards others, a near-unpardonable sin for one about to embark upon a novitiate – but in the morning the benevolent Superior would spare the verbal rod, recognizing that both girls were far from home and that the pretty, dark-haired Cornish lass must be feeling more lonely than anyone, because she spoke no French.

Yet Rose was proving remarkably adept at picking up the words and phrases being spoken around her. Was it, she wondered, because she had French antecedents – or was it just that she was naturally quick to learn?

The Vicomte de Champèniers, whose slow-moving progress, together with that of his Vicomtesse, had been the reason for Rose's capture when fleeing for the waiting lugger, had given it as his opinion, when consulted by

Alethea, that Rose's much-valued locket was undoubtedly a 'Toutin', and that the miniature portraits inside bore a remarkable resemblance to members of the de Villecourt family formerly resident in the Lorient area. Unless his memory served him falsely, one branch of that family had left the country many years ago in search of greater religious freedom.

The strength of this intriguing information was somewhat diluted, however, by the guarded opinion of other aristocratic captives that the Vicomte's memory was frequently found to have played tricks with him. Nevertheless, Rose stored the Vicomte's words in her mind – and every so often she pondered them in her heart.

But the enforced inactivity of daily life in the Château Fontanelle was eating into her soul. For Alethea, delightful companion that she was proving to be, the contemplative routine of the cloister was clearly enough. For Rose, it threatened atrophy. Day after day went by – week after week. No news of the outside world; not a sound from Ashley. Nothing but confinement to that long, unfurnished room; monotony relieved only by the daily exercise periods in the gardens.

It was Sister Aloicius who suggested Jacques Dubois. Was he not still in touch with the smuggling fraternity – those 'gentlemen of the trade' whose patriotic duty could so easily be diverted by the gleam of pecuniary gain. And did not his cottage garden conveniently border the château's 'garden of meditation' in which the Carmelite sisters were allowed to perambulate unmolested during their daytime exercise? With the connivance of that same Jacques Dubois, might not some kind of message be transmitted to that very special person 'over the water' who had so bravely effected the rescue of Alethea's father as well as of others? Sister Aloicius found herself entering whole-heartedly into the role of subtle schemer. If, at times, she wondered whether the Almighty – and also the Mother Superior, for that matter – would entirely approve of her intended deceptions, she quickly smothered such doubts beneath the warm blanket of her affection for Rose. After all, she was doing no more than opening the door of the cage so that the little bird could fly out.

It will surprise no one, therefore, to learn that of all those held captive at the Château Fontanelle in the year of Our Lord, Seventeen Hundred and Ninety Three, the most frequent visitors to 'le jardin de méditation' were the gracious, high-spirited Sister Aloicius, the empyreally-minded Alethea MacKenzie of Trevadne in Cornwall, and the one-time Cornish barmaid, Rosie Roskruge, of St Keverne.

Spring was already bursting asunder the bonds of a joyless winter, and beneath the spidery branches of white-barked silver birch, wild daffodils, their petals still tightly furled, thrust yellow-tipped buds towards the pale sunshine. From the tree-tops came the joyful reminder that once again birdsong was coming back into fashion. The raucous 'caar' of the rook and the monotonous 'clack' of the jackdaw had given way to the tinkling twitter of the goldfinch and the rollicking cadence of the chaffinch, while even the companionable little redbreast had reluctantly yielded his winter-held sway to the triumphant notes of the blackbird. And every now and then the sombre hues of the lingering winter would be relieved by the darting flash of a yellowhammer. The garden of meditation, especially in the Spring, abounded with the urgency of bird-life.

It was Sister Aloicius' firm belief that the birds talked to each other in the dialect of the district. She was laughed at, of course, but she firmly maintained that the melodious notes of the blackcap and the garden warbler were lower and sweeter in the wooded areas around Saumur than ever they were in Northern Finisterre. Moreover, she was quite convinced that birds as a whole, particularly songbirds, were acutely aware of social status, and that young males coming into a new district with a different dialect had to learn that new dialect in order to be successful in finding a mate. Thus the females, when serenaded, would consider the timbre of the song when selecting the most socially acceptable partners.

After all, she claimed, did not St Francis of Assisi talk to the birds in their own language; might not, therefore, others of a similar propensity discover, in the solitude of the cloistered life, yet more divine mysteries of the universe? Some might think her mad, she would laugh, but although God had seen fit to withold from her the benefit of good looks, he had endowed her with a merry heart and a very acute sense of hearing.

It was that same highly-developed faculty that detected the sound of fork striking flint in the cottage garden of Jacques Dubois.

Sister Aloicius, Alethea and Rose were together making the most of the short time allowed them to promenade in the grounds of the Château Fontanelle by making straight for 'le jardin de méditation' as usual. At the welcome sound picked up by the sharp ears of Sister Aloicius they quickened their step. As they reached the rustic stone bridge fording the stream that meandered gently through the garden, the long-awaited sound was confirmed. Jacques Dubois was undoubtedly digging in his garden. He was separated from them only by the high stone wall.

Making sure that they were not being overlooked by any of the guards patrolling the grounds, and brushing aside protestations from her companions, Sister Aloicius immediately offered herself as the 'go-between'. One Breton-speaking accomplice to another, she felt, would hold out more hope of success. Using the clasped hands of both Rose and Alethea as human stirrups, Sister Aloicius scrambled up the wall so that she could just look over the top. Attracting Jacques' attention with a sibilant 'Psst!', she immediately gained his surprised response, and flashing her long-lashed eyelids at him – the good Lord had blessed her with most attractive eyes – she quickly had him agreeing to do whatever he could to assist the captured mam'selle anglaise to escape. He remembered her well. She was the one with the clever idea of the girdle-rope, yes?

By chance, it was a good moment to seek a favour of this kind. Robespierre's Reign of Terror was at its height.

Danton had just been guillotined, and the rumour was that the late King's sister, Madame Elizabeth, would very soon suffer the same fate. The country was becoming sick of the never-ending bloodbath. And Jacques Dubois detested Robespierre. Yes, of course he would help the little English lady to escape.

But first he must consult with his friends – to ascertain the best method of conveying a message to England. Now that the two countries were at war it would not be so easy, but he would do his best. The day after tomorrow he would make a point of being in his garden at the same time and he would then let the Sister know what success he had achieved.

He then shambled off, muttering that the good Sister should have a care. It would go ill for both of them, he and she, if they were caught talking to each other. The city of Brest was less than sixty leagues distant, and it was there that 'les saluds' had set up their infernal guillotine. Already, prisoners were being moved from Morlaix and St Pol de Léon to the prisons in and around Brest – never, he added darkly, to be heard of again.

But Sister Aloicius was not frightened. She calmly assured Monsieur Dubois that someone – one of the three of them – would be in the garden of meditation at the appointed hour two days hence, to hear what progress had been made and to transmit to Monsieur Dubois the message to be sent to a certain gentleman in England. Then she jumped down from her makeshift platform into the waiting arms of Alethea and Rose, the latter showering her with thanks for her boldness.

The three of them were then returning to the château, their precious allocation of promenading time having elapsed, when, upon turning the corner of the hedge surrounding the garden they found their way barred by a bayonetted musket. One of the château guards, it seemed, had been watching them from the shadow of a tree.

'Attempting to escape!' the prison governor snarled at them later when they were arraigned before him in the ornate luxury of the withdrawing room. 'And who is the ringleader?' He stared at them, like a snake about to strike.

Sister Aloicius was about to claim responsibility when Alethea quickly intervened. 'Non, non, citoyen. C'est moi.'

'Mais non!' Sister Aloicius contradicted. 'C'était moi!' She tried to push Alethea behind her, into the background, as far as possible from this weasel of a governor.

Unhesitatingly, Rose stepped forward. Under no circumstances could she allow these two unselfish people to take the blame for her. Making no attempt to speak in a language which even now she only occasionally understood, she declared firmly, 'No, sir. It is I. The responsibility is entirely mine.'

It had little effect. Immediately, the verbal wrestling broke out again. Simultaneously, Sister Aloicius and Alethea began protesting once again, and in a torrent of words not fully intelligible to Rose, that the mam'selle from England was *not* responsible; she was merely a spectator.

The prison governor, M. Belette, a petty despot promoted from bureaucratic obscurity in nearby Brest, prided himself on his astuteness. For several minutes he surveyed the three women sourly. He wondered what the Carmelite nuns wore under those unattractive brown habits. His mind constantly dwelt on such things. He contemplated using his authority to find out – by force, if necessary. But he had to be careful. His authority was derived from a former senior officer at the Hôtel de Ville, Monsieur – now Citoyen – Bousillier, recently promoted to the governorship of the more prestigious prison, the Château de Pontrechat, at Brest. And Citoyen Bousillier was extremely jealous of his position because not only was he in charge of all the émigré prisoners incarcerated within the confines of the Château de Pontrechat but he had also been given overall responsibility for his junior, Citizen Belette, at the Château Fontanelle, near St Pol. As a result, he expected certain favours from M. Belette; such as the transfer to the Château de Pontrechat of any desirable young females who might provide Citizen Bousillier with satisfying sexual opportunities.

He felt reasonably certain that Citizen Belette would be happy to comply with such a demand – for the very simple reason that not very long ago Citizen Bousillier had caught his junior, Citizen Belette, with his hands in the coffers at the Hôtel de Ville. Out of the kindness of his heart, Citizen Bousillier had kept quiet about the matter, deeming it possible the day might come when Citizen Belette would remember that one good turn deserves another. The advent of the Revolution had lifted both M. Bousillier and his junior out of the humdrum rut of clerical drudgery at the Hôtel de Ville and placed each one of them in situations of hitherto unimaginable power. It had also put M. Belette in a position to fulfil his tacit obligation to his senior officer, the governor of the Château de Pontrechat.

Citizen Belette, stroking his chin in lascivious contemplation, looked appreciatively at Rose.

'Hmm!' he mused, 'now *there's* a ripe little plum if ever there was one! And caught in the act of trying to escape, eh? Very convenient! Transfer her to the Château de Pontrechat "for reasons of greater security" – and for the governor to use as he chose – why, what better way to wipe clean the slate of moral indebtedness between M. Belette and his senior officer, M. Bousillier.' Those guilty hands once found in the municipal coffers at the Hôtel de Ville would surely be cleansed for ever if M. Bousillier were to indulge his erotic fancies with the pretty little 'anglaise' sent to him from the Château Fontanelle.

Citizen Belette picked his nose reflectively. 'Those two,' he commanded the attendant soldier, 'the Carmelite and the civilian, there – lock them up in the gun room.'

The dunderhead in uniform jerked his bayonet enquiringly in the direction of Rose and Alethea. 'Celles-ci?'

'No, no, you stupid pig!' the governor exploded, 'The real Carmelite,' he snapped, pointing at Sister Aloicius, 'and that one there – the English aristo.' He made as if to spit as he indicated Alethea. 'Do as I say. Take them away and lock them in the gun room. That'll teach them not to try to help others to escape.'

He picked the other nostril, contemptuously flicking the extraction over his shoulder. 'This one,' he went on, wagging a finger at Rose, 'the one so anxious to get back to England. I have other plans for her. She is clearly in need of a change of atmosphere. The sea breezes wafting over the Château de Pontrechat at Brest will do her much good, I fancy, and the surrounding walls are thicker and higher than anything we have here. It will provide her with a more interesting challenge.

'But even more interesting yet,' he went on, an evil grin slitting his weasel face, 'is the fact that my good friend, Citizen Bousillier, the governor of the Château de Pontrechat, just happens to be particularly fond of English ladies.'

'Oh, no, no!' protested Sister Aloicius. 'You must not send her to Brest, Monsieur – I beg you!'

'Silence, woman!' the weasel snarled, 'or I will send you there as well.'

'Send me in her stead,' Sister Aloicius pleaded, 'but do not send the young English maid!'

But Governor Belette, his face turning purple at the threat to his authority, shouted at the thick-headed soldier to obey his command. 'To the gun room, blockhead! – and lock them up!'

The dim-witted soldier then began herding the three women together, forcibly urging them towards the door.

'Not all three of them, you nitwit!' screeched the governor. 'Just those two, there,' he indicated, pointing accusingly at Sister Aloicius and Alethea. 'Celles-là! Can't you understand your own language, idiot!'

Like a suspect ewe – or a lamb earmarked for the slaughterhouse – Rose felt herself being physically separated from the flock. Governor Belette had placed himself between her and the only two friends she had in the world at this moment, and with no time for words of heartening encouragement or even farewell commiserations, Alethea and Sister Aloicius were bundled at bayonet point out of the room and down to confinement in the gun room.

Rose was left standing defiantly in front of Citizen Belette.

Few only of his words had been intelligible to her. But she had got the meaning of his instructions. She, it seemed, was to be transferred to another prison – a prison at Brest whose governor had a partiality for young girls, especially if they happened to be English, and from Sister Aloicius' outburst of protest, it seemed likely that the experience would be distinctly unsavoury. Governor Belette had not said *when* she would be moved, but Rose felt sure it would be sooner rather than later. She had but one thought in her head therefore when she was allowed to rejoin the rest of the captives in the long room, and that was to convey the crucial message to Jacques Dubois.

Time and opportunity were clearly limited. She might be moved from the Château Fontanelle tomorrow. Now that she had been forcibly separated from Alethea and Sister Aloicius there was no chance to make contingency plans. Somehow or other she must make contact with Jacques Dubois this very evening. But on her own, how could she attract his attention – even supposing she could escape for a few minutes to the garden of meditation. She could never hope to climb that wall on her own. And even if she still had possessed that once useful girdle-rope – long since cut down and confiscated – there was no convenient tree near Jacques Dubois' cottage garden on which to hang it. But *somehow* she must get a message to him before they carried her off to Brest.

She bided her time. She knew that at nine o'clock in the evening the Carmelite sisters would gather round their Mother Superior, and they would sing with that celestial sweetness which she and Ashley Penberth had first heard together nearly six months ago – their evening hymns of praise and prayer. She had noted that at such time the soldiers and that horrible concierge-woman were usually off their guard. That would be the moment to slip out of the château and race down to that blissfully peaceful garden of meditation. Just what she would do when she got there she had only the haziest of ideas. She would have to rely on the inspiration of the moment. She prayed that it would come.

When at last the Sisters were all gathered around their Superior – all, that is, except Sister Aloicius and the novitiate Alethea MacKenzie – and had burst forth into full vocal praise and adoration, Rose tiptoed along the passage to the head of the staircase, and looked down into the hall below. Her heart leapt with joy. The concierge-woman was nowhere to be seen.

Sidling out through the heavy oak doorway, she picked up the hem of her cumbersome make-believe Carmelite habit and ran for all she was worth. She arrived at the garden of meditation, breathless but bubbling over with hope. She had reached her objective – apparently without being seen.

But now what? She listened intently. Not a sound emerged from the other side of the high wall; not so much as the faintest indication that Jacques Dubois was in his garden – not even taking an evening stroll to inspect the progress of his vegetables, or enjoying a final sniff of the night air.

So, what could she do now? Foolishly, she chided herself, she had made no definite plan for such a situation. Her one aim had been to escape from the château and to reach the garden of meditation undetected, and before she was taken away to Brest. She had not stopped to think what she would do if Jacques Dubois was not in his garden.

But she *must* do *something*. It might well be her very last chance. But what? Certainly, she dare not call aloud. That would immediately alert the guards billeted on the nearby lodge-keeper. Feverishly she cast about in her mind for some means of conveying a message to Zeph Curnow's old smuggling friend, and through him, she hoped, to Ashley.

Suddenly an idea came to her. First of all she tore a strip of material from her underskirt. Then, deliberately scratching the forefinger of her right hand on a sharp flint, she squeezed enough blood to write the words – 'Prisoner at Brest'. It was a rough and ready message, but it was just readable; it would have to do.

After that, she found a large stone, and tied the piece of cloth around it. She was about to toss it over the wall, aiming it to land as near as possible to the back door of Jacques

Dubois' cottage . . . when she paused. Would a ragged piece of underskirt with a message scrawled in blood be enough . . . enough to tell the man she loved that it was she, Rose, who was now in such dire need of him! Suppose the message became blurred . . . unreadable . . . meaningless. What could he be expected to make of just a ragged piece of cloth?

Anxiously she fingered the locket and chain that, throughout her life, had meant so much to her and from which she had never been parted. Could she bear to risk sending this, her only precious possession, this jewel that had so often sustained her in moments of despair? But she had to be practical; at least it would leave him in no doubt about who had sent the message.

Quickly she untied the knot around the stone. Then, firmly, resolutely, she unclasped the gold chain, removed the locket and threaded the cloth through the suspension ring.

Rewrapping the cloth around the stone, she once again secured it with a knot.

Then, with a silent prayer to send it on its way, she tossed it over the wall.

CHAPTER TWO

Homeward Bound

Captain Euan Robertson, Master of the Packet Ship 'Elizabeth-Ann', leaned against the poop rail, cocking a highly-polished ankle-boot onto the rim of the wooden fire-bucket at his feet. Then, idly picking his teeth with a gold toothpick, he casually surveyed the passengers thrusting their way up the gangplank.

The usual motley collection, he concluded. Failures, probably, all of them; returning to the mother country, defeated by the rigours of colonial existence; glad to be going 'home' − even if it meant, as it almost certainly would, the spiritual suffocation of religious intolerance and the sordid enslavement of penury.

To the disillusioned colonist, for ever looking back over his shoulder, the retrospection of eighteenth-century England − despite its impenetrable barriers of class and its grinding poverty amidst glittering wealth − seemed preferable to the backbreaking toil of those five-acre plots of General Oglethorpe's 'Great Experiment'. Having suffered the death of his friend, Robert Castell, in a debtors' prison in England, the noble-minded General had decided to establish a haven for others, similarly in debt, by opening up a new colony in America just 18 miles upstream from the mouth of the Savannah River. The General's project had attracted much sympathy; the cash began flowing in; and in 1733, thirty-five families sailed with General Oglethorpe, landing at Charleston before moving on to Savannah and those five-acre plots granted to each family.

Captain Robertson knew the story well. At first, 'The

Great Experiment' had seemed a correspondingly great success. Repressed, debt-ridden families leapt for joy in their new-found freedom. Favourable reports filtering back to England soon brought others, similarly fleeing from the grim clutches of the Marshalsea and the Fleet prisons, and within six years of the original landing at Port Royal, the Savannah colony had grown to as many as five thousand souls.

But General Oglethorpe, a philanthropic, well-meaning man, had frowned on slavery and rum. Religious tolerance – yes; but no slaves, and no rum. He had high ideals; so had the colonists; but having come from backgrounds of severe deprivation, and after enduring the forty-three day uphill trip across the Atlantic in the bowels of an emigrant ship, they were short of stamina. Undernourished even before they left England, they found the hard, unfamiliar work in the fields more demanding than they had ever imagined. They began casting envious glances in the direction of the much older colony at Charleston where slaves were available and where there was always plenty of rum.

As a result, General Oglethorpe's philanthropic dream, which had flourished so encouragingly during its first six years of life, soon began to dwindle until the population was down to no more than five hundred. Indeed, it was only when the British had permitted the introduction of both rum and slavery that the fortunes of Savannah began to rise once more.

Captain Robertson's sea-tanned features twisted into a wry smile. Of those passengers now struggling up the gangplank of the 'Elizabeth-Ann' nearly all of them, he reflected, would have found colonial life, even in easy-mannered Charleston, a bitter disappointment. That 'great experiment' had proved to be a great strength-sapping delusion, an intolerable physical burden. Better now to cut your losses and return to familiar surroundings, they would have concluded – even if it might mean tails between legs, red faces and hangdog expressions for the homecoming.

As 'live cargo' they would have emigrated, bubbling over with hope and expectancy, their passage money of £5 each having procured for them nothing more than a place in which to cook, a supply of foul-tasting water, and an over-crowded, ordure-ridden area in the 'steerage' in which to eat, sleep and have their daily being.

And now, having failed to make a success of that great experiment, they were returning once again as 'live cargo', and in conditions little better than those of a slave ship.

Just a few of them, the Captain mused, would have been able to amass – by begging, borrowing, or even stealing – sufficient funds to purchase the luxury of a cabin, four feet, four inches by six feet, six inches of satinwood-panelled privacy and comfort. But not many, for aboard the 'Elizabeth-Ann' such cabins were indeed a luxury. Six only – three between the Dressing Room and the Master's cabin on the port side, the other three adjoining the Captain's Stateroom on the starboard side and aft of the Pantry.

But no passengers, neither 'cabin' nor 'steerage', were allowed on board until the 'Elizabeth-Ann' was fully loaded, and the turnround on this particular trip had been slower than usual. But from past experience, Captain Robertson knew how useless it was to try and hurry inhabitants of this enlightened but easy-going South Carolina seaport. They would take their time; even a slave-master with a whip could scarcely make them hasten.

And as for the emigrants waiting for a passage back to their native land – well, they would just have to be patient.

So, the 'Elizabeth-Ann', her massive bowsprit seeming almost to nudge the pantiled roofs of the waterside buildings, lay idly alongside the quay. Her tall, majestic masts towered silently above the colourfully stuccoed houses with their ironwork balconies and Venetian door and window blinds, while anxious passengers made frequent but fruitless enquiries about when the ship would sail.

Captain Robertson was not greatly concerned. All along Tradd Street, King Street and in East Battery there were elegant new houses, brick-built since the devastating fire of 1740, whose merchant owners were happy to entertain a Packet captain from England. They liked to show him their pine-panelled parlours, their combination living and dining rooms, their tall, banister-back chairs and their mahogany and pine secretary-bookcases with bird's-eye maple veneer and coloured rosewood borders. Upstairs he would be shown with pride to a guest bedroom resplendent with four-poster bed and draped with homespun linen hangings embroidered with colourful crewelwork. Downstairs again he would listen reverently to a reading from the Bible in the family's Keeping Room.

But it was not all reverence and polite appreciation. There were races; there were many balls and dinners; there were well-educated young ladies happy to escort him – suitably chaperoned, of course – to concerts performed by professional musicians and to regale him with all the news of the very latest Paris fashions.

And then there were the men's clubs – friendly, easy-going, welcoming – for, after all, was it not a sea captain who had brought from Madagascar less than a hundred years ago that package of seed rice which had founded so many Charlestonian fortunes. Wherever flooding was possible – two or three times a season, and achieved by raising the levee, damning a stream and creating a reservoir – a rice crop could be obtained. Wealth, abundant and undreamed of, had followed. As tobacco was to Maryland and Virginia, so rice had proved to be for Charleston. It created an aristocracy of planters and merchants; it fastened slavery upon the region; it enriched both town and countryside with expansive houses, imposingly pillared and gabled, and it made possible a life of indolent refinement for all the most prosperous families.

In short, Captain Euan Robertson was never bored by an enforced sojourn in Charleston. Not for the first week or so, that is. After that, he began to get irritable. It was time to move on. Although it might flatter his ego to be so hospitably entertained by southern belles and their exuberantly wealthy fathers, it did nothing to swell the contents of his purse, and now that the full consignment of cargo was securely stowed, it was time to bid farewell and make for the Atlantic ocean – even though it was a Friday.

So, he had let it be known that the 'Elizabeth-Ann' would sail with the tide that evening – and any who were not aboard by then would be left behind.

Some of the bolder passengers, hearing that he intended sailing on this traditionally unlucky day, tried to persuade him to postpone sailing until Saturday. But he would have none of it. 'Nothing but an auld wives' tale!' he had snorted contemptuously. The 'Elizabeth-Ann' would sail with the tide that evening, Friday or no Friday, and be damned to the superstitions of a gaggle of 'Live cargo'! It was the homeward run they would be setting out on – the 'downhill' run, so called because the prevailing winds blew from west to east, and the east-flowing Gulf Stream always helped a ship to make good time. Given reasonable weather, they should be entering Falmouth harbour in twenty-five days' time.

Thus ran the thoughts of the Master of the 'Elizabeth-Ann' while he watched the humble, the meek and the lowly – as well as the truculent and proud of heart – as they came aboard his ship. Just another bunch of unexceptional folk, he mused – a few of them successful in life, perhaps, but most of them broken-down failures. 'Live cargo', indeed! A very apt description.

The Captain continued to pick his teeth contemplatively. But then his attention was captured by the advent of a young woman – seemingly little more than a girl – mounting the gangplank with firm, sure-footed strides. She was quite strikingly beautiful. In her arms she carried a tiny baby wrapped in a shawl.

Increasingly, packet ships like the 'Elizabeth-Ann' were crossing the Atlantic to the rapidly developing colony of America carrying passengers of considerable renown – wealthy merchants, diplomats, international celebrities, and even well-known ladies from the London music halls – but Captain Robertson, canny Scot that he was, felt certain that the vision now coming up the gangplank – like an artist's dream of a 'Madonna and Child' – was no ordinary passenger.

That small, oval-shaped face, framed by the hood of her loose, sack-type quilted jacket with its long sleeves tight-fitting from the elbow downwards; that pert, yet proud, set of the head; the trim ankles, cased in fine cotton stockings and thrusting boldly from beneath the green Mantua silk gown and scarlet petticoat; the laced shoes, and that necklace bearing such a distinctive, oval-shaped locket.

Captain Robertson, having travelled the world, prided himself on his accurate perception of nationality. French . . . that was it, he concluded. Something about the fine bone structure, the slender neck, the elegant yet impulsive hand grasping the rail of the gangplank. And those large, expressive eyes.

Undoubtedly French, probably Huguenot, he thought. There were still many of them in Charleston. Driven out of France by Louis XIV's revocation of the Act of religious tolerance, the Edict of Nantes, they had fled to neighbouring Protestant countries, especially to the Netherlands and England, taking with them their industrious habits and manufacturing skills. Most of the refugees to England had settled around London and Canterbury, but there were also sizeable congregations at both Plymouth and Exeter in the flourishing serge industry and making the famous Passavant carpets. From these English communities came the four hundred and fifty or so French Huguenots, sent out in the late seventeenth century under the royal patronage of King Charles himself for the express purpose of cultivating wine, oil and silk. That they had failed signally was unfortunate but not catastrophic. Many of them found alternative and lucrative occupations – to which the colourfully stuccoed houses with their pink and deep purple pantiles, typical of the Bordeaux area of France, bore distinctive witness.

They had not all been artisans. Noble families – the de Chastaigners, the de Vervants among others – had bought estates running into thousands of acres, and it was from among blue-blooded families of that ilk, that the beautiful young woman now coming aboard his ship was descended – or so Captain Robertson surmised.

He pocketed his toothpick, descended the brass-inlaid steps leading down from the poop deck, and moved smartly to the head of the gangplank. He wanted to take a closer look.

As she carefully stepped off the projecting end of the plank, lifting the hem of her petticoat and displaying to even greater advantage the slender elegance of stockinged leg and ankle, the young woman fluttered her long-lashed eyelids shyly at the imposing figure of the Captain.

'Welcome aboard, ma'am,' he greeted affably, 'I trust that both you and the bairn will enjoy a pleasant crossing.'

'Thank you, Captain. I trust we shall.' The voice, though barely audible, was well-modulated and cultured. It bore only the merest trace of a foreign accent.

The Captain leaned forward, very gently drew back the edge of the woollen shawl, and purred appreciatively at the sleeping baby. 'Charming,' he beamed, with genuine admiration, 'Quite charming!' Wisely he refrained from tickling the soft, rosebud cheeks; instead, he transferred his gaze to the mother. With a rhythmical rocking motion she quietly cradled the infant in her arms.

'I assume, ma'am,' the Captain enquired politely, 'that you have already been acquainted with your cabin number?' He found himself looking down into a pair of cool, blue-grey eyes beneath finely-arched eyebrows. High cheekbones tapered prettily to a firm yet delicately pointed chin. Throwing back the hood of her quilted jacket, and with a slight flush colouring her milk-white skin, she half-turned towards him. With the merest shake of disavowal, she said simply, 'I have no cabin, Captain.'

Fumbling in the inside pocket of his braid-edged frock coat, Captain Robertson extracted his personal passenger list. 'Some mistake, perhaps,' he muttered into his beard. 'A misunderstanding at the agent's office, no doubt.' He quickly ran his eye down the list, confidently expecting to find at least one de Rochefoucauld, or de Villeneuve, or even just a plain Dubois. But no name on his list could boast even a modest French connection.

Frowning deeply, Captain Robertson went on, 'May I have your name, please, ma'am. I'm afraid I havena had the pleasure . . .'

'Smith,' came the firm, almost defiant reply. 'Mrs Lucy Smith, Captain.'

Captain Robertson cocked one bristly, ginger-coloured eyebrow in her direction. 'Oh, aye,' he said disbelievingly, 'Mrs Smith, d'ye say?' He scanned the names on his list of cabin passengers. There was no 'Mrs Smith'. Then he glanced at the much longer list of those travelling 'steerage'. Yes, there it was; almost at the bottom, 'Mrs L. Smith and infant daughter'.

The Captain stroked his beard, pensively. 'Oh, aye,' he murmured, as though speaking only to himself. 'So I see.' Once more, from beneath those ginger-coloured, shaggy eyebrows, he regarded the delicate beauty of the woman and her baby. He was thinking of the filth and stench that inevitably built up in the 'steerage' quarters during a long voyage; of the ever-present disease risk attendant upon mounds of uncleared ordure; of the cynical boast of some ship's captains of the day that they had more births than deaths among their passengers.

He let out an involuntary snort of disgust. Then, replacing the list in his inside pocket, he called to his First Mate, 'Mr Hanson . . . Be so good as to show this lady and her bairn to their quarters, if you please.'

He was about to remount the poop deck stairway when, pausing with one foot on the bottom step, he called back over his shoulder, 'And, Mr Hanson! Have a care. Remember the child is but a babe.'

He stood for a moment, watching the retreating figure of the woman. He noticed that the hem of her gown was frayed; that the heels of her shoes were worn down. And yet she walked proudly.

He climbed the remaining stairs to the poop deck; leaned against the rail once more, deep in thought.

*   *   *

Later that afternoon – that September Friday afternoon – the ship having been cleared of all visitors, company agents and port officials, the 'Elizabeth-Ann' was prepared for leaving harbour. Gangways were hauled in, head and stern ropes cast off, and slowly, under the watchful eye of Captain Robertson, the ship was towed away from the quay, swung round, and then pointed out to sea. Sails were loosed, let fall and sheeted home, and as they caught the wind and filled, the ship began to pull away majestically from the English colony of America.

On the Charleston quayside, small groups of relatives and well-wishers watched her until she was hull-down on the purple horizon. ''Tis bad luck to sail on a Friday,' they murmured among themselves. 'Cap'n should have waited until the mornin'. I told him so – indeed, I told him, and told him, and told him. But he'd have none of it. Swep' it aside, he did. ''Nothin' but an old wives' tale,'' he said, ''Nothin' but an old wives' tale''.'

And that, too, would have been the First Mate's opinion, had he been asked – except that, having been born within sight and sound of Bow Bells, he would probably have used one of his more favoured expressions, saying that such superstitions were 'nought but a lot o' cock and no balls!'

But he was not asked. Even if he had been, he would certainly have agreed with his Cap'n that they had been in port quite long enough – Friday or no Friday!

Having duly carried out the Captain's request to show this remarkably beautiful woman to her unsavoury quarters, Jim Hanson had returned to the poop deck and reported that he had settled 'the young person and her baby' as best he could. He also reported having heard grumblings among other like-situated passengers about the special attention apparently being paid to her.

'Och, bugger the passengers!' the Captain had exploded, 'I'll teach 'em to complain!' His mouth set in a hard, grim line. 'Ony mair bluidy nonsense o' that sort, an' we'll put em' all on hard tack!'

From long experience of sailing with Captain Robertson,

the First Mate knew when to keep silent. The red-haired Scotsman possessed a fiery temper to match his colouring. He could explode. But this evening he seemed unusually preoccupied.

Presently, having set the course, the Captain handed over to his second-in-command, and went below. Fingering his beard reflectively, he once again drew the passenger list from his pocket. His eyes flew straight to the entry, 'Mrs L. Smith and infant daughter'. No name for the child, he observed. Not yet christened, he supposed. Her own name she had said was 'Lucy'. Rather commonplace, wasn't it, for such an uncommonly distinguished-looking lady. And, of significance possibly, no mention of a husband; no 'Mrs William Smith' or 'Mrs Henry Smith' – ordinary enough names, to wit. Just Mrs L. Smith – the 'L' presumably standing for Lucy.

Uncharacteristically, Captain Robertson found himself absorbed by the mere thought of that woman. Never before had one of his passengers so intrigued him.

At dinner that evening he made his usual polite conversation with the cabin passengers at his table. But his thoughts were elsewhere. Even the steward, serving fresh meat and vegetables for the first meal at sea, noticed it. Normally, his Cap'n was full of good-humoured bonhomie – after all, a large proportion of his cabin passengers' fares went directly into his pocket. But that evening, Captain Robertson seemed unusually withdrawn.

And when, at length, he excused himself from the assembled company and retired to his cabin, he found he could not sleep. His thoughts kept returning to that vision – that Raphael-like incarnation of 'Madonna and Child' – which, in the persons of 'Mrs L. Smith and infant daughter', had so recently boarded his ship. Try as he would, he could not get the woman out of his mind; the constantly recurring thought of that arresting, seemingly almost immaculate beauty, suckling her infant child down there in the bowels of the ship, inhaling the stench of excrement and exposed to the inevitable risk of disease.

Throughout the night he tossed, sleeplessly, upon his comfortable bed. Then, in the early hours of the morning, an idea took root in his mind.

'Mr Hanson,' he commanded briskly, when once more he stood beside the First Mate on the poop deck, 'be sae guid as to request the presence of Mrs Smith . . . Mrs L. Smith . . . You are acquainted with the lady to whom I refer . . . Be sae guid, Mr Hanson, as to require the lady to come to ma cabin. I wish to converse with her.'

'Mrs Smith, Captain? Yes, sir. Very good, sir.' With no more than the semblance of a smirk, the First Mate set off towards the part of the ship he least liked to visit. Even before he reached the companionway hatch leading to the steerage quarters, the stench of unwashed human bodies assailed his nostrils. Without descending the steps, and keeping well back from the aperture, he called, 'Mrs Smith! . . . Cap'n wants yer . . .', adding with a fruity gurgle, 'wants yer in 'is cabin, see. So, look lively!'

He waited, peering down into the murky quarters, and smothering the up-wafting odours with a handkerchief placed firmly over nose and mouth. Several faces appeared out of the gloom, but not the right one.

'Mrs Smith!' he bellowed once more. 'You wot's got the child, there. Mrs L. SMITH!'

Presently, the young woman appeared, her cheeks flushed from the heat of the hold. She held the baby in her arms. Glancing up gratefully at the welcoming sunshine and the delicious wafts of fresh air, she smiled – and even the hard-bitten seaman of many summers, many ports, many women, felt moved by the picture presented. Under his breath he muttered, 'Cor! . . . but the Cap'n aint arf picked hisself a ripe plum there.'

Then he helped the lady up the ladder and led the way aft.

'Och, but do come in, Mistress Smith,' Captain Robertson greeted, with what he hoped was his most winning smile, 'I just wanted to have a wee word wi' ye.' He rose from behind the table in his well-furnished stateroom, at the same time motioning his guest to a chair. 'Do, please, sit down, ma'am.'

Observing the hesitation, and the enchanting flush colouring her finely-chiselled cheekbones, he sought to put her at her ease by adding, 'May I offer ye a beverage o' some kind . . . a cup o' hot coffee, perhaps?'

Clearly the lady was somewhat discomfitted. It was most unusual for the captain of a trans-Atlantic vessel to entertain a lower-class passenger in his cabin at any time – and if he did so it usually cloaked some dubious intent. Nevertheless, the young woman gracefully accepted the proffered chair, and while composing her features as best she could, she said quietly, 'Thank you, Captain. I should relish a cup of coffee.'

Captain Robertson nodded to the Mate who had been hovering enquiringly in the doorway. 'Very good, sir,' Hanson responded, 'A cup of coffee for the lady, sir . . .' and then glancing at the wriggling baby, he added, 'and what about the little mite, Miss . . . er, I mean "Mrs" . . . Anything for her, like?'

The polite refusal left Jim Hanson no alternative but to close the door, curiosity unfulfilled, and make for the galley. As soon as he had gone, Captain Robertson opened the conversation by enquiring after the baby's health. 'In fact,' he went on, not entirely truthfully, 'it's really on account o' the wee bairn that I wanted to have a word wi' ye.'

'Oh, she's very well, thank you, Captain. No trouble at all.' The mother gazed down lovingly at the lively little face of her child.

'Aye,' the Captain said slowly, regarding the young woman narrowly from beneath bushy eyebrows. 'And I'm anxious that it should stay that way, ma'am.' He leaned back in his leather-buttoned armchair, put his fingertips together, and stared up at the deck head. 'I'm a wee bit concerned for the bairn's health and wellbeing, d'ye understand,' he dissembled convincingly. 'As ye must be well aware, certain parts of the ship are not notably salubrious . . .' He paused, watching the lady's reaction. Clearly she was on her guard, wondering just what this conversation was leading up to. In reply, she merely nodded her head.

41

'Naturally,' the Captain continued, embarking upon yet another half-truth, 'I am concerned, of course, for the health of all my passengers on these long voyages, but I feel a particular responsibility for the young, especially the wee bairns, d'ye understand.'

He felt a sudden quickening of the pulse as the woman smiled her appreciation. He cleared his throat loudly before continuing. 'For that reason, Messus Smith, I've decided to move yersel' and the wee bairn from your present unsavoury quarters to the more healthy atmosphere o' cabin accommodation.'

'But Captain . . .' the woman protested, her cheeks colouring prettily, 'I understood no cabins were available, even if I could have afforded . . .' She broke off, lowering her eyes from the Captain's gaze.

''Tis true, ma'am,' he broke in, saving her embarrassment, 'that all passenger cabins were fully reserved quite some considerable time ago . . .'

'How then,' the woman was quick to counter, 'can you move me and my daughter from our present quarters?'

'Because, my dear ma'am,' Captain Robertson beamed, a little too readily, 'I've decided to make my own bed place available tae ye.'

Immediately the words were out of his mouth he realized his mistake. He could have bitten out his tongue. The shadow of distrust clouding the woman's face spoke far more eloquently than words. She thought he was inviting her to sleep with him – a common whore, willing to barter her favours in exchange for a few creature comforts. Seeking to dispel her obvious disquiet, the Captain blundered on, 'My meanin' is, ma'am . . . that is, what I mean ta sae . . .' He felt his own cheeks reddening ridiculously. 'Wha' I'm tryin' ta tell ye, ma'am, is that I shall, of course be moving out so as to leave you and the wee one entirely untroubled in the more comfortable surroundings o' my cabin.'

He sat back in his chair, confident that he had successfully assuaged her worst fears. But, just to make sure, he added,

'And besides, ma'am, 'twould be a great deal more healthy for the bairn.'

To his surprise and mounting chagrin, he watched her slowly shake her head. 'It is very kind of you, Captain Robertson,' she demurred, 'but I could not possibly accept your offer . . .'

'If 'tis the stupid claver ye're thinkin' on,' he broke in, 'then banish it from yer mind . . .'

'No, no, Captain,' she replied with a shake of the head, 'that kind of thing does not bother me . . .'

'Well, wha' is it then?'

'For one thing, sir,' she retorted politely, 'if I were to do as you suggest, where would the captain of this ship take his rest?'

Captain Robertson spread his arms expansively. 'All *this* is also my cabin, ma'am. As ye see,' he demonstrated, indicating the lockers with bed places above them, running along the starboard side of the cabin, 'there's really an abundance o' room – even for a man o' my size.'

'Oh, but no, Captain,' she protested, 'I could never consider turning you out of your own quarters.'

Cocking one eyebrow, and fixing her with a mock-severe scrutiny, the Captain growled good-humouredly, 'Ma'am! Do I have to remind ye that *I* am Master of this ship . . .'

'Oh, yes, I know, Captain, but I could never feel happy if . . .'

'No "ifs" nor "buts", ma'am, if you please! I'm sure ye must be well aware, once aboard ma ship, everyone – an' I do mean "everyone" – has to obey ma commands.' The voice was stern, but the accompanying smile radiated an undeniable warmth.

Mrs Smith meekly bowed a submissive head. 'As you say, Captain,' she concurred, 'I will obey your commands.'

If Captain Euan Robertson had successfully deluded himself concerning his motives for installing the lady and her child in his cabin, the delusion was not shared by his shipmates. That Mr Hanson, the First Mate, should be sceptical was not surprising. Enforced celibacy on a long sea voyage was a tedious fact of a sailor's life. If it could be alleviated without blatant impropriety, well then . . . And besides, who was he, Jim Hanson, to indulge in moral censure . . . especially where his Cap'n was concerned. Drive a ship to the very limit of safety, could Captain Robertson, and crowd on sail until it was more than a man's life was worth to go aloft, but it was the Captain, and he alone, who had to decide how much punishment 'Elizabeth-Ann' could take from freezing winter gales and mountainous Atlantic waves – and he had never let his crew down yet. A hard man, yes – and sometimes a hard taskmaster – but after sailing with him over many years, Jim Hanson not only liked the man but also held him in high respect.

As for the crew, they reckoned the skipper had found himself a 'right dainty little tart', and while regarding him with acute, at times almost unbearable, envy in what they assumed were his nightly escapades in his bedplace, they grumblingly conceded that it was a captain's privilege to pluck what fruit he could from the orchard of his passenger list. It was unusual, though, for a captain to make his pick from among the sludge of the steerage. No matter; a good trollop was a tasty morsel . . . from whatever class of passenger she came.

Not surprisingly, it was from among the privileged cabin passengers that resentment was strongest. How dare the Captain flaunt his profligacy before their very eyes! It might not have been so insufferable – indeed, it would have been almost acceptable – had he chosen someone from their own class. But that he should blatantly cohabit with some slattern from 'the lower orders' was well-nigh intolerable! – even if, grudgingly, they had to admit she looked more like a queen than a chambermaid. It was really quite astonishing how a mere servant girl, these days, could dress herself up to look as good as her betters; prettier, in fact. But what was even more galling was the sneaking feeling that the menfolk seemed to prefer them to the well-brought-up ladies of their own class – in bed, at least!

But although he was aware of the damaging clashes and

clavers going on behind his back, and that such tittle-tattle might jeopardize his future as a sea captain once the gossip machinery slipped into gear back in England, it bothered Captain Robertson not at all. He was determined that 'Mrs Smith and infant daughter' should have every comfort his ship could provide. When he was not needed up on deck, he happily dandled the baby on his knee; when he could safely leave the running of the ship entirely to the Mate, he would play draughts and dominoes with the child's mother; and nightly at his table he made sure that the lady of whom, unknowingly, he was becoming dangerously fond, was always seated at his side.

While other voyagers in the 'Elizabeth-Ann' might be finding this twenty-five-day Atlantic crossing a lengthy and tedious experience, to Captain Robertson it seemed no more than an evening gone.

And yet he felt a strange sense of urgency creeping into his soul; a feeling that each day, each minute of every hour, must be lived to the uttermost; an awareness – call it a premonition if you will – that his and her tomorrow might truly never come.

For Mrs Smith and her infant daughter, tho', the first twenty-one days of that Atlantic crossing passed smoothly and happily. The sea was calm, the wind blew steadily but not too strongly, and 'Elizabeth-Ann', a truly majestic sight under full sail, sped across the ocean. As though encapsulated within the broad freedom of the seas, Mrs Smith felt able to forget the past and hold back the future. If other female passengers regarded her as a scarlet woman, brazenly sharing with the Captain not only the comforts of his bed-place but also, of course, the sensual delights of his bed as well – if they chose to dub her 'the Captain's whore', making contemptuous asides and shunning her company – if that was to be their attitude, well, so be it. For her part, she was content merely to enjoy, in a manner which only mothers can fully understand, the growing beauty of her baby child; to watch it kicking its sturdy little legs, flexing its tiny fingers, and laughing at her from the cot which

Captain Robertson had improvised from the lowest drawer of his heavy sea chest. To the dark-haired, bright-eyed little bundle ensconced within the Captain's best-quality merino blanket, the makeshift cot was as good as any highly polished mahogany cradle.

But then came the storm. For three whole days it raged; whipping the hitherto docile sea into mountainous, threatening waves; tearing at the greatly reduced canvas like a demented terrier; howling through the rigging, night and day, like a pack of starving wolves. Even Jim Hanson, veteran of many Atlantic storms, had been apprehensive. And the crew, never at its best in a crisis, had required exceptionally firm – sometimes even violent – handling.

To the Captain it seemed like confirmation of his worst fears. That premonition of disaster which, since a few days out from Charleston harbour, had been eating into the very fibres of his rugged being, now seemed about to be fulfilled. He had never feared a storm before. Indeed, he had almost gloried in the challenge; man's courage and man's endeavour pitted against the worst the elements could do.

But not this time. Begrudging every moment his presence was required on deck, he longed to be down below; with her – in that domestic warmth with which she and her baby had so endearingly invested his cabin. Fellow sea captains would undoubtedly accuse him of having gone soft. He did not care. Let them think as they liked.

But having regarded himself as a confirmed bachelor of long standing, Captain Euan Robertson felt ill-prepared for the emotional impact of those first twenty-one days. At the outset he had convinced himself that the glow within him was nothing more than the warmth engendered by the unselfish act of having given up his cabin, but as the days slipped by at such an alarming rate he began finding more and more excuses for being with her in his private cabin. He loved to play with the baby girl; to pick her out of that improvised cot and dandle her upon his comfortable knee; to feel the warmth of her soft, strawberry-like cheek against the sea-tanned leathery roughness of his own. He would tickle her tummy, running his strong, erstwhile seaman's fingers up over her well-swathed chest, and then up under her chin. He found himself making the most ridiculous noises to amuse her. He never tired of it. Nor did he ever tire of the baby's response – a gurgle of delight and a roguish smile. Unquestionably, undeniably, the little dark-haired, rosy-cheeked mite had captured his heart.

More disturbingly, so too had her mother. Captain Euan Robertson, hard-bitten ship's Master, confirmed bachelor and distrustful of any emotional involvement ever since a silky temptress in Oporto had once torn his young heart to shreds before unfeelingly casting it away, now found he could not sleep at night for thinking of the baby's mother. That first sight of her, carrying her precious bundle up the gang-plank – that Raphaelian vision of 'Madonna and Child' – would float before his eyes as he lay in his temporary berth, staring through the darkness at the deck head. Gradually he came to realize, almost with a sense of disbelief – yet wondrous awareness – that for the first time in his life he was falling truly, deeply in love. In the twenty-one days since clearing Charleston, 'Mrs Smith and infant daughter' had become the core of his being, the centre of his universe.

And then had come the storm. During those three long days and nights, with 'Elizabeth-Ann' scudding before the wind, reefed down and trysail set, Captain Euan Robertson had remained staunchly beside the steersman at the wheel. No matter what privations of weather or sleeplessness had to be endured, he was determined to bring the 'Elizabeth-Ann' and her now more than precious cargo through the storm and safely into port once more. Although the thirty fathoms of trailed hawser had succeeded in breaking up the waters astern as well as lessening the ship's tendency to yaw, it was not possible to prevent her from rolling and lurching with sickening monotony. And with the great foaming mountains of sea surging up astern and hurling the ship onwards there was the inevitable anxiety that she might be pooped, or bow down into the sea with too much headway as a result of carring an excess of canvas.

But Captain Robertson accepted it all as a challenge to his seafaring skill. A new sense of purpose stirred within him; a trenchant desire to survive. Surprisingly, too, the years seemed to be slipping from his shoulders. He began to feel young again.

After three days and three nights of constant battering, trying its utmost to destroy everything that got in its path, the wind was at last dying down again, leaving the former turbulent seas to compose themselves into a long, heavy swell rolling north-eastwards beneath a gathering sea mist. Captain Robertson felt able to hand over to his second-in-command, and leaving the First Mate with orders to keep the 'Elizabeth-Ann' on her present course, north-east by north, he thankfully left the poop deck and went below.

Never before had he looked forward to the completion of a trans-Atlantic passage with so little pleasure. By his reckoning, 'Elizabeth-Ann' could now be no more than a bare twenty miles or so from the Western Rocks and the most south-westerly conglomeration of the Scilly Isles – although in the gathering mist it was difficult to be precise. But time was passing so quickly; they had been making a fast passage. In less than twenty-four hours they would be docking at Falmouth. A new sense of urgency gripped him. He felt an overwhelming desire to spend the last evening of this momentous Atlantic crossing with the woman who now so completely enthralled him.

When he entered the cabin, the baby was being given its nightly immersion in the canvas bath rigged by the boatswain and filled with hot water by the sandy-haired galley boy. The baby's mother, kneeling beside her wriggling, gurgling child, an apron tied around her waist and a most becoming flush highlighting her cheeks and eyes, looked up as the Captain entered.

'I hardly expected to see you so soon, Captain,' she smiled. 'I was afraid, in this worsening weather, you might have to stay on deck.'

Throwing his cap onto the cushion-covered locker, the

Master of the 'Elizabeth-Ann' muttered, 'Och, no. 'Tis nought but a wee bit o' sea fog, and Hanson's a verra experienced man. He'll be gettin' his Master's Certificate at the completion o' this voyage. In fact, I shall be sorry to lose him. In any event,' he added, reverting to her original enquiry, 'he knows where to find me – should there be any trouble.'

'Trouble?' she asked, looking both surprised and alarmed. 'What kind of trouble, Captain?'

'Och, whisht ma'am! There's no' a thing wrong,' he soothed, easing off his storm jacket and laying it alongside his cap. 'Dinna fash yersel', lassie.'

He knelt down beside mother and wriggling baby; watching them both quietly for several moments. Then he drew a deep breath.

'It'll no' be long now afore we pick up the Cornish coast,' he began hesitantly, 'and tha' means we're nearly at the end o' the voyage.'

He paused, anxiously watching for the mother's reaction. She merely nodded understanding; did not look up.

'I felt I needed the time to spend wi' you and the wee one,' he continued almost gruffly; then added in a much softer tone, 'afore the partin' o' the ways, ma'am.'

This time she looked up, smiled her warm, ingenuous smile, saying, 'I'm glad you came, Captain.' Then she went on bathing the baby.

Clearing his throat rather loudly, the Captain blundered on. 'I'm a plain man, ma'am, no' given to polished manners and smooth talk like some o' ma fellow captains, but I speak as I feel.' He coughed nervously, the effort of speaking his mind on this occasion having suddenly parched his throat. 'During these past few weeks,' he stumbled on, '. . . ever since we sailed from Charleston, in fact . . . ye must surely ha' noticed that I've been spendin' mair an' mair time down here in the cabin when, perhaps, I should ha' been up on deck. The plain truth is, ma'am, I've grown exceptionally attached to yersel' an' the wee bairn. Between the two o' ye, I do believe ye've changed ma life. Ye've turned this drab old cabin o' mine into . . . into . . .' he fumbled for the right word, 'well, into a hame, ma'am . . . into a real hame. Why, I do declare it'll never be the same again wi'out ye.'

He floundered on, groping for the words. 'Wha' I mean is, ma'am, I'll never want to put to sea . . . I mean, things can never be the same wi'out . . . Och, dammit, woman! Wha' I'm tryin' to tell ye is . . . that I've fallen in love wi' ye! There, now,' he concluded breathlessly, 'I've spaked ma mind . . . an' I'm glad to ha' done sae.'

He sat back on his heels, staring down at the deck planking – and waited.

The woman lifted the baby from the improvised bathtub, wrapped it in one of the Captain's towels, and began drying the squirming, frog-like little body. She did not look up; for a long while she did not speak. Then, in a low, almost inaudible voice, she said, 'Captain Robertson, you have been wonderfully kind to both me and my daughter. You have never tried to take advantage of a situation which others, in a similar position to yourself, might not have been able to resist. For that alone I am truly grateful. But I never thought . . .' She broke off, frowning deeply and staring unseeing at the deck while rhythmically drying the baby's legs. Then she turned her head; looked straight at him, her large, soulful eyes holding his unflinchingly.

'Captain,' she went on, 'you have been so good to me. You have undoubtedly incurred the opprobrium of all your other passengers – true cabin passengers who have paid for their accommodation and who are entitled to expect your consideration. You may, for all I know, also have incurred the wrath of your employers . . . for, heaven alone knows what tales will be told against you by those self-same passengers when finally we reach our destination. They could, I fancy, do you immeasurable harm in your career as a sea captain.

'You have done all this for me, Captain,' she went on, slipping the infant child into its flannel nightdress, and allowing its tiny fingers to play with the gold-enamelled locket which, Captain Robertson had noticed, she always wore around her neck, 'You have been kindness itself. For this reason alone – and especially in view of what you have just said about your feelings for me – I think you should know the truth . . .'

Sensing some unfavourable revelation, the Captain blurted out, 'Whatever ye say, it wadna make a wit o' difference to the way I feel about ye.'

'I think it might, Captain,' she replied quietly, 'I think it might. But in any event, you're entitled to know.'

Without any apparent feeling of embarrassment or impropriety, she put the babe to her naked breast and gently rocked from side to side. 'As you see me now, Captain,' she continued, 'you probably believe me to be a devoted mother returning home to show off my baby to a welcoming family . . . You also probably believe that I have left behind me in our American colony an equally devoted father.'

The mention of a husband caused a sharp, involuntary intake of breath by Captain Robertson. He got to his feet; paced across the cabin to the square port, and stared out at the misty horizon. He stood, with his hands behind his back, flexing his fingers uneasily. He did not like the look of the weather. He knew he should be up on deck, taking control; but he also knew that he must hear the truth about the woman; whether or not his feelings for her were reciprocated.

Still speaking softly, the woman went on, 'Half of that picture is a true one, Captain. But, sadly, only half. It is true that I am returning to my family in England, with what reception I know not, because I have to tell you, Captain Robertson, that I have left behind me no husband in Charleston, nor, indeed, will there be one awaiting my arrival in England. In short, Captain, I am unmarried!'

She paused to allow her words to sink in. At the same time, she gazed down lovingly and without shame at the child in her arms. 'If you wish to know the details, I will tell you,' she offered. But then, seeing the violent shaking of his bowed head, she concluded by saying, 'Perhaps it is enough to admit that, being young and foolish, I loved a man – the bearer of an honourable title – who could not

51

make me his wife. He died in action before he could make good his promises.'

Captain Robertson turned to face her, leaned against the highly polished cabin table. 'Aye,' he sighed, 'I thocht it wad be something akin to tha'. I never believed the name o' Mrs Smith from the start.'

The mother laid the baby in the makeshift cot, then sat back on her heels. Folding her hands in her lap and staring down at the deck, she explained simply, 'I have a very dear, good friend in Charleston – she used to be my nurse as a child, before she married and emigrated – and when I realized I was with child, I knew she would never let me down. So, I decided to save my mother and father, both of them of strict Huguenot descent . . .'

'Och, yes,' the Captain interjected, 'I fully understand tha'. You wadne wish to hurt them. But what is to become of you and the wee one now . . . after we dock, I mean?'

She spread her hands, gave the merest shrug of her shoulders, and smiled sadly. 'I know not, Captain. I must leave it in the hands of . . . of Fate, I suppose.'

For a moment Captain Robertson seemed dazed and irresolute. Instinct told him that matters were urgent. In a little while he must concentrate on bringing his ship into harbour; there would be the inevitable excitement and bustle of a dockside arrival; unless he acted at once, the moment would be lost for ever. He must again declare his love.

Sinking to one knee in front of the kneeling mother, and looking her steadfastly in the eye, he said, 'I know I'm only a plain man, ma'am . . . a roving sea captain at that. I realize also that in age ye may regard me as being too greatly your senior, and I'm certain that in looks I'm no' a match for your youthful beauty . . . but, as I've already told ye, during these last three weeks I've come to love ye, ma'am, like I've never loved afore, and there is no greater desire in ma heart than to be granted the privilege o' looking after you and the bairn. In short, ma'am, I'm asking ye to be ma wife.'

The effort of this proposal had brought beads of perspiration to the sea captain's brow. While waiting for her reply he dabbed at his forehead with a cream silk handkerchief.

But even before she had time to speak, a hoarse shout sounded from above. 'On deck, Captain! Danger ahead!'

Tearing himself away from the now thoroughly frightened mother, Captain Robertson rushed up the companion stairway. It became obvious at once that the 'Elizabeth-Ann' had run into really thick weather. Their position was now uncertain, but all too soon the sullen thunder of an ocean swell hurling itself against a rocky shore could be heard. It sounded ominously close.

'Och! Wha' the de'il?' the Captain exploded, momentarily confounded. But then, quickly recovering, he barked out the commands: 'Shorten sail! Stand by to take in royals and flying jib!'

Peering through the murk, and pointing over the starboard bow, he said to First Mate Hanson, 'And wha' in hell's name is that over there?'

Following the direction indicated, Jim Hanson could just make out the dim outline of a rectangular shape lying low in the water. 'Well, blister m' tripes!' he exclaimed loudly. 'It looks like the hull of a ship . . . a fishin' smack, perhaps, . . . But it can't be . . . surely. It ain't movin' in the water. Sea's washin' over it. Must be a wreck, or somethin' . . .' His voice trailed away, indecisively.

'Whatever it is, Mr Hanson, it's now too close for us to clear it on the seaward side. So, "Steady ahead!" then, man . . . Leave it on the starboard beam, and as soon as we've left it astern, prepare to "Wear ship" and then make for the open sea.'

But as they closed with this phantasmal outline, the awesome truth gradually loomed into unmistakable clarity. Far from being a harmless coaster plying its trade off the Cornish coast, or even an abandoned wreck, the fog-shrouded object slowly transformed itself into a group of murderous-looking rocks.

'Godsteeth!' the Captain swore roundly. 'But where the de'il can we be!'

'Too bloody close inshore for my bleedin' likin',' Jim Hanson's cockney accents asserted. 'And the sooner we gets the bleedin' 'ell out of it, the better it'll be for all of us, eh, Captain!'

Captain Robertson's response was immediate.

'Stations for wearing ship!' he commanded, 'Leadsman to chains. Arm the lead!' In stentorian tones the First Mate relayed the orders.

Instantly the ship became alive; men racing to their stations; swarming up the rigging like ants up a webbing brace.

Then came the second command. 'Brail up spanker!' followed at once by 'Up mainsail!'

Below, in the cabin that had been her home for the past three weeks, the woman anxiously watched over her child. The commands being issued from the poop deck above her head, muffled by the ship's planking but still clearly audible above the sounds of squeaking blocks, creaking timbers and sluicing water, meant absolutely nothing to her. She stared down at her sleeping baby, wondering what was to become of them, quietly praying that they might survive.

The Mate's voice sharply broke in upon her prayers.

'Brace in afteryards! Up helm!'

He sounded positive enough. Under Captain Robertson's orders he would be totally in command of any situation. After all, they had both been at sea for many years; both were widely experienced. All would be well, she felt sure. Perhaps she could relax a little. Everything seemed under control.

'Let go after bowlines! Man the weather afterbraces!' The orders continued to flow – unhurried, precise, and reassuringly authoritative – but to the young woman from Charleston, South Carolina – as, indeed, to most other passengers aboard the packet ship 'Elizabeth-Ann' – these commands were as a foreign language; sailors' special language, the language of ships and the sea. But, issued with

54

such commanding authority, they allayed the fears of an anxious soul.

Unseen, except by those on deck, the 'Elizabeth-Ann' now began her majestic swing round to starboard; the wind beginning to draw forward on the starboard side.

Again, the Mate's voice penetrated to the cabin below – powerful, commanding, nursing the ship round on to her seaward course.

'Square the headyards! Man the main tack and sheets! Set mainsail and spanker! Haul aboard! Haul out!'

So the commands continued. They must all mean something to the ship's crew, the woman reflected with a fleeting smile. It was just as well, she thought ruefully, because without such commands the ship could not sail. To a mere landlubber, however, they were nothing but unintelligible gobbledegook; the language of seamen since the days of long ago.

But scarcely had the 'Elizabeth-Ann' set out on her bolt for the open sea and safety than a sudden, sickening crunch brought her progress to a halt. Total confusion followed. Unsuspecting seamen were shaken from the rigging like apples from a tree. Most of them thudded to the deck, writhed momentarily, and then lay still. Others, hardly more fortunate, were catapulted into the foaming seas, only to be swept to a watery grave.

Within minutes of the ship striking, a giant wave had slewed her round so that the whole length of her hull lay broadside-on to wind and weather. Temporarily interrupted in their mighty shoreward surge, huge seas began cascading over the bulwarks, flooding the lower deck and swirling down into the hold. Like sandhoppers flushed by the incoming tide, the steerage passengers scrambled up on deck. Some sought a precarious foothold in the rigging while others made a mad rush for the boats.

A gigantic wave then caught the bow of the ship, and with a hideous screeching and a horrifying shivering and shuddering of timbers, it lifted the hull yet more firmly on to the reef, leaving bowsprit and spars pointing drunkenly upwards. The impact brought the foremast crashing down on the seaward side, thus holding the ship at a dangerous angle and exposing her decks and cabins even more nakedly to the oncoming seas.

'Cut away the rigging,' the Captain shouted to the carpenter, the only member of the crew still retaining a semblance of calm. 'Let go the foremast!' he yelled, knowing from experience that a floating mast or spar – something to cling to – had saved many a life in similar disasters. 'And man the boats, Mr Hanson,' he roared above the turmoil. 'Get one out on the lee side if you can. And, Mr Hanson . . . control the crew. You may have to use force!'

Clambering back to his cabin, he found the woman he loved huddled in a corner, clutching her baby – terrified. At the first impact of ship against rock, every unfixed object in the cabin had gone slithering and crashing to the deck, and had not the mother made an instinctive grab, the improvised cot containing the sleeping child would have been violently hurled against the bulkhead.

Stepping over the debris, Captain Robertson gathered both mother and baby into his arms, and in an attempt to sound reassuring, he said, 'There's nae need to be afeart. Just cling tae me, and ye'll be a' richt.'

As he began climbing the companion stairs once more – the woman with one arm around his neck while with the other she clung tightly to her child – the ship shuddered, and then came more upright.

'Oh, Captain!' she gasped apprehensively, but trying hard to be brave. 'But what is going to happen to us!'

'Whisht, ma'am!' he replied, with an assurance he was very far from feeling, 'dinna be feartie! That was only the foremast being cut awa! It'll lessen the drag on the ship, d'ye ken. Just you keep a tight hold on me,' he repeated, as he emerged from the cabin, 'and ye'll be quite a'richt.'

But as he feared, pandemonium had broken out on deck. Having succeeded in lowering a boat on the lee side, both panic-stricken passengers and crew were jostling to get into it. Despite the Mate's best efforts to restore some sort of order, the imminence of catastrophe and the basic instinct of self-preservation – coupled with the fact that very few could swim – had transformed rational human beings into a herd of stampeding animals. Shouting and screaming – and fighting among themselves – they all saw the boat as their last possible chance of survival, no matter that it was already dangerously overloaded. If there was room for only one more, then at least two would be competing for it.

With one arm gripping the lee rail while in the other he carried the woman with her child, Captain Robertson waded through swirling cascades of sea water, along the still perilously sloping deck.

As he neared the frantic scramble alongside the ship's lifeboat, he pulled the pistol from his belt. The woman's body, as he carried her, had shielded it from the lashing spindrift, thus keeping the powder dry. Firing above the heads of the crew, he yelled, 'Stand back! Make way for the woman and child!' – but he still had to force his way through the crowd until he reached the stern of the longboat bobbing dangerously alongside the stricken vessel.

Having handled the drenched mother and baby into the boat, accompanied by a silent prayer for their miraculous deliverance, he then made no further attempt to hold back the avalanche of bodies scrambling over the side.

He knew that his ship was doomed. Pounded relentlessly now by massive Atlantic seas she was already beginning to break up. Within the next few minutes – possibly fifteen at the most – 'Elizabeth-Ann', the ship he had always loved, would slither beneath the waves, never to be seen again.

What right had he, Captain Euan Robertson, to prevent a last desperate bid for survival.

CHAPTER THREE

A Rose is Born

Sampson Roskruge sat dozing by the fire. He and his wife Amia had just finished their tea – saffron cake, thunder 'n' lightning splits, and generous helpings of star-gazey pie.

It was the familiar routine. Invariably, as soon as tea was over and the wooden platters cleared from the well-scrubbed table, Sampson would be joined by his wife, one of them on each side of the fireplace, firstly in companionable silence, and then, ultimately, dozing.

And 'tea' was no fanciful designation because, unlike so many other poor souls, inland and up-country, who either couldn't obtain the precious tea leaves or else could never afford to buy them, the seafaring inhabitants of St Keverne in Cornwall were seldom without the wherewithal with which to brew a welcome dish of tea.

For eleven years, now, Sampson and Amia Roskruge had been following the same daily routine in their cob and thatch cottage at Rosenithon, just over a mile on the seaward side of the village of St Keverne and overlooking Godrevy Beach. Every day they would follow the same well-organized, steady routine – every day, that is, except when Sampson and his friend, Wilmot Tripconey up at Trevallack, went off in their fishing boat and stayed away several nights at a time. It was after such nocturnal absences that Amia would find her stock of tea leaves miraculously replenished. Like the widow's cruse, it never seemed to dry up.

And there were nights, too, when Sampson was away on other business – village business. And if, during those nights, Amia should hear the sound of trotting ponies coming up from Godrevy Beach and on past their cottage towards the village, she would turn her face to the wall, as she had been taught at her mother's knee long ago, so that she never saw more than just the shadows of the horsemen as they went riding by.

Amia, like all other good Cornish womenfolk, had learnt to be discreet.

On the whole, they had been good years for Amia – those eleven years with Sampson as her husband. He was a good man, hardworking, wresting for both of them a fair living from his modest smallholding and the fishing boat which he owned jointly with Wil Tripconey, and they never seemed to be without those small luxuries that make a woman's life worth living – a roll of silk from which to make a pretty dress, and a little bit of lace for trimming the edges; a drop of brandy to keep out the cold in winter; and, of course, that indispensable adjunct to all occasions traumatic or mundane, a steaming hot cup of tea.

No, all things considered, Amia Roskruge was contented with her lot – except, that is, for just one thing.

Every night throughout those eleven years, and before they climbed into their rough wooden bed, Amia Roskruge, with Sampson kneeling beside her, had prayed that their union might be blessed by the birth of a child. So far, those prayers had remained sullenly unanswered, and although Amia could scarcely be described as being well-stricken in years, by now she had almost given up hope. Like the biblical Hannah, it seemed, the Lord had shut up her womb.

But still she prayed.

Her thoughts, however, were elsewhere as she now joined her husband beside the open fireplace and slipped into an untroubled doze. The evenings were beginning to draw in; and it had been getting colder of late. Apart from an occasional crackle from a log on the fire, a blissful stillness descended upon the kitchen of Thorn Cottage. Not even the tick of a clock disturbed the quietness; only Sampson's deep, rhythmical breathing could be heard.

Outside, despite the strength of the wind, a typical late

October fog was rolling in from the sea, but within the sturdy cob walls of Thorn Cottage all was peace and warmth. Tranquillity reigned.

But not for long. A banging on the front door, and the familiar voice of young Gwydel Roskelly from Chenhale shouting, 'Brig in trouble, Mester! She'm drivin' on the Manacles! Better come quick!' brought both Sampson and Amia Roskruge suddenly wide awake.

Reaching for the lifeline which he always kept coiled and slung behind the front door, ready for just such an emergency as this, Sampson Roskruge, with his wife not far behind him, ran through the trees in front of Thorn Cottage and then down the golden-brown leaf strewn pathway that led to Godrevy Beach. Through the gaps between the trees, and beyond hedgerows bordering the rocky coast, he could just discern the outline of a ship help fast on the Manacles. Her foremast had gone, and she lay now like a broken-winged sea bird totally at the mercy of thundering seas. In a few minutes she would begin to break-up, and unless all those on board had got away in one of the ship's lifeboats, Sampson knew all too well that there could be a heavy loss of life. He had seen it so many times before.

As he ran across the grey-sanded foreshore and down to the pebble beach, one thought only was uppermost in his mind – to save as many lives as possible, and to deny that watery graveyard yet further names to its roll. Never mind the proceeds from the wreck – God's gift to hard-pressed Cornishmen, the Harvest of the Sea – that would come later; hogsheads of wine, spirituous liquors, cotton, oil, fruit, anything, in fact, that could be salvaged. But that must wait. First of all, Sampson, together with other St Keverners now flocking to the beach, must save life – if it could be saved. And there always had to be a large question mark against that, because, against a raging sea, there was little that men could do from the shore. Perhaps someday, someone would devise a means of getting a line aboard a stricken vessel – but it hadn't happened yet.

So, Sampson felt relieved, when he reached the water's

edge, to see that a ship's lifeboat had at last pulled away from the brig and was heading for the shore. But it looked fearsomely overloaded. Lying low in the water, the coxswain was having the greatest difficulty in keeping the boat stern to weather, and preventing it from lurching round, broadside-on to the tumultuous waves. In the bow, Sampson could just make out the slender figure of a woman clutching a bundle to her chest. Could it be a child, he wondered; so small, so vulnerable in that hostile sea.

But even as he watched, mesmerized by a sense of impending disaster, a mammoth breaker swept up astern of the lifeboat, lifted it on high like some sacrificial offering to the gods, then dashed it down into the trough, slewing it around and leaving the whole length of its side at the mercy of the oncoming tumult.

Within seconds, a following gigantic wave, even more hell-bent upon destruction it seemed, crashed over the seaward beam, completely overwhelming the small boat and throwing all the occupants into the raging surf.

Immediately, Sampson Roskruge, the lifeline tied round his waist, plunged into the foaming turmoil. He had been watching that slender figure with the bundle clasped tightly in her arms. If he could save one poor soul from this tragedy, it would be her; and if that bundle proved to be a baby at breast, then he would save both of them.

Battling his way through mountainous breakers, he managed to get close enough to the near-exhausted woman to see that the bundle she carried was, in fact, a small child. And as the backwash from a huge wave swept him towards the two of them he was able to grasp the baby from the mother's outstretched hands and tuck the little thing under one arm. But just as he tried to grab the mother with his free hand, the power of the sea swept them apart. He tried again, skilfully using the back-surge of the water to bring them together once more. Their fingers touched; he thought he had her; but again, in the moment of success, she was dragged from his reach. He could see she was getting weaker; she could not survive the cold and the battering much longer.

He must make one more supreme effort; it would have to be his last because he, too, was becoming exhausted, and unless he now allowed himself to be pulled ashore, he would lose his own life as well as that of the baby he held in his arm.

Flailing away with his free hand and kicking fiercely with his legs, he got himself into position to make a last desperate effort. For the third time, and as if in some macabre, watery paean of praise, they were swept together by the jousting waves. For a brief moment Sampson felt the woman grab hold of his sodden sleeve. Now, he thought, if she can just hang on tightly while I haul on the lifeline, I may yet be able to save them both.

But almost at once he felt her additional weight dragging them all under. Which one to let go . . . mother or child? Agonizing decision . . . but it had to be made – and made quickly – or all would be lost.

Mercifully, it was the mother who made the decision for him. Realizing the impossibility of his saving them both, she gathered up every last ounce of her remaining strength to wrench from around her neck the gold-enamelled locket which she always wore, and which she now thrust into Sampson's outstretched hand. For one brief moment their eyes met – and held.

To the end of his life, Sampson would never forget the expression in those eyes. The message was clear; her two most precious possessions she was handing into his care.

Then, with a look of relief and resignation on her young and still beautiful face, she surrendered herself to the awesome power of the sea.

*   *   *

That night, as the baby lay by the fireside, warmly wrapped in a soft woollen shawl and sleeping soundly in yet another wooden drawer – unpolished, this time, and brought down from a rough-hewn chest upstairs – Sampson and Amia Roskruge knelt down beside her. For several minutes, pre-occupied with their own thoughts, neither of them spoke.

No one knew exactly how many lives had been lost when the brig, 'Elizabeth-Ann', had foundered on the Manacles, but it was feared there had been no survivors . . . none, that is, except the tiny baby now sleeping peacefully in front of the fire in a humble cottage overlooking the disaster.

It was Sampson who broke the silence. Gazing down at the dark hair, the flushed, dimpled cheeks, the long, curly black eyelashes, he murmured softly, 'She'm bonny, ain't she, Ame? She'm just like a fresh-sprung rose.'

His wife smiled lovingly at the sight of the tiny head lying so quietly, so innocently on the hastily prepared pillow. 'You'm right, Sam,' she said at last, 'she'm just like a rose.'

She continued to stare, wonderingly, deep in thought, for several more seconds. Then, with an air of finality, she added, 'And that's just what us'll call her, Sam. Us'll just call her . . . Rose.'

Possessively, she pulled the shawl a little closer around the sleeping baby.

The good Lord had answered her prayers.

CHAPTER FOUR

The petals unfurl

Melder Tresooth was waiting patiently. She always did. She always waited — and it was always with monumental patience. Her parents, with that mystic prescience reserved for members of the Celtic race, could not have named their daughter more appropriately. Melder was the very essence of sweetness.

Every day, as soon as lessons were over, she would wait for her little friend, Rosie Roskruge, at the entrance of the charity school at Lan-Keverne. Set in a field of just over an acre, part of which had been given by Squire Locryn Sandys at the turn of the century, the school was the practical expression, like hundreds of others throughout the country, of the growing awareness by the aristocracy and the well-to-do — the pricking of conscience, perhaps — of the need to educate the poor. Not surprisingly, St Keverne was rather proud of its charity school. Its children were being taught to read and write, and some of them were even being taught to do a little arithmetic. The boys were less attentive than the girls; they wanted to be away down at Porthoustock or Porthallow, fishing from the rocks, or helping the menfolk with mending their nets or caulking the fishing boats. And one of the least attentive of the boys was Myron Pinnerton. He was large for his age, but his brain had not kept pace with the rest of him.

Melder Tresooth was older than Rose — not by much, but just enough to make her feel protective. Having taken after her father who, in his younger days, had been a formidable wrestler, Melder was strong for her age. And although she could never have explained it – would not even have tried to do so – ever since she had first set eyes on the little dark-haired girl from nearby Thorn Cottage she had quite taken to her.

The affection was firmly reciprocated. Being an only child, without anyone to play with at home, Rose had come to look upon Melder as her big sister. They did everything together; they scoured the beach at Godrevy for unusual seashells, as well as anything valuable that the tide might have washed up; they climbed the Giant's Quoits overlooking Porthoustock and watched the seagulls swooping and turning in search of the smallest morsel; and when it came to harvest time they would decorate the very last sheaf of corn with bright red poppies and yellow cornfield flowers, and then join in the age-old ceremony of 'Crying the Neck'.

The fact that Rose was very much the prettier of the two girls mattered not one wit to Melder; the very sweetness of her nature precluded any jealous thoughts from her mind. She merely rejoiced in Rose's beauty; she was content to be her bosom friend.

But being the elder of the two, and being unusually good at reading and writing, Melder and Rose were separated from each other during school hours. It mattered little, though, because as soon as lessons were finished they would link arms and walk home together, Melder going out of her way a little by taking the Rosenithon lane before turning off along the footpath to Trythance. Mostly they would part there – to meet again at the same spot next morning; but quite often the one would go home for supper with the other, and they would play together until it got dark.

But today, although Melder waited in her usual place just inside the school gate, Rose failed to join her. Melder wondered what had detained her. Nearly all the other children had come tumbling out of the modest school building and were already hopping and skipping joyfully on their way home – but there was no sign of Rose. It was all the more surprising because they had agreed to go home by Long Meadow Lane in order to see Mistress Nancy's pet monkey, and they would need to hurry otherwise they would be late getting home for supper.

After waiting for several minutes, Melder decided she must go and look for Rose.

Unknown to Melder, her friend had been waylaid upon emerging from the building by Myron Pinnerton and the gang of much smaller boys of which he was the overgrown leader. Grabbing a tress of Rose's long dark hair, Myron had pinned her head against the wall so that escape was impossible. With the fingers of his other, ham-like fist he stroked the underside of Rose's chin in an unpleasantly familiar manner. His face was threateningly close to hers, and as he spoke, his foul-smelling breath assailed her nostrils. Egged on by his jeering supporters, he taunted, 'So you reckons you'm a bit differ'nt from we, don't ee, Rosie? Bit more cleverer, like, eh?'

'Aw, arse,' grinned his idiotic-faced henchmen. 'You'm allus a bit differ'nt from we, aren't ee, Rosie?'

'An' you *am* differ'nt from we,' Myron continued, stupidly. 'You really *am*, Rosie.'

'Aw, arse,' agreed the jeering semi-circle. 'You really am differ'nt, Rosie. You'm cleverer'n we. Teacher says so, don't her, Myron? ''Top o' the class Rosie'' – that's what teacher do call ee, Rosie. I'nt that right, Myron?'

Rose, frightened but defiant, said nothing. Her silence merely provoked the bully.

'An' shall I tell ee why you'm so differ'nt?' Myron grinned foolishly.

'That's right, Myron,' bayed the pack. 'Tell Rosie why her'm differ'nt from the likes o' we.'

Myron's moon-shaped, unwashed face brushed against Rose's unblemished cheek. She tried to push him away, but her hair was virtually rivetted to the wall. She was his prisoner, and he knew it.

'An' if you'm a good girl, Rosie, I'll tell ee why you'm so differ'nt from we,' he offered, winking hugely at his admiring supporters. 'Ais, I'll tell ee – out o' the kindness o' my heart.' He paused, letting his words sink in, revelling in his power over his victim.

'Tedn that you'm only a girl, and ain't got 'xactly the things what us've got,' he went on, deliberately trying to titillate the lascivious imaginations of his pubescent cronies. 'It's because you'm not really Rosie Roskruge, see, Rosie.' He swept his accomplices with a sly grin. 'You didn' know that, Rosie, did ee,' he continued artfully. 'But I'm telling ee now, out o' the goodness o' my heart. You ain't really Rosie at all.' He paused, watching for the effect of this information. Rose stared back at him, bewildered but still defiant.

Myron's dirty, smelly fingers caressed the softness of her skin. 'And if you'm a very good girl, Rosie,' he confided, warming to the possibilities suggesting themselves in his mind, 'and do 'xactly as I say, I'll let ee into a secret 'bout who you'm be.' His face oscillated inanely, close to hers. 'An' you'd like that, wouldn't ee, Rosie? I think ee'd like that very much, eh?'

It was at that moment that Melder Tresooth came round the corner. She took in the scene at a glance; it was all too familiar . . . that dreadful Pinnerton boy, overgrown for his age, surrounded as ever by his gang of younger boys, and deliberately persecuting a child much smaller than himself – and always with a ratio in his favour of at least five against one.

'Leave her alone, you great bully,' Melder flared. 'Leave her alone at once!'

Myron turned; saw it was only a girl – and a girl on her own, too – and like a dog scenting success with a pliant bitch, he refused to be separated from his prey. Over his shoulder, he spat, 'Fart off! Melder – you festering arse-hole! Fart off!'

In that instant, all the sweetness drained from Melder like liquid from a broached and upturned barrel. From being a naturally gentle, loving Cornish maid she suddenly became transformed into a tigress defending her cub.

She positively flew at Myron, grabbing his shoulder with

her right hand and digging the fingernails of her left hand deep into the flesh of his neck. 'Leave her alone, you filthy bullying bastard!' she screamed, clawing her left hand down his neck. 'Leave her alone – or I'll gouge your bloody eyes out!'

The fury of her attack, and the uncharacteristic venom in her words, so frightened the little gang of cowards over whom Myron ruled that they fled like rats abandoning ship. Without so much as a backward glance, they left their powerful leader to his fate. Their concern was only for the preservation of their own skins.

Myron, a fellow-coward at heart, and deserted now by his fair-weather friends, released his hold on Rose and shambled off, ruefully nursing the ugly scratches on his neck. But not before Melder, still in the full adrenalin flow of her anger, hurled her parting shot . . . 'And if anyone's a bastard around here, it's you, Myron Pinnerton!'

She should never have said it, of course – and as soon as it was out, she felt ashamed. It was a village secret that she happened to know, and in the fury of her pent-up anger at Myron's persistent bullying and persecution of younger children, she had been unable to prevent herself from blurting it out. But she shouldn't have done so – and immediately she felt contrite.

Hugging the still trembling Rose tightly to her, she made straight for Thorn Cottage, and supper with the Roskruges. It was no time to play with Nancy's monkey.

That evening, after Melder had left for Trythance, and Rose had gone unusually early up to bed, Amia Roskruge's sharp ears caught the sound of sobbing coming from above.

'Ssh!' she cautioned, replacing the flat-iron on the hearth. 'That be our Rosie, Sam. There'm somethin' wrong, I reckon.'

Sampson stroked his chin reflectively. 'Ais,' he agreed, 'I thought her were extra special quiet at supper. 'Twas that bullyin' the Tresooth maid was tellin' of, I don't doubt.'

'Well, us'll soon learn,' she announced, hoisting the hem

68

of her plain linsey-woolsey skirt and beginning to mount the
narrow stairs, candle in hand.

'What is it, Rosie?' she soothed, as she entered her
daughter's small, sparsely furnished bedroom. 'What is it,
my love?'

All that was visible on the bed was a tousled mass of dark
hair. Rose's face, tear-stained and buried deeply in the
down-filled pillow, was completely covered by her long dark
curls. Amia knelt beside the bed; took Rose's hand in hers;
and began gently stroking it.

'What is it, my love?' she repeated softly. 'What be ailin'
thee then, Rosie? Tell your mama.'

For a long time Rose remained unresponsive, burying her
head still further into the pillow while Amia continued
soothingly to stroke her arm. Then, at last, a tear-stained
face appeared through the damp curls, and a voice, scarcely
audible, asked, 'Why am I different, mama?'

'Different, my love? What 'xactly do ee mean – different?'

But she knew her reply was no more than procrastination.
Many times during the last few years she and Sampson had
talked privately about whether, and if so, when, they should
tell Rose the truth concerning the unknown circumstances
of her birth, and of how she came to be their daughter. The
village had kept the secret well – as Cornish villagers can
when it concerns one of their own – out of respect and liking
for Sampson and Amia Roskruge, but particularly because
of Sampson's bravery in trying to rescue not only the child
but also the mother as well. But whenever Sampson and
Amia discussed the problem, they would find the most
cogent of reasons for doing nothing. They recognized that
the dreaded moment would have to come someday – but
not just yet. After all, Rose seemed so happy with them as
her mother and father; she had never known any other. And
it was bound to upset her when eventually they told her the
truth. Better leave it until she was a bit older – until she
was making her way in the world, perhaps – it would be
less of a shock to her then.

So they reasoned; and so they thankfully postponed the inevitable.

But they reckoned without the intervention of Myron Pinnerton.

Rubbing her eyes to dispel the salty tears, Rosie continued, haltingly, 'They just said I was different, mama. The boys and Myron . . . they captured me . . . and they said I was different. What did they mean by that, mama?'

Amia gathered Rose into her arms; soothed her; comforted her. 'Aw, them good-fer-nuthin' boys! They'm just a teasin' of ee, Rosie. That's all 'twas. They'm no good fer nuthin', they ain't.'

'But why am I different, ma,' Rosie persisted, 'I don't want to be different. I want to be like everyone else, mama. So, why do they say I'm different?'

A creak on the stairs told Amia that Sampson was on his way up. It was in character, Amia reflected. He had obviously heard the conversation from downstairs; had recognized that the moment had come. It was just like him – that he should wish to share with his wife the burden that was about to descend on them. They had gone into this thing together, and together they would see it through.

He quietly entered the room, sat on the opposite edge of the bed, and took hold of Rose's hand, caressing it gently between his own, gnarled, toil-hardened palms. He glanced across at his wife – and nodded. The time had come.

'It all happened quite a long time ago now, Rosie,' he began softly, 'when you were no more'n a babe. There were a brig . . . her went on the Manacles, her did. Wrecked, her was . . . a total loss. Broke up within a few minutes of striking. Well, and then . . . and then . . .'

'An' 'twas like your daddy says,' Amia put in, seeking to take her share of the story, 'there you was, only a tiny baby, out there in that terrible sea . . . in those thunderin' waves . . . an' your daddy, he went into they roarin' breakers and saved ee, my love . . . saved ee from bein' drowned, like . . .'

'But 'twere all a long time ago,' Sampson hastily interposed, not wishing to be cast as a hero, 'and us've been

70

meanin' to tell ee 'bout un for quite a while . . . as soon as ee were old 'nough to understand, like . . . and perhaps us oughta've told ee sooner . . . but somehow,' he ended lamely, 'us just seems to have let un go by . . .'

Soothing words, conforting hugs – no matter how lovingly bestowed – can never quite make up to a little girl for the sudden realization that the two people most dear to her, and whom she has come to regard as her parents, are not, in truth, her mother and father.

And although that same little girl bravely dried her tears and gave her lovingly concerned parents a positive assurance that she was now quite all right, as soon as they had gone downstairs once more, she covered her head with the blanket and quietly sobbed herself to sleep.

* * *

It was later than usual when Rose left Trythance, after supper, to walk home across the fields to Thorn Cottage.

She had been helping to harvest the last field of wheat on the Tresooths' farm – she and Melder, along with many others, tying and stooking the sheaves of corn after the reapers had done their work. She always loved the ancient custom of 'Crying the Neck'; she had witnessed it, and been a part of it, ever since she could remember, and at this particular time it gave her a feeling of permanence, a sense of belonging, a reassuring confirmation of her roots.

As the reapers neared the end of their task, they would leave a small patch of wheat in the middle of the field to be cut down by all the harvesters, men and women, boys and girls included. Then someone, usually farmer Tresooth himself, would raise the handful of wheat stalks high above his head, exclaiming, 'I 'ave un! I 'ave un!' Someone else would immediately ask, 'What 'ave ee? What 'ave ee? What 'ave ee?' and the farmer would joyfully reply, 'A Neck! A Neck! A Neck!' to be greeted by a great cheer from all in the field, reapers, harvesters and those who had just come for the fun.

The 'Neck' having been properly 'Cried', it would be preserved until the following year.

All this, coupled with the warming sensation engendered by the cider and croust which invariably followed the ceremony of 'Crying the Neck', filled Rose with contentment and a feeling of kinship with her surroundings as she now wended her way homewards.

Away to her right, and still just visible in the gathering twilight, lay the curving sweep of Godrevy Cove; and there, like the crustated back of a half-submerged sea monster, and looking deceptively harmless amid the gently rippling waves, were the dreaded Manacles.

Nearly three weeks had gone by since that fateful night when she had learnt the full story of how she came to be the daughter of Sampson and Amia Roskruge. Perhaps, in the whole of her life, she would never make a more traumatic discovery. In the space of a few minutes, the very ground upon which she had hitherto walked seemed to have been cut from under her feet. For several days she could scarcely touch a crumb of food; she felt as though her tummy had been comprehensively squeezed and then put through a ringer. Her insides felt too twisted and flattened to absorb anything solid. To placate her mother, as well as to hide her inward distress, she drank a little warmed milk and pecked at the nourishment placed lovingly in front of her.

Throughout those days – and nights – when she had walked the lonely path of anonymity – a nothing belonging to nobody – she had clung to the vision, so vividly created by the story told to her, of the man on the beach, Sampson Roskruge, who had risked his own life to save her from the sea. Ever since she could remember, she had always felt a special affinity towards the man she believed, without any question of doubt, to be her natural father, and if she loved him then, she loved him even more so now.

Strangely, she thought to herself, even had the choice lain with her she would not have chosen anyone else for a father. He had cuddled her when she was a baby, told her bedtime stories before she went to sleep, and simply by the

72

solidity of his presence he had given her, she realized now, even at her still tender age of girlhood, a wonderful feeling of security.

And as she grew older, it was he who brought the sparkle into her life, the excitement. He would take her with him in the fishing boat he jointly owned with Mr Tripconey up at Trevallack; he had shown her how to catch bream, hake, cod and conger with hook and line. And after harvest-time, when the wheat was in the stook and the Neck had been Cried, he would take her up onto the cliff where the huer had his little hut from which he kept constant watch for the approaching shoals of pilchards. A great thrill would run through her as she heard the man shouting through his speaking trumpet, 'Hevva! - Hevva!', warning the waiting seine boats that the fish were coming. Eagerly she would scan the sea for the tell-tale red-brown flurry in the water, the unmistakable sign of the approaching shoal. With mounting excitement she would watch the huer directing the seine boats with his white flags until, at the precise moment, he would bawl through his trumpet, 'Shoot the seine!', and the boats, as rapidly as possible, would encircle the shoal, gradually drawing it closer and closer to the excited villagers waiting on the shore.

If, at times, she felt sorry for the helpless fish struggling furiously within the net, she would remind herself that fishing had been the staple industry among seaboard folk for countless generations – indeed, had not the Christ drawn his disciples from among fishermen. 'I will make you fishers of men,' he had said, and he had founded his church on Peter, the big fisherman. So, there couldn't be anything wrong or cruel about fishing, otherwise Jesus would have said so – and so far as she, Rose, could remember, he never had. At least, if he had, the vicar had never mentioned it in any of his long sermons.

So, fishing was all right. It was a wholly acceptable way of life. 'Let down your net for a draught', Jesus had told those disciples who had toiled all night and caught nothing. And when they did as they were told, they caught so many fishes that their net broke – the very thing the excited villagers of Coverack, Porthallow and Porthoustock most feared as they waited expectantly while the menfolk dragged the nets inshore.

Yes, it was exciting, Rose reflected; it was things like that – excitement, activity – which she associated with her father. A man's world.

But, if Sampson was her girlish idol, it was to Amia's ample bosom that she flew in time of trouble. It had never failed. Always ready with warmth, comfort and soothing words, her mother knew just how to apply healing balm to lacerated feelings, injured pride, sagging prestige. Rose knew she was lucky in her parents, Sampson and Amia Roskruge, but she couldn't stop herself wondering . . .

She had just gone through the second field separating Trythance from Rosenithon when, from behind the tall hedgebank, a dark figure emerged, barring her way.

'Hullo, Rosie,' a voice purred at her out of the gathering gloom. 'Just on your way home, are ee, Rosie?' The words, the voice – immediately, alarm bells started clanging in her head. 'I thought I might catch ee on your way home.'

Unwisely Rose had backed against the coign of the hedgebank, instinctively distancing herself from the unmistakable figure of Myron Pinnerton. 'What are you doing here, Myron?' she enquired, trying hard to disguise the fear in her voice.

'Aw, I just come to say I were sorry, Rosie. I thought I might catch ee goin' home,' Myron repeated, a stupid, conciliatory cadence in his tone.

'Sorry for what?' Rose asked – again, unwisely. It would have been better to accept the apology without query before hurrying on. But we are not always wise, especially when frightened.

'For sayin' you was differ'nt at school the other day.' Once again, by stretching out his left hand, Myron had caught a tress of Rose's hair and pinned it against the granite gatepost. 'Just come to say "Sorry", Rosie,' he added, without so much as a grain of repentance in his fatuous voice.

'That's all right, Myron,' Rose replied, gradually regaining her natural courage. 'I accept your apology, and we'll say no more about it.'

She tried to move away, but her head was held fast against the post. 'Let me go, please, Myron,' she said, politely enough – but then, as panic took root, she flared, 'Let me go!'

''Ere, 'old on a minute!' Myron countered, in that deliberately assumed voice of a simpleton which he used when he sought to beguile. 'I got somethin' to show ee, Rosie, I got somethin' extra special to show ee.'

While he was yet speaking, his right hand was fumbling with the falls of his breeches, unbuttoning them, and then displaying precisely what they were intended to hide.

At his birth, the fairy godmother perched at the end of the rough-hewn cot had clearly decided to withhold from Myron the benefits of brains and good looks. Instead, she had made up for this deficiency by granting him an abundance of muscle and brawn coupled with a phallic appurtenance of truly gargantuan proportions. It was enormous.

'There y'are, Rosie,' he drooled. 'Take a good look at ee. I'nt un a real beauty! I brought un out specially for ee. Just look how un's risin' see. All for you, Rosie. I'll wager ee'll never see anything bigger'n this un,' he added, with genuine pride.

To a young girl, bordering upon the age of puberty, such a revelation was nothing less than horrific. Like other carefully brought up girls of her age, Rose was aware of the anatomical differences between the sexes, but apart from the very occasional sight of celestial cherubim – either in the sculptured form or as background to some religious painting, and nearly always with a strategically placed oak leaf preserving modesty – she had never before been rudely confronted with the male sexual organ. In its normal, quiescent, flaccid state it would have been upsetting enough, but Myron Pinnerton's procreative equipment, when presented for inspection, could always be relied upon to do its owner's bidding. In short, without fail, it rose to the occasion.

Thus, at a tender age of innocent girlhood, Rose found herself being invited to inspect the physical expression of growing manhood in its most provocative form. And, worse still, not only to inspect . . . for Myron Pinnerton was even now inviting her to touch it.

'You can stroke un, if ee likes, Rosie,' he purred, imbecilically. 'As a special favour to ee, Rosie, you can stroke un.' And when she drew back in disgust, he urged more forcefully. 'Go on, Rosie . . . stroke un!'

Drawing back even further, and placing one hand over her eyes, she cried, 'No! No! It's horrible! It's vulgar! I'll not have anything to do with it.' Despite the enormity of the whole grotesque situation, some kind of devilish magnetism compelled her to unshield her eyes as this perverted youth went on, 'Look, Rosie! Look what un'll do for I.' With a swoop of his free hand, he picked up the hem of her rough-woven dress and, with a foolish giggle, he hooked it over his swaying protuberance. 'There, see!' he gurgled proudly. 'See what a fine clothes peg 'er can make.'

This display of lewd humour might just possibly have been tolerated from someone of such restricted intelligence and limited sense of propriety as Myron Pinnerton – after all, ever since the beginning of time, both children and animals have been intrigued by genitalia – had it stopped there. But it didn't. Myron knew what he wanted; and having successfully lifted Rose's still pathetically childish skirt and underskirt, he proceeded to press home his advantage. Before Rose fully realized his intention, his thick, stubby fingers were fumblingly exploring her most private area.

'Stop it!' she screamed, trying furiously to wriggle free of his groping hand. 'Leave me alone, you brute!'

But still he pressed his body against hers, his fingers forcing themselves between her upper thighs. 'Oh, Rosie,' he breathed hoarsely, with mounting ecstasy. 'Oh, Rosie, Rosie!'

Instinctively, and without proper knowledge of the effect

of her action, Rose brought one leg sharply upwards, digging her knee into his groin.

The result was instantaneous. The rampant youth let out a squeal of anguish, released the tress of Rose's hair, and backed away, doubled up with pain and clutching his testicles. Simultaneously, the terrified girl saw her chance and was gone, fleeing not only for the retention of her virtue but most likely, she thought, for her life as well.

Once again she arrived back at Thorn Cottage in a state of near hysteria. Once again – and this time even more so – it fell to Sampson and Amia Roskruge to comfort and to soothe – and eventually to coax from their sobbing, frightened daughter, the reason for her overwhelming distress.

Later that evening, when time, that unfailing friend of the abused as well as the bereaved, had started to work its healing process, and when Rose, still in those strong, all-embracing arms of her simple-hearted mother, had finally fallen asleep, Sampson Roskruge jumped on the back of his favourite mare and galloped off into the night, through the village and then over to Trevallack Farm.

His friend, Wilmot Tripconey, was just finishing a late supper.

*　　*　　*

Myron Pinnerton hauled in his line and prepared to return home. He had been fishing from the rocks off Manacle Point all afternoon, but now it was beginning to get dark, and he was feeling cold. He gathered up his tackle and began the steep climb up from Porthoustock.

As he breasted the Rosenithon Quoits, his inglorious mind reviewed once more the subject which had been exercising it for most of the last two days – the thought of Rosie Roskruge. The excruciating pain arising from the fortuitous blow she had dealt him in the most vulnerable part of his anatomy had now worn off, but the memory of how close he had come to the consummation of his most burning desire still coloured his every thought. How very near he had been to success! And Rosie had clearly been most impressed by what he had shown her. Why, then, had he failed? It was very puzzling. After all, what were young girls for if not to satisfy a lusty fellow's normal appetite? – and Rosie was certainly growing into a very desirable fruit! What had gone wrong, then? he wondered. It had always been his under-standing, based on information passed to him by the older lads of the village, that all you had to do was to show a girl your credentials, and provided they were substantial enough, and ready enough, then the rest was easy. And Myron Pinnerton's 'credentials' were certainly very impressive!

As he passed the entrance to one of Farmer Tripconey's off fields he noticed a haycart standing just inside the gateway. He wondered why it was there, but the thought quickly vanished from his mind as he began planning how best to mount his next attack on the girl whose young but developing body he now found so fascinating.

His lascivious mind was still contemplating all manner of the lewdest schemes when he felt his arms and shoulders forcibly gripped from behind, and before he knew what was happening he found himself being bundled through the gate-way and into the field. He was then thrown to the ground, face downwards while his hands were tied behind his back and a gag put into his mouth. Out of the corner of his eye he caught sight of his assailants. Each man was of strong, muscular build; each was masked and hooded. Not a single word had been spoken between them. One of them had laid an ominous-smelling wooden tub on the stubble nearby.

Having tied and gagged the precocious youth, they set about removing his breeches – nothing else. No further removal of clothing was necessary; his shirt, like the legendary 'Cutty Sark', was of no great length, and he wore no underpants.

The wooden container, smelling strongly of its contents, was then placed beside the prostrate figure. The two men knelt down. Swiftly, and with farm-bred thoroughness, they smeared the buttocks all over with the sticky, tarry substance.

Then they rolled him over onto his side. One man's boot went over the youth's ankles, pinning them to the ground;

the other man similarly anchored the victim's neck, as with a sheep about to be sheared. A gnarled, work-hardened hand went deeply into the tub of pitch, brought out a fistful of the black, strong-smelling pitch, and smeared it comprehensively all over the lower abdomen – and, most comprehensively of all, over the private parts.

To add the final indignity, the other man felt in his pocket to produce a handful of poultry feathers. Buttocks, abdomen, and especially the genitals, were then carefully and systematically festooned.

Again, throughout the whole operation, not one word had passed between the two men.

Having completed their task, they then carried the youth to the nearby cart and laid him on a bed of hay. Then they set off for the village.

Next morning, as Myron Pinnerton's cronies entered the square on their way to school, they were astonished to see their leader securely tied to the wooden railings outside the White Hart Inn. He had his boots on; his socks were in their usual bedraggled position around his ankles; his chest and upper abdomen were covered in the normal way by his shirt.

But he had no breeches. And as usual, when Myron Pinnerton's pride and joy was available for inspection – even though it might be covered with black pitch and decorated with feathers – it never failed to rise to the occasion. Despite its recent indignity, it remained rampantly defiant.

It was too much for the small boys. As each one passed on his way to school, the giggles and the smirks were frequent and unrestrained.

'Ooh, Myron!' they squirked. 'Oooh, oooh, Myron!'

But the rest of the village pilloried the youth. They guessed what he'd been up to! It was rough justice, but they reckoned he deserved it.

CHAPTER FIVE

Once to every man and nation . . .

Ashley Penberth sat astride his favourite mount, gazing out across the English Channel.

How many times had he sat there before, on the highest point of Rosemullion Head, murmuring aloud to the faithful Puncher – talking to him as though to an old friend, confiding his innermost thoughts – as he had done so often in days gone by when he was riding the coastline from Helford down to Cadgwith as His Majesty's Riding Officer for the district.

And that district had included the parish of St Keverne.

Once more, as he sat astride the patient cob, the memories came flooding back. That first time – as a newly appointed officer of H. M. Customs – when riding from Gillan Creek down to Porthoustock, he had pulled up to allow Puncher a bite of fresh grass, and the little pantomime of the red shirt had been played out before him in a cottage garden down there in Porthallow. The grey-haired woman had come out of her back door, gathered in the washing but left the red shirt lazily fluttering on the line. Then something – Puncher jingling his bridle, perhaps – had caught her attention; she had spotted a 'King's Man' astride his horse, up there on the cliff – and straightaway she had removed the red shirt from the washing line.

It was the time-honoured signal, Ashley knew, to an incoming ship loaded with contraband goods; red shirt hanging on the line meant 'The coast is clear!' – and no red shirt signalled 'Danger! There's a goddamned Riding Officer on the prowl!'

A few moments later, a young lad had emerged from the cottage, jumped on a pony and galloped off up the hill in the direction of St Keverne – a village, Ashley had been told, with a very healthy appetite for smuggling.

It had been all the more of a surprise, therefore, to find that the news of his approach did not appear to have reached the Three Tuns Inn by the time he arrived there shortly afterwards.

Having seen to Puncher's stabling, he had clattered in to the bar with as much noise as possible. He was a 'King's Man', new to the job, and he did not believe it would add to his credentials if he were to creep about apologetically. He was being paid – pittance though it was – to enforce the law; to ensure payment of revenue to His Majesty, King George the Third, so that the country could afford, among other things, an incomparable Royal Navy with which to defend our shores. It was a thankless task, admittedly, and a lonely one. Every man's hand, it seemed, was agin you. Nobody loved a 'King's Man' – because it was his daily business and his duty to seize contraband goods which included all those little 'extras' – a drop of brandy to keep out the winter's cold, a bit of lace to trim a pretty dress, and a nice hot cup of tea to cheer a dreary day – none of which a poor body could afford unless it had been smuggled in from across the sea.

But for Ashley Penberth it was a job. Someone had to do it. And by taking it on, Ashley had made it possible for the faithful Zephanaiah Curnow – he who had been the only survivor from the wreck in which Ashley's father had perished, and who had subsequently supported his widowed mother so staunchly in the years thereafter – to remain in his cottage at Treworden. Times were not good on the land then, and if Ashley had remained at home and farmed the Treworden acres himself, Zeph would have had to find another job. Small thanks, Ashley reckoned, for unstinted loyalty.

So, having failed to obtain a commission in the Navy on account of an injury sustained at school, he had done the

81

next best thing – or so he thought. He had become one of His Majesty's Riding Officers in the Customs Service. At least he would be working out of doors. No dusty ledger, no high office stool, no endlessly scratching quill pen for him. His ceiling would be the sky, his walls would be no more claustrophobic than a cluster of granite rocks; and with the salty tang of the sea in his nostrils he would be riding the most beautiful coastline in the world. He would certainly be unpopular, but at least he would be *free*.

As he sat now astride the faithful Puncher, staring out across the sea, his mind went back to that first official visit to the Three Tuns Inn at St Keverne.

It had been his intention that gloriously sunny June day to ride on down to Cadgwith – another hotbed of smugglers, so he'd been told – but he had been dawdling, up there on a small plateau above Porthkerris beach, lying in the bracken while Puncher dragged at a patch of succulent pasture, well-shaded by a tall clump of furze. His thoughts then had revolved around the lovely Alethea MacKenzie, his childhood love – the girl who had enchanted him ever since he had first gone over to Trevadne, to share lessons with Sir Andrew MacKenzie's two little daughters, Jeannie and Alethea. Jeannie was the elder of the two. She was lovely, as well; dark-haired, vivacious, and even at that comparatively tender age, sexually precocious. But Alethea had been the one he had fallen in love with – she with the corn-coloured hair and eyes like the sky of a cloudless summer's day. She had taken his hand on that first morning of lessons with the MacKenzie governess, Miss Proudfoot – or just 'Pruddy' for short – and led him round to her side of the table, saying, 'You shall sit by me, Ashley', and to the shy, self-conscious farmer's boy that was the Ashley Penberth of yesteryear, the messsage transmitted by that soft little hand of hers in his was one of 'friendship for life'.

At least, that was how it had seemed to that 'farmer-boy', set down as he was in the awe-inspiring surrounds of that impressive squire's residence. Through childhood, into youth, and then on into early manhood, that 'friendship for life' had grown into love – on Ashley's side, by any measure – and if, in maturity, Alethea had felt a higher calling, a more sanctified betrothal, then that was one of the perplexing mysteries of life.

But as he lay in the bracken, head cradled in his hands, a stem of juicy grass in his mouth, and staring up at the azure sky on that peerless June afternoon, he had no foreknowledge of Alethea's decision to take the veil. All the world then seemed at peace with itself – and Alethea, that lovely younger daughter of Sir Andrew MacKenzie, was the girl for him.

Indeed, it had required a conscious effort of mind to drag his thoughts away from the love of his life and get on with the job for which he was being paid.

Remounting Puncher, he had ridden down into Porthoustock and then up the steep hill into St Keverne.

He had pushed open that stableyard door of the Three Tuns Inn with a roughness and a clatter calculated to announce his arrival. He had no intention of being overlooked.

When he stalked into the bar the scene that greeted him was familiar enough; dun-coloured walls half-panelled with varnished timber; a faded picture above the empty fireplace; a high-backed settle and a few rough-hewn chairs beneath a sagging plaster ceiling blackened by years of ascending tobacco smoke. There were many such inns and kiddleywinks throughout the length and breadth of the county – dimly lit, cheerless and uninviting.

But then he saw her – standing behind the bar and buffing the highly polished surface with an old woollen stocking.

As his eyes became accustomed to the subdued lighting of the inn he had noticed that she was wearing a dark magenta-coloured silk dress – and that she was exceptionally pretty.

Even then he had wondered who she was and how such a remarkably pretty girl came to be serving behind a bar in St Keverne. And how often had he wondered that, since!

He had not been very kind to her on that first meeting –

he had made her and her employer, the spindle-shanked landlord, Will Trenethy, manhandle the tubs and ankers of spirits down in the cellar during his inspection, and in doing so she had torn a nasty gash in her new silk dress. He had felt a brute at the time; but now, the memory was like a dagger in his heart.

That had been their first meeting. Understandably, she had loathed the sight of him. He couldn't blame her. In the interests of his official business he had behaved, from her point of view, unpardonably.

Next day he had been able to perform some small service by helping her put back a wheel that had come off the haycart she was driving. It was nothing, really, but she had seemed impressed. She had even tried to thank him the following day as he rode back from Cadgwith – but she had caused Puncher to shy, and he, Ashley Penberth, Riding Officer for the district, had been unseated. He had *not* been amused.

And then, one day, he had come upon her bathing in a small cove near Porthoustock. Shamelessly, he had manoeuvred himself into the position of a Peeping Tom as she undressed behind some inadequately concealing rocks. His dissolute gaze had devoured the beauty of her nubile young body – the shapely thighs, the voluptuous curve of the hips, the bravely uplifted, pert young breasts. It had quickened the rising power of his manhood; it had been most disturbing. Try as he would, he could not obliterate the memory of that sexually exciting revelation, despite the frequent reminders to himself that Alethea was the girl he truly loved – and desired.

Then had come the night of the fire.

Looking back now – and with all the advantage of hindsight – he wondered why he had not realized more readily that something was afoot. True, the village had seemed unusually quiet, and the atmosphere had felt charged with an air of expectancy – but you often had that feeling on a hot summer's evening, especially if there was a storm brewing out to sea.

And the bar of the Three Tuns Inn contained its usual sprinkling of 'regulars', perched expectantly like sparrows on a branch and eager to applaud vociferously any shaft or sally of humour from the 'King's Man'. He had realized they were only trying to keep him in a good humour, but he was enjoying himself. After a long day's riding, a deep draught of Will Trenethy's best porter was washing the tiredness out of his limbs, investing his view of life with an iridescent hue, and filling him with a sense of ever-growing bonhomie.

And, as he leant against the bar, the close proximity of a delicately perfumed Rosie, her provocatively cut bodice displaying more than just a hint of what lay beneath, had done nothing to diminish his pleasure. He was enjoying himself. And even if he suspected they were lacing his porter with something a little bit stronger . . . so be it! He had a good, strong head; he could stand it. And besides, a Riding Officer's job was an extremely lonely one; he made few friends, and was frequently outnumbered by his adversaries, and the opportunities for a little revelry among good-hearted Cornish countryfolk were few and far between.

And that barmaid, Rosie! She really was extraordinarily attractive!

When, later, having laid his supper up in the one and only guest bedroom at the inn – the one with that immaculate view of Falmouth Bay and Rosemullion Head – she had tended him so charmingly, bringing him that deliciously creamy, brandy-laced trifle and refilling his tankard with Will's heady brew, he had made little resistance.

He had resisted even less when, with the gentleness of a purring kitten, she had slowly divested him of his clothes and laid him down on the simple wooden bed. Already the room was spinning round alarmingly as he sank back on to the pillow . . . but through the steamy vapour of his befuddled brain he had heard the sound of trotting ponies.

Too late, he realized what was happening; too late he understood why the drink had been so potent; too late, he knew just what those ponies would be carrying strapped across their willing backs!

But when, despite rapidly blurring vision, he saw that Rosie had pulled the silk-taffeta dress over her head and was slowly moving towards him clad only in gartered stockings and diaphanous chemise, his resistance had finally flown out of the open window.

His Majesty King George the Third might need his revenue to pay for his army and his navy, but when a red-blooded Riding Officer feels the warmth of a seductive young body against his, its fragrant owner beneath the coverlet on the bed, then who can blame him if he decides, for just this once, to let the bloody ponies thunder by!

But the fire had very nearly ruined everything! – not only the thatched roof of the Three Tuns Inn. Burnt to a cinder, it was; nothing but the shell left standing, despite the gallant efforts of the villagers and their hand-to-hand water bucket chain.

Sitting astride Puncher now, and gazing yet again out over the bay, from Rosemullion Head to the clearly visible sailors' landmark of St Keverne church spire, Ashley was remembering how he and Rose, after first freeing Puncher and the other two horses from their smoke-filled stable, had then fought with the rest of the village to quench the raging fire.

He was remembering also that night, nearly three months later, when she had surprised him outside the Angel Inn at Helston. From the deep shadows of the side yard she had glided like some hooded spectre, touching his arm and saying, 'I had to see you. It's urgent!'

What could be so urgent, he had wondered – and what could demand such a clandestine meeting. Had she come to tell him that after that one night of love, so rudely interrupted by Will Trenethy's shout of 'FIRE', she was nevertheless with child.

A rueful smile flickered across his face at the recollection that it had turned out to be nothing of the kind. She had come to warn him that a notorious gang of wreckers was about to pillage a stricken vessel down at Porthleven. The smile softened as he remembered how she insisted on coming with him on that dangerous mission – and how helpful she had been in overcoming that wicked little villain with the lamp, and how tenderly she had staunched the bleeding and bound up his wounds after that bloody affray with the wreckers.

Each memory stabbed afresh at his heart. But the one which plunged the knife most deeply and twisted it until the pain became almost unbearable was the re-enactment in his mind of that errand of mercy – that adventurous rescue of the prisoners from the Château Fontanelle.

Against his better judgment – if not against the sub-conscious dictates of his heart – he had allowed Rose to come with him in his lugger, 'Heatherbelle II', when, together with Zeph Curnow, they had crossed the Channel to the Baie de Morlaix in an attempt to snatch Alethea MacKenzie and her father, and as many others as the lugger could carry, from the bloodthirsty clutches of the Convention and, ultimately, the blade of the guillotine.

Thanks to Zeph's knowledge of navigation – acquired on former smuggling trips to Roscoff with Ashley's father – they had found the Château Fontanelle without difficulty and, under the cover of darkness, they had tied up alongside a nearby jetty. But it was thanks to Rose's forethought that they were able to scale the high wall which surrounded the château. Dressed in a home-made Carmelite habit – they had received intelligence that a whole convent of Carmelites had been imprisoned in the château – Rose had cleverly thought of substituting for the usual nun's girdle a strong, knotted rope. Within minutes, an overhanging tree branch had been found, the rope looped over it, and Ashley first, then Rose, were over the high wall and within the precincts of the Château Fontanelle.

But it was when they were coming away, their mission of rescue almost accomplished, that the tragedy happened.

Rose was leading the escaping party – or so Ashley had thought – while he and Sir Andrew MacKenzie, armed with a pair of flintlock pistols each, were delaying the pursuing soldiers. Rose knew where the knotted rope had been left hanging. She would guide the fleeing prisoners down to the quay where Zeph would be waiting, ready to cast off the lugger at a moment's notice.

All seemed to be going well. The first, unexpected volley of fire from Sir Andrew and Ashley had momentarily thrown the soldiers into confusion. Valuable time had been bought; time enough for the fugitives to gain their objective. By now, Rose and her escaping companions should be over the wall and safely aboard the lugger.

But time was becoming acutely precious. The tide would be receding rapidly. 'Heatherbelle II', probably overloaded with an excess of passengers and therefore drawing a greater depth of water than usual, could not remain afloat much longer. And if she were to be left high and dry, all then would be lost!

Time, therefore, for Ashley and Sir Andrew to loose off a final volley – and then cut and run.

No time then to bother about the knotted rope; up and over the wall they had scrambled – somehow. And there was the lugger looking uncomfortably full of huddled fugitives, and Zeph at the tiller, saying anxiously, 'Only just in time, zur. Water be runnin' out fast!'

It was only then, as his eyes swept over the passengers aboard, that Ashley had realized that Rose was missing!

'Where's Rosie!' he had shouted. 'Where is she?'

Nobody knew. She'd been with them down to the wall, they said. But then . . . well, she'd just disappeared.

Since that moment, scarcely a day had passed for Ashley without the memory of it returning to haunt him. True, he had done his best. He had set off immediately in search of her, despite the pleadings from the boat that they would be stuck on the mud and 'caught like rats in a trap!'

'Then sail without me!' he had ordered as he ran back along the path beneath the high wall, seeking once more the knotted rope. 'If I'm not back in time . . . sail without me!'

But he had been shot by one of the guards . . . and after that, he remembered nothing.

Nothing, that is, until he regained consciousness . . . only to find 'Heatherbelle II' under way, and making a spirited bid for freedom.

* * *

Sir Andrew MacKenzie was in the library at Trevadne, scanning the pages of 'The Tatler' when Ashley walked in.

'Aha, there, laddie,' Sir Andrew breezed. 'Guid to see ye.' He carelessly flung the periodical on to the library table. 'And how is ma wee dochter, Jeannie, then. I hae na set ma een on her for a wee while.'

Ashley glanced at 'The Tatler', open at one of the society pages. He thought it strange that his father-in-law should be interested in matters so largely connected with London.

And then he remembered Madame de Levoisier.

'It's about Jeannie – at least partly about Jeannie – that I'd like to speak to you, Sir Andrew,' he said, moving towards the leaded windows overlooking the rose garden. Every time he entered that room it brought back vivid memories of the days when he had shared lessons with Jeannie and Alethea under the tutorship of Miss Proudfoot; when he had met the two girls for the first time, and when, as a shy, uncultured boy, he had fallen in love with Alethea.

'Oh, aye,' Sir Andrew queried, his bristly ginger eyebrows shooting up into his forehead, 'she's not been giving you any trouble, I hope.' His eyebrows descended as he assumed a mock-serious expression. 'Mind you,' he continued, half ruefully, 'she's always been a lively lassie. Oh, aye, a braw wee lassie, is ma Jeannie – as well you must know.'

Ashley decided he must come to the point at once. He took a deep breath.

'You remember the rescue from the Château Fontanelle,' he began, turning to face his father-in-law.

Sir Andrew looked surprised. 'D'ye think I shall ever forget it, laddie,' he challenged, his tone changing from banter to one of the utmost seriousness. 'As my brother, Ranald, said in his speech when you and Jeannie were wed, we all owe you and your man, Curnow – but especially you, laddie – a debt of gratitude we can never repay.'

Ashley nodded grateful appreciation. But then, fixing Sir Andrew with a pointed stare, he said slowly, 'Me . . . Zeph Curnow . . . and there was one other . . .'

The Scotsman looked away; gazed, unseeingly, out of the mullioned window. After a long pause, he acknowledged softly, 'Aye, I know who you mean. The wee lassie that came wi' ye.'

'And helped me,' Ashley added, '. . . stood by me . . . shared with us all the dangers . . . helped you and the others to escape.'

With a sharp intake of breath, Sir Andrew nodded agreement. The reminder had touched him on a raw spot. He remembered it all so clearly. Upon finding that Rose had not returned to the lugger, Ashley had declared forcefully that he could not leave without her . . . that he would *never* leave without her . . . and it was Sir Andrew himself who, knowing that only a few minutes remained before the ship would be left high and dry by the receding tide, had roughly declared, 'Then we're all as good as dead. Caught like rats in a trap!'

And when Ashley, notwithstanding, had made it clear he could never leave without Rose and that he was going back for her, it had been Sir Andrew who had decided to stop him. It had been a split-second decision. If they waited until he returned – with or without Rose – the lugger would have dried out at the quayside; the soldiers, at their leisure, would then have recaptured the boatload of fugitives; they would all have been marched back to the Château Fontanelle, either to be shot as escaping prisoners, or carted away to Brest as further fodder for the guillotine. The whole daring rescue exploit would have foundered – there, on the mud, beside the quay.

In that fleeting moment of decision, when seconds rather than minutes counted, Sir Andrew MacKenzie had decided it was better that one young girl – brave though she had been – should be left behind, rather than that many more innocent people, including the owner of the rescuing lugger, himself, should be ruthlessly murdered without justification and without trial.

So, with Zeph Curnow at his side, Sir Andrew had set off in pursuit of Ashley, determined to bring him back to the boat before it was too late – and prepared to use the butt of his pistol to knock him senseless, if need be. In the event, it was a soldier's bullet, hitting Ashley in the leg and bringing him to the ground, which had saved Sir Andrew from that necessity.

But the intention had been there.

Now, from beneath a pair of bushy, ginger-coloured eyebrows he regarded Ashley minutely. He thought he could divine, etched in the younger man's face, something of the remorse which was racking his soul. Sir Andrew understood. He felt no small measure of guilt, himself.

After that brave and gallant rescue from the Château Fontanelle, Sir Andrew had felt he owed a great deal more than just gratitude to Ashley Penberth in whom he had taken a special interest ever since as an unborn child he had lost his father, shipwrecked on the Manacles. Indeed, he felt he owed Ashley Penberth his very life.

As a result, and after discussion with Ashley's widowed mother, Marianne, Sir Andrew had offered to Ashley the more lucrative and prestigious post of Manager of the Trevadne Estate. It would mean that he no longer needed to continue as a Riding Officer in His Majesty's Customs Service. He had done well for His Majesty in seizing, single-handed, a valuable haul of contraband goods which had elicited a grudging word of praise from a hateful senior officer; he had done well for innocent seafaring folk as a whole by apprehending a gang of bloodthirsty wreckers and sending them to their just deserts. In the process, he had been badly wounded. He had been wounded again – shot in the thigh – while going back for that little barmaid girl during the rescue from the Château Fontanelle. And if that were not enough, the laddie had suffered a broken leg while a schoolboy and, as a result of incompetent

91

medical attention, had been left with a permanent limp.

Ashley deserved a quieter life, Sir Andrew had thought; and so did his mother. But even more importantly, so did Sir Andrew's dark-haired, vivacious and sexually precocious elder daughter, Jeannie.

And Jeannie had a habit of getting her own way.

Neither Sir Andrew nor Ashley's mother were so naive as not to see the risk – but as the weeks went by, and the war with revolutionary France made contacts across the Channel increasingly difficult, they did nothing to hinder the developing relationship between Ashley and Jeannie. A boy and girl friendship of long standing soon became something much stronger. While she most deeply desired his manhood, for him, in the loneliness of his remorse and guilt, her sensuality acted like an obliterating drug.

Marianne Penberth was delighted. She had always hoped – and often prayed – that her son would one day marry one of the MacKenzie girls. And on a glorious early summer's day, in the church on the cliff overlooking the Helford River estuary – in the sight of God and a goodly congregation – her prayers were answered and her dream came true.

Ashley Penberth and Jeannie MacKenzie became man and wife together, 'to have and to hold from this day forward . . .'

Still gazing out of the library window, and with his hands thrust deep into his breeches pockets, Sir Andrew now said quietly, 'And it's bothering you, laddie. I can see that.'

'She's still alive,' Ashley replied, 'and she's in prison.'

'How d'ye know that?'

'She got a message through to me.'

'She did?' Sir Andrew queried in surprise. 'And when did you get it?'

Again Ashley drew a deep breath, whistling through his teeth. 'On the very morning after Jeannie and I were married,' he said flatly.

'Och, laddie!' Sir Andrew retorted sympathetically. 'And ye've kept it to yersel ever since, eh?'

'I've had to. No one else to confide in – except Zeph. He knows. It was one of his old friends who got the message through.'

'And wha' did the message say?'

'It just said "In prison at Brest".' The catch in Ashley's voice told Sir Andrew more than could a whole volume of words.

'Aye,' he breathed, in a surprisingly understanding tone, 'and ye've been living with that knowledge all the while.'

'Trying to suppress it,' Ashley groaned. 'Trying to put it away . . . not to think about it. After all, I'm married now to Jeannie,' he blurted. 'It's not fair to her . . . and I can't give her . . . I can't be to her . . .'

He broke off; began pacing the room. How could he tell his father-in-law that he was unable to give his full, loving attention to his daughter . . . that, with the image of an imprisoned, endangered Rose continuously in his mind, he could not even fulfil the frequent demands of the marriage bed.

Again, with an unusual depth of sympathetic understanding, Sir Andrew merely commented, 'Aye. I ken what you mean, laddie.' After a pause, he added, 'And what do you plan to do?'

'I must go for her,' Ashley replied, simply. 'I've wrestled with the problem but I know now I shall find no peace unless I go over and, somehow, bring her back.'

Sir Andrew stroked his chin, deep in thought. 'It'll not be easy, now the war's growing more vicious,' he said at length. 'The French are watching their coastline very closely – escaping émigrés, you know. And what about the navigation into and out of Brest? It could be hazardous slipping past those two Pointes guarding the entrance to the Rade.'

'I know it'll not be easy,' Ashley replied firmly, 'but I also know that I shall never rest until I've tried.'

Sir Andrew nodded. 'No. I don't think you will.' He continued to stroke his chin contemplatively. 'I don't believe you will.'

'What troubles me very much, tho',' Ashley went on, 'is

the problem of Jeannie. I may be away for quite a while . . .
I may not be able to effect a rescue straightaway . . . but
how can I explain my absence to her?'

'Gone to buy sheep in Scotland?' Sir Andrew mused –
but immediately saw the impracticability of the suggestion.
'But no, you may be away for several weeks; it would be
hard to attribute that to sheep buying.'

He frowned; continued to stare out of the window, deep
in thought.

'Of course,' he said, brightening, 'the very fact that we
are at war might well provide the solution. Secret government
business . . . knowledge of the Brittany coastal waters,
etcetera, etcetera . . . all very clandestine, d'ye ken.'

A rueful smile spread across Ashley's face. He was seeing
his father-in-law in a very unfamiliar light. Sir Andrew
seemed to be almost enjoying the prospect of deception. Was
it something to do with the Highland ancestry, he wondered,
or was it just that he appreciated the romance of a daring
rescue?

As if realizing his son-in-law's thoughts, Sir Andrew
MacKenzie flashed him something very nearly resembling
a conspiratorial wink as he added, 'Leave it with me, laddie.
I have an idea I may be able to help you.'

CHAPTER SIX

The Château de Kerjean

Outside the pillared front entrance the cart was waiting. Those familiar heavy oak doors. How they brought back memories! That first evening, now seeming so long ago, when she had stood among those tall dark trees, her hand firmly held in Ashley's powerful grip as she gazed forlornly at those formidable doors – when she and Ashley had come to rescue Alethea MacKenzie, the girl now languishing in the gun-room alongside Sister Aloicius.

The sight of the farm cart, too, now standing there in this comfortless dawn, sent a searing shaft of nostalgic memory burning into Rose's heart. How long was it since that contrastingly glorious summer's morning when she, with a haycart of similar size, had so grudgingly accepted assistance from the once-hated Riding Officer, Ashley Penberth!

How long ago was it that they had shared that soft, mossy patch of turf on the cliffside above Porthoustock, devouring the romantic beauty of the Cornish seaboard, and exchanging the innermost of thoughts.

How long, too, since that unforgettable night of the fire when, to protect her much-loved father and 'to do her duty by the village', she had brazenly set out along the unfamiliar trail of seduction up there in the bedroom of the Three Tuns Inn!

It seemed such a long, long time ago – and yet it was all less than a year!

And, surprisingly, in that time – during the seemingly endless weeks of captivity at the Château Fontanelle – she had come to know and admire the girl she had once regarded

95

as her rival in love. She could now understand – even if she could not share – Alethea's desire for the life of the cloister. If it was her devout wish to become a nun – to become not an earthly bride but a bride of Christ – then it was not only an awesomely beautiful vision, it must also reveal a very deep and true vocation. And for that, Rose could only love and admire her – even if she felt no such calling for herself.

And Sister Aloicius. Was there ever a lovelier person! Deprived of great physical attractions – apart from those prettiest of eyes – her whole personality radiated a gaiety of spirit. And yet there was a delightful calmness about her, suggesting, Rose thought, a degree of inner peace for which throughout the ages misguided mankind has been inwardly longing.

Now, there she was – Alethea beside her – at the window of the gun-room, watching prayerfully as Rose, together with four other prisoners, was bundled into the cart.

The unshaven, raggedly dressed carter, having chained his charges to the sides of the vehicle, now climbed to the driving position and whipped up the horse. As the wheels began to revolve, Rose tried to encapsulate within her mind the picture of those two who had shown her so much love, waving to her now from that window and so clearly sending her unspoken words of concern and affection. She wondered if she would ever see them again.

With this gloomy thought merely adding to the greyness of the dawn, Rose stared about her.

The roughly constructed cart, with its five prisoners chained together as well as to its sides, was now rattling out past the massive iron gates at the entrance to the Château Fontanelle. Instinctively Rose glanced upwards. There, starkly visible against the lightening sky, were the intricately interwoven letters of the monogram. What were they? Could they be the 'L de V' she had once before been so eager to discern. And did it now matter any longer! What good would an aristocratic lineage serve her now? – indeed, in revolutionary France of 1793 such a background could well mean but one thing – death!

Outside the prisons, life was becoming almost more dangerous than within. News had just penetrated the high surrounding walls of the Château Fontanelle that a young, auburn-haired twenty-four-year-old had come to Paris from the Normandy city of Caen, and had plunged a butcher's knife into the heart of the 'Friend of the People'.

Jean-Paul Marat, editor of the revolutionary news-sheet, 'L'Ami du Peuple', was easing his syphilitic condition in the comfort of a hot bath when Charlotte Corday burst into his room and struck him dead. This intrepid young girl – inspired by the theories of Rousseau, and idolizing the brilliant and romantic Madame Roland – believed fanatically in the noblest principles of liberty and equality. But she was utterly appalled by the mounting terror ceaselessly being fostered by this self-styled mouthpiece of the people. She saw it as her duty – her destiny – to rid France of this festering scourge.

Within thirty-six hours of arriving in Paris, it was said, she had purchased a carving knife from an ironmonger's shop near the Palais-Royal, and hiding it under her dress she had taken a cab to the Rue des Cordeliers where Marat lived with his mistress, Simone Evrard. With one tremendous thrust, straight to the heart, she had plunged the knife into Marat's chest.

Four days later her pretty, auburn-haired head had dropped into the basket beneath the guillotine set up in the Place de le Révolution.

Danton – he of the butcher-like head and the booming voice, the bristling eyebrows and the florid complexion – Georges-Jacques Danton, Tribune of the People, had gone the same way. The butcher himself had been butchered.

And as if that were not violent enough, ugly rumours were already abroad that the Queen of France would soon be following them to that same insatiable guillotine.

Party-loving Marie Antoinette – the play-actress and pretend milkmaid at her beloved Petit Trianon – had been imprisoned in the Conciergerie since August of the previous year. Torn from her young children, and suffering frequent haemorrhaging as well as rapidly failing eyesight, the thirty-eight-year-old Queen had been lodged in a cell with but one heavily-barred window at near ground level, and with no more light than that given off by a pair of candles. Her husband had already been beheaded, and now without her children she was a woman bereft of all hope.

They said that her son, the eight-year-old dauphin, was still alive – still alive, yes, but being cared for by a callous cobbler named Simon who had received assurances from the 'Comité de Sûreté Général' that the child's death would be welcome to them. For, so long as the boy lived there would remain hope for the many royalists and émigrés who had escaped overseas.

Such thoughts were passing through Rose's mind as the cart rumbled into the broad square of St Pol de Léon, past the towering Kreisker, and then out on the road to Le Folgoet.

Only then did she begin to take note of her fellow-travellers.

On the rough-hewn bench opposite her sat a delightfully antique-looking couple whom Rose had come to know, but only distantly, as the Comte and Comtesse de Ploumanoir. Their faces were like finely chiselled marble, their expressions were those of utter disdain. Whatever terrible fate might lie ahead of them, they would meet it with the same aristocratic fortitude as that being shown by their queen in the Conciergerie.

They sat on their own, speaking to no one, but staring out across the featureless landscape as though anticipating the peaceful oblivion which could not be far off. So long as they had each other, they had no fear.

Alone and afraid, Rose could not help feeling envious. They looked so calm, so resigned. They had seen it all. They were together.

Although spiritually bereft and feeling so horribly alone, Rose was squeezed between an abundant physical presence

98

on each side of her. On her left, and almost overflowing on to her, sat a wealthy tobacco merchant from Morlaix, Monsieur Duvivier. During her short acquaintance with him in the Château Fontanelle, Rose had discovered his secret. In early manhood he had acquired enormous wealth, first as a slave-trader and then as a privateer. Having made his fortune by the most dubious of means, he had then clothed himself in respectability by purchasing a thriving tobacco business and an impressive riverside residence to go with it. Unfortunately for him, he had not been good to his servants – he could not prevent his former slaver instincts from breaking the surface of his carefully cultivated gentlemanly calm whenever he felt crossed.

Now, the pigeons were coming home to roost. Those embittered servants were the masters. Condemned to the bleakest of prospects within a high-security prison at Brest, Monsieur Duvivier was being given a taste of his own medicine. He was sunk in gloom.

On Rose's other side, and also overflowing copiously onto her thighs but at least trying to minimize the discomfort, sat a priest. Middle-aged and exceptionally well-built, he displayed a ruddy, healthy complexion seeming to deny the privations of captivity. He appeared taciturn, withdrawn, introverted. In the Château Fontanelle he had kept himself very much to himself. But when, shyly, Rose smiled at him, seeking only the solace of brief companionship, his face momentarily brightened like a sudden shaft of sunshine flitting across a bleak winter landscape.

'You are English, yes?' he enquired in a clear but Breton-intonated voice, and when Rose responded affirmatively, he went on to ask how she came to be in such a sorry situation.

He listened carefully while she described the rescue attempt with her friend, Ashley Penberth, and when she had concluded with her capture and incarceration at the Château Fontanelle, he commented wryly, 'I think you must be a very brave lady to help your friend so. Yes, a very brave lady indeed.'

'And I think you speak English very well,' she complimented with as much cheerfulness as she could muster. 'How do you come to speak it so fluently, if I may enquire?'

'For some years I was in England, you know,' he answered drily, 'I stay with some kind people in your county of Devon.'

'Oh, yes,' Rose responded wistfully, 'that's next to my own county of Cornwall. What part of Devon do your friends live in?'

'In the north of the county, yes. Not far from the town of Bideford,' the priest enlightened. 'I stay with some friends in the village of Hartland. We have for long time had . . . er . . . connections in that part.'

Despite the dismalness of their circumstances and prospects, Rose clapped her hands delightedly at the mention of English place names, especially West Country towns and villages.

'And what misfortune is it, Father . . .?' she began.

'Lemaître,' he prompted, 'Père Lemaître.'

'Thank you,' Rose smiled. 'Although I have seen you, of course, in the prison we have just left, I was unaware of your name.'

He nodded. There was infinite sadness in his eyes, Rose thought, as he stared out across the fields of grey, lifeless vegetables.

'May I enquire what misfortune has brought *you* to this sorry pass, Père Lemaître,' Rose asked.

He paused for a moment, contemplating the straw on the bottom of the cart, aimlessly shuffling it with his feet. Then he said the one word, 'Cowardice.'

Rose turned; looked at him in astonishment. The powerful build, the healthy complexion spoke of nothing but strength and determination. 'I find that hard to believe,' she said.

He shook his head sadly. 'But it is true. I was with the Carmelite friars in Paris – the Couvent des Carmes, in the rue de Vaugirard, you know – that is, I was there until the second of September, almost one year ago, when the massacres began.'

Rose's hand flew to her mouth. 'Oh, no!' she breathed

with horror. 'The September Massacres! I've heard of them. But you escaped!'

He nodded, his features lined and drawn with remorse. 'That is why I am a coward.'

'But why?'

'Because, if I had been brave, I would have died with all the others. Instead, I am strong and powerful . . . and so I escape. But I do not feel it is right that I should.'

Rose watched, helpless, as the torment of memory clouded his eyes. 'Would it be of any help for you to talk,' she asked quietly, '. . . to tell me about it?'

While the cart slowly wound its way through the Breton countryside, alongside the river Quillec and on towards the small 'ville' of Berven with its square-towered church and its triumphal arch, Père Lamaître began to unburden his soul. Rose saw little of her surroundings, so intrigued, so appalled was she by the account being unfolded by the priest.

'They swarmed in off the streets,' he was saying, shading his eyes as though trying to shut out the horror, 'drunk with cheap wine and the lust for blood, and yet more blood. They spared the friars – and those friars were truly wonderful; they did everything they could to protect us, but the mob had heard there were priests and royalists sheltering within the convent, and they just went mad. It was the priests they were after, really, because we had refused – er – we refuse to take the oath to the Republic.'

He paused; the memory almost too painful to bear. But eventually he went on:

'We waited in the chapel, expecting at least a fair trial. We had nothing to fear, we thought. We had committed no crime.'

Another pause. Père Lamaître blew his nose loudly on a piece of linen that had once been a handkerchief.

'There is a passage leading from the chapel to the garden of the convent, and in a small recess beneath the stairs, Monsieur Maillard – may God rest his devilish soul—' the priest went on, involuntarily crossing himself, '—it was there that this Monsieur Maillard had set up his judgement table.'

'Judgement table!' Rose exclaimed incredulously, 'You don't surely mean to tell me the trial took place in a passage!'

'If you could call it a trial!' Père Lemaître scoffed. 'We were already condemned before we even got to open our mouths.'

'Why? Because you refused to sign this oath?'

'We had all declared that our oath was to none other than to God. We repeated that we had committed no crimes. Then the so-called judges all laughed.' Père Lemaître again covered his eyes. 'It was unbelievably horrible!'

Rose waited quietly for him to continue. 'And then what happened,' she asked softly.

'We were pushed along the passage towards the garden door outside which there is a small platform and then some steps down to the garden.'

The priest paused, pressing a clenched fist against his mouth, trying to control emotion. Then, with a pitiable crack in his voice, he went on:

'The murderers were waiting for us as we came through onto that platform. They slashed at us – with swords, with machetes, with cutlasses – anything, until nearly all of us were dead. Only a few – the younger and stronger ones, like me, made a fight of it, fought them off and made a dash for the wall. How we ever got over that wall I will never know! But somehow we did – just a few of us.'

'And you were one of those lucky ones,' Rose breathed.

But the priest shook his head. 'No,' he said wearily. 'For me – I have known no peace since that day.'

'But you escaped!' Rose burst out. 'You outwitted those terrible murderers! Why have you known no peace?'

Père Lamaître gave a long-drawn-out sigh. 'Because,' he said at last, 'it is not enough to be free only in the body. You must also be free in the spirit – and I cannot cease to remember those who fell. I cannot help but be thinking I should have been one of them.'

'And now you are a prisoner again,' Rose observed, with a puzzled expression. 'How do you come to be in that situation. Did you deliberately allow yourself to be caught?'

He shook his head. 'No,' he said sadly. 'I did not even have enough courage to do that. Foolishly, I tried to escape to England – to my friends at Hartland, you know. They have sheltered me before now in time of trouble, and I expect . . . I expect*ed* they would do the same for me now. But, for my sins, I suppose,' he concluded with a rueful smile, 'I was caught at Roscoff – they are watching the shipping very closely now, it seems – and then I was brought back to St Pol.' He spread his hands. 'How is it you say, "Man proposeth, but God disposeth" – is that right, yes?'

Rose offered no comment. She had never heard the saying. She supposed it was correct. He certainly seemed to be very knowledgeable. Well, priests usually were, weren't they? But she didn't like the sound of the shipping being so closely watched at Roscoff. If they were taking that much trouble at a small place like Roscoff, how much more interested might they not be in an English lugger feeling its way into the important harbour of Brest! And that, precisely, was what Rose was hoping – no, praying fervently – that Ashley would shortly be doing.

She fell silent for a while, engrossed with her own thoughts – pondering what the priest had been telling her and wondering about Ashley – while the cart slowly jolted across the open countryside towards the ancient capital of the Léon.

At Berven, a fresh but only slightly less emaciated horse was substituted for the now exhausted original, and during the changeover each prisoner was handed a bowl of watery soup and a hunk of stale bread. As sustenance it was totally inadequate, but at least it provided a welcome relief from the monotonous jolting of the cart. It also allowed Père Lamaître, by way of diversion from the former gloomy topic of conversation, to draw Rose's attention to the sixteenth-century church.

'You will see, mam'selle, how the tower of the church it is square and it is crowned, as you might say, with a dome and – er – the small "lanternes et les balustrades décoratifs". I only mention it to you because it is – no, it *was* the first one like it in Brittany, I believe. It soon became

103

the example – the "modèle", yes – for many others.' He smiled thinly. 'Or, at least, that is what they say.'

Surveying the ornate building and trying to take an intelligent interest in what the priest was telling her, Rose could not help being plunged into nostalgic memories of that other square church tower that she knew so well – the one with a soaring spire ascending into the fathomless blue of a Cornish summer sky – the familiar church tower at St Keverne.

Oh, how she longed to be back there now – among all those kindly Cornish folk, those gossiping, laughing villagers, even those lecherous old yokels with their suggestive glances – her 'regulars' at The Three Tuns Inn.

But above all, she longed for the warm, protective embrace of Amia and Sampson Roskruge. The very thought of them – the loving care with which they had surrounded her all her life – brought an unassuageable ache to her heart.

They had done their best to dissuade her from accompanying Ashley Penberth on his errand of rescue; they had tried to paint an attractive picture of the alternative – the simple life of the village, with marriage to a local boy, then children and even grandchildren. But in their heart of hearts, Rose guessed, they knew such a life would not be enough for their adventurous daughter. She loved them all the more for letting her go – allowing her to 'ford her own streams, climb her own mountains' – but at this particular moment she was angry with herself for having done so. Just look where it had landed her!

As an antidote to these feelings of nostalgia and regret, which were making her feel more and more depressed, she was glad to have the company of Père Lemaître. His conversation not only lightened the burden of her own thoughts, it also seemed to relieve his own gloomy forebodings. If nothing else it helped to dispel the tedium of the journey.

Some time after leaving Berven, the cart turned off the lane onto a long entrance drive, at the end of which pepper-pot towers could be seen rising above the ramparts of a castle. All around lay the emerald-green fields of extensive parkland.

With uncharacteristic enthusiasm, Père Lemaître slapped his thigh. 'Aha! Voila!' he exclaimed. 'I wondered if they would throw us in here for the night. This is the Château de Kerjean – still some distance from Brest. I thought it would be too much for the poor old horse to pull us to Brest before dark. So, I think they lock us all up in here for the night.' A smile flickered across his face. 'But I shall not mind. It means one more day to think about things, one more sunset, one more dawn . . . and besides, it is an interesting château; there is an amusing story . . .'

The priest's speculation proved correct. Unceremoniously, the prisoners were unloaded like cattle and then goaded towards the stable block forming one side of a rectangular courtyard. There they were chained to the iron bars forming the top section of stalls normally occupied by a single horse. The Comte and Comtesse de Ploumanoir were allowed to share a stall; the unfriendly Monsieur Duvivier was given one also; and when it came to the allocation of a resting place for the night for Rose and Père Lemaître there appeared a distinctly mischievous gleam in the gaoler's eye. He would put these two together in a single stall – yes, he would – this lovely, nubile young girl, and this celibate priest. It would test the strength of the priest's vow of celibacy to the uttermost, would it not; just the two of them, chained together and lying there side by side in the straw on the cold floor of the stable. Might they not seek each other's close . . . very close . . . proximity – just for the sake of warmth. Might it not torture the priest with carnal desire! The turnkey thought it might provide his sharp ears with an abundance of salacious amusement during the night.

Père Lemaître was not deceived. He correctly guessed what was passing through the gaoler's mind. He recognized the danger. He began to doubt his ability to resist. But, ah! what bliss if the temptation should prove too strong – and he were to succumb! Oh, get thee behind me, Satan!

'There is a story about this castle,' he began, when he

105

and Rose, still chained together, had bunched the straw against the wooden partition and made themselves as comfortable as possible. 'It is a story of long ago,' he went on, his mind dwelling, no doubt at the behest of the devil, on the former tempting theme, 'but I think it might perhaps amuse you. Yes?'

'Oh, please go on,' Rose encouraged, thankful for any alleviation of the weary hours ahead and quite unaware of the tenor of his thoughts. 'You are familiar with this castle, then, are you?'

'I have been here once before – just the once – when I was a young curé at St Pol, you know. It was then in the ownership of an elderly lady, Madame de Coatanscour, but I believe she was bothered too much by the soldiers of the National Guard so she go to stay with her sister at St Pol de Léon. I cannot be too sure of this but I do not think – er – how you say – I do not think – er – things have gone too well for them in St Pol. I do not think either of them approved of the Revolution – and that, I am afraid, may not be too good for their health, no.' He paused for a moment, reflectively, before continuing, 'But I hope they will be all right, yes. I most sincerely do.'

'But what is the story about the castle?' Rose asked, fearing that he might be losing his thread. Like so many priests, Father Lemaître had a beautiful voice and, notwithstanding the language difference, a remarkably fluent delivery. She would have been content to listen to it almost indefinitely.

'Oh, yes,' he said, more cheerfully, 'the story of the Château de Kerjean.' He clasped his hands behind his tonsured head, and leant back against the partition. 'Well, the story says that a long, long time ago – about two hundred years, I think – a Monsieur Louis Barbier inherited much moneys from his uncle, who was a very wealthy abbot, you know, and he decided to build a castle which would be the envy of all the people of the Léon. He succeeded, don't you think – because the Château de Kerjean, where we are now temporarily imprisoned, was the result.'

Even in the growing darkness Rose could see that he was smiling at her – as though that were the end of the story.

'Is that all?' she asked, surprised. 'Is that all there is to tell?'

He laughed warmly – affectionately. 'No, no. That is not the story. That is just the beginning, you know. But now I tell you.' Moving a fraction closer, he settled himself more comfortably before continuing:

'A descendant of the original Monsieur Louis Barbier, a Monsieur René Barbier by name, had married a very beautiful lady, Françoise de Quélen, but as time went on he became over-confident of the lady's love for him, and when he went to the court of Marie de Medici, he began boasting of the great love between himself and his lady wife and how true they were to each other.'

The priest gurgled mischievously. 'That was Monsieur Réne Barbier's big mistake. Oh-ho. Because, you know, his boasting was overheard by four other young courtiers who proposed, er – how you say – a wager, a bet, yes – that each one would go to Kerjean and seduce the beautiful young Françoise, the trophies of success being an engagement ring, a brooch, a ribbon, and a lock of the fair lady's hair – four young men, you know, and four tokens of success.

'Very well,' he went on. 'Monsieur Réne was so confident of his wife's fidelity that he accepted the wager. The four young gallants left for Kerjean. But they had agreed to obtain the tokens by means of a trick, and in due course the four trophies arrived at court – the ring, the brooch, the ribbon, and the lock of the lady's hair. Well, you can imagine the horror of Monsieur Réne Barbier when he received them! Not just the one – but all four! Monsieur Réne was in a ferment, I can tell you. He immediately leapt on a horse and rode to Kerjean as fast as he could travel.'

Once again came the priest's throaty chuckle. And the rustling of straw on the far side of the partition suggested that even the morose M. Duvivier was becoming interested.

'But the beautiful Francoise was not only virtuous,' the storyteller continued, 'she was also very shrewd, you know.

And when she discovered the trick being played on her husband, she very skilfully lured the four rascally courtiers to a room in the château – dangling the bait of her virtue before them, I suspect – and when they were all there, she left the room on the pretext of changing into something more suitable for the occasion, you know – in the way that ladies have, yes – and then she shut the door on them *and turned the key in the lock*!

'Next day, the clever Françoise set the swashbuckling young courtiers to work with spinning-wheel and loom, making the kind of coarse cloth which is only suitable for prisoners, and when her anxious husband returned she was able to lead him to the room in which the four ''seducers'' were hard at work on their menial task.'

He chuckled appreciatively once more, and then sat upright and rubbed his shins. His feet were feeling cold. The chill of the night was setting in on the Château de Kerjean.

'Well,' he said at last, 'that is the legend of Kerjean. It is a true story, so I am informed – and, well I hope it has helped at least to pass a little of the time, yes?'

'Most certainly,' Rose assured him, 'and a very amusing story it was, too. "Très amusante" yes?'

'You learn to speak a little French, then,' Père Lemaître praised. 'That is good. You must speak more.'

He clasped his hands behind his head once again, and then sank back into the straw. He closed his eyes, a beatific smile upon his face – presumably at the recollection of those would-be seducers being thwarted in their rampant desires, Rose supposed. 'Très amusante', she had said, and she meant it. An amusing story, typical of the pranks played by young bloods of the day with nothing else to do but swagger and boast at the court of their sovereign, she imagined. But quite a daring story – especially coming from the lips of a Jesuit priest.

Supper that night was the best they had been given for a very long while. Better by far than anything served up to them at the Château Fontanelle. The gardens of the Château de Kerjean were well stocked, and the soup they were brought that evening consisted of a broth containing leeks, onions and potatoes. The gaoler had seen to it that the priest and the young girl chained to him should have the largest portions. He wanted them to feel well satisfied. He thought it might stimulate their fancy for a frolic in the straw. After all, no man can make love on an empty stomach – and the gaoler was looking forward to a little bit of titillating voyeurism.

Darkness fell, and the temporary prisoners being lodged at the Château de Kerjean made themselves as comfortable as they could for the night. Rose glanced across at the rotund figure lying beside her. Even in the diminishing light she could see that his eyes were open. He was looking straight at her.

She wondered just how strong were the bonds of celibacy restraining a healthy middle-aged priest. Almost imperceptibly, as evening lengthened into night, he had edged a little closer. She could now feel the warmth of his breath on her cheek.

She shifted her position; moved away from him as far as the restricting chains would allow; turned over onto her side, facing away from him, removing temptation. She could do no more. After all, he *was* a priest!

It had been a long, exhausting day. The jolting cart seemed to have disjointed every bone in her body. She drew the straw up around her; closed her eyes.

After a while – and with the swaying movement of the jolting cart still fresh in her mind – she fell asleep.

And she dreamed.

She was back with her loving parents at their cottage at Rosenithon, St Keverne . . . and she had only just met Ashley Penberth.

CHAPTER SEVEN

The Other Side of the Coin

'What be doin' today, then, Sam?' Amia Roskruge asked her husband. 'Goin' fishin' again?'

'Naw, naw, Ame. There be too much else to be done today.'

'An' what would that be, then?'

'Aw, well, there be that thur load o' hay up five-acre needs bringin' down afore the weather breaks.'

'Couldn' ee leave un go a day or two? 'Twouldn' hurt, would un?' his wife suggested. 'Seems a shame to miss a good day's fishin'.'

But Sampson Roskruge shook his head, finished his breakfast, and then got up from the well-scrubbed kitchen table. 'Naw, naw, Ame. Us'd betterways haul un down while 'tis fine.'

Wiping his mouth with the back of his gnarled fist, he moved across towards the door and apse leading out to the back yard, and was about to take down his farming jacket from off the hook when Rose appeared at the top of the stairs. She was still in her night-clothes, her dark hair playing carelessly around her face, her cheeks flushed with sleep.

She yawned expansively, stretched luxuriously, saying: 'I'll go fetch un for ee, Papa.'

Sampson chuckled, 'Aw, no, Rosie. You doan want to go gettin' yourself all covered wi' hay.'

Not for the first time he thought he had never seen a prettier young girl. Tousled, she might be, but there was a freshness about her, even first thing in the morning – a kind of desirable nubility. Since working as barmaid up at the Three Tuns Inn she had visibly bloomed. The 'regulars' had warmed to the sparkle of her light-hearted personality, to her readiness always to match banter with telling riposte, and to that generosity of spirit which made old men feel young again, and young men feel handsome. Whoever was lucky enough to get her for a bride, Sampson reflected – and again, not for the first time – would indeed be a fortunate man.

But it was she who chuckled now. 'Get away with you, Pa. I don't mind a bit o' hay in me hair, an' well you knows it.' She was standing on the bottom step, cupping chin in hand, and resting her elbow on the lowest stair-post. 'I'd be glad of somethin' useful this mornin' . . . especially after last night's affray up at the Tuns.'

'Affray?' Her father, on his way out into the wash-house, stopped in his tracks. 'What sort of an affray was that, then, Rosie?'

'Didn' Mam tell ee, then?' Rosie queried, sleepily, running a hand through her dark curls. 'Oh no, of course; you were out in the boat last night, weren't ee?'

'Ais,' her mother confirmed, 'an' you was asleep, Rosie, by the time your father come in.'

Rose nodded, rubbing the sleep out of her eyes as she shuffled across to the table at which her mother still sat.

'Well,' she began, sliding on to her usual chair and then cutting herself a slice of bread to nibble while she talked, 'us had a visitor up at the Three Tuns last evening.'

'Aw, ah,' her father said, rather losing interest. 'That ain't anythin' extra special, inna?'

'No—,' Rose smiled, 'We do sometimes have 'em from foreign parts, 'tis true. But this one were a bit special, like.'

'Aw, ah,' echoed her father. 'An' who were that, then?'

Rose idly broke off a large piece of bread and popped it in her mouth. ''Twere a Customs man,' she said.

Sampson stiffened. 'A Customs man, did ee say?'

'That's right, Papa. He said he were the new Ridin' Officer for the district, or somethin'.'

'Aw – a new man, then,' her father observed – interest clearly rekindled.

Rose nodded. She went on nibbling, keeping her father on tenterhooks while her mother poured her a cup of goat's milk. 'He told Will Trenethy that th'old un's now *re*-tired, an', evidently, this un's taken his place.'

'Taken the place of th'old un, has ee,' Sampson said, darkly. 'An' what sort of a man would this one be, then?'

'Real nasty!' Rose retorted with feeling. 'A real stuck-up, arrogant sort o' bully of a man.'

'Not like the old un, then?'

'I don't know, Papa,' Rose answered, 'I don't think I ever see'd un.'

Sampson snorted. 'That were the best part of un,' he muttered, half to himself. 'Knew what was good for un; knew when to stay away.'

'Well, this one don't seem to,' Rose retorted sharply. 'Pokin' his nose into everythin'. Made poor old Will turn the cellar inside out, he did. Wouldn't lift a finger to help – not one finger! And what's more,' she went on angrily, 'for that very same reason he caused me to go and spoil my lovely new dress – the one that Mama an' me've only just finished makin'! I tell you, it isn't fair,' she added, near to tears. 'It just isn't *fair*!'

'An' how did that happen, then?' her father enquired sympathetically.

''Twas a gert, rusty nail stickin' out of the barrel,' Rose sobbed. 'It got caught up in me front while I was helpin' poor Will.'

Amia Roskruge patted her daughter's hand, soothingly. 'Not to worrit, Rosie,' she purred. 'Us'll soon put un to rights, you'll see. Us've got a bit o' the same material, an' us can soon put in a new piece, like. So don't ee fret yerself, love.'

While his wife placated their distressed daughter with her soft, comforting words, Sampson's thoughts moved elsewhere. He did not like the sound of this new Riding Officer for the district. He decided it would be prudent to confer with his friend, Wilmot Tripconey, up at Trevallack; more prudent, in fact, than either going fishing or, indeed, bringing home those last few cocks of hay from five-acre.

Sampson Roskruge was a man of action. No sooner was his mind made up than . . .

''Twould be good of ee, Rosie, if ee could bring down that thur hay, like,' he said firmly. 'There do be a pile o' things for me to see to – other things, if you understand me – an' I'd be real glad if you could put Belle in the shafts an' bring down a load or two.'

'That's all right, Papa,' Rose replied, visibly more cheerful. 'I said I would, and I will.'

'There's a good girl,' her mother encouraged. ''Twill do ee good to have somethin' else to think about instead o' ponderin' over that thur new Ridin' Officer all the time.'

Rose glanced up into those gentle, loving eyes – into that plain yet perceptive face which had been her refuge and her solace throughout the years of her childhood. How was it, she smiled to herself, that her mother seemed able to divine even her innermost feelings; and had she guessed already that, no matter what else engaged her daughter's attention throughout the day, the image of that Riding Officer, infuriating though it might be, would never be very far from her thoughts.

*　　*　　*

Rose turned left into Tregellast Lane and, somewhat unwisely in view of the heavy load of hay piled high on the farm cart, she allowed Belle to pick her way homeward. It was foolish, perhaps – but it was one of those peerless mornings when spring gives way to summer and the world, for a moment, seems to have rid itself of care.

It was a day to dream dreams, to scent fragrances, to smell the salt tang of the sea. For, away to her right, shimmering lazily in the caress of early-morning sunshine and less than a mile distant, lay the silver-blue waters of the English Channel.

113

Singing at the top of her voice, and throwing her arms skywards as though to embrace the whole cosmic beauty of the morning, Rose was unaware that Belle had momentarily strayed from the paths of righteousness in order to snatch a succulent mouthful from the hedgebank. In doing so, she had pulled the haycart off the well-worn track, perilously close – far too close – to the deep ditch running alongside. Before Rose could pull the mare back on course, the off-side wheel of the cart had plunged into the ditch. Not only was Rose sent slithering off the hayload and into the hedge, but worse still, as Belle, frightened by the unexpected disturbance, lunged forward to pull the cart out of the ditch, the off-side wheel came off and the linchpin went flying into the undergrowth.

Having painfully extricated herself from the prickly hedge, Rose first of all set about quietening the over-excited Belle, who was still trying to drag the wheel-less cart from the ditch.

Then she surveyed the damage. The cart lay drunkenly on its side, while much of the laboriously loaded hay now festooned the hedge like a dishevelled old lady's hair. A moment's aberration had undone a large part of the morning's work – quite apart from the much more serious problem of an un-wheeled, immovable haycart.

It was while she was pulling thorns out of her arms and hands, and considering what best to do next, that she heard the sound of horse-hoofs coming along the lane in her direction. Surely, she thought with relief, whoever it was would help her. St Keverne, like most other Cornish villages, was a close-knit community, and there was scarcely a single soul for miles around who would not readily come to her assistance.

As the unhurried 'clip-clop' of hooves came gradually nearer, her spirits rose. Whoever it might be, he or she would either help her to right the cart and re-load the hay – or they, themselves, would summon additional aid as might be necessary. All would soon then be set to rights.

But as she prepared to hail the rider coming round the bend in the lane, the first thing she spotted above the top of the hedgerow was a black tricorn hat and then a sky-blue jacket.

'Oh, no!' she wailed aloud. 'Not him!'

Of all people, the last she expected to see – and the most profoundly unwanted – was the pompous, arrogant, and thoroughly unhelpful new Riding Officer for the district, Ashley Penberth.

'Woo'ah, there, Puncher!' He reined, coming alongside. 'And what have we here? Why, 'tis Mistress Rose, of the Three Tuns Inn – unless I'm very much mistaken.' He politely raised his hat but remained firmly, irritatingly, in the saddle. 'Some kind of a mishap, eh?'

'A haycart on its side without a wheel,' Rose replied tartly, 'I should have thought any fool could see that!'

Infuriatingly, the man continued to sit, elbow on saddle pommel, saying nothing – but with an amused smile tugging at the corners of his mouth. He was obviously restraining an inclination to laugh out loud.

'Well, well,' he said at last, 'I suppose any fool *could* see that – unless, of course, he was determined not to get involved in rendering any assistance.'

He clicked his teeth, and his horse obediently began moving off.

'The brute!' Rose flared under her breath. 'He's not going to lift a finger! Just like he was last evening!'

The poisonous thought had no sooner taken root in her mind than she realized the man had pulled his mount to the lane verge and was dismounting. Throwing the reins over a convenient branch, he then sauntered slowly back to where Rose stood forlornly beside the sorry-looking haycart.

'Now, then,' he began, unhurriedly, 'let's see what we can do to set Mistress Rosie on her way again.'

He proceeded to examine the cart with a seemingly expert eye.

'Well, the axle's not broken,' he observed with a grunt. 'At least that's something. Now let's have a look at the wheel.'

He stalked back to where the wheel lay upright against

the hedge. As he did so, Rose noticed that he walked with a pronounced limp, and that the heel of his left boot was built-up considerably higher than the right. She had not noticed it the previous evening.

'And the wheel appears to have survived,' he remarked, pulling it out of the hedge and bowling it back towards the stricken cart. 'So, the question is, how do we get it back on to the axletree?'

The man's actually going to help, Rose thought to herself with growing astonishment; this bullying, officious 'King's Man' is about to help someone in distress! She could hardly believe her eyes.

But then, when he leaned the wheel up against the steeply-listing vehicle, Rose saw, with a mixture of dismay and unworthy satisfaction, that the hub of the wheel and the naked end of the axletree were irreconcilably far apart. 'Now what are you going to do?' she found herself thinking – and immediately felt ashamed. Even though the man was an obnoxious interloper and an enemy of all inoffensive country folk, he *was* trying to help. And that was something to be thankful for – even though it was quite apparent he would be unable to succeed; at least, not without additional help from someone familiar with the peculiarities of farm carts. Such knowledge, she felt sure, would not come within the ambit of a mere Riding Officer. Searching premises for contraband liquor and bullying unsuspecting landlords, yes; but not the repair of a broken-down haycart, especially if it meant helping a nobody – like a mere chit of a barmaid.

Reluctantly she had to admit to herself that she might be wrong when she saw the man for whom, hitherto, she had felt nothing but loathing and contempt, slowly divest himself, first of his tricorn and then of his sky-blue jacket, each of them thrown casually onto the hay remaining in the haycart. Then, to her absolute astonishment, she watched His Majesty's Riding Officer sink to his knees and crawl underneath the axle.

'Now then,' he called from beneath the cart, 'when I lift the axle, you slide the wheel on. Understand?'

Rose grasped the heavy wheel. 'Oh, but you'll never be able to lift this load,' she said, genuine concern in her voice. 'It's far too heavy!'

'Do as I say!' came the succinct response. 'And don't dally! I may not be able to hold it up for long.'

Placing his broad shoulders along and beneath the axle, Riding Officer Ashley Penberth prepared to test his strength.

'Ready?' he called – and receiving an anxious acknowledgement from Rose – he began to take the strain across his back and shoulders. Every muscle seemed to be quivering, every vein standing out alarmingly on face and neck as, slowly and with continuous, powerful exertion, he raised the side of the cart.

But, struggle though she would, Rose could not force the hub over the axle-end. A matter of less than an inch prevented the marriage of the two.

'I can't get it on!' she cried, despairingly.

'Try harder!' came the strangulated voice from below. '*Harder!*'

Furiously Rose wrestled with the obstinate wheel. Frantically once more she tried to push it over the axle tip – to bridge that infuriatingly small difference between success and failure. But the axle was just too low, while the hub was a fraction too high. And the wheel felt damnably heavy.

'I can't, I can't,' she wailed. 'It just won't go on.'

Almost in tears, she watched the cart's side slowly subside to its former, drunken angle.

'Oh, I *am* sorry,' she moaned, as the Riding Officer crawled out from underneath. 'I just could *not* get them to marry up!'

He was perspiring freely, and Rose noticed with horror that his white cambric shirt was horribly stained with the underside filth of a cart used for all manner of farm duties.

Pausing only to regain his breath and, with the back of his hand, to brush the sweat from his brow, he said curtly, 'Unload some of the hay. Then we'll try again.'

'Why, yes, of course,' Rose readily agreed, relieved at

the not unfriendly tone of his voice. 'Why ever didn't we think of that before, I wonder.'

'Because I thought I was stronger than apparently I am,' he grimaced, flashing her a sardonic smile. 'But we'll do it next time – you'll see.'

And they did.

Once more the hitherto overbearing, inconsiderate Riding Officer – 'King's Man', and scourge of humble folk who had only wanted to enjoy a drop of brandy and a nice cup of tea without it costing more than they could afford – got down on his hands and knees, and crawled under the axle of the cart.

Once more, with a groan of concentrated energy, and straining every sinew in his muscular frame, Ashley Penberth raised the side of the heavy wooden cart so that the male stub of the axle came level with the female orifice of the wheel hub. Feverishly, Rose tried to effect the union.

But now the axletree was fractionally too high. Less than half an inch stood between successful consummation and frustrating failure. She struggled to lift the wheel – to bring it into line – but it was too heavy.

'Down a little,' she panted. 'Only a fraction.'

He lowered it. Too much! Nevertheless, she tried again, frenziedly using every ounce of her strength to match the orifice with the axle stub. She nearly succeeded; she so nearly got it on. But the two components must be exactly in line; any deviation from the precise, harmonious plane makes a successful union impossible. The female must come sweetly to the male.

'Up again,' she gasped. 'Just a tiny bit.'

Slowly, painfully and vibrating in every muscle, he raised the cart. 'For God's sake, be quick!' he anguished. 'I can't hold it much longer!'

And in the split second, the fleeting moment, when successful union became possible, Rose acted quickly and positively. It was a moment, she knew, that might never recur.

With a long-drawn-out gasp of satisfaction, she pushed the wheel firmly back into position.

'It's all right,' she said triumphantly. 'You can let it down now.'

Groaning with relief, the Riding Officer lowered the cart, and then sprawled, exhausted, on the soft verge-side turf beneath the cart.

After a few moments he joined Rose who, still recovering her breath, was leaning back against the hedgebank. For a while he remained silent, also regaining composure and mopping the perspiration from his brow. Out of the corner of her eye Rose looked at him; saw him for the first time, not as the Riding Officer, the 'King's Man', the enemy of the community, but as someone – an ordinary human being – who had been willing to get down on his hands and knees, to ruin a freshly laundered cambric shirt, and to use every ounce of his physical strength, just to help her. She realized she was looking at him through a different pair of eyes.

In a rugged sort of way he was quite handsome, she concluded. Fair, crinkly hair, scraped back and tied at the nape in the current fashion; short, slightly uplifted nose; powerful build – especially about the shoulders and arms; fresh, healthy complexion; steely-blue eyes.

Last evening, and first thing this morning as he came round the bend in the lane, she had seen him only as a ruthless servant of the Crown, a bullying sadist, and the very last word in arrogance and insensitivity. Now, as he leaned back against the hedge beside her, mopping his brow and recovering his strength, she saw him as a completely different person.

She looked down at his left boot; the one with the heel made up; and she wondered . . .

But before she had time to crystallize her thoughts, he was picking up the hay fork and purposefully – expertly – pitching back onto the now righted cart as much as possible of the scattered hay.

'Oh, please . . . please don't bother about that,' Rose protested. 'You've done more than enough, already.'

His answer was merely to continue swiftly and energetically completing the task. Then, as he struggled back into his

119

jacket and redeemed his discarded hat, he said, 'There's one other thing. We must find the linchpin.'

He began searching around, scuffing the long grass backwards and forwards with his boot, thrashing at the branches of the hedge with his riding crop, Rose joining him in the search. But the linchpin was not to be found.

'Oh, never mind,' Rose said at last, feeling that the man had really done quite enough already, 'I'm sure I shall be all right now.'

He smiled at her – the first warm, friendly smile she had seen on his suntanned face – and shook his head. 'You'll not get far without a linchpin, I'm afraid. The wheel'll be off again before you even get home.'

He produced from an inside pocket of his sky-blue jacket one of the wickedest-looking knives Rose had ever seen, and while she watched with increasing surprise and not a little grudging admiration, he quickly fashioned a makeshift linchpin from the branch of a nearby tree.

'This'll do for the time being,' he grunted, knocking the pin into the hub, 'but I'll see you safely home, nevertheless.'

Despite her protests that she only had a short way to go and would, therefore, be perfectly all right on her own, the Riding Officer insisted on accompanying her all the way back to Thorn Cottage.

Then, without another word, he raised his hat in polite salute, and galloped off down the track towards Godrevy.

CHAPTER EIGHT

A Wild Goose Chase

Rose woke early next morning. Already the sun was streaming in through the small, square window of her sparsely furnished bedroom.

Sitting up in bed, hugging her knees, she could look straight down through the narrow avenue of trees bordering the footpath to Godrevy Cove, and there, in the distance lay the sea.

Nearly a day had gone by since she had reluctantly, but in the end gratefully, accepted assistance from Riding Officer Ashley Penberth, and although she would not have cared to admit as much to anyone else in St Keverne, he had scarcely been out of her thoughts ever since.

He had even invaded her dreams. After that first encounter at the Three Tuns Inn, she had finally gone to bed thinking of him as the most unpleasant man she had ever had the misfortune to meet. That night, as she dreamt, he had appeared as a horned demon brutally chastising a hunchbacked Will Trenethy with a rusty-nailed goad. As the dream proceeded, the hump in poor Will's back had turned into a keg of contraband liquour under his jacket, while the nails in the goad had become the kith and kin of the one which had torn her dress.

Then, within a few hours of that dream ending, he had been displaying kindness itself while helping her from a most tiresome and frustrating situation. In little more than the twinkling of an eye he had become, not an ogre doing His Majety's bidding, but something far more akin to a knight in shining, if somewhat axle-stained armour.

And she hadn't even thanked him!

True, he had ridden off somewhat peremptorily – but she could have found an opportunity to thank him properly, and yet she hadn't!

And he really had behaved rather nobly, she mused – getting down under that cart, probably ruining his shirt in the process; and then risking serious physical injury by lifting the cart off its grounded axle. He had seemed quite a different person, then; no longer imperious and disdainful; just like a normal, rather likeable human being. Quite attractive, in fact.

She really didn't know what to think. No one in their right senses would ever dream of being friendly with a Riding Officer – a 'King's Man'! – at least, not if they knew what was good for them! – especially in a village like St Keverne!

But, at the same time, he *had* been extremely helpful – when he could so easily have passed her by.

As a matter of common courtesy, she really ought to make an opportunity to thank him for his trouble. Yes, that was it; as a matter of common courtesy. She liked the expression; said it over to herself several times – 'as a matter of common courtesy'.

The only question was – when would she be able to thank him, and how?

Sitting up in her bed on that immaculate June morning, with the birds in tumultuous chorus beyond her open window, and the silvery-blue sea shimmering in the distance, she formed a plan.

The infallible local news-agency – the coastal grapevine – confirmed that after spending the night at the Three Tuns Inn, and then assisting a certain damsel in distress in Tregellast Lane, the Riding Officer had travelled by the Three Brothers of Grugith, across Crousa Downs, and after making surprise searches at Trelan, Carnpessack and Ponsangath, he had ridden into Coverack where he had put up for the night. It was, therefore, an evens bet that in the morning he would be riding back along the coast by Lowland Point, Porthoustock and Porthallow, before spending the

122

night at the inn at Manaccan. On the other hand, Will had suggested, he could decide to ride back by the inland route, making searches at Polcoverack and Trevithian before making a courtesy call on the local magistrate, Colonel Bouchier, at Lanteague. You never could tell, of course; not until the Riding Officer was actually on his way. Then the grapevine sprang into life, and started shaking!

But Rose decided that although it might be a long shot, it was worth a try. It could be weeks, or even months, before he returned to the Three Tuns Inn and by that time he would probably have forgotten all about the help he had rendered in Tregellast Lane. Worse still, he might have forgotten all about the girl he had helped!

So, that morning she put on her prettiest summer dress – pale lemon cotton with a square, low-cut neckline trimmed with lace. It had short, puff-sleeves, also lace-trimmed, and it was tied at the high waist with a pale blue ribbon. She knew she looked pretty in it, and it went well with her floppy, shepherdess-style straw hat, tied under the chin with a matching blue ribbon.

Standing in the open doorway of Thorn Cottage, after breakfast that morning, she threw her bare arms heavenwards and stretched luxuriously. Away to her left and beyond the steep valley that runs out onto the beach at Porthoustock, the broad expanse of Falmouth Bay lay twinkling in the morning sunshine. She took several deep breaths, filling her lungs with the intoxicating freshness of salty coastal air, and expelling each one slowly with a long-drawn-out sigh of contentment. She lazily crossed her arms and gave herself a big hug. The birds sang, the sun warmed, and the sea beckoned. The day, it seemed, was made for romance.

She would see.

'Mama, dear,' she called over her shoulder, 'it's such a lovely day, I think I'll take a walk.'

Her mother, strong forearms flecked with flour as she kneaded the dough for the day's baking, called back from inside the cottage, 'That be aw right, then, Rosie my love.

You do as you see fitty. You'm not required up at the Tuns before noon, I 'spec, so that'll be aw right. Which way'll you be goin', d'you 'magine?'

'Oh, down Godrevy, I expect – then up over and down round Lowland, p'raps. I'll see how I feel about it.'

'Bravish ole walk, Rosie, love,' came the reply, 'so mind how you go – watch your footsteps along that rough old track.'

'No need to worry, Ma,' Rose called back gaily as she pulled the simple, wooden gate behind her and latched it. 'I'll be mindin' how I go.'

She set off down the tree-lined, boulder-strewn footpath leading to Godrevy Beach, but when she reached the gateway overlooking the cove, she paused. Over the years, this gateway had become for her a private and very personal shrine. She always stopped there for a few minutes whenever she came down this way because there, straight ahead of her and jutting skywards like some lurking sea-monster's fangs, were the dreaded Manacles rocks.

It was on those rocks, she had been told – there, on that half-submerged group known as the Gwinges and looking now so innocent among the gently rippling waves – that the packet ship 'Elizabeth-Ann' had foundered, taking with her all on board; all, that is, except one tiny baby girl plucked from the raging turmoil on that terrible evening. Among those lost in the tragedy had been her mother.

How long and how deeply she had wondered just who that mother was. What was she like? That she must have been pretty and loving and gentle, she felt sure. But was she dark or fair; was she tall and slim, or was she short and, perhaps, even a little bit dumpy? Where had she come from, and where was she going, with such a young child? From King George's late-lamented colony of America, they had said. But why? Had she relations out there – a husband, no doubt – and was she perhaps bringing the baby home to show to loving parents and family in England? But no one had come forward to claim the child; no doting grand-parents, no caring aunts and uncles, nobody. No one seemed

124

to know – or if they did, they would not tell her.

Time and time again she had built up in her mind an idyllic picture of her natural, loving parents, of her true background.

But then a dark thought would come creeping in to challenge the illusion. Was it really an idyllic picture – or was her mother running away from some deep-rooted fear, or even disgrace! And why should she think that, anyway? No one had ever suggested it – it was entirely her own imagination – but no one had ever denied it, either.

A thousand times she had pondered these and many other unanswered, and seemingly unanswerable, questions, but nobody had even been able to satisfy her natural curiosity and her deep longing to know her identity. Indeed, she had been afraid to ask, for fear that the truth might shatter her dream.

And now, as she gazed out across the water to those harmless-looking rocks – and as on so many other similar occasions – her hand felt for the gold-enamelled locket which she always wore around her neck, and which she knew had once belonged to her mother.

For the thousandth time her fingers traced the letters inlaid in gold on the back. They had become smooth with age and frequent fingering but it was still quite possible to decipher the intials 'L de V'.

For the thousandth time she wondered what they stood for, and whether they held the secret of her birth.

Brushing a tear from her cheek, and taking a last backward glance at that terrifying reef of half-submerged rocks which, over the centuries, had claimed so many lives, she dragged herself away from the gate and continued down the path towards the beach. Impulsively, she broke into a run. She often did, if momentarily she was feeling depressed. It helped to lighten her darkness, to remind her just how lucky she was; lucky to have such loving parents as Amia and Sampson Roskruge, lucky to be as pretty as she knew she was, but above all, especially on a day like this, just lucky to be alive.

Reaching a favourite stile in the hedgebank beyond Dean Point, she arranged herself decoratively along the top crossbar, and gazed soulfully out to sea. The lazy wash of the incoming tide lapped rhythmically around, and occasionally over, the craggy Maen Land rock away to her left. Further out, the Carn-dhu and Minstrel rocks, all part of the Manacles group, looked slightly more menacing but even they could not contrive, on this still, peaceful summer's morning, a more vicious appearance than just a cluster of ochreous-coloured rocks off the Cornish coast.

And yet, to Rose, now gracefully adorning a rough-hewn wooden stile in her pretty lemon-yellow dress, they were as headstones every bit as meaningful as any granite slab in a graveyard. If she had been able to read with the eyes of the Almighty she would, she felt sure, be able to decipher the names, ages and dates of all those who lay buried beneath those waves which now so mildly lapped the jagged Manacles rocks; able to read them as clearly as though they had been carved by the village mason. And somewhere amongst that myriad of rock points, both submerged and awash, would be engraved in celestial handwriting the name of her very own mother. Would that name, she had so often wondered, bear any relation to the initials inlaid on her gold-enamelled locket.

The sound of thudding horse-hoofs, coming from the direction of grassy Lowland Point, broke in upon her reverie. She looked up sharply. Unmistakably, a black tricorn was visible, bobbing up and down above the brambles bordering the coastal track. Immediately, and for no sensible reason she kept telling herself, her heart began pounding. Her carefully thought out plan was about to materialize. He was coming her way.

Emerging from the thicket, on to the grass-covered plateau, he reined in his mount and for several minutes sat loosely in the saddle, gazing out to sea. Admiring the view? Rose wondered. Surely not. He must have seen it a thousand times or more.

Her curiosity was soon satisfied. From an inside pocket

of his sky-blue jacket he drew a telescope; extended it, and put it to his eye.

Following the direction of his view, Rose could just make out a two-masted vessel on the horizon. So that was his interest, was it. A ship coming over from Roscoff or one of the Channel Islands with contraband on board, perhaps; an object of considerable interest to a Riding Officer, no doubt, but of no consequence to a pretty girl in a pale lemon dress.

She wondered whether he would swing his telescope on to her. She smoothed her dress, patted her hair, and allowed the semblance of a smile to soften yet further the already soft line of her lips.

But he snapped the telescope shut with an air of finality, returned it to his inside pocket, and then gathered up the reins of his horse.

He hadn't even given her so much as a cursory glance.

Even more disturbing was the emergent realization that now, instead of riding along the seaboard track and right by the stile upon which she was sitting, he seemed to be intending a more direct route across the top side of the field, through the gate in the dividing hedgebank, and then off up the short cut to Rosenithon.

The sudden realization that the whole of her carefully conceived 'chance meeting' was about to evaporate into a 'might have been' unless she acted quickly brought her slithering off the stile. Somehow she must attract his attention. Picking up her skirts she began to run, keeping to the far side of the hedge so that she would not be seen. When he came to open the gate, she would be there to do it for him. She would take the opportunity to thank him for his invaluable assistance with the broken-down haycart. In return, he would thank her for opening the gate, to which she would reply that one good turn deserves another. All rather mundane, she realized, but at least it would open the way for a longer conversation. And she wanted to talk to him again; to hear his deep, well-modulated voice. It was ridiculous, of course – but she did. Above all, perhaps, she wanted him to understand that in some way, she knew not how, she was something other than just a village barmaid.

As she hurried towards the gate she was startled to hear him urging his horse into a canter. 'Gerrup, Puncher! Gerrup, laddie!' sounded from the far side of the hedge. Hooves began pounding soft turf; bridle jangled; leather boot tops rubbed sqeakily against saddle flap; it was obvious the man was about to jump the gate.

In a flash, Rose visualized the whole scene. He would fly the gate with the ease of a practised jumper, and without even being aware of her presence, he would gallop away up the hill, leaving her speechless under a shower of hoof-thrown mud.

At all costs she must do something . . . anything . . . to attract his attention. She quickened her pace, and as she ran she removed the floppy-brimmed hat. She would use it to flag him down.

She arrived at the gate post at precisely the moment when Puncher was about to make his jump. Not surprisingly, her sudden, unexpected appearance from behind the hedge, waving a hat, made the horse swerve violently to the left. His rider, equally taken by surprise, shot out of the saddle and crashed against the gate. For what seemed to Rose like an eternity he lay there, motionless, his head against one of the crossbars, his hat poised drunkenly over one eyebrow.

The horse, quickly recovering from his fright, trotted back to where his master lay, and began tossing his head with menace while angrily jingling his bridle. Several seconds elapsed before the faithful animal would allow Rose to go near the prostrate figure of his master.

When at last she persuaded the cob that she intended no harm, Rose knelt beside the inert figure. In a flash, the whole gloomy picture of her failure flooded into her mind. In that moment of thoughtlessness, she had utterly ruined her plan – she, of all people, who had been riding ponies ever since she could remember, and who, on more than one occasion, had silently cursed some unthinking, non-riding person for a similarly thoughtless act! Silently she castigated herself;

128

stupid fool that she was! He would *never* forgive her.

She was greatly relieved to find upon closer inspection that he was not seriously hurt; more dazed than damaged. Already he was struggling to his feet and brushing away the bits of earth and grass from his jacket. There was a nasty-looking graze where his cheekbone had hit the fence, and there would be colourful bruising around his eye next morning, but otherwise he appeared to be intact.

'Oh, sir!' Rose blurted out, overcome with confusion and shame. 'I am so *dreadfully* sorry! It was all my fault. I should ha' known better than to come from behind the hedge like that!'

As he continued to brush himself down and straighten his belt, she sensed that it was not the bang on the head or the graze on his cheek that was hurting. It was the loss of official dignity. A *Riding* Officer, of all people, to be unseated! It was intolerable.

Hurriedly she sought to soften the indignity. 'It was all my fault,' she repeated. 'I should ha' known it would make the horse shy like that. It was stupid of me. An' 'twas enough to have anyone off!'

He glanced at her; nodded briefly – but said nothing. Instead he gathered up the reins and swung into the saddle once more.

Seeking to detain him for at least a few more minutes, she began, 'I really came to say . . .' but he was already moving back the way he had just come.

In a last attempt to be helpful, Rose called out, 'Hold on a minute. I'll open the gate for ee.'

But over his shoulder, he called curtly, 'Leave it!' – and as he wheeled his horse round to face the gate once again, he added, 'And this time stand well clear, please.'

He dug his heels into Puncher's flanks, flew the gate with deceptive ease, and then galloped off up towards the village.

CHAPTER NINE

Never a mistake . . .
Never a discovery!

Rose retrieved the floppy-brimmed, shepherdess-style hat which she had flung away when going to the aid of the fallen Riding Officer. She flicked off a few bits of soil and grass, and then, as she watched the mounted figure disappearing in the direction of St Keverne, she angrily banged the hat against her thigh.

'Idiot!' she cried aloud. 'You blithering idiot!' She regarded the innocent hat as though all her troubles were the hat's fault. In a sudden surge of frustration, she bashed the hat against her thigh once more. 'I've a good mind never to wear you again,' she threatened, irrationally. 'D'you hear me!'

She was answered only by the plaintive screech of a seagull wheeling high above her head. In defence of the hat knocked senseless through it's owner's anger, the bird, like an old crone scolding a wayward child, seemed to be saying, 'It was you-ooh, you-ooh, you-ooh!'

'Oh, I *know* it was my fault, really,' Rose flared back. 'All my fault! But there's no need to keep rubbing it in!'

She stamped her foot on the soft, mossy turf. It relieved her feelings. So she did it again. 'There! That's better!' she exploded, pursing her lips very tightly. The gull, now suddenly silent, seemed content to hop along the top of the sea wall on one leg, evidently regarding the incident as closed.

With a last backward glance at the rock-strewn seaboard, Rose began retracing her steps towards Rosenithon. The day which had started so brilliantly now seemed, irretrievably, to have clouded over – even though the sun might still be shining from a clear blue sky. Her plan, so eagerly devised in the early morning, now lay in ruins; the man she most wanted to impress with her charm and her gratitude – and she *had* wanted to impress him, despite her conflicting emotions – would even now be cursing her for the stupid little fool which, in her moment of impetuousness, she had undoubtedly been. There could be no denying it – she had been a thoughtless idiot.

By the time she reached the gateway with its view across Godrevy Cove and the Manacles, her spirits as well as her self-esteem had plummeted, and as she gazed out at the Carn-dhu rocks and the Gwinges – her especial and very personal shrine – her eyes became awash with tears. 'Oh, Mother . . . true mother . . . Oh, Mother in Heaven, or wherever you are,' she breathed, 'do you understand . . . Do you understand that although I am surrounded by such loving people . . . and I know I'm lucky . . . there are times, mother dear, when I feel so lonely. I feel I don't truly belong. Can you understand that, Mother dearest?'

For several minutes she listened; listened intently, deeply within herself. She was answered only by the distant murmur of the sea, and the scolding 'clack' of a jackdaw high up in a nearby elm.

With a despairing sigh, she gathered up her skirts and began delicately picking her way back up the rough tree-shaded footpath leading to Thorn Cottage. Her mother – her mother on earth, Amia Roskruge – was, reassuringly, precisely where Rose expected her to be; in the kitchen, preparing the table for dinner. She looked up as Rose entered, her large comfortable presence filling the room with a feeling of permanence and stability.

'You'm back sooner that I 'spected, Rosie my luv,' she purred, the mere timbre of her voice acting like a soothing balm. 'I didn 'spect ee quite so early.'

Rose stood in the doorway, aimlessly swinging the floppy-brimmed hat. 'No,' she said wistfully, 'I just thought I'd come home.'

131

Her mother shot her a quizzical glance. She knew her daughter; she'd loved her and cared for her since babyhood. Something was wrong. She recognized the unusual flatness of voice; she noted the tear stains on the cheeks.

'Ez anythin' the matter then, my luv?' she asked gently. 'Tedn a bit like ee to sound so sad.'

Rose felt the strong, well-covered arm go round her shoulders; felt the work-hardened hand pressing her head against the ample bosom; smelled the familiar apron-smeared smell of farmhouse butter, pastry, and the earthiness of unwashed sweat. She was Rosie once more; the little girl who would run to this wonderfully comforting person whenever she was troubled or sad, or when she had been teased by the older children at the charity school in the village. And, as always in the past, all her troubles came pouring out – all her doubts, all her fears, and nearly all her hopes – they all came tumbling out onto that massive, comforting bosom. And as always, too, this sympathetic mother turned them all inside out. In her cosy, unhurried voice, she made them all seem like nothing more disturbing than the little molehills in the field which her father and old Prince, the plough-horse, would scatter with the chain-harrows.

'Why, you've got nothin' to be worryin' over, my luv,' the soothing voice continued. 'If you wants to see that fella again – to thank un for helpin' ee – you'll not have long to wait; an' that's for zertin! After all,' she added with a wry smile, 'they Customs gints don't leave the likes o' we in peace for very many moons, now do 'em?'

'He's different, Ma,' Rose defended, recognizing the thinly veiled disapproval in her mother's voice. 'Not a bit like th'others. Even Will Trenethy has to admit that.'

'Well,' Amia countered enigmatically, 'that's as may be. But my guess is, it'll not be more'n a week or two before he'm around these yer parts again.' She smiled at her daughter indulgently. 'Especially,' she thought to herself, 'after settin' eyes on a girl like you!'

The prophecy proved more accurate than either mother or daughter expected.

Indeed, it was no more than a fortnight later when Rose, having spent nearly all morning working on her father's and Mr Tripconey's boat down at Porthoustock, decided to take her 'croust' – the pasty and saffron cake that her mother had put up for her in the wicker basket – up to her favourite grassy ledge on the track leading over the hill to Porthallow.

It had been very hot working down there on the boat, mending nets, sorting tackle, and she knew that she must be smelling distinctly fishy. So, she decided to have a bathe.

She often did this, in the seclusion of the small, sandy little cove at the foot of the cliff. It was so secluded that it was like a private beach; you couldn't be seen by anyone – except someone on the sea, of course, and also from the narrow track along the cliff edge.

But the track was only seldom used, and so Rose felt quite safe. Even so, no decent girl would ever dream of being seen bathing in the nude – it was quite bad enough for a fully developed young lady to be seen bathing at all!

So, Rose and her mother had made up what they considered an appropriately modest bathing gown. It was voluminous. Despite the fact that fashionable people, having formerly confined themselves to the warm spring waters of Bath and Harrogate, were now venturing into the sea at Brighton, Margate or Scarborough – all because some up-country doctor had been extolling the therapeutic virtues of salt water – it was still considered highly immodest for a lady to display the contours of her figure; below the waist, that is. Above the waist, tight-fitting, décolleté bodices were not only permissible, they were positively 'de rigueur'. But below the waistline, the most intimate configuration of the feminine form, even down to the ankle, must forever remain a tantalizing mystery. So, the bathing gown had to be voluminous. Propriety demanded for the male, a pair of billowing drawers reaching down to below the knee; a lady's gown must have a skirt so large that it would balloon in the water in such a way as to preserve intact the secrets of her figure.

''Tis all very well to talk about modesty,' Rose had

remarked to her mother, as they began cutting out the skirt for her bathing gown, 'but there's nothin' very modest about the amount of material we'll be needin'.'

'No, but tedn right to go bathin', else,' Amia Roskruge observed. 'Why, they do say the ladies an' ginelmen up country is so concerned 'bout bein' seen undressed on the beaches up there that they've invented these yer things they call bathin' machines.'

'What be they, then?'

'Why, they'm like little houses on wheels, so they say. Seems they'm dragged up an' down the beach by horses, accordin' to whereabouts the tide is, see.'

'And what be the idea of that, then?'

'Aw, 'tis so's the ladies and ginelmen don't have to display themselves on the beach, like. They can come out o' these yer bathin' machines all ready an' undressed, if you understand me, an' step right down into the water.'

Rose, who had never been shy of her figure, and whose feet had long since become hardened by the shingle beaches of the Lizard, looked at her mother in astonishment. 'Well, I never did,' she laughed. 'Sounds a funny old idea to me.'

' 'Tis more'n that,' her mother continued, warming to her subject. 'They do say that for anyone who's a bit afeard o' goin' in the water, like, there's a couple o' women – washerwomen sort o' women, if you follow me – waitin' outside these yer bathin' machines, ready to give un a duckin'!'

Mother and daughter burst into laughter.

' 'Tis true, Rosie,' Amia Roskruge had continued, 'true as I'm yere. An' they call these yere women – these yere duckin' women – they do call un "dippers", I believe.'

'Where did you learn all this, then, Mama?'

'Why, vicar was tellin' us, up in the village one day. He'd been up that way recently, so he said. Seems that our church's beginnings was connected in some way with an abbey in those parts. Booley Abbey, did he say? I'm sure I don't know.'

'Oh, yes. I believe I've heard Charles Incledon sayin'

something about it, over at The White Hart. He learned about it when he was singing in the cathedral choir at Exeter, I think. Beaulieu Abbey, that's right.'

'Where would that be, then, Rosie?'

'Oh, 'tis up that way, somewhere. Somewhere near the Isle of Wight, I believe.'

Amia Roskruge looked at her daughter with undisguised admiration. 'You'm clever, Rosie. I always said you'd be the clever one. I never was much of a scholar, meself – never had any real schoolin', like. But you . . . you'm really clever, Rosie, and I'm proud of ee.' Then she added rather sadly, 'I wish I'd had a bit o' schoolin', like you.'

Rosie sighed too. 'I wish I'd had a lot more schooling,' she said wistfully. 'I'm not nearly clever enough. I wish I knew more about . . . oh, all manner of things. I wish . . . I wish . . .' Then she checked herself, thinking that her mother might feel hurt. 'But I'm very lucky,' she added, 'very lucky indeed.'

There had been a brief, awkward pause. Then the conversation had flowed on – easily, uninhibitedly, in the warmth of a companionship between mother and daughter that had grown up over the years.

And the voluminous bathing gown had been finished, tried on amid much merriment and, finally, thoroughly approved of.

But that was all quite a long time ago. The costume had been worn and well salted many times since then. Today, Rose had no thoughts of bathing machines or buxom female 'dippers' in mob-caps and décolleté bodices – no thoughts, in fact, of anything other than the sheer joy of bobbing about in the gentle wavelets that lapped the secluded, grey-sanded beach near her home. Nothing to disturb her peace of mind; nothing, that is, until the moment she espied a horse and rider slowly descending the steep, mountainous track on the far side of Porthoustock.

For a moment her heart seemed to miss a beat. The light blue riding jacket; the black tricorn hat. Not for a second had she thought he'd return to the locality so soon.

135

As he emerged into full view she knew for certain that it was Ashley Penberth.

Panic seized her – momentarily, at least. Here she was, in the water – albeit in her swirling, voluminous bathing gown – but if she wanted to make absolutely sure that this time he would see her, then she must be up on the grassy verge beside the track when he came by. And there must be no movement whatsoever to frighten the horse. But how could she possibly get undressed, dried and back into her ordinary clothes in the time available. It would hardly be proper for her to appear before him – and at close range too – clad in her wet bathing costume. Although it was expansive enough when ballooning in the water, it clung to her body like a kind of outer skin when she walked up the beach. Every intimate curve and contour became distressingly visible. It mattered little that her well-formed, fresh young breasts should be delicately etched in outline – after all, what else were fashionably cut, low-neckline dresses designed to display – but it was her hips and her thighs, her ankles even, that posed such a problem. It was the intimate revelation of these very aspects of feminine anatomy which could turn a relatively docile male into a lecherous beast – or so she had been warned.

By the time the Riding Officer clattered up the flinty pathway leading to the grassy plateau, Rose was leaning against an outcropping rock, drying the ends of her hair. She had modestly covered herself from the waist down. Only her bare toes peeped out from below the red and white striped calico overskirt which she wore when working on the boat. Beneath it her long wet bathing drawers felt uncomfortably clammy; worse still, she was beginning to itch in a very personal area.

But the smile with which she greeted the man she most wanted to see revealed none of her physical discomforts. This time, she made not a sound; she waited for him to speak first.

As soon as he saw her Ashley reined in his horse.

'Hullo there, Rosie.' The greeting was cheerful enough. 'I hardly expected to see you this side of Porthoustock.' To her surprise as well as delight she saw he was dismounting. 'Giving the Three Tuns a miss this morning, eh?' he called over his shoulder as he loosened Puncher's girth.

'It's my morning off,' she lied. 'Will won't be expecting me until this evening.' If the Riding Officer was prepared to stay and chat, so was she. She'd just have to risk Will's wrath; she'd plead illness, or something; she'd deal with that problem when it came. For the moment it was enough that he had thrown the reins loosely over the saddle, leaving Puncher to crop a nearby patch of grass.

As he sauntered over to where she was sitting he remarked casually, 'So you've been bathing, eh?' He gave her figure an appraising glance. 'Very aristocratic. All of a sudden it's become fashionable among the up-country gentry, I understand. Salt water, and all that.' His eyes twinkled as he added. 'Distinctly "à la mode", as you might say.'

Rose laughed. She had no idea what he meant, but it had broken the conversational ice.

'I don't know about it bein' aristocratic,' she countered. 'But what I do know is that I love it. 'Specially on a day like this – even though the water *is* rather cold.'

'Bound to be, at this time of year,' he sympathized, sitting cross-legged on the turf and gazing appreciatively across the bay. 'I take it you can swim?'

'Oh, yes, indeed. My father taught me when I was quite young. Said he wouldn't take me out in the boat until I could swim.'

Ashley raised a quizzical eyebrow in her direction. 'That was sensible. You can't be too careful on this coast.' Involuntarily his eyes strayed towards the Manacles. 'You like boats, then, do you?'

She nodded vigorously – more vigorously than she really intended, but at that moment she shivered. She was feeling increasingly clammy. She wondered how much longer she could endure it; she was determined to detain him as long as she could, but there was a limit.

The shiver had not gone unnoticed, and although the clinging tendency of the bathing gown was being fully

137

appreciated, especially where it emphasized the contours of her ripe young breasts, Ashley took pity on the girl by saying:

'You must be cold, Rosie. Wouldn't you like to get changed back into something warmer?'

Rose blushed prettily, shrugging her shoulders and spreading her hands to indicate that there was really nowhere sufficiently private for a modest young girl to change.

Sensing her embarrassment with considerable, though disguised, amusement Ashley remarked, 'Oh, am I the problem, perhaps? Well, in that case I'd better be on my way.'

'Oh, no, no,' Rose blurted out a little too hurriedly. 'You're not really a problem at all. I mean . . .'

'Well then,' Ashley said, coming to the conversational rescue, 'what about those rocks down there? Wouldn't they provide enough cover?' Leaning back against a low outcropping rock and half closing his eyes, he added mischievously, 'And I promise not to look.'

It was a promise easier made than kept because the rocks proved not quite so preclusive as they had appeared. Between the two largest ones, behind which Rose began to divest herself of her clammy garments, there was a fairly narrow gap. By shifting his position slightly to the right Ashley found himself with an inquisitive bird's eye view of what he was not meant to see. It made for compulsive viewing. First, the tight-fitting bodice was unlaced and discarded, revealing the well-formed vibrant young breasts; then came the voluminous skirt, pulled over the head and cast aside; finally, and most seductively, the long ankle-length drawers were wriggled out of, displaying all too briefly the forbidden fruits – the temptingly rounded hips, the shapely thighs and the dark mysteries of the lower abdomen. Ashley could not drag his attention away; it was arousing within his loins the disturbing sensation of raw sexual desire.

Then, like a warning cloud rolling in from the sea, the vision of Alethea MacKenzie floated in to his conscience – dear sweet, gentle, lovable Alethea, the only girl he had really loved since childhood.

Firmly, resolutely – reluctantly – he shut out that beguiling vision down there on the beach; he tightly closed his eyes.

When eventually Rose emerged, fully dressed once more and with her hair beginning to dry into enchanting little ringlets around her face, she looked even prettier than ever, Ashley thought. A rich glow illuminated the limpid whiteness of her smooth skin, and her eyes seemed to be sparkling with the lustre of the sea.

But he could no longer regard her in quite the same light as before. Those brief glimpses of her nakedness had given him a carnal knowledge of her body to which he knew he was not really entitled. He had stolen something from her. Yet he felt neither guilt nor shame. Unknown to her, she was known to him; and in a curious sort of way it made him feel possessively protective.

As she settled herself beside him on the soft, sea-sprayed turf she opened the wicker basket and offered him a piece of saffron cake. Accepting it gratefully he lay back against the rock, munching the cake and gazing speculatively at the pale blue sky.

'Have you lived round here all your life, Rosie?' he asked casually.

Her mouth was full of pasty, and as she had no wish to shower him with bits of flaky pastry she just nodded. Then, finishing the mouthful, she said, 'Yes, nearly all my life.'

She noticed him cock an enquiring glance at her. 'Nearly, but not all,' he questioned. 'Sounds interesting. Where else?'

Rose responded with an expansive, sweeping gesture that embraced both sea and sky. 'Out there – somewhere,' she indicated.

Ashley continued to munch. 'A mermaid, I suppose,' he grunted. Receiving no encouraging rejoiner to his rather poor attempt at humour, he lightheartedly conceded, 'Oh, well, them that asks no questions don't get told no lies, I guess.'

For several moments Rose sat hugging her knees. Should she tell him, and if so, how much. Continuing to stare out to sea, and with a wry little smile playing about her lips, she informed him, 'As a matter of fact, I was washed up on the beach when I was a baby.'

From the sudden jerk of his head she knew she had captured his interest.

'The ship was called the "Elizabeth-Ann", so I was told,' she went on, quietly, 'and she became a total wreck out there on the Manacles. I was the only living thing saved.'

He lay back against the rock again, shading his eyes from the sun. 'Go on,' he encouraged, sympathy softening his deep voice, 'tell me about it.'

In a few brief sentences she told him all she knew of the catastrophe – none of which she could remember herself, she explained. But she told him how Sampson and Amia Roskruge had taken her in and brought her up as their own child; she told him how much she loved and admired them both.

'So there you are,' she concluded, with a valiant attempt at a merry laugh. 'Or perhaps I should say "Here I am", the village barmaid, with two lovely parents – and yet I don't really know who I am.'

'And does that bother you?'

'No, not really, I suppose. But . . . .' She stared wistfully out to sea.

'But what?' he asked.

She hesitated, frowning slightly, uncertain how much to confide. Then, with a gesture of trust, she removed the locket and gold chain from around her neck and handed it to him.

'It's this,' she said in a small, half-apologetic voice. 'It's the only thing I've got that belonged to my mother. In that last moment of tragedy it was all she was able to pass on to me, and I've always had the feeling that she meant it to convey something to me – some kind of message, perhaps.'

Ashley took the gold-enamelled locket and gold chain from her, and examined it carefully.

'Hmm,' he murmured at last. 'It's attractive . . . and very unusual.' He continued to turn the jewel over in his hands. 'Quite valuable as well, I should say – apart from the obvious sentimental value. I rather like this picture on the back. Some sort of naval engagement I should imagine, wouldn't you?'

Rose watched him, fascinated, as he minutely inspected both chain and locket. He seemed particularly interested in the design of the locket.

'I don't know very much about these things,' he went on, 'but I would hazard a guess that this one is French. These initials in fine gold on the front here – this monogram "L de V" – that rather suggests that I might be right.' He rummaged about in his waistcoat pocket and produced a small magnifying glass. 'There was a French master gold-smith by the name of Toutin – Henri Toutin, I think it was – who became quite famous for this kind of jewellery. Originally I think he had a workshop in Blois but eventually he had one in Paris as well. He was flourishing in the middle of the last century, I would say.'

'You seem to know more than just a bit about it,' Rose admired. 'Where did you learn all that?'

Ashley shot her an enigmatic smile. 'Picked it up as I went along,' he said airily. 'I had to; it's more or less our line of business, jewellery – if you know what I mean.'

He peered through the magnifying glass as he continued, 'This fellow Toutin, he usually managed to engrave his name on his work somewhere – but I can't see it on the outside. I wonder if it's on the inside. Have you ever looked?'

'On the inside? Oh, no,' Rose replied anxiously. 'I don't think it opens. It's not meant to, surely. It's just the picture on the back, and the initials . . .'

But Ashley was fingering the suspension ring at the top of the locket. 'They usually do, you know. This is a locket, not just a pendant.'

He continued to work at the ring through which the chain was looped, saying, 'This one's a bit stiff – probably got thoroughly salt-encrusted – but it's beginning to work free. Ah, there we are.' He indicated to Rose how the two tiny arms of the swivel had swung clear of the top of the locket. 'Now then, let's see what we can find.' He produced a knife from beneath his riding jacket – the very one that had cut the makeshift linchpin from the hedge – and proceeded to insert the razor-sharp edge between the tightly closed sides of the jewel.

'Oh, do be careful,' Rose burst out. 'I couldn't bear for it to be damaged in any way. It's the only thing I've got . . .'

'Have no fear, Rosie,' was the seemingly thoughtless reply. 'Monsieur Toutin was a master craftsman; he made his hinges admirably strong.'

Rose edged closer, to watch what he was doing. Despite her anxiety, she felt instinctively that they were on the point of making a momentous discovery.

'Aha, here she comes,' Ashley announced triumphantly, as he very carefully prised open the two halves of the locket. 'Gently does it.'

'Ohhh!' Rose groaned excitedly. 'I'd no idea!' Impulsively she placed one hand on Ashley's as he held out the opened locket. 'Let me see, let me see!'

She could scarcely believe her eyes. Inside were two – one on each side – most exquisitely painted miniatures; on the right, a bearded stern-faced gentleman with an aquiline nose; on the other, facing him, the ageing but still beautiful face of a woman. For such small paintings, the features were incredibly clear. Both the man and the woman wore powdered wigs, and the clothes – what little could be seen of them – appeared to be seventeenth rather than eighteenth century.

'Oh-h, just look at that!' Rose exclaimed, a note of awe creeping into her voice. 'What marvellous little portraits – just look at them! Perfect in every detail.' She took the jewel, gently cradling it in her hands. Then, turning to Ashley with a look of admiration and gratitude in eyes that were moist with emotion, she blurted out, 'Oh, Mister Ashley, I *am* so grateful! I never knew . . . Well, I suppose I never thought to try . . . I was just so thankful to have something belonging to my mother that I never thought about whether it would open or not.'

Ashley, his delicate task completed – there had been a few anxious moments concerning the strength of the hinges

142

– lay back on one elbow and regarded Rose with amusement. There could be no doubt but that she was a very pretty girl. The dark hair, drying in the sun and clustering all over her head in disorderly curls; the creamy white skin, now suffused with the afterglow from a bathe as well as the excitement of a new discovery; the ingenuous radiance in those sparkling eyes. He was more than pleased to have been some help.

'Rather important-looking people, I'd say,' he suggested, leaning over to get a closer look at the miniatures. He trained his magnifying glass on the opened locket.

'Hmm,' he murmured pensively. 'I wonder who they are.' The distinctive smell of her freshly salt-washed body and the dying fragrance of an expensive perfume – so incongruous on a simple, country girl – taunted his nostrils as he leaned towards her. He wondered where the perfume had come from. He thought he could guess. Roscoff was only the other side of the Channel, and many a smuggling boat came ashore with a few phials of scent to beguile a lady.

'Hmmm,' he said again, this time more appreciatively. 'A very distinguished-looking couple. French aristocracy, unless I'm much mistaken.'

'Oh, do you really think so?' Rose burst out excitedly, gazing at the portraits with an entirely new interest. 'Oh, wouldn't it be wonderful if they were!' She was like a small child rediscovering a long-lost toy, Ashley thought. He lay back on the turf once more, contentedly enjoying the sight of her unabashed pleasure as, alternately, she pressed the locket against her bosom and then held it out to look at it again.

Rose remained in that same position for quite a long time, saying nothing, just savouring the beauty of the delicately wrought locket and the two aristocratic-looking portraits inside. Were they, perhaps, her grandparents; was she really French, not English – or half French, possibly? She examined both faces minutely. But even with the aid of Ashley's magnifying glass she could see no recognizable likeness to herself. Well, then, perhaps they were her great-

143

grandparents; it would be difficult to see a likeness from that distance. She decided to ask the man who had opened up for her these exciting possibilities.

'Can you see any likeness in either of them – to me, I mean?'

He took the locket and magnifying glass from her, and with mock solemnity scrutinized both portraits. He kept looking backwards and forwards from them to her – and then back again. Finally, teasingly, the flicker of a smile playing about his mouth, he shook his head.

'Oh-h-h,' she groaned. 'Not any resemblance at all?' It was as though the sun had suddenly gone behind a cloud.

To her surprise a broad grin was creasing his face as he handed her back the locket. 'No, no,' he laughed, 'I was only teasing.' Then more seriously, 'Yes, there is a likeness – only slight, I would say – but distinct, nonetheless. The eyes and the brow – yours and hers are alike. A couple of generations between you I'd say.' She felt his eyes upon her as she lovingly examined once more the face of the woman who might perhaps be her grandmother.

'Does that please you?' she heard him ask. She turned and looked straight into his slightly-mocking eyes. Obviously he had no idea what this meant to her – just how much it meant to discover even the smallest fragment of one's roots. And why should it – to someone who almost certainly knew exactly who he was and where he came from.

'Would you not be pleased – if you were me?' she asked simply.

He clasped his hands behind his head and lay back in an attitude of contemplation. 'An interesting question,' he remarked. 'I've never really thought about it.'

It was probably foolish of her, Rose thought, but she couldn't help feeling a small glow of pride that she, the humble barmaid with very inadequate schooling, could 'ask an interesting question' of someone who was so obviously far better educated.

'It'd be different for you, of course,' she interposed, 'because you know all about your family, I expect. You have

144

a mother and father – I expect – sisters and brothers as well, perhaps?'

The reply seemed a long time coming. 'No, as a matter of fact, I haven't,' he said, at length. 'Neither brothers, sisters, nor even a father. Only a mother.'

Rose bit her lip. She rather wished she hadn't asked. He would think she was prying. But before she had time even to murmur an apology, he went on, 'No, it's rather a curious coincidence, perhaps, but just as you lost your mother out there on the Manacles, so too I lost my father.'

'Oh, no – oh, I *am* sorry,' she whispered. 'I shouldn't have asked.' But she was secretly glad that she had; inevitably it must create a bond of mutual sympathy between them.

He seemed not to notice the apology because he was already saying, 'Yes, my father was shipwrecked on his way back from Roscoff. He'd been over there on business of some kind. It happened just a few days before I was born, so I never knew my father.'

'Would you rather not talk about it?'

He shook his head. 'No, no, I don't mind. It was all a long, long time ago.'

He plucked a succulent stem of fresh green grass and began chewing it. It was a peerless morning. The sun was hanging high in the sky like a molten ball against a backcloth of azure vastness; the gulls screeched lazily above the rocks, the bees hummed with expectation among the early foxgloves and the purple loosestrife; the gentle rhythmical murmur of the waves on the pebbly beach induced a timeless sense of peace and well-being – a moment, in fact, for nostalgic reverie.

Rose, propped up on one elbow, watched every expression on his strong, virile face as, with eyes still half closed, he began to reminisce.

On the proceeds salvaged from his father's cargo, he told her – and on the recommendation of squire Sir Andrew MacKenzie who had befriended his widowed mother – he had been sent away to boarding school 'to make a gentleman of him'. It had been his desire, ever since childhood, to become an officer in the Royal Navy – to follow in the footsteps of boyhood heroes like Hawke and Boscawen. Unfortunately, while at school he had broken his leg, and the drunken school doctor had failed to set it properly. As a result, one leg was slightly shorter than the other and it had left him with a limp. When he went up before the Navy Board they'd been kind – but they hadn't liked his limp.

He sat up then and stared out across the bay towards Falmouth where the tall masts of the Channel squadron were clearly visible.

'So,' he concluded, a hollow ring of cheerfulness creeping into his voice, 'as *they* didn't want me, I did what I thought was the next best thing. I joined His Majesty's Customs Service.' He turned, enveloping her in the warmth of his half-apologetic smile. 'I know it's a good deal less glamorous than the Navy, but at least it's a job that allows me to keep an eye on things at home – and, of course,' his eyes developed a wickedly mischievous glint, 'it brings me into contact with pretty girls in alehouses – like the one at St Keverne, for instance – so there can't be very much wrong with it, now can there?'

It was a somewhat laboured compliment, Rose thought, but it brought a pretty little blush to her cheeks, nonetheless.

'Unfortunately,' he continued, jerking himself to his feet once more, 'they don't pay me to sit around all day chatting to pretty barmaids and talking exclusively about myself. So, I must now be about my proper business.'

He gathered Puncher's reins into his left hand, swung himself easily into the saddle, and with a farewell nod and a cheery wave, he clattered off up the flinty coastal track.

CHAPTER TEN

The Big House

Rose paused at the top of the rough granite steps set into the footpath up from Laddenvean. She leaned against the tall grassy hedgebank to draw breath. Adjusting her brown-paper parcel to a more comfortable position, she glanced back the way she had just come. Piercing the gloom of the heavily overcast sky, and dominating the scenery for miles around, was the tapering spire of St Keverne church. Even as far away as Pendennis Castle, guarding the entrance to Falmouth harbour, that church spire could be seen rising from the cliff-tops above Porthoustock. It was a beacon to the weary traveller, a landmark to the homecoming sailor, and it had formed part of the background to Rose's daily life for as long as she could remember.

Away to her right, down there in the valley, ran the stream from which the monks of St Keverne must have once drawn water for their daily needs. But that was a very long time ago – more than five hundred years, so the vicar said – and a whole ocean-full of water must have gurgled its way down to the outfall at Porthoustock since those faraway days. By comparison, Rose reflected, a mere trickle had gone by since that peerless June morning when she had lain stretched out on that springy turf alongside Ashley Penberth.

Even if the abruptness of his leaving had left a few lacerated feelings, there had remained with her the knowledge that for a few brief moments they had shared each other's innermost thoughts. With flattering candour he had told her of the accident which had subsequently altered the whole course of his life, while she in her turn had recounted how

147

she came to be living at St Keverne. It must, surely, have forged a bond between them.

She could still picture him clearly, lying there against the rock – eyes half closed, fair, curly hair tied at the nape by a black satin ribbon, strong-featured if not classically handsome good looks, and with laughter lines radiating attractively from the corners of his eyes. And it was not until he had disappeared over the hill above Pencra Head, and while she was still basking in the afterglow of his companionable presence, that she realized that she *still* had not thanked him for his help with the broken-down haycart. But, somehow, it no longer seemed important. That short time together must surely have carried their relationship beyond such a need.

Having now recovered her breath, Rose transferred the parcel to the other arm and set off once more in the direction of Lanteague. But not before taking a last backward glance at the church spire. Now that she was leaving it behind, she suddenly felt overcome with nostalgia. It might be quite a long while before she saw this reassuring part of her background again because, although Colonel Bouchier's manor was only a few miles from St Keverne, it was surrounded by a thick and rather forbidding belt of fir trees. You could neither see into it, nor could you see out of it.

Her father had not been very keen on the idea of her going to Lanteague; her mother was in two minds about it, but she could see the possible advantages.

It was just a bit of stray gossip that Rose had picked up – not at the Three Tuns Inn for a change, but outside the baker's shop in the village square – that the Colonel's Lady was in need of a new seamstress. Poor old Lena Milren, who had been with her ladyship for many years, was now so stricken with the rheumatics in her hands that she could no longer do the intricate needlework which Lady Bouchier required. And if there was one thing in particular that Amia Roskruge had taught her daughter it was how to handle a needle and thread.

So, Rose had applied for the situation. 'When one door

closes, another opens', she had been told – and it had done so in the nick of time for her because when eventually she had reported for duty at the Three Tuns after that hour of dalliance with Ashley Penberth on the cliffside beyond Porthoustock, Will Trenethy had not been best pleased with her. If she thought so little of her job as to turn up more than an hour late, he had told her, then she had better start looking for another one elsewhere. There were plenty of other girls in the village who would jump at the chance of serving behind the bar at the Three Tuns Inn!

In a fit of huff, Rose had picked up the hem of her wool-embroidered dress, and swept out – never, she had vowed, to darken the doors of the inn again.

It was an ill wind, tho', she conjectured, because Colonel Sir Francis and Lady Arabella Bouchier were, without doubt, quite the most aristocratic couple in the district, and they were known to entertain some very exalted people. Although they had no family of their own, they had many friends in high places. Indeed, it was confidently rumoured – in the way rumours grow – that if ever His Majesty, the King, should deign to set foot in the extreme south-western parts of his domain, he would almost certainly stay with the Bouchiers.

So, to be employed in any capacity up at 'the big house' added a certain cachet to one's personality – and to be employed as seamstress to Lady Bouchier was to stand very much nearer the top of the domestic hierarchy than the bottom. It was, in fact, quite a feather in one's cap – and it was far and away above the rank of an ordinary housemaid.

With this comforting thought in her mind, Rose set off along the footpath that would eventually bring her to the Manor of Lanteague.

It wasn't, of course, that she expected or even hoped to meet any of the highborn friends of the Colonel and his Lady – not, at least, on the same social footing – but, nevertheless, she felt it would be a step in the right direction. It would bring her into more sophisticated company. Deep, deep down inside she felt that, in some way or other, she really belonged in an atmosphere of greater elegance and charm – greater, that is, than anything the confines of a village inn could provide. It was the same at home – at Thorn Cottage – and this was the thought that hurt. She loved her parents so much that any idea of wanting something different seemed so disloyal. Both of them, Sampson and Amia Roskruge, had given her everything; often it had been more than they could really afford. But they had given it willingly, unselfishly. Above all, throughout the whole of her remembered existence, they had given her the priceless gift of security. Theirs was a simple life, never an abundance of material things, but there were always fish in the sea to be caught, crops in the fields to be harvested – had not the good Lord promised there would always be seed-time and harvest – and if there was never any money to spare at Thorn Cottage, there were those little unexpected luxuries that miraculously appeared in the upstairs cupboard after Sampson Roskruge had been a-fishing overseas.

So, the thought of wanting something better seemed ungrateful; yet, it was always there, it could not be stifled, and in taking the situation as seamstress to Lady Bouchier, Rose was trying to resolve it.

She climbed over the stile at the edge of the field opposite Trevallack and decided to pay the usual courtesy call on Mrs Tripconey. The Tripconeys had been good friends to the Roskruges for many years and it would have been unthinkable for Rose to go past Trevallack without going in for a chat.

'Why, hullo there, Rosie, my dear,' Mrs Tripconey called through the kitchen window as soon as she recognized her visitor. 'What be doin' out this way, then?'

She was already wiping the flour off her hands and on to her apron when Rose entered the warm, homely kitchen. 'You'm not just takin' a walk, I reckon, not wi' that gert parcel under your arm.'

Rose dumped the package on one of the empty high-backed kitchen chairs and sank down onto another. 'No,' she puffed, 'I'm not just out walkin' for pleasure. I'm on my way to Lanteague.'

'Oh, my!' Mrs Tipconey exclaimed. 'So you'm consortin' wi' the gentry, then?'

Rose threw back her head and laughed – that merry, deep-throated laugh that Mrs Tripconey always loved to hear, and which always surprised her coming from someone as refined-looking, and fine-boned, as Rose.

'No, no, not corsortin', I'm afraid, Mrs Trip,' Rose answered. 'Just doin' a bit of needlework for her ladyship.'

'Aw, ais,' Mrs Tripconey breathed, all ears. 'Well, let me get ee a dish o' tay, then, my dear.'

'Lady Bouchier's been needin' a seamstress, it seems – ever since Mistress Milren found the work too much for her – and so when I offered for the position, her ladyship agreed to take me on. Had you not heard, then, Mrs Trip?'

'No, no, my luv, 'tis news to me,' Mrs Tripconey shook her head. Then she put one finger on the end of her nose and corrected herself, 'No, that edn quite trew – I do tell a lie – because I did yere somethin' about you not bein' at the Tuns any longer.' She looked at Rose enquiringly.

'That's right, Mrs Trip,' Rose agreed, shifting uncomfortably and hoping to avoid further questioning. 'Shall we just say Will an' me had a little difference of opinion.'

Mrs Tripconey peered over the top of her steel-rimmed spectacles as she infused the tea.

''Twas somethin' to do with a hanzum Ridin' Officer, or so I yerd,' she teased.

'Aw, now, Mrs Trip,' Rose blushed prettily, 'you shouldn't say such things. 'Twas nothin', really.'

Mrs Tripconey handed Rose her cup of tea, and sat down conversationally at the kitchen table.

'Well now, my luv,' she coaxed, folding her massive forearms on the well-scrubbed table beneath her equally massive bosom, 'tell us about this new situation of yours up at the big house.'

Eleanor Tripconey was the motherly sort; she had borne seven, lost four to the dread disease of diphtheria and reared only three – two lusty farm boys, Aaron and Tom, and

151

a rather sickly daughter called May. She had known and loved Rose ever since the child had been brought ashore at Godrevy – indeed, if Amia and Sampson Roskruge had not taken the baby for their own, then Eleanor and Wilmot Tripconey would gladly have added to their own large, but sadly diminishing brood. As things had turned out, the Tripconeys often reflected, it was probably for the best that Sampson Roskruge was first into the water on that fateful night, otherwise the poor little sea orphan might have followed the four unfortunate Tripconeys to yet another sad little grave.

So, Eleanor Tripconey had always taken a special interest in Rose's progress – she had often remarked to husband Wilmot what a refined, intelligent girl Rose was becoming, and pretty with it, too – and she was particularly pleased now to see Rose sitting there, sipping her tea and looking so bonny. In return, Rose had always looked upon 'Mrs Trip' as her second mother. She felt she could tell her anything; Mrs Tripconey would never be censorious.

By the time Rose had finished her tea she had recounted how Lady Bouchier had interviewed her in the opulent surroundings of Lanteague. Rose had been unusually nervous but her ladyship had gone out of her way to make the young girl feel at ease. As a result, Rose was really looking forward to working for such a refined lady, and in such elegant surroundings. Even though she knew she could never be regarded as of equal social status, at least she would be working with the finest materials and for educated high-born folk.

'Well, but I don't know so much about that,' Mrs Tripconey chaffed, sensing once again the underlying yearning for knowledge of her true background which Rose, unwittingly, had increasingly revealed as she had grown to womanhood. 'Chance be a fine thing, my luvly, and there be plenty of young gents that be ready enough to partake of the Colonel's hospitality – especially after they bin out huntin'. Young "bloods" they do call 'em, I believe.'

'Oh, Mrs Trip,' Rose countered deprecatingly. 'I can't

see any o' the likes o' they takin' a shine to a girl like me. After all, I'm only going to be the seamstress – nothing like a young lady o' the house.'

Mrs Tripconey wagged her head knowingly. 'It might not seem all that fitty to you, my dear, but you'm a purty wee thing, Rosie. As I've said to Mr Tripconey more'n once, "Wilmot," I've said, "there be somethin' – I don't rightly know just what 'tis – but there be somethin' a little bit special about our Rosie. Can't say zackly what 'tis, mind, but 'tis somethin'." '

Rose smiled shyly, wistfully. She was fingering, absent-mindedly, the locket on the gold chain.

'But mind you,' Mrs Tripconey went on, 'that's not to say you mustn't be a bit careful – have your wits about you, like, because there be plenty o' they young bloods'll come offerin' ee all sorts o' niceys and things they nivver ought to be considerin', see. So, you just watch out, Rosie, my dear, an' doan' ee go offerin' any favours to young gents wi' one thought only on their wicked minds – and that's to have your shimmie off!'

Both of them burst into peals of laughter – indeed, the sound was still echoing among the cups, plates and saucers decorating the kitchen dresser when Rose retorted, 'You needn't worry 'bout that, Mrs Trip. I had plenty o' that sort down at the Three Tuns.'

'Aw, ais,' Mrs Tripconey snorted, 'but they'm no more'n a passel o' lewd yokels down thur. Whereas them as you'll be meetin' up at the Manor, now they'll be a whole pile different. Smoother with it, like, and all dressed up like fine mabyers. That thur nephew of the Colonel's, for instance. What do they call un? Lef-tennant Yewbert Loxley-Gregg, isn't it? Gert big fellow, ee be – 'im in his fancy uniform, spurs an' sword an' all. Quite a young turkey-cock, they do say.'

The smile disappeared from Mrs Tripconey's motherly face as she fixed Rose with a meaningful look. 'But I'd be wary of ee, Rosie my luv, if I was you. I've yeard tales about ee . . . so, I reckon you've best be a bit careful, see.'

But, unwisely perhaps, Rose was only half listening. Her thoughts had strayed to another uniform – a sky-blue jacket, a black tricorn hat, and a cutlass suspended from a broad leather belt. Less socially acceptable than the glittering scarlet and gold disported by the Colonel's nephew, no doubt, but that was of no consequence to Rose. What mattered to her was, simply, that she should acquire the speech and the mannerisms, if not of the gentry then at least of the middling sort because in this way – and in this way only – she felt she could raise herself in the estimation of Ashley Penberth.

She thanked Mrs Tripconey for the cup of tea and the friendly chat, and then went on her way. But not before promising that if ever she should find herself in need of a sympathetic ear she would not forget that Trevallack and the Tripconeys were less than a mile from Lanteague.

She continued along the lane for a quarter of a mile and then struck off to the left along the footpath leading past the curious, prehistoric object known as the Standing Stone which the vicar had told her was the same as the ones up at Stonehenge – some kind of religious shrine, or something. So far as Rose was concerned, it merely provided the cattle in the field with a convenient means of relieving an itch.

Shortly after leaving the Stone, the footpath entered a narrow gulley overhung with tall trees. There was something eerie about this shady, boulder-strewn part of the short-cut across the fields to Lanteague – almost as though the spirits of those pagan worshippers of long ago still sought to inveigle you in their dubious practices. As you walked along, the air suddenly seemed to grow colder. Rose picked up her skirts and hurried on. She would be using this footpath quite frequently in future, and she just hoped that this spooky feeling was not an omen of things to come.

Reaching the lane again, she was glad of the reassuring stolidness of the two humble estate-workers' cottages at the end of the footpath. There was nothing spooky about them; in fact, with their whitewashed cob walls beneath low, thatched roofs they seemed almost to be smiling. Rose found herself clinging to the memory of those two little cottages when, a few hundred yards further down the lane, she came face to face with the massive and rather forbidding gates of Lanteague.

Considering it inappropriate to make her entry by such an exalted route, she continued along the road until she found the servants' entrance at the back of the mansion. Tucking the brown-paper parcel containing her clothes more securely under her arm, she boldly knocked on the back door. It was eventually opened by a spotty-faced young under-footman wearing black breeches and a slightly soiled waistcoat.

'I'm Rose Roskruge, Lady Bouchier's new seamstress,' she announced, the firmness of her voice betraying over-anxiety not to appear nervous. 'Is her ladyship at home?'

The under-footman regarded Rose insolently. 'Have you an appointment with her ladyship?'

'Well, no, not exactly an appointment but . . .' Rose felt she was foolishly blustering.

'Her ladyship don't see nobody that's not got an appointment,' the young man sneered.

Stung by his rudeness, Rose drew herself up to her full height and thrust out her chin. 'Kindly inform Lady Bouchier that her new seamstress has arrived.' It sounded rather over-important, but the young man's insolence riled her.

'Follow me, then, dearie,' he replied familiarly, and turned on his heel.

Rose followed his loping figure along an ill-lit passage which eventually gave on to a large rectangular hall, its towering walls all liberally hung with hunting trophies and relics of the Colonel's military ancestry.

'Wait here,' the under-footman commanded. 'I will enquire as to whether her ladyship will see you.'

He stalked across the highly-polished wooden floor towards a heavy oak door at the far end of the hall where he halted and knocked. Rose felt sure he ought not to be

155

entering her ladyship's presence dressed in that greasy waistcoat. But it was no concern of hers, she concluded; she could only wait, feeling increasingly nervous and insignificant amid such exalted surroundings.

Presently the young man reappeared, somewhat chastened, Rose thought, and considerably more deferential, to announce, 'Her ladyship will see you now, miss. Step this way, please.'

Lady Arabella Bouchier was seated, quill pen in hand, at an ornately decorated Louis Quinze bureau over by a window on the far side of the elegantly furnished room. Standing nearby, legs a-stradle, and gazing out at the formal rose garden, was a young man dressed in well-cut country clothes. He remained motionless, back to the room, as the under-footman formally announced: 'Miss Roskruge, the new seamstress, my lady.'

'Come in, Roskruge,' Lady Bouchier commanded, laying down the quill pen and half turning in Rose's direction. 'I'd quite forgotten you were coming.'

'But you did say I was to start today, my lady,' Rose ventured, in a small voice.

'Oh, yes, yes,' her ladyship boomed. 'I'm sure you must be right. I have an appalling memory.' She turned full-face towards Rose, welcoming her with a warm smile. 'Indeed I'm most pleased that you've come. There's a great deal of work awaiting you – especially with the Hunt Ball only a few weeks away. Now then,' she continued, her eyes sweeping approvingly over the neatly dressed figure of her new servant, 'let me see, your name is . . . er . . . Rose, is it not? Well, now, Rose, in a moment I shall send for the housekeeper and she will show you your room, but first of all I think we should have a little talk about your duties and what will be expected of you.'

At that moment the figure in the window turned slowly and draped itself along the chintz-covered window seat near Lady Bouchier. The sandy moustache drooped languidly around the corners of the mouth; the fleshy lower lip curled sensuously chinwards. Beneath spiky yellow eyebrows, pale blue eyes wandered lasciviously over Rose's figure.

With a dismissive wave of her hand in his direction, Lady Bouchier introduced: 'This is my nephew, Mister Loxley-Gregg – on leave from the 46th Foot, and down for a few days' hunting.'

Rose smiled politely, and inclined her head.

The Lieutenant's eyes continued to devour the shapely contours of her bodice.

CHAPTER ELEVEN

The Ball

It soon became clear to Rose why Lady Bouchier needed a hard-working seamstress so urgently; she had to have a whole new wardrobe of clothes. In addition to the London Season, when she and the Colonel would be doing the usual round of theatre parties and important City balls, another date had been ringed on the calendar in the New Year – the South-West Cornwall Hunt Ball would be taking place at Lanteague. During that weekend Colonel Sir Francis and Lady Arabella Bouchier would, by tradition, be entertaining a large house-party. It would be quite unthinkable for Lady Arabella to be seen during that weekend to be wearing anything remembered from last year.

So, no sooner had Rose been installed in her new surroundings – a light, airy workroom on the first floor at the back of the house, and a small but modestly comfortable bedroom on the second floor, high up under the eaves and overlooking the front courtyard – than she found herself almost literally up to her neck in satins, laces, silks and patterns, and of course a whole workbox full of sewing materials. A very far cry, she thought to herself, from the bombards and blackjacks and pewter tankards of an alehouse.

Every morning, just before eleven o'clock, Lady Bouchier would pay a visit to the sewing room to see how the new seamstress was progressing. On the very first visit, when Rose was new to the task and feeling intensely nervous, her ladyship had been understandingly considerate. Although they discussed fashions and styles which even then were

158

taking Paris by storm, Lady Bouchier had not asked her to attempt anything too elaborate for her first effort. Nothing more intricate than a blue and white striped silk gown with a sack back, elbow length sleeves trimmed with lace, a long bodice, and a full skirt held out at the sides by panniers.

From a very early age Rose had demonstrated a natural aptitude and uncommon skill with needle and thread, and Amia Roskruge had encouraged it. Together they had spent long hours companionably engaged in dressmaking and embroidery. In the winter months they would sit in front of the furze and log kitchen fire; in the summer they would be outside the front door of Thorn Cottage, with the attractive view of Godrevy Beach in front of them. The knowledge and dexterity which Rose had developed in those early days was now to stand her in very good stead. Lady Bouchier was delighted with her work. Very soon she was encouraging her new seamstress to attempt one of the latest and most becoming of current fashions – the polonaise. The gown was to be worn over a petticoat, as before, but the overskirt was to be kirtled up into a bunch at the hips and held in position by tapes tied together inside the skirt.

'I think the petticoat should be of the same creamy-coloured cotton material as the overskirt, do you not agree, Rose,' Lady Bouchier observed, gently fingering the fine-spun fabric.

'Oh, indeed, my lady,' Rose readily agreed, 'especially as it will be worn beneath a very open gown. A pretty petticoat is intended to be seen, is it not. It should never be regarded as an undergarment.'

Lady Bouchier nodded approval. She was warming to the girl's enthusiasm – indeed, she found herself almost looking forward to her daily visits to the sewing room.

'And the embroidery, Rose? A flower motif, do you think?'

'Yes, my lady,' Rose answered thoughtfully. 'I can quite visualize that. In a matching shade of wool – I would do a sample first, of course.'

Lady Bouchier pondered, idly fingering the creamy material. 'A lightish brown wool, I think, Rose. And you could highlight it with an amber colour, perhaps. It would complement the dark brown silk calash protecting my hair out of doors, do you not agree?'

'Oh, yes, my lady. I can see it exactly.'

Lady Bouchier smiled indulgently. She was really getting quite fond of the girl. 'You've made a propitious beginning, Rose. I hope you will be happy here.'

Rose coloured, prettily. 'Oh, I'm sure I will, my lady. I only hope I shall be able to give satisfaction.'

With an encouraging nod of agreement, Lady Bouchier swept elegantly out of the sewing room.

It was the kind of work Rose really enjoyed. She felt entirely at home among all the exquisite materials – silks, satins, cottons and taffetas – that Lady Bouchier had had sent down from London.

As the seamstress, in direct daily contact with her ladyship, the rest of the household staff tended to treat her with veiled hostility. She was entitled to certain rights denied to them – one of which was the doubtful privilege of taking her meals separately with the housekeeper.

But she did not mind; it was a small price to pay for the other freedoms she enjoyed, and the opportunity to express her natural creative ability. Yes, there was no doubt about it, on the whole she was very happy with her situation.

There was just one ripple that sometimes disturbed the otherwise tranquil waters.

Ever since that first occasion when Lieutenant Loxley-Gregg had cast an approving eye over the face and figure of his aunt's new seamstress, he had found reasons for visiting Lanteague with a far greater frequency than ever before. Indeed, Rose had overheard Lady Bouchier remarking the fact to her husband, and while the Colonel had expressed himself flattered by his nephew's attentions, he also confessed to having become heartily sick of the young man's face.

And it was not a very pretty face, either. Chinless, and with a nose like a piece of roughly moulded putty, it seemed devoid of expression as well as character. And the protruding lower lip was perpetually moist, and frequently flecked at the corners with saliva.

Moreover, it was a face which was appearing rather too often round the door of the sewing room. On the flimsy pretext of being in search of his aunt, Lieutenant Loxley-Gregg would inflict his presence upon Rose for long periods of time, to such an extent that on more than one occasion she had to ask him to leave in order that she might get on with her work. It had become embarrassing.

But today, she could leave all that behind; she had completed her initial probationary period – entirely to the satisfaction of her ladyship, she understood – and she had been allowed her first afternoon off. It seemed such an incalculable age since she had seen her beloved parents, and she could hardly wait to tell them all her news.

She hurried along the lane, past the imposing wrought iron gates at the entrance to Lanteague, and then on until she reached the friendly-looking pair of estate workers' cottages. There she turned off left, on to the footpath leading to the prehistoric Standing Stone, and along the spooky, overhung track behind Tremenhir.

But she was in no mood to be scared today; she was going home. She had the whole afternoon ahead of her during which time all the words, the thoughts, the hopes and fears could come tumbling out into the ever-receptive ears of her anxious-to-hear mother and father. She even caught herself gabbling away under her breath as she skipped along past the gaunt, odd-shaped Menhir stone. Very soon the tall spire of the church came into view, and she felt a little thrill of excitement to see once more this homely, familiar landmark. As she hurried across the Square, one of her old 'regulars' staggered out of the inn and, catching sight of her excitedly flushed, pretty face he shouted a lewd but welcoming greeting. Oh yes, she was home again all right, she reflected wryly. With a friendly but dismissive wave she increased her pace, and very soon she was almost running along the short lane to Rosenithon. At the foot of the steep hill leading 'up-over and down-round' to Porthoustock, she turned right, down the lane leading to Thorn Cottage. For the last hundred yards, and despite the roughness of the track, she picked up her skirts and ran. She burst in through the cottage door and there, quietly snoozing beside the gently smouldering fire, were her parents. She was home, at last.

'Oh, my, my!' Amia Roskruge exclaimed, rubbing the sleep from her eyes and struggling to get up from the rough-hewn but sturdy rocking-chair, 'You'm quite a stranger, Rosie. But let's have a good look at ee.' She clasped her daughter's shoulders, holding her at arm's length. 'My, my!' she repeated cosily. 'You'm bonnier than ever. I'nt she, Sam?'

Sampson Roskruge nodded agreement. Standing beside his wife he placed one hand on Rose's shoulder, and with the work-swollen, tar-ingrained forefinger of his fisherman's hand he gently stroked the unblemished softness of Rose's neck. 'Ais,' he purred, 'she'm bonny all right. Bonnier than a flower – allus has been.'

Rose flung her arms around first her mother, then her father; the warm, homely smell of the oven still clung to her mother; the stronger, more permeating smell of tarred fishing nets faintly intermingled with the smell of the milking pail was, symbolically, her father. She loved them both. They meant 'home'.

After the hugs and greetings, the questions. 'Now then, Rosie, how be doin'? What be like up there at the big house? Am you kep' busy, like, all day long?' Both mother and father were eager to hear the smallest titbits of information.

Divesting herself of her warm woollen shawl, Rose drew up a chair between her two parents, and taking their hands in hers she enthusistically set about satisfying their curiosity – about the size and expansiveness of the manor itself, the magnificent draperies in all the main rooms, the ornaments, the pictures by great artists, the seemingly endless range and variety of china and silverware, but above all the spacious, lofty splendour of the main hall.

'And 'tis there,' she declared excitedly, 'in those truly fittin' surroundin's that the Hunt Ball will be held.'

Sampson and Amia Roskruge sat gently nodding approval. They knew that a Hunt Ball was something splendidly important – something to which, even in their wildest dreams, they themselves could never be invited. But they were glad for Rosie.

'All the gentry'll be there,' Rose continued, 'all the beautiful young county ladies and their squires'll be there; all the bigwigs from the towns like Helston and Penzance, all them'll – all they, I should say – all they will be coming. Why, everyone of importance will be there.'

'Oh, my, my!' her mother exclaimed.

Wide-eyed, and thoroughly enjoying the image she was creating, Rose went on, ''Tis going to be a really grand affair, her ladyship says, and I'm already busy on makin' her a very special new gown for the occasion. And the hall's all got to be made ready, all the curtains have got to be took down and shaken, and there'll be a thousand candles in the chandeliers! And then there'll be the minstrels up there in the gallery, come all the way from Falmouth, they say.' Scarcely allowing time to draw breath, she eagerly elaborated; 'And Colonel Bouchier says it'll be a kind of celebration for his nephew – the one that's in the army, that is – because he's just been promoted, or something.'

Sampson Roskruge interrupted with a snort. 'What, him? Promoted? Lieutenant "Nose-in-the-air" Hannibal Loxley-Gregg promoted? Well, well! Th'army must be in poor shape if they have to promote a fellow like ee.'

'Why, do you know him, Papa?'

Sampson chortled. 'Aw, ais. I see'd un a time or two. Ee bin out huntin' a bit, lately. Not much of a rider, though.' Sampson's shoulders began to shake; the memory was obviously one of some hilarity. 'Ais, I mind seein' un put his 'orse at a fence out Crousa way – twern't much more'n a few sticks o' furze, like, but th'old 'orse tipped un out

163

o' the saddle, all right. I were doin' a bit o' rabbitin', I mind, an' I see'd it all. Aw, no, he'm no more'n a shadow o' the old Colonel.'

'Well, to be truthful, I'm not too sure just what it is,' Rose admitted, far too excited at the prospect of the forthcoming ball to note the contempt in her father's voice, 'but whatever it is, the Colonel says there'll be cause for celebration. And as for her ladyship – well, she says it'll be the finest ball in the county for years.'

*   *   *

When at last the evening of the great day arrived, the hall at Lanteague had been transformed. For days beforehand the household servants, as well as some of the estate workers and their wives and daughters, had been swarming like honey bees all over the large, rectangular-shaped ballroom, dusting, cleaning and polishing until the whole room, from floor to ceiling, radiated a hitherto unimaginable magnificence. The massive chandeliers, supreme examples of the glass-cutter's art, had been gently lowered so that each delicate ear lobe, each peardrop, each dangling glass swordblade could be carefully washed in soapy water, then dried and polished until the whole cascading brilliance of cut glass artistry danced and shimmered with ever-changing shafts of coloured light. Exotic pot plants and flowering shrubs, specially brought on in the greenhouses for the great occasion, were banked high in each corner, filling the whole atmosphere with their heady, intoxicating fragrance. The large, oval-shaped carpet covering the stone-flagged floor of the vestibule, where Colonel Sir Francis and Lady Bouchier would receive their guests, had been subjected to an onslaught by housemaids. Armed with dustpans and spent tea leaves they had sprinkled and brushed until the carpet glowed with a richness more befitting a palace than a country manor house.

For over an hour before the first guests would be arriving, Rose had been closeted with her ladyship making small final adjustments to the cream muslin gown on which she had been working almost up till the very last moment. It was short-sleeved, high-waisted and had an elegant train; it would be worn with a muslin stole and a black fichu to complement the black tambour embroidery. Lady Bouchier still favoured heavy brocaded shoes, and she had chosen a pair in a rich cinnabar colour.

'Oh, my lady!' Rose burst out impulsively, standing back to view the finished creation. 'You *do* look lovely!' Then, deferentially, she quickly added, 'If you'll forgive me for saying so.'

Lady Bouchier bestowed a generous smile on her new young seamstress; the girl was so eagerly pleased, so flushed with the success of her first major creation. 'She's a great deal prettier than many of the belles at the ball tonight,' she thought to herself. 'She would turn more than one young blood's head, I'm sure – even in that plain black dress she wears every day.'

But out loud she merely said, 'Thank you, Rose. Of course you may say so. After all, the effect is entirely due to you.'

She had become fond of the girl, even after so short a period of employment. Her intelligence was clearly above that of the usual type of sewing girl. She was so quick to understand and appreciate a new fashion trend, so endearingly anxious to please. Undoubtedly the girl could go far, Lady Bouchier reflected – always provided that she played her cards aright.

'When you've finished tidying up, Rose,' her ladyship was saying, as Rose knelt once more at the hem, adjusting to her satisfaction the final sweep of the train, 'I expect you'd like to watch the dancing – the servants usually watch discreetly from one of the doorways – and I shall be interested in your opinion of some of the dresses.'

Rose swallowed hard. It was a disappointment that she was being classed with 'the servants' – even if only by implication – but she said, 'Very good, my lady. Yes, I

165

shall enjoy that.' She gathered up her workbox, and rose to her feet.

Later that evening she joined a little bunch of household staff huddling inconspicuously in a doorway of the ballroom. She, too, felt she should be as unobtrusive as possible, but if she were to carry out her ladyship's injunction she must at least position herself so as to be able to take a good look at the fashions.

At first she was so fascinated by the breathtaking spectacle of glamour and glitter swirling and twirling on the dance floor in front of her that she was quite unable to concentrate on anything more precise than the broad canvas of this fabulous scene. But after a while, as she stood there gently swaying to the lilting music of the orchestra up in the minstrel's gallery, her eyes began to focus on the individual dancers and the clothes they wore; the magnificently embroidered silks and satins worn by the ladies, some with bodices cut daringly low, others more demure with an elaborately frilled fichu to give the fashionable pouter-pigeon effect. Hair styles, piled high, were becoming even more striking, some sprouting carefully chosen feathers as well as fruit or flowers – there was even one young sparklet with the emblem of a ship in her hair and a dashing young naval lieutenant on her arm.

But, like their feathered counterparts in the natural world, it was the menfolk who provided the dazzling streaks of colour; the scarlet of the hunting 'pinks', the blues, the greens, and again the scarlets of the regimental jackets with their glimmering buttons and their gold or silver trimmings; the scarlet stripes down the outer seams of their dark blue trousers; the jangling spurs, the gleaming boots. Across the English Channel the 'sans-culottes' of Revolutionary France might be ominously sharpening their knives, but the British Army could still find time for dalliance.

As if to highlight the brilliance of the military uniforms and the hunting scarlets, the less startling velvets and broadcloths of the men in civilian life – the notaries, the parsons, and the more prosperous burgesses – stood out in sombre relief. It was among these less guadily attired young gallants that Rose, with a sudden, alarming realization, caught sight of a familiar figure. Involuntarily her hand flew to her mouth. 'Oh, no!' she exclaimed under her breath. 'Surely not!' Not among all these titled, highborn, wealthy people!'

He was dancing with an ethereal-looking goddess dressed in a pale blue silk gown with a broad skirt and fashionable sack back. The colour of the material was reflected in the eyes of the girl as she smiled – elusively, tantalizingly – at her partner.

That partner, whose hand she held, and into whose eyes she dreamily gazed, was unmistakably – and for Rose, heart-sinkingly – Ashley Penberth.

Next to them in the line of dancers, and squired by a rather dilettantish-looking officer of dragoons, another Venus glided lightly over the floor. Darker, more voluptuous, her hair piled high in elaborate style, the likeness proclaimed that she must surely be the elder sister of the fair-haired vision.

As the two couples drew nearer, Rose melted into the shadows. Emphatically, she did not wish Ashley to see her; her plain black dress singled her out, as nothing else could, as being one of the household staff, not one of the guests. All the more she wished to remain unobserved when, as the couple danced by, she saw the look on Ashley's face as he devoured the beauty of his blue-eyed partner. It was, Rose felt despairingly, the look of a man deeply in love.

Her immediate inclination was to run away and hide; up to her meagrely appointed bedroom, to fling herself onto her comfortless bed, there to give way to the bitter tears she was now forced to hold back. During those short – but for her, idyllic – moments she had spent with Ashley Penberth above that little cove beyond Porthoustock she really felt she had captured, if not his heart, then at least his interest. Yet here he was, in front of her very eyes, totally enraptured by someone else – by that landowner's daughter that Will Trenethy had warned her about, presumably; the one who lived with her father and sister in the large mansion overlooking the Helford River, and who had everything a young girl could desire – beauty, wealth and an impeccable social background.

Rose turned away; she could not bear to watch. But she could not run away. Her ladyship had asked her to observe, and observe she would – even if it stunned her heart to do so.

Scarcely had the music of the stately cotillion died away than Rose noticed the orchestra conductor, high up in the minstrel's gallery, tapping his baton on his music stand and announcing that the next dance would be a country dance.

This was the signal for the pink-coated hunters to go mad. With whoops of delight they began wildly cavorting around each other, some blowing strident notes on hunting horns, others pretending to be galloping furiously across open countryside. If the sedate, older burgesses looked on with less than approval, the young army officers lacked nothing of the hunter's high-pitched exuberance. The free-flowing wine was undoubtedly taking effect. Full-grown men were acting like children; the party was beginning to warm up.

But the rousing gaiety served only to increase the numbness in Rose's heart. Out there on the ballroom floor, together with his most beautiful partner and so much an intrinsic part of the colourful scene, was Ashley Penberth, while she, Rose, her foot tapping instinctively in time with the music, was condemned to watch from the shadows.

The country dance had just got into full swing when Rose observed a less than welcome figure, champagne glass in hand, moving unsteadily in her direction.

Hubert Hannibal Loxley-Gregg, nephew and heir-presumptive of Colonel and Lady Bouchier, had just been gazetted Captain, and he had decided there could be no better occasion to celebrate his promotion than the Hunt Ball at Lanteague.

By contrast with some of the other gentlemen at the ball, and certainly most of the ladies, Captain Loxley-Gregg was not beautiful; far from it. Moreover, during the whole of his adolescent years he had never had any success with members of the fair sex. But 'sex' was a word that occupied his thoughts exceedingly. It burned him. So much so that in his desire to become better acquainted with the mysteries of carnal enjoyment he was wont, in the officer's mess sometimes, to become somewhat indiscreet. Indeed, he had been subjected to an unwelcome amount of provocative ridicule by fellow junior officers on account of his lack of consummated prowess in that particular sphere.

He had come to the Hunt Ball with one thought uppermost in his mind; what better way to celebrate his long-awaited promotion – and to silence the recurring mess-room taunts – than by crossing the Rubicon of sexual enlightenment?

And as he steered his way uncertainly across the ballroom floor his sights were firmly, if blurredly, fixed on a pretty young seamstress in a plain black dress. He had spotted her standing unobtrusively among the servants.

Shortly after his arrival on the previous day, Rose had almost bumped into him while returning from a fitting in her ladyship's boudoir. He was emerging from one of the guest bedrooms. Rose deferentially stood aside to let him pass but he pinned her to the wall, albeit in a supposedly playful manner, by putting one arm on each side of her head.

'Aha, now! Caught you at last, Rosie,' he slobbered, attempting a winning smile, 'and a pretty little cage-bird you make, I'm bound to admit.'

Keeping her eyes demurely downwards, Rose spoke quietly. 'If you'll excuse me, sir, I have work to do for her ladyship.' She made as if to move, but he kept her pinned.

'Little birds can't be let out of the cage without paying the forfeit, y'know.'

'If you'll excuse me, sir . . .'

'And you know what the forfeit is, don't you, Rosie?'

Rose knew all too well. She flashed him a warning stare. 'Sir, if you'll excuse me . . .'

With a characteristically sheepish grin, he let one hand drop. 'All right, Rosie. I'll let you go now. But you're coming to the ball tomorrow evening, aren't you?'

Having escaped from his embarrassing attentions, and with a safe distance between them, Rose felt she could afford to be polite.

'Oh, no, sir. It would be quite improper for me to attend the ball. It's not my place . . .'

She had dropped him the semblance of a curtsey, and then hurriedly disappeared round a corner of the corridor.

Now with the ball at its height, and having liberally fortified himself with his uncle's champagne, he was seeking her out.

'Aha, there you are, Rosie! I've been wonderin' where the devil you'd got to.' He lurched towards her, grasping her hand and pulling her towards the ballroom. 'Come along, now. Can't have you standin' there all evenin' like a blighted wallflower. Wouldn't do at all. Positively wouldn't do . . .'

'Oh, no. No, sir!' Rose protested. 'No, I couldn't. It wouldn't be right. I've already told you, it's not my place.'

'Whadjer mean, "not my place"! You're place is wherever I say it is.' He tightened his grip on her arm. 'You're just as good as any of those old fo . . . hic . . . fogeys out there, Rosie. Egad! but I do swear you're a dashed sight prettier than any . . . hic . . . any of 'em.'

Rose was still protesting as he dragged her to the edge of the highly-polished ballroom floor. But then she caught sight once more of Ashley Penberth and his flaxen-haired goddess gently swaying to the intoxicating strains of the music. It was too much. Throwing caution to the winds she melted into the arms of the surprised but delighted Captain Loxley-Gregg. She would show them! Especially Ashley Penberth! She would show him and his captivating partner that she could dance as well as any of them. She would show them all . . . all those horror-struck, highborn ladies with their disapproving glances down their long straight noses, so aghast at the sight of a mere seamstress in a simple black dress sharing the colourful ballroom with them. Unwisely perhaps, Rose threw herself into all the excitement and hilarity of the country dances – first, 'My Lady Bouchier's

170

Delight' in honour of the hostess, then 'Parson's Farewell' which elicited much chaffing of the reverend members of the cloth, and finally, to the delight of the younger dancers, the fashionable and somewhat risqué 'À la Mode de France.' Twirling, pirouetting and swaying, her head held proudly high, Rose felt as though she had been dancing, dancing, dancing all her life.

At every opportunity Captain Loxley-Gregg's hand found her waist and drew her close.

'Thought you said you didn't know how to dance, Rosie,' he slavered, an inane grin splitting his flushed, perspiring face from ear to ear. 'Egad! but I do dec . . . declare you quite put all those stuffed dum . . . dum . . . hic dummies to sha . . . ame.'

His face was unpleasantly close; alcoholic fumes almost overwhelmed her. But she did not care. She did not care about anything! The lively tempo of the music, 'andante' moving into 'allegretto', was infusing the blood in her veins. Even the orchestra conductor, sensing the unusual, was enjoying her blatant defiance of decorum. What did it matter to him; music was for everyone, for rich and poor alike, for maidservant as well as master, it recognized no social barriers. Spurred on by the welcome sight of her infectious gaiety he urged his players to an even greater crescendo of melody – 'allegro vivace' – and beamed encouragement to the pretty young dancer in the plain black dress.

Some of the older red-coated hunters were grinning surreptitious encouragement; many of the younger ones were openly applauding her boldness in flaunting established conventions. Subversive breezes – fanned by the quill pen of Jean Jacques Rousseau – had already wafted across the English Channel from France. 'Liberté, Egalité, Fraternité' – that was the mood of the moment among the young.

Suddenly, Rose realized that she had become the very centre of attraction. All eyes were on her. For a few very brief moments it was intoxicating. She, Rose Roskruge, humble seamstress of no known pedigree, was holding the stage. Everyone was looking at her – even, yes, even Ashley Penberth!

171

Then like a douche of ice-cold water, she felt the unwavering stare of Lady Bouchier. It was the end of her dream. If she wanted to remain in her ladyship's service, she must leave the ballroom forthwith.

Disengaging herself from the clasping arms of Captain Hubert Hannibal Loxley-Gregg she threaded her way through the gyrating dancers, back to the seclusion from which she had emerged. On the way she passed right beside the man she most wanted to impress. But he did not look at her; he had eyes only for the girl in his arms.

Rose remained within the shadows of the passage for a few minutes while the heady excitement of a few seconds ago drained out of her. She felt utterly deflated. Even the orchestra seemed to have lost its sparkle. The conductor no longer threw his arms about with frenzied abandon. Sadly he searched in vain for the proud figure, so light on her toes, so conspicuous among all the colours in her plain black dress.

The dancers soon resumed their former, staid expressions. Just a few still chattered animatedly about the extraordinary departure from acceptable etiquette. No-one would envy that unfortunate seamstress when confronted by her mistress in the morning. But it had been no more than a momentary diversion. As the evening progressed, no one would give it a second thought. No one, that is, except the newly promoted infantry Captain. He was delighted to have created something of a stir, to have shared the limelight – and to have advanced his cause, as he thought, with his aunt's delectable handmaiden. But, damme! Why the devil had she gone and left him like that? Dashed uncivil, begad! Well, I mean to say, damme!

Rose watched the dancing for a few more unhappy moments – until she saw the Captain determinedly coming in search of her – then she disappeared down the long passage, and went up to bed. She felt completely exhausted by the evening's excitement and all the preliminary preparations, and within a few minutes of donning her warm flannel nightgown she had fallen fast asleep.

She had been in that blissful state for what seemed like

172

only a short while when she was disturbed by the creak of a floorboard. A further creak . . . then another . . . getting nearer. Instantly she was wide awake, one hand to her throat. Heavy breathing . . . coming closer. She opened her mouth and tried to scream, but no sound emerged. She tried again. This time she made a noise . . . but not a proper scream . . . more like a violin bow being drawn across a slackened string. She tried to raise herself on one elbow . . . but she felt frozen to the spot, petrified. A hand closed over her mouth . . . a large hand with a flabby palm. Stertorous breathing brushed her cheek. The smell of brandy assaulted her nostrils. At last she found her strength; she tried to wrench herself free but the hand on her mouth pinned her down. As she struggled she heard the familiar voice.

'It's all right, Rosie. I won't hurt you. I've just come to say goo'night – a proper goo'night.'

She tried to dig her teeth into the flesh of his flabby hand. But he had her jaw in a vice-like grip. His fingernails sank deep into her cheek. It was hurting.

'Now, now, Rosie, don't be naughty. And it was very . . . very . . . naughty of you to run away like that this . . . hic . . . this evening. Very naughty. But if you're a good girl now, and do as I say . . . then you won't get hurt.'

In the pale moonlight filtering through the half-drawn curtains of the dormer window she could see that he wore only a dressing gown. In forcing her head down on to the pillow he allowed the gown to fall open. It merely confirmed that he had nothing on underneath. Under any circumstances – and notwithstanding her earlier experience with Myron Pinnerton – the revelation of total male nakedness would have come as an extremely unpleasant shock. To be confronted now in a bedroom at night by the risen expectation of unassuaged male lust was horrific.

Frantically she struggled; in doing so she kicked the bedclothes off her prostrate body. It was exactly what he wanted. Her nightgown had risen up around her waist revealing her thighs, sensuous and shapely, the more to inflame, still higher, his long-frustrated desire. He threw

173

himself on top of her, grasping and squeezing painfully the soft, rounded flesh of her hips, forcing her against his naked loins. Desperately she tried to wriggle free; it merely spurred his determination, and she found herself tightly pinned beneath the whole weight of his body. He was within reach of that supreme conquest. Nothing would deprive him now.

Momentarily he relaxed the near-suffocating grip on her mouth; once more she tried to scream. But before she could make any semblance of prolonged sound, his wet, slobbering lips had found hers in a revoltingly probing kiss.

At the outset she had been frightened – then terrified – by the sudden, stealthy awakening and the subsequent realization of the intruder's intent. But now, fear had been overtaken by a deep-rooted, animal determination to survive. She suddenly became like a wildcat, biting and scratching with every ounce of her strength, and digging her fingernails deep into his flesh. All the while she was trying to extricate herself from beneath his body. But he was too heavy; she could make no impression. In the extremity of her distress she remembered an old crone saying to her once, in the confidentiality of the Three Tuns Inn, 'If you ever find yerzel in a fix, dearie, allus remember to keep your legs tightly crossed.' She was trying to do that now. But she was not succeeding. He was too powerful. Already he was forcing one knee between her thighs, prising them apart like a blunt axe splitting a log, and although she was now fighting like a demented animal, his enraged brute strength was becoming too much for her.

Then she remembered something else the crone had said.

Choosing her moment, she suddenly relaxed the tension in her legs, and summoning every ounce of remaining strength she brought her right knee up into his groin with a vicious impact, at the same time using her right hand to force his shoulders off her body. With an agonized gasp of surprise and pain, he rolled to one side. It was long enough. In a flash, Rose was off the bed and making for the door. But he had grabbed at her nightdress. Gripping it with the fury of a deprived tiger, he held on. He would *not* be denied. If it was the last thing on earth he did, he would . . .

But his grip was too tight; Rose's determination too strong. A sudden rending sound broke the silence of the early morning. Even the seams sewn by an experienced seamstress could not withstand the strain. The nightdress was in shreds. Rose was free – but naked.

Foaming at the mouth with frustration, the infuriated Captain made a last, despairing lunge. But she was too quick for him. Snatching her old woollen dressing gown from the hook on the door, she was out into the corridor, running for her life along the passage.

Already the first streaks of dawn were lighting the eastern sky.

CHAPTER TWELVE

Summary Justice

The glimmer of light from the cowhouse at Trevallack was like a beacon to a homecoming sailor. It meant that the Tripconeys were up – some of them, at least – doing the early milking.

Shoeless, and clad only in her well-worn, almost thread-bare dressing gown, Rose hurried along the lane towards that light. The rough, flinty surface lacerated her feet; the north-easterly blowing in from the sea shrivelled her flesh and pinched her cheeks. But she pressed on, head down, determined. That light meant not only shelter, it would mean succour and comfort and sympathy.

As she turned off the lane and onto the footpath leading past the Standing Stone, now so gaunt and eerie in the half-light, she could not help remembering the excitement of that first afternoon off when she had started out along the same route for Rosenithon and home. The Hunt Ball and all the hustle and bustle surrounding it was then still in the future. She remembered how she had regaled her loving and attentive parents with the details of the various preparations taking place at the manor, and how much she was looking forward to her very first experience of such a glittering occasion.

What could she tell them now? How could she explain, as she returned to Thorn Cottage at this early hour, naked – or at best in borrowed clothes – that all her high-flown hopes of improving herself were now as blossoms in the dust. As she hurried towards the refuge of Trevallack and the Tripconeys she thought of the Old Testament story of how David's son, Amnon, first tricked and then forced his sister,

Tamar. More than once, sitting in her usual place in the choir, Rose had listened to the vicar reading the story of the Old Testament. She remembered now how Tamar, arising from her bed of rape, had cried aloud, 'And I, whither shall I cause my shame to go?'

The words rang round and round in her head, bridging the distance of many thousand years as though it were only yesterday. 'And I, whither shall I cause my shame to go?'

But Tamar had been raped – yes, raped. And even if Rose had escaped the ultimate physical humiliation, she knew that it had been only – and almost literally – by the skin of her teeth. She felt soiled; she felt unclean; and although she knew that no shame could be attached to her, deep down inside she understood the utter despair of Tamar's cry.

'And I, whither shall I cause my shame to go?'

When she reached the entrance to Trevallack farm she paused for a moment, leaning against the granite gatepost. Yes, there was no doubt about it, the Tripconeys were up; the familiar sounds of an occasional rattle of halter chains, and the intermittent hiss of the milk into the bucket, confirmed that the early-morning ritual had begun.

Up till that moment, flight had been the single thought uppermost in her mind; to get away as quickly as possible from Lanteague and from that slobbering ogre of a Captain. But now that she had reached the haven of the friendly Tripconeys, her resolve and her resistance suddenly gave way and she burst into tears. Uncontrollable sobbing; the natural reaction to an ordeal overcome.

It was the sound of her sobbing that brought Mrs Tripconey to her bedroom window. Even in the half-light she could see the girl at the gate, and the heartrending sounds left Mrs Tripconey in no doubt about the child's distress. She hurried into her clothes and went downstairs.

Snatching up one of the candle lanterns already alight in the kitchen, she bustled out of the back door, turned left in the yard, and hastened towards the farm entrance.

'Now, now, now then,' she soothed, putting a sympathetic

arm around the shoulders of the figure still wracked with sobs. 'What be the matter, then, child?'

She turned the girl to face her, holding up the flickering lamp as she did so.

'Oh, my dear Lordy!' she exclaimed. 'I do declare 'tis Rosie. Oh, my poor child,' she went on, clasping Rose to her ample bosom, 'whatever ails thee?'

She enveloped Rose in her strong, comforting arms and propelled her towards the farmhouse. Within the privacy of Trevallack kitchen, and after a restorative cup of tea, Rose tearfully recounted to a most sympathetic listener the lurid details of her frightening experience. Mrs Tripconey's face, normally smiling and good-natured, gradually assumed a terrifying severity as the story unfolded. At the end, she gave Rose a great big hug of compassionate sympathy, poured her another cup of tea, and told her to stay by the warming log fire while she went upstairs to find her a few clothes. She returned in a few minutes and handed a bundle to Rose.

'They'll not fit ee too special, my luv, but at least they'm warm. Slip 'em on, then us'll take ee back to Thorn.'

She went out of the kitchen, carefully closing the door to shut out the wind, crossed the yard to the shippen, and peremptorily summoned her husband.

'Trip,' she commanded, in a voice that warned her husband no back answers would be tolerated, 'I want ee to put Betsy in the cart right away. We'm goin' down to the Roskruges.'

Bewildered, but obedient, Wilmot Tripconey did as he was bid, leaving his two sons to finish off the milking. Only very seldom did his good wife address him in that manner, and over the years he had learnt that when she did, the wisest thing was to obey. It was while putting Betsy into the shafts that Mrs Tripconey enlightened him.

''Tis young Rosie Roskruge,' she murmured in an undertone. 'She's been interfered with up at the big house.'

Then she told him.

Wilmot Tripconey's mouth formed into a hard, inflexible line. For several moments he said nothing. But his breathing

178

became heavy. Making the final adjustment to Betsy's harness with an unusually strong-armed jerk, he muttered fiercely. 'The bloody young bastard! I allus knew that whelp was a wrong un! By God, but we'll make un pay for this.'

His wife laid a restraining hand on his arm. 'But Wil,' she cautioned, 'we must be careful about tellin' Sampson. He'm sure to be after killin' that young man – and us don't want a murder to deal with as well.'

Her husband grunted. As usual, his wife was right. However careful they were in the telling, Sampson would see red. He loved Rosie as though he had sired her – more, perhaps. No man had a greater love for his daughter than had Sampson for Rosie. So, he would need to be restrained if they were to save him from the gallows.

Wilmot Tripconey led the mare and the cart up to the back-door porch where his wife and Rose were waiting. Without bothering to divest himself of his milking smock he climbed up into the driving seat, holding the reins while his wife and Rose clambered up behind. Then he touched Betsy lightly on the rump with his whip, and they set off in the direction of St Keverne.

At the junction with the lane leading out to Tregowrie they turned right, past the site of the old priory at Laddenveen, and then up the hill into the square. There was more than a hint of frost in the early morning air and Rose was glad to huddle close to Mrs Tripconey. The familiar sight of the Three Tuns Inn nestling beneath the towering church spire was balm to her jangled nerves. She was among friends again; she was going home.

The trotting pony's hoofbeats echoed loudly as they rattled out of the square and along the road to Rosenithon, and Rose observed the curtains of more than one upstairs window being discreetly drawn aside. Before the day was out, she guessed, everyone in the village would know of her early-morning homecoming. And the reason? Well, individual imaginations would provide a variety of explanations – and each retailing would no doubt become more and more lurid.

But Rose was past caring. Within minutes she would be in the arms of the mother who had loved her and nurtured her for as long as she could remember; she would be embraced and supported by the man who had snatched her from the sea. At the moment, nothing else mattered.

Sampson and Amia Roskruge were just stirring from their bed when they heard the pony and cart cross the stream and clatter up over the flinty track in front of Thorn Cottage. Peering out of the small, square-paned bedroom window, Sampson exclaimed:

'Yere, Ame, 'tis Wilmot an' Eleanor from Trevallack! And, bless my soul if they haven't got our Rosie wi' em. Yere,' he repeated, more anxiously, 'there be somethin' wrong, Ame. We'd best be downstairs right away.'

Without waiting to throw anything over their nightclothes they descended the narrow wooden stairs, and were just in time to open the front door as Mr and Mrs Tripconey came up the short garden path, each with a protective arm around Rose.

'Oh, my darlin', darlin'!' Amia Roskruge burst out, 'Whatever's befallen thee, my loved one, my precious?' She gathered her daughter into her massive arms, clasping her tightly to her chest as though the very force of her embrace might squeeze out the distress all too apparent in Rose's face. The strong, homely smell of her warm breath evoked such a surge of emotional childhood memories that Rose found it impossible to be brave any longer. She gave way to a fresh outburst of tears.

Quietly but firmly Amia Roskruge led her daughter up the stairs to her bedroom. And when Sampson made as if to follow, he received an equally firm signal from his wife which made him hesitate. 'This' his wife had clearly implied, 'is woman's business.' Sampson knew better than to interfere.

It was Mrs Tripconey who told him. After a brief discussion she went upstairs to join mother and daughter, and to see if there was anything she could do to help. This left Sampson and Wilmot Tripconey alone downstairs.

Half an hour later, Wilmot and Eleanor Tripconey were

on their way back to Trevallack. They had fulfilled their role as friends in need; for the moment there was nothing more they could do. Besides, the milking had to be finished and the milk delivered; the calves had to be fed, the sheep to be shepherded.

But three hours later, Wilmot Tripconey was waiting in Trevallack's kitchen, dressed in his market suit.

Presently, he was joined by Sampson Roskruge, also dressed in his best. When Amia Roskruge had asked her husband why he was so attired and where he was going, Sampson had returned the meaningful look as he replied, ''Tis man's business we'm about.'

'Oh, mama,' Rose enquired nervously, 'where's he going?'

'Never you mind, Rosie. Your father will see to it. Leave it to him,' was all Rose got in reply.

Now, the two men set off in Wilmot Tripconey's dog-cart. It was good of Wil to offer to accompany him, Sampson reflected, and Wil's shining market cart was much more impressive than anything Sampson could produce. And it was important to look impressive, because they were on their way to see the Colonel.

While Amia Roskruge and her friend Eleanor Tripconey had been upstairs comforting Rose at Thorn Cottage, their husbands had been making a plan.

Sampson was all for physical retribution; to waylay the newly promoted bastard of a Captain and tan the hide off him! But Wil had counselled caution; wiser not to take the law into their own hands – at least, not yet. Better by far to approach the Colonel who, as the local magistrate, must surely see that justice was done.

'Will you be spokesman, then, Wil?' Sampson had asked.
''Twould be better that way, you bein' a parish representative, like. Besides,' he added feelingly, 'I might not be able to keep my temper.'

They pulled up outside the main gates, and Sampson jumped down to swing one of them wide open. No slinking in by the servant's entrance for him; they would enter in style or not at all. He owed it that way to Rosie.

181

A supercilious footman opened the massive front door and disdainfully enquired their business. In a firm voice Wilmot Tripconey announced that they wished to have speech with the Colonel. The usual question followed: 'Have you an appointment?'

'We wish to see the Colonel, him bein' our local magistrate,' Wil replied firmly again, colouring in the face and not really feeling at all sure of himself. But he added, ''Tis a matter o' considerable urgency.'

Colonel Bouchier received them in his study, standing in front of a blazing fire and beneath the stuffed, heavily antlered head of a red deer.

'Good morning, gentlemen,' he greeted, with punctilious courtesy. 'You wish to see me, I believe.'

'Yes, sir. That's right,' Wil assured.

'Let me see,' the Colonel went on, screwing up his eyes. 'Tripconey, is it not?'

Wil nodded. 'And this be Sampson Roskruge of Thorn Cottage, Colonel.'

'Ah, yes. Overlooking Godrevy Beach, eh?' With finger and thumb he meticulously parted and smoothed his pepper-and-salt moustache. 'Well, now. What can I do for you?'

He did not invite them to be seated – left them standing just inside the door from the hall.

Wilmot Tripconey fingered his hat uneasily. ''Tis a matter of considerable seriousness we be here to see ee about, Colonel.'

'I didn't imagine it would be something trivial,' the Colonel retorted, bristling. 'Please continue.'

''Tis a matter concernin' Miss Rose Roskruge, Colonel. That is Mester Roskruge here's daughter, like.'

Sampson nodded vigorously. 'My daughter, Colonel.'

Colonel Bouchier searched the ceiling, gently swaying backwards and forwards on his riding-booted heels. Clearly, he was trying to remember who Rose Roskruge was. One of the servants, he supposed.

Anticipating his difficulty, Sampson enlightened, 'Her's bin seamstress to her ladyship, sir.'

'Oh, ah! Yes, of course.' He remembered her now. Quite a pretty little thing. Perky too, he wouldn't wonder. 'In that case, a matter best dealt with by Lady Bouchier, no doubt,' he suggested, relieved at the prospect of being able to delegate a low-level domestic matter to his wife.

'No, sir,' Wilmot replied firmly. 'Beggin' your pardon, but 'tis certainly not a matter for her ladyship. Leastwise, not at this pertikler moment.'

Colonel Bouchier regarded the two men narrowly. 'Very well, then,' he commanded. 'Pray continue.'

'Well, sir, 'tis this way,' Wil went on, nervously shifting from one foot to the other, 'It seems that Miss Rosie, Sampson Roskruge here's daughter – well, sir, it seems like she's been . . . er . . . she's been . . .'

'Come along, man. Out with it,' the Colonel barked.

Sampson could tolerate the suspense no longer. 'Her's bin hinterfered with, Colonel. That's what's about it. Our lovely little Rosie's been hinterfered wi'.'

'For heaven's sake, man! What the devil are you talking about?' The Colonel looked angrily from one to the other.

Wilmot Tripconey took a deep breath. In his gravest manner, he announced, 'I be sorry to have to tell ee, sir – an' I be tellin' ee as a magistrate – that it's a case of attempted rape.'

'Rape!' exploded the Colonel. 'Good God! Are you telling me that this . . . this rape . . . or attempted rape took place here, under my roof?'

'Yes, sir.'

The Colonel let out a gasp of exasperation. 'Ohhh! One of the footmen, I suppose.'

Both Wil and Sampson slowly, accusingly, shook their heads.

'Well, who was it, then? One of the estate staff?'

Again, the two simple countrymen shook their heads.

'Now look here, my man,' the Colonel warned with asperity, 'you've made a very serious accusation against someone. I demand to be told who it is.'

Trying to control his mounting annoyance at being

183

bothered with such a tedious domestic problem, Colonel Bouchier began pacing the floor. He was trying to recollect, also, the judicial penalties for rape. Since time immemorial it had been regarded as a heinous crime; in the Conqueror's time it had been punishable by mutilation and the putting out of the rapist's eyes, and although in later years it had been mitigated somewhat, conviction could still mean transportation or penal servitude for life.

The Colonel's characteristic habit of pacing the floor was abruptly terminated when Wil, clearing his throat nervously before speaking, said, 'I'm sorry to have to inform you, Colonel, but it was your own nevvy.'

'My nephew!' the Colonel stared, incredulously. 'My nephew, Captain Loxley . . .' but he never finished the sentence. Instead, with his chin buried deep in his chest, he resumed pacing in front of the fire.

Abruptly, he came to a halt, and turning to the two accusers he fixed them alternately with a cold, penetrating stare. 'You do realize, do you, what a serious accusation you are making?'

'Yes, sir,' Wilmot replied with firmness, 'that be why both of us is come.'

Again the Colonel paced the floor, hands behind back, deep in thought. 'When did this happen?' he asked eventually.

'Last night, sir.'

'Last night? The evening of the ball?'

Both men nodded. The Colonel turned, staring out of the window. In the silence that followed, the ornate clock on the mantelpiece monotonously, ominously ticked away the minutes. Still gazing out of the window the Colonel eventually asked, quietly, 'What proof have you got that it was my nephew?'

This was Sampson's cue. He had been rehearsing it in his mind on the drive out to Lanteague. With an encouraging nod from Wilmot he launched into what he felt was damning evidence.

'Rosie's a courageous maid, Colonel,' he said, thrustingly. 'Her's full o' courage, like. Her'd have put up a brave old

184

fight, I tell ee, and you'm best have a good look at that nevvy of yours and see if he hasn't a fair number of marks on 'is face, like.'

It was a telling shaft, and the Colonel recognized its worth. If his nephew was the culprit, and there had been a fight . . . With military precision he made up his mind. He would send for the young man. But first of all he would inspect the battleground – always a sound strategic principle – he would see for himself. With a curt, 'Remain here, please, until I return,' he strode from the room.

He found his wife finishing a late breakfast in the morning room. A place had been laid at table for Captain Loxley-Gregg, but it had not so far been used. Lady Bouchier was in earnest conversation with Mrs Arbuthnot, the house-keeper, but she looked up when her husband entered.

'Oh, Colonel,' she greeted concernedly, addressing him formally as was usual in front of the servants, 'Mrs Arbuthnot has just been telling me some rather distressing news about my seamstress, Rose. She's flown, it seems. Apparently, she left in something of a hurry.'

The Colonel, seldom guilty of verbosity, merely beckoned to his wife. 'Come with me, please.'

He waited, stiffly at attention, moustache bristling, while his wife put down her table napkin and rose from the table. Then he held the door for her. With measured, determined strides he marched across the great hall where the household servants and some of the gardeners were still busy clearing up the remnants of the previous night's revels, and then he mounted the broad staircase with its heavily carved balusters. Lady Bouchier, following, knew better than to ask any questions while still within earshot of the servants, but as they mounted the back stairs leading up to the domestics' bedrooms, she felt free to ask, 'What is it, Francis? Why are you taking me all the way up here?'

'To have a look at your seamstress' bedroom. To see if there is any evidence.'

'Evidence? Evidence of what, for heaven's sake?'

The Colonel paused on the top step of the narrow staircase,

turned and fixed his wife with the most quelling magisterial eye, and then uttered the one word, 'Rape.'

He led his wife into Rose's bedroom and marched over to the bed. The bedclothes were exactly as Rose had left them – rumpled and in total disarray but, the Colonel noticed with judicial perception, not stained.

For her part, Lady Bouchier observed that Rose's day clothes were still neatly folded on the plain, upright chair, and that there was no dressing gown hanging on the back of the door.

'Well, my dear,' the Colonel enquired, 'what is your opinion?'

Lady Bouchier, a look of increasing horror on her aristocratic face, was turning over the bedclothes. From beneath the crumpled pillow she pulled the torn nightdress, and examined it. Colonel Bouchier joined her, and they both looked at it – and at each other – in consternation.

The Colonel took the garment from his wife, folded it, and stuffed it in the capacious pocket of his riding coat.

'Thank you, my dear,' he murmured. 'Vital evidence. I'm glad to have you with me. You may be needed as a witness.'

'Oh, my God, Francis,' Lady Bouchier expostulated, 'don't say there'll be a court case. The whole county will hear about it – and under our roof, too. Oh! it's too horrible!'

'The law must be upheld, my dear,' her husband rebuked, 'especially by the magistracy.'

'But, Francis . . .'

Colonel Bouchier took his wife's arm and began firmly propelling her towards the servants' staircase once more.

'I appreciate your feelings, my dear, but I can only repeat, the law must be upheld. However,' he went on, his florid brow puckering with thought, 'I think perhaps there might be another way. Hmm. Leave it to me, my dear. After all, I'm not entirely without experience in such matters.'

Resuming once more his former stance in front of the

study fire, booted legs a-straddle, hands clasped behind back, he prepared to address the two patient plaintiffs.

'Gentlemen,' he began, conferring upon them again the status to which they were quite unaccustomed, 'I have made my inspection, and I have come to a decision. There are two courses open to us in order to resolve this dastardly affair. Either you can make a formal complaint, laying an information before me now, and then the law will inevitably take its appropriate course.'

He very deliberately parted and smoothed his moustache while fixing the two men with a penetrating stare.

'I must warn you, however,' he continued gravely, 'that such a course would undoubtedly mean a full hearing in a court of law, and with all the attendant publicity which that entails. Do I make myself clear, gentlemen?'

The two men nodded dumbly. The awesome prospect of a courthouse began looming alarmingly.

'I should also add,' the colonel went on, 'that such court action would inevitably require the attendance, as principal witness, of Miss Roskruge herself. It might not be a very pleasant experience.'

Sampson shuddered. The very thought of his Rosie being subjected to cross-examination in the witness box by one of those clever lawyers – and Captain Loxley-Gregg would certainly be able to afford one of the most skilfully unscrupulous ones who would twist the truth and tie her up in knots – the very idea of his Rosie being subjected to an ordeal like that was abhorrent. He would do almost anything to prevent that.

'The other alternative,' the Colonel was saying, 'and one which may possibly appeal to you rather more than having to make an appearance in court, is for you to leave it to me to conduct a private enquiry and to administer such summary punishment as I think fit.'

The Colonel could not fail to observe the gleam of hope dawning in the agonized Sampson's eyes.

'I can assure you, gentlemen,' Colonel Bouchier continued, 'that if I find the alleged culprit to be guilty, I shall

187

have no hesitation in making the punishment fit the crime. You may rest assured on that point.'

It seemed to both Sampson and Wilmot Tripconey that as Colonel Sir Francis Bouchier gave them this assurance a gleam of a different kind came into his steely-grey eyes. It was a gleam of relish at the prospect of physically avenging a loathsome deed.

'So, gentlemen,' the Colonel concluded, 'I leave it to you. The choice shall be yours.'

The two countrymen looked from one to the other, nervously hat-twiddling. This was a situation neither had foreseen; the need to make a decision – and in front of the Colonel, too. Both men wished they had their womenfolk handy to advise them.

In the end, it was Sampson who spoke out firmly for his daughter. ''Twould be best to leave un in your hands, Colonel. You'm more 'customed than we to dealin' wi' matters o' this sort. We'm content to leave ee to do what's best.'

For a fleeting moment the sternness which normally characterized the Colonel's whole demeanour relaxed as he gazed at the plain, trusting face of Sampson Roskruge. He remembered the story; how the man had dashed into the sea to rescue the drowning child; how he and his wife had brought the child up as their own and given it life when otherwise there would certainly have been death. And now, here he was, hat in hand, standing before him and demanding nothing more than that his child should be avenged. A thunderous look of determination crept over the Colonel's face. 'And by God!' he vowed silently to himself, 'she *shall* be avenged!'

'Very well, Roskruge,' he said out loud, his face resuming normal inscrutability, 'it shall be as you wish. I shall conduct the interview, establish the facts, and administer the punishment.' He gazed thoughtfully out of the window, parting and smoothing his moustache again, and rocking back and forth on his heels. He suddenly appeared to arrive at a decision, and turning to the patiently waiting supplicants, he barked, 'And furthermore, I shall make it possible for you, gentlemen, if not actually to see the proceedings, at least to hear them, in order that you may be satisfied that justice has been done. Kindly follow me.'

He led the way from the study into the adjoining library where he indicated two leather-bound armchairs, saying, 'Make yourselves comfortable, gentlemen. This may take a little time.'

He returned to the study, leaving the door ajar. Then he moved across to the bell-pull and tugged at it impatiently.

'Inform Captain Loxley-Gregg that I wish to see him here, in the study,' he instructed the answering under-footman.

'Very good, sir,' the servant bowed, 'but I think the Captain is not yet up, sir.'

'Well, get him up, man!' Colonel Bouchier retorted, testily. 'Tell him I wish to see him at once. *At once*, d'you understand?'

The footman departed in a hurry.

Colonel Bouchier was impatiently pacing to and fro in front of the study fire when the door from the hall opened to admit his nephew. Captain Hubert Hannibal Loxley-Gregg was attired only in nightshirt and dressing gown. He held a towel up to the left side of his face.

'Sorry to be so late getting up, Uncle,' he began defensively, 'but it was really quite a party last night. The ball, I mean,' he added rather too hastily, before blundering on. 'Never known a livelier one, Egad! Quite the most outstanding occas . . .'

But the Colonel cut him short. 'Why do you keep holding that towel up to your face like that?'

'Oh, this!' The Captain tried to sound unconcerned. 'Spot of bother with the razor, don'cher know. Unsteady hand, and all that. Must have been that absolutely superb champagne you gave us. Terribly senior of you, sir. What!'

The Colonel eyed his nephew severely. His wife's sister's whelp. Never cared for the fella. Couldn't stand the sound of his drawly voice.

'Take that towel away from your face, please.' He spoke

politely, but he was coiled like a cobra, ready to strike.

'Oh, no, I say, Uncle,' protested the Captain, 'really a too awful sight for words, don'cher know.' He sank down wearily into a chair.

'*Stand up, man!*' the Colonel thundered. 'Stand up when you address a senior officer,' he repeated in a slightly more temperate voice, 'and take . . . that . . . towel . . . from . . . your . . . face.'

Captain Hubert Hannibal Loxley-Gregg struggled to his feet, still protesting. 'I say, Uncle, dashed uncivil, I must say.' But he still clutched the towel to his face.

'*TAKE THAT TOWEL AWAY!*' the Colonel bellowed, his own face colouring an alarming shade of crimson-magenta. But his nephew still refused to obey. It was too much for the Colonel. He strode across the room, caught hold of the towel and snatched it from his nephew's hand.

A deathly silence followed as the Colonel stared at the livid scars down the side of his nephew's face. Unquestionably they were the fighting scratches of a desperate woman's fingernails. The Colonel's expression assumed the texture of granite. Very slowly, and very deliberately, he walked over to the wall behind his desk and took down a horsewhip. Turning to the newly promoted Captain, he said with icy deliberation, 'Last night a young woman in my wife's service narrowly escaped being raped.' He paused just long enough for his words to achieve full effect. Then he went on, 'I intend to discover the culprit and to exact punishment. I shall do this myself in order to avoid, as far as possible, the unsavoury publicity which otherwise would inevitably arise. However, the punishment will be no less severe, for all that. Do I make myself *absolutely* clear?'

'Oh, ah, positively so, Uncle Francis. But why are you telling *me* all this?'

'Do you deny any knowledge of this heinous crime?'

'Ooh, ah, absolutely so. As I've already recounted, the old razor must have slipped rather badly, what! Dashed unfortunate, don'cher know, Uncle – but positively the razor.' He gingerly felt the side of his cheek.

'Are you prepared to prove your innocence?'

'Oh, goo' Lord yes. Absolutely so. Swear on the Bible, any old day!'

Like a rapier thrust came the demand. 'Very well, then. Take off your dressing gown and nightshirt.'

Captain Loxley-Gregg permitted himself a sickly grin. 'Oh, I say, Uncle! Goin' a bit far, aren't we? I mean to say, dash it!'

'Take off your clothes!' The command had a steely insistence. The Colonel meant to be obeyed.

Shuffling towards the door, Loxley-Gregg tried the artifice of procrastination once again. 'But I say, hang it, Uncle! A fella really can't be asked to strip. I mean to say, hang it!'

Hand on the door knob, he was about to make a dash for his aunt's protection when an ear-splitting crack from the Colonel's hunting crop warned him of the consequences. The thong had come perilously close.

'*Take off that nightshirt!*' Clearly, the Colonel's fuse had already burnt dangerously short; the long, thin whip lay snake-like on the highly-polished floor – quivering.

Captain Hubert Hannibal Loxley-Gregg at least had enough sense to realize that further resistance could only exasperate his uncle to the point of apoplexy. Moreover, he had his eye on the Lanteague estate; as the only surviving male relative, he must surely stand a very good chance of inheriting his uncle's wealth. He must on no account throw that chance away by antagonizing the old boy.

He decided to fall back on the unwritten code of honour between fellow officers and gentlemen. Momentary indiscretions must be kept strictly a secret between them.

Casting aside the dressing gown, and drawing the nightshirt over his head, he shot what he felt to be an endearingly conspiratorial glance at his uncle.

'I suppose you're going to say I shouldn't have done it,' he simpered, 'but you must admit she's a very perky little wench, what!'

For no more than a few seconds the Colonel stared at the

deep, incriminating weals which Rose had managed to inflict on her assailant. Then he erupted.

'I'll give you "perky little wench"!' he snorted, standing well back and bringing the whip down sharply across the naked Captain's back. 'You unspeakable blackguard! Take advantage of one of my staff, would you! You deserve to be *horsewhipped* – and, by God! *so you shall*!'

With relentless fury he pursued the hopping, leaping, protesting figure around the room, whirling and cracking the whip, and every so often landing a searing blow on the tenderest parts of the Captain's anatomy.

'You unmitigated scoundrel, you! Abuse my hospitality, would you – desecrate my house! I could have you tried by a jury in a court of law. Attempted rape. Sounds pretty, doesn't it! Humble seamstress violently assaulted by army officer. And, by God! ya didn't even succeed! A hideous crime under any circumstances, but to *fail* . . .'

The Colonel's opinion of military failure was succinct – and extremely painful. The quivering buttocks of the newly-promoted officer sustained yet another scalding lash.

'Bring disgrace on your family, would you,' – CRACK – 'and on your friends,' – CRACK – 'and worst of all, you've disgraced the regiment! And this . . . is what . . . the regiment . . . thinks of you!' Each pause was punctuated by a lacerating whiplash, scorching the already sorely afflicted skin and causing the Captain to let out a succession of blood-curdling screams.

'Ha! A squealer, eh?' the Colonel shouted, now implacably pursuing his jibbering nephew. 'Cryin' before you're really hurt, eh? Well, perhaps it'll teach you not to go forcing your lechery on innocent girls in the dead of night.' A terrifying gleam crept into the Colonel's eye as he brought the whip down with a final, never-to-be-forgotten lash. 'You snivelling, whimpering nincompoop, you! I'll teach you!'

Exhausted, he threw the whip down on the desk and walked back to the fire. Beads of sweat were running down his high-coloured face. Placing one hand on the mantelpiece for support, and without looking at his nephew, he said quietly, 'Now get out. Out of this room, out of this house – and out of my life. I never want to set eyes on you again.'

He waited in silence while his nephew, clasping his dressing gown around his sorely stinging nakedness, shuffled out of the room. Then, mopping his face and neck with a large cream silk handkerchief, Colonel Bouchier walked slowly, wearily across to the door of the study. Pushing it open, he regarded sanguinely the two countrymen sitting forward uneasily on the edge of the leather armchairs.

'Gentlemen,' he said at last, after taking a deep breath, 'I trust you are satisfied.'

Mulling over the astonishing events of the morning while returning, eventually, to Thorn Cottage, Sampson decided not to tell Rosie all the details of the Captain's punishment.

He knew his daughter well enough to realize that if he told her everything she might, with that perversity which has characterized womanhood since the Garden of Eden, even feel sorry for the man who had so nearly raped her – despite the fact that, in Sampson's opinion, he had been given not a lash more than he deserved.

CHAPTER THIRTEEN

The Château de Pontrechat

Early morning mist still shrouded the tall chimneys and turrets of the former home of Monsieur René and the redoubtable Madame Françoise Barbier when the five prisoners were once more bundled into the waiting cart.

Whither now? Rose wondered.

'To the Château de Pontrechat, it is my guess,' Père Lemaître announced, anticipating her thoughts – and while still chained to her person.

'You seem to know much about these ancient castles,' Rose observed. 'Can you tell us anything about this château to which you think we are now being taken?'

The priest shrugged his massive shoulders. 'Nothing of any particular interest, I do not think.'

And then, shooting her a suggestive glance, he added, 'No . . . er . . . how you say . . . no "juicy bits", yes?'

'Nothing so interesting as a ring, a brooch, and a pretty blue ribbon,' Rose suggested somewhat archly – and immediately wished she hadn't. The look in the priest's eyes clearly indicated a resurrection of lustful thoughts, and she had no desire to stretch even further the restraining ties of his celibacy.

'No,' he said sadly, flashing a glance of repressed yearning, 'Nothing so . . . er . . . exciting as a piece of blue ribbon.'

He fell silent after that, consumed by his own thoughts and only occasionally permitting himself a sideways glance at Rose. Overnight the bonds of celibacy had held – but only just. It had been for Père Lemaître a terrible struggle.

None of the other chained occupants of the cart seemed

disposed to converse. The Comte and Comtesse de Ploumanoir sat huddled close together to keep out the early
morning cold, their eyes seemingly glazed against the
inevitability of their fate. Monsieur Duvivier, so accustomed
to an over-burdened table, was showing outward signs of
gnawing hunger. His normally fat cheeks were unusually
pinched and blue with cold, and every now and then he
would clutch his protuberant belly, as though to squeeze it
might lessen the intensity of his longing. But he, too,
said nothing.

Temporarily bereft of a conversationalist, Rose looked
around her. Kerjean had long since receded into the distance,
and having recently passed through the hamlet of St Derrien,
they were now entering the equally unremarkable village –
if worthy of such a title – of Plounéventer. She could not
help contrasting the flat, featureless countryside with her own
beloved part of Cornwall. True, there was an abundance
of flat heathland on the Lizard between St Keverne and
Helston, but since leaving St Pol de Léon there had been
nothing to compare with the secret charm of Gillan Creek
or the mystic beauty of the Helford river.

In the far distance, away to their right, a tall tower rose
above the woolly carpet of low-lying mist, and in an attempt
to relieve the monotony of this forlorn journey, Rose gently
nudged the priest's arm. 'Monsieur,' she asked, pointing,
'qu'est-ce que cela?'

He smiled, clapping his manacled hands in appreciation
of her hesitant attempt to speak his own language, and
saying, 'Bravo, mam'selle. You speak very well, yes. You
must try to speak more and more, then you will get good,
yes.' He followed the direction of her pointing finger, and
said, 'That, mam'selle, must be the belfry of le Folgoët.
They say it is a copy of the Kreisker at St Pol, you know.
But I am not sure.'

'Le Folgoët,' Rose repeated, 'Can you tell us anything
of interest about le Folgoët?'

Père Lemaître thought for a moment. 'Again . . . no
blue ribbons, I think,' he said, glancing sideways, his

eyes twinkling wickedly, 'but there is a legend . . . if I can remember it.'

Gazing at the distant church tower, and screwing up his eyes as though prising the story from his store of Breton legends, he went on, 'The name "le Folgoët", it means "the Fool's Wood", you know, and the legend says that a poor, half-witted boy once lived in a hollow tree by a spring at the nearby Lesneven, not much more than a stag's leap away.'

He cleared his throat noisily before continuing. 'This boy, whose name I believe was Salaün, could speak only a few words which, being translated into English, meant, "Oh, Blessed Virgin Mary!" These were the only words the simple-minded lad could say, but he repeated them very frequently. The legend tells that after the boy's death a lily was seen to be growing from his grave, and that the . . . er . . . the seed-forming parts . . . how you say, the "pistil", yes . . . they made the words "Ave Maria" in beautiful gold letters. So you see,' the priest concluded, 'that was the miracle. Even in death the boy could speak to the world.'

'What a charming little story,' Rose commented. 'In life he could not speak clearly, but in death his message was unmistakable.

'But that is not all,' Père Lemaître went on. 'Do you like that I continue?'

They were now approaching the outskirts of what looked like a sizeable market town. Rose had no idea how much further they had to travel, but she found the priest's stories interesting and the tone of his voice soothing. These legends of his, recalling the distant past, seemed to throw the present into more acceptable perspective. They softened the sharp outlines of today's picture; they muted the jarring colours of the contemporary scene.

'Oh, yes,' Rose replied with genuine enthusiasm, 'do, please, go on.'

'Very well,' he said, clearing his throat again. 'The news of this miracle spread throughout the whole of Brittany, and when Jean de Montfort . . . you English would call him a "Pretender", yes . . . after he had won the battle of Auray

196

he ordered a chapel for the Virgin to be built with its altar standing above the spring from which the simple-minded Salaün used to drink. And if you go to le Folgoët now you can see Salaün's fountain to this day, yes.'

'So that poor simpleton is remembered still,' Rose observed thoughtfully, '. . . while nearly all the great and powerful are long since forgotten.'

Père Lemaître smiled ruefully. 'How is it you say . . . "There must be a moral in it, somewhere", yes. And I say "God moves in mysterious ways", you know.'

By now they were rumbling along the main street of a busy market town. At the end of the street a bridge, with overhanging houses, crossed the river, and the whole atmosphere was redolent with the smell of fish. Market stalls lined the street, and succulent-looking fruit and vegetables were much in evidence.

'À quel village sommes-nous?' Rose tried tentatively.

The priest laughed. 'Very, very good, mam'selle. Once more, you are improving. "Voilà Landerneau!" This is the town of Landerneau.' His face suddenly clouded over. 'It means,' he added with a deep sigh, 'that we cannot now be far from our destination . . . unless I am mistaken.'

While the near-exhausted horse was being allowed a much-needed drink at the trough in the centre of the town, a group of small boys gathered round the cart, pulling grotesque faces and jeering at the prisoners. One of them picked a squashed artichoke from off the ground and flung it, with deadly accuracy, at the somnolent figure of Duvivier.

Briefly the fighting spirit of the former privateer flickered. 'Allez-en! Canaille!' he shouted, angrily shaking an impotent fist at the urchin. But the boy just laughed. If there had been another piece of putrefied vegetation to hand he would no doubt have flung that, too. It was fortunate there was no recently deposited ordure nearby.

'And what can you tell us of Landerneau,' Rose asked, deliberately ignoring the taunts of the children. 'Your tales are such a welcome diversion, monsieur. They greatly alleviate the tediousness of the journey.'

Père Lemaître smiled his appreciation. He felt flattered that such a pretty young girl should find his conversation interesting. It said much for her intelligence, he thought; unusual in someone of her age.

'I cannot tell you very much,' he said with a weary sigh, 'except that, as you see, the town has a busy market for vegetables and fruit as well as fish. It is the only port on the river Elorn and it was once the capital of Léon. But, apart from that, I can really tell you nothing.' He lapsed into a brooding silence as the cart rumbled on alongside the river, past the ancient bridge and along the Quai de Léon.

Rose studied the priest's face, trying to read his expression. It was an interesting face, she thought; one moment humorous, the next full of sadness.

He was staring out across the now widening Elorn river towards the Plougastel peninsula. Nodding sadly in that direction, he said, 'I used to play there as a boy, you know – at St Jean. We used to frolic around the fountain nearby. It was at one time a well-known gathering place for Druids.' After a moment's pause he added with a forlorn, fatalistic shrug, 'I suppose you could say that I at least return to my roots for my burial.'

'You mustn't *say* that,' Rose admonished. 'You must *never* give up hope!'

He shook his well-shaped, tonsured head. 'For you it is possible, mam'selle,' he added resignedly, 'but not for me. I am a priest, you see – and the Tribunals they do not like the priests.'

'But why ever not?' Rose exclaimed. 'What could they possibly have against priests?'

Père Lemaître drew a deep breath, then turned and fastened his long-lashed, soulful eyes on his chained companion. 'Because, mam'selle, as I told you – we will not swear an oath of allegiance to the Republic. Our allegiance is to God, and to God alone.'

'And is that your only crime?'

The priest shook his head. 'No. They do not like us for other reasons. At first, we welcomed the Revolution. At

198

least, we were not against it. In God's name, who can be against liberty and equality for all men – and those of us worldly enough to take an interest in our country's affairs had belief in the Girondins. They were the dreamers, the men of intellect – they mostly come from the Gironde, south of Bordeaux, you know – and they had the true vision of freedom and equality.' His expression changed from that of visionary to that of disillusioned priest. 'And if you had been born, mam'selle, as I was, of poor peasant folk with scarcely enough food to go round and little hope of a better way of life, you would perhaps understand how some of us felt . . .'

Rose smiled inwardly. 'Yes, monsieur, I understand better than you imagine.'

'But then,' the priest went on, absorbed by his own reflections, 'the men of violence took control. The Dantons, the Robespierres, and the Desmoulins of the Revolution, they created the monster which we now have – and monsters must always be fed on human blood and yet more human blood.'

Again the sad shake of the head. 'Alas, that is the way with revolutions, it seems. They begin in the minds of men dedicated to the betterment of the oppressed, but once the river of blood and carnage has started to flow, no one can stop it. It has to run itself to a standstill. And in the process, those who started it are devoured by it in the end. Marat, the so-called "friend of the people" has gone already, as you probably know; the great Girondins: Vergniaud, Brissot, and even Madame Roland are all now facing death. Before long,' he continued, gazing prophetically into the future, 'it is my belief that all the most violent men of the movement will follow in the bloodstained footsteps of those they have already murdered.'

Rose shuddered. Even as she followed the direction of the priest's gaze across the broadening waters of the Elorn estuary a cloud moved across the sun.

It was still casting its deep shadow over the land as the cart turned into a steep track leading up to a castle.

'I have made the mam'selle sad,' the priest's voice purred in her ear, 'and I have no wish to make for unhappiness – especially in the present circumstances. Let me try to cheer mam'selle a little. I tell you a story, yes?'

Receiving encouragement from Rose – anything would be better than those gloomy references to blood and death – Père Lemaître continued:

'The château we now approach, it is called Le Château de Pontrechat. Please don't ask me why because I do not know. But there are some who say it is really the château de Garde-Joyeuse, and that it contains the tomb of the famous lovers, Tristan and Iseult. I expect you are familiar with the story.'

Rose reluctantly confessed she was not. Though she had always devoured avidly the knowledge imparted to her at the charity school at St Keverne, it had not included the story of Tristan and Iseult. And yet she felt sure she must have heard it because in her bones she knew it to be a legend of powerful romance.

'Tell me,' she said, careful not to display her ignorance. 'I would like very much to hear it from your lips.'

The priest smiled. He was delighted by her ingenuousness; he had not been deceived for an instant. 'Very well,' he agreed, 'I tell you. Tristan, you see, he was a Prince of Léon. He was also the nephew of Mark, who was the Duke of Cornouaille, you know. There now! Did you not say you were from Cornwall in England, yes?'

Rose nodded.

'That is very interesting,' Père Lemaître went on, 'because it was King Gradlon, coming from Cornwall in the first place, who called his new kingdom "Cornouaille" – but then that is another story, as you say. I must not wander too much. I must return to Tristan, Prince of Léon.

'Very well,' he continued, wiping his mouth with a handkerchief extracted from the folds of his tattered cassock, 'the legend is that Tristan was sent to Ireland to seek, on behalf of his uncle, Duke Mark of the Cornouaille, the hand of Iseult, the most beautiful Princess of Ireland, and to bring

her back to his eagerly awaiting uncle. That was the arrangement, yes; the uncle trusting his nephew to bring him back
this beautiful maid for him to wife.'

Rose smiled. She could see the possibilities.

'Very well,' the priest continued, sensing his listener's
interest and warming to his story, 'the beautiful Princess
accepted the proposal brought by Tristan on behalf of his
uncle, yes, but on the boat coming back to Cornouaille, these
two young people accidentally – yes, the legend says it was
an accident, but of course, you may believe as you wish,'
he added with a twinkle, 'they accidentally drank the love
potion that was intended to bind Iseult to Duke Mark in
eternal love.'

The priest paused – tantalizingly.

'And what happened?' Rose urged.

Père Raoul Lemaître turned to look at her. His long-
lashed, soulful eyes washed over her – smouldering with
repressed desire. 'Passion, mam'selle, can sometimes prove
stronger than duty.'

Involuntarily, Rose moved a fraction further from him.
In a deliberately conversational tone, she asked, 'And how
does the story end, Monsieur?'

Quickly recovering his former attitude as dispassionate
raconteur, the priest gave a throaty chuckle. 'As you can
well imagine, mam'selle, the Duke was not very pleased with
his nephew, and the legend has it that Tristan and Iseult
hid from him in the forest which we are even now looking
at – the forest surrounding the Château de Pontrechat.'

Following the sweep of his arm, Rose observed, 'It
certainly looks thick enough to hide anyone. But what
happened to the two lovers in the end?'

'There are many different versions,' Père Lemaître
continued. 'Some say that Tristan was murdered by the
revengeful Duke Mark, while others declare that after
hiding for several years in these forests, Tristan and Iseult
eventually marry and live in Tristan's castle – possibly
this very castle that is before us now. Sometimes they
make each other very, very happy – sometimes they are

201

very sad. But always it is Iseult who follows Tristan to the grave.'

Once again a cloud obscured the sun. Prophetically, it seemed, it was still spreading its gloom as the cart rattled across the drawbridge and into the courtyard of the Château de Pontrechat.

Built for the express purpose of guarding the upper reaches of the Elorn river, and to protect the port of Landerneau, the capital of ancient Léon, the Château de Pontrechat was of an unusual triangular shape. Two large round pepper-potted towers stood at the extremities of the side overlooking the river, with a smaller turret making up the third angle. On all sides the land fell sharply away from the outer wall, while the main quarters of the château and the entrance thereto were guarded by a moat.

As soon as the cart became visible, trundling up the steep track, the drawbridge began creaking to its lowered position. The moat, Rose noticed, was covered with a thick carpet of vivid green pond weed. It looked suffocatingly uninviting, and it smelt strongly of excrement.

Upon arrival within the inner courtyard, the prisoners were taken to a room at the foot of the west tower, and searched. Just what the gaolers thought they would find on a bunch of prisoners coming from one prison to another Rose could not imagine. She supposed it was an invariable routine, ordered by the governor, which must on no account be dispensed with. She realized that perhaps it was not so futile after all when she saw the Comtesse de Ploumanoir being ruthlessly stripped of the few jewels she had been able to retain from her previous incarceration at the Château Fontanelle. And then when the aged prison officer stood in front of Rose his eyes went straight to the gold chain around her neck.

He held out his hand – waiting.

'Non, non!' she protested, backing away and clutching the chain firmly in her fist.

The brutish-looking man stared back at her; moved a step closer, still holding out his hand.

'Non!' she persisted. 'Non, non! C'est un bijou très precieux!'

The officer continued to stare. Then, like the strike of a cobra, his hand shot out; tried to grab the chain. Simultaneously, the priest who had been watching with the eyes of a hawk, intervened. His powerful fist gripped the man's hand; held it away from Rose. A rapid, threatening conversation followed, none of which Rose understood. Eventually the man backed away, leaving Rose defending her gold chain like a tigress guarding her cub. Had the priest threatened the man with eternal damnation, or what? Or had the ageing officer recognized the raw muscular power residing in the priest's arm – realized that with one lightning crunching twist he could snap the brittle bones of a forearm.

Rose did not know. It mattered little because within the next few minutes all five prisoners were being paraded before the prison governor, Citoyen Henri Bousillier.

It soon became apparent that Monsieur Belette, governor of the Château Fontanelle, had ingratiatingly advised his former superior at the Hôtel de Ville, that one of the prisoners now coming under his authority might be worthy of 'special treatment'.

Monsieur Bousillier, having heard the arrival of the cart in the forecourt, was waiting in the prison governor's office. In age, he was a man already well down the slope from peak virility; in appearance, although once able to present a manly figure, he had now completely lost control of his girth through over-indulgence in food and wine. His cheeks were flabby.

He had no difficulty is recognizing 'la prune très agréable' – the delectable plum - which the obsequious Monsieur Belette had sent him. His rheumy eyes swept appreciatively over the contours of her figure. Lascivious contemplation of what might lie in store for him with this young 'anglaise' were already causing saliva to dribble from the corners of his mouth. He was impatient to taste this English fruit.

Yes, M. Jacob Belette, that aptly named snivelling weasel of a junior of his, had served him well in this instance, he felt bound to concede. But what was it the Good Book said, 'Cast your bread upon the waters . . .' – although, of course, he had long ago burnt his copy of Holy Writ in order to be in tune with the spirit of the Revolution – but the wisdom of Ecclesiastes had declared that 'thou shalt find it again in many days'. Monsieur Bousillier congratulated himself. Overlooking that little misdemeanour so foolishly perpetrated by his junior at the Hôtel de Ville was about to pay handsome dividends, unless he was much mistaken. 'Cast your bread upon the waters . . .' Indeed!

But Citoyen Bousillier was no fool. At least, not so far as feminine conquest was concerned. He had learnt that a certain amount of patience usually brought the richest physical rewards.

Moreover, he disliked virgins. A messy business, he found. Before dipping his own toe in the water he preferred someone else to break the ice – to ease the way in for him. It wasted less time. Monsieur Bousillier looked long and hard at 'la petite anglaise' – and licked his lips.

Yes – from long experience – he thought she was probably a virgin.

Monsieur Bousillier stroked his fleshy jowls contemplatively. That great hunk of a priest she was manacled to – he'd be no good at deflowering a maiden! Vows of celibacy, and all that. No good at all.

Or would he! Might it not add a touch of the macabre! The celibate priest chained to the delectable virgin – the ultimate temptation, the Garden of Eden all over again. The terrible remorse that would follow the breaking of the sacred vow! It would certainly add spice to an otherwise tedious existence; the cat playing with the mouse – before finally devouring it!

The governor of the Château de Pontrechat rubbed his swollen hands in pleasurable anticipation. He gave orders for the Comte and Comtesse to be imprisoned in a room in the east tower, together with the surly Monsieur Duvivier, but the 'jeune fille' and the 'prêtre' were to remain chained to each other while sharing an upper room in the west tower.

Immediately, Père Lemaître objected. The governor should at least respect the tenets of Holy Church – even if he did not embrace them for himself. Besides, in all humanity it was not right for a young girl to be forced to share with a man – any man – all the functions of daily life – eating, sleeping, and those other necessary performances for which every human being was entitled to a little privacy.

It made no difference. It merely increased the nefarious pleasure with which Citoyen Bousillier regarded the prospect.

'Allez! Allez!' he commanded, ordering the prisoners from his presence. He would allow the priest just one night in which to squeeze the plum – to make it soft and juicy. Then he, Monsieur Bousillier, governor of the Château de Pontrechat, would devour it at his will.

The room in the west tower was not unpleasant. Although it contained no furniture – apart from two roughly made wooden chairs and a few straw-filled palliasses – the rectangular slit-type windows looked out over the moat and across sloping fields towards the Elorn river. At one time it had probably been a guest bedroom. Around the wall beneath the windows was a stone slabbed seat projecting outwards above the moat. Conveniently placed, and covered by a square block of timber, was a round hole for use as a 'cabinet', and through which excreta would have a clear drop to the moat below. It was regarded as being highly civilized.

Flung into the room by a surly gaoler, Rose and the priest heard the key turned in the lock and bolts rammed home.

Père Lemaître looked forlornly at his chained companion. 'I am sorry, mam'selle. I did what I could.'

'Of course you did,' Rose replied, trying to inject some cheerfulness into her voice. 'It's not your fault.'

'But I do not trust that governor,' the priest observed. 'I think he is a wicked man. I think he is scheming something evil, but I do not know what.'

'Oh, well,' Rose sighed philosophically, 'there doesn't seem to be very much we can do about it.' For the hundredth time she surveyed the chain which secured them to each other around the ankles.

'It is criminal,' he burst out, 'to keep a beautiful young girl like you, mam'selle, chained to a middle-aged priest like me. It is barbaric. It is a complete denial of the "liberté" which the Revolution is supposed to stand for. It is the kind of bestial treatment that stirred the great Linguet to spring to our defence. Originally, he was a supporter of members of the Cordeliers club, but it was when they butchered Le Barra, plucking out his tongue before cutting off his head . . .'

'Oh, don't!' Rose cried. 'It's too horrible! Please don't tell me any more.'

The priest hung his head. 'I am sorry, mam'selle,' he said, full of contrition, 'Sometimes I get – how you say – carried away, yes. I am sorry. But Monsieur Linguet, he came to our rescue – he defended us when the Pope issued a decree abolishing our order some years ago. After that, of course, we had to – er – to "go to ground", you know, and some of us had to flee the country. But Monsieur Linguet, he defend us. Indeed, when the King was captured and thrown into prison, it was Monsieur Linguet who offered to plead for him as an advocate in the court.'

Père Raoul Lemaître's dissertation was interrupted by the sound of bolts being drawn back and a key being turned in the lock.

The huge door was pushed open by the gaoler to admit a youth of about seventeen or eighteen years of age carrying a tray bearing a hunk of bread and two bowls of soup.

The youth looked from Rose to the priest – and then quickly back to Rose again. He smiled at her – and, grateful for the warmth of his expression, she smiled back. The boy then glanced in the direction of the window ledge, and raising his eyebrows questioningly, he moved across and laid the tray on the ledge beneath the window. Again he looked at Rose, obviously seeking her approval.

As a matter of courtesy, the priest nodded a gruff 'Merci', but the youth made no acknowledgement. He continued to hold Rose in a long, appreciative stare.

He smiled at her, diffidently. She smiled back. He smiled again, this time with greater confidence. Again Rose returned his smile. He said nothing.

The youth glanced over his shoulder at the gaoler who was lolling against the open door, idly whittling a piece of wood and apparently unheedful of anything occurring within the room.

Once more the boy smiled at Rose, and fumbling in the folds of his ragged smock he produced two large apples. With a delightfully impish glance, he handed them both to the girl from whom he seemed unable to drag his eyes.

Rose was about to express her delighted surprise when the gruff voice of the gaoler barked, 'Armand! Allez!'

With a lingering backward glance at Rose, the youth slowly went back towards the door. As he went through the doorway, the gaoler, with an obscene expletive, gave him a vicious kick.

'Ohh! You brute!' Rose exploded. 'Leave the lad alone!'

But the gaoler merely leered at her as he pulled the door behind him.

Once more the bolts were rammed home, the key turned in the lock. Rose and Père Raoul Lemaître were left alone with their supper – and with themselves – for the night.

The supper, consisting of pieces of beef floating in a thick soup containing potatoes, onions and carrots, was of a distinctly higher quality than anything served up at the Château Fontanelle, and the gratuitous addition of the two red-skinned apples turned the meal into something almost resembling a pleasure.

'That was good of the lad,' Rose remarked, savouring the rich, juicy flesh of the fruit. 'I wonder where he got them from and why he gave them to us.'

'There are many orchards in Brittany,' the priest smiled, 'and boys have been good at stealing apples since the beginning of time.'

'But there can't be an orchard within this castle, surely?'

'No, perhaps not, but there will be plenty in the surrounding countryside.'

'But how does the youth get to them? Is he not a prisoner like ourselves?'

The priest shook his head. 'I think not. He will be allowed to come and go as he pleases – always provided that he performs his duties when required, yes. He is just a serf, you know. He will be paid nothing for his work. All he will get in return for the menial task of serving the prisoners will be such food as he can – how you say, "purloin", yes – is that not a polite way of saying that he steals, ha – and of course he will be allowed to sleep in his kennel like a dog. But I do not think he minds very much. He knows no other life – and, besides, I think he is probably "muet" – how you say, a mute, yes.'

'You mean he is deaf and dumb? But what makes you think that?'

'From the way he looks and behaves,' the priest said. 'There is much flexibility in our order, you know. We have been encouraged, ever since Saint Francis Xavier, to become involved with different ministries all over the world, and we have been especially concerned for young people, as well as for the sick, for prisoners, for prostitutes and for soldiers. Our founder, Ignatius, was a soldier, you know, and it was while he was recovering from a wound received in battle that he experienced his religious conversion.'

'And you think that poor boy, so heartlessly kicked by that horribly turnkey, is deaf and dumb?'

'It is probably *because* he is deaf and dumb that he was kicked. Have you noticed, mam'selle, that in the animal kingdom it is always the injured, or the deformed, or the sick that are maltreated by the others?'

'Oh, yes,' Rose readily agreed, 'I have seen it many, many times at home. It is always the little runt that gets pushed away from the trough, always the injured or the sick fowl that gets mercilessly pecked by the healthy ones.'

'And it is the weakly lamb that is taken by the fox,' the priest added with a rueful snort.

'But that is among animals,' Rose retorted. 'Surely human beings must be less cruel than animals.'

Père Lemaître drew a deep breath; gave a long-drawn-out sigh. 'After what I saw in Paris, mam'selle, I am beginning to have doubts.'

For a long while after that they remained silent, each preoccupied with thoughts of their own. Inevitably, as the light began to fade and yet another night of imprisonment approached, Rose's thoughts returned, as they always did, to her home, her devotedly loving parents – and to Ashley. Would he ever come for her; had he forgotten all about her; was he now in the arms of another woman?

As the full moon slowly climbed into the darkening sky, casting strange, elongated shadows through the small rectangular windows of the tower, Rose could not help remembering that night, now so long ago yet seeming as fresh in her mind as though it were only yester-eve, when she and Ashley, and old Zephanaiah Curnow had slipped into the Baie de Morlaix and then silently glided to that inlet below St Pol de Léon. That adventure, nerve-tinglingly exciting though it had been, must be counted as the beginning of all her troubles. Until then, her life with those simple, loving-hearted parents of hers in the remote Cornish village of St Keverne had been idyllically secure and with only brief moments of unhappiness. Just what would they be thinking and wondering now – that lovely warm-bosomed mother, that rugged, forthright father who had plunged into the raging seas to rescue her from the shipwreck all those years ago, and who had loved her unfailingly ever since.

Now, as she sat chained to a Jesuit priest in the fast-fading light of evening, and in the confines of a well-guarded castle on the banks of the Elorn river, the surging memory of those loving parents overcame her. She began to cry. At first, silently; she did not wish the priest to pity her. But then, as she thought of the distance now separating her from the love and security of her homeland and all that she most treasured, the silent tears gave way to uncontrollable sobbing.

She felt the priest's arm go around her shoulder. He pressed her head gently but firmly against his massive chest, comforting her.

They remained in that position for quite a long time – she sobbing like a child, he rhythmically patting her with the tenderness of a loving parent. Nothing was said; words were unnecessary. Quietly he allowed – and by his unspoken sympathy he encouraged – the reservoir of pent-up emotions, which had been steadily building up during the past frustrating months, to overflow. He was wise enough, and experienced enough, to know that the most effective balm for an overwrought soul is the comforting arm, the sympathetic ear.

For a while, again like a child, and one who realizes that the wound is no longer hurting and who tries to stop crying but cannot, Rose was unable to control her sobbing. It was as though the clockwork toy, wound to its tautest and then released, could no longer be controlled.

But eventually, as the stream of emotion ran dry, the sobbing became gradually less intense – then intermittent only – until finally it ceased altogether. Exhausted, Rose lay back on one of the straw-filled palliasses which must be her bed for the night. Inevitably, being chained to her, the priest must lie nowhere but beside her. And because of the comfort he had already given, she made no protest when once again his arm went round her shoulders. Indeed, she was consoled by his presence, glad of his nearness, and when he offered once more his chest as a pillow for her head, she found it solidly reassuring.

For a considerable time they remained thus – he gently patting her shoulder, occasionally stroking the lobe of her ear, while she gradually regained her composure.

It was not until she felt his lips brush her cheek that she fully realized the danger. Until then, she had been totally preoccupied with her own distress. She had not recognized the effect her proximity might be having on him.

She felt him move even closer – so that his body touched hers for its entire length – and once again she felt his lips brushing her cheek before burying themselves in her hair.

'Monsieur,' she said, moving herself away from him so that their bodies no longer touched, 'is this not rather dangerous?'

He gave a deep sigh – and for a long while he did not speak. Then, at last, he murmured, 'Mam'selle, I would be less than honest if I did not confess that I find you infinitely desirable. I know that I am a priest, and that I ought not to entertain such feelings – but we men – how you say – we are all the same, cassock or no cassock.'

Inwardly, Rose smiled to herself. What a delightfully comic way to put it, she thought. That it was true, she had no doubt, for there was no logical reason why it should be otherwise. And it was the first ray of humour to lighten the gloom of their dismal surroundings. Instinctively, she found herself warming to him.

At the same time she recognized the moment when she should move right away from him, as far as their chained state would permit. She knew that; she was fully conscious of the need; but she was too tired, too exhausted to do so.

His voice was purring in her ear once more. 'You may wonder, perhaps, why I am saying this to you now, yes – especially when you remember that, although I was sorely tempted last night while we were also chained together at the Château de Kerjean – and I believe that old rascal of a gaoler was hoping for a bit of fun – nevertheless, I succeeded in restraining my desires.'

Again, she knew she should have told him that of course he must do so again this night – and, indeed, every night thereafter, so long as through the iniquity of their captors they remained chained together.

But she did not. Perhaps it was because she now felt overwhelmingly tired. Perhaps she was able to persuade herself that a priest of the church would never so blatantly break his vows of celibacy. Perhaps, at the very back of her mind, there was just a tinge of curiosity.

Whatever the reason – and 'le coeur a ses raisons . . .' – she said nothing.

Instead, it was he who continued:

'I am telling you this now, mam'selle, because I no longer feel sure that I can contain the desire that is welling within me. You cannot understand, of course, the impelling

211

strength of such masculine desire. You are young and beautiful – very, very beautiful, yes – and one day you will meet and fall in love with a handsome young man of your own age. Indeed, I hope that you do – because, then you will understand, I think, something of the deep desire which I feel for you now.'

She moved a little further from him; crooked her arm behind her head; stared up into the moonlit, slanting shadows.

She knew that she should either do or say something calculated to cool his obviously mounting ardour – but she knew not exactly what. Sheer exhaustion was beginning to take its toll; resistance ebbing from every fibre. She just hoped that he would accept her inert response as indication of her lack of corresponding feeling. There was really very little else, in the circumstances, she could do. After all, they were totally alone; he was far stronger than she, and a man aroused was virtually unstoppable; he could over-power her with ease. Immediately, the vision of the newly promoted Captain Loxley-Gregg flashed odiously back into her consciousness.

But there was a difference. Whereas the mere proximity of Loxley-Gregg's body had been utterly repulsive, she could not feel the same about Père Raoul Lemaître. He had been kind to her; he had been honest with her; he was not forcing himself upon her body.

And after all, was it so very important. Did it really matter all that much? She was tired; she was utterly alone, apart from him; and, most depressing of all, she seemed to have been forgotten.

When she felt the tattered hem of her home-made Carmelite habit being lifted; when she felt his hand sliding up her leg, caressing the soft flesh of her thigh, she knew she should be making some kind of protest, some measure of resistance, limp and exhausted though she was. And when she realized, as she undoubtedly did, that he was fumbling with his cassock, pulling the front of it high around his waist and exposing, as she could see in the pale moonlight, the full power of his manhood, swollen, extended and erect, she should have protested even further.

She should properly have been shocked, she knew – but into her mind's eye, simultaneously, flashed again the memory of that childish encounter with Myron Pinnerton as she walked home across the fields between Trythance and her home at Rosenithon. Then it had been a traumatic experience; she had been frightened, shocked and horrified. But now she felt nothing; no sense of alarm, no feeling of shame or disgust, no will to resist. She was slithering, she knew, into an irreversible situation. She felt drained – no feeling left except one of mild curiosity. She wondered what it would be like – almost as though she were another person, outside her own body, watching the enaction of a scene in which she was taking no part.

His breath was hot on her cheek; his mouth was searching for hers – penetratingly – voraciously devouring with the power of sheer animal desire. And even when she felt the full strength of his risen manhood pressed against her loins – when she heard his agonized groan, 'Ah! mais je ne peux pas m'arrêter!' – even then she still felt emotionally dead. She neither resisted nor tried to resist. Bracing herself for the moment of entry, she wondered briefly how she would respond, how she would endure. She felt no stirring of corresponding desire, no vision of souls meeting in climactic bliss . . . She felt nothing.

But then, at the moment of abandon – at the very point of final surrender – she heard the agonized cry of 'Non, non! C'est sacrilège!' as he rolled away from her, covering his face with his hands, his whole body racked with sobbing.

In the eerie, moonlit stillness of the ensuing moments, broken only by the sounds of his slowly descending remorse, Rose lay alongside him, staring up at the darkened ceiling. She had just come within a hair's breadth of losing what little personal pride she still possessed, and yet, apart from a sense of relief at the escape from purely physical demands, she still felt emotionally numb. If she retained any feeling at all, it was one of pity for the distraught priest at her side.

While she remained inwardly undisturbed, he was obviously going through a spiritual hell.

Presently, he rolled over again; clasped her in his arms; clung to her. There was no passion; only remorse.

'Ah, mam'selle,' he groaned. 'How can I ever be forgiven. With my flesh I wanted you so much. The whole of my earthly body, it longed for you with a passion greater than anything I had ever known before. So deeply I yearned to possess you, to devour you, to subliminate myself within your body. But always, always, my sin was ever before me – even at the height of my rising passion. I tried, and I tried, to send it away – but it would not let me go. And then, at the very point of physical consummation, it dazzled me with its brilliance. I could not hide from it any longer.'

He broke off, momentarily overcome with emotion. Then, in a strangulated voice, he added, 'You see, mam'selle, it was a vision of the Cross – my crucified Lord – and within sight of this vision, I could not break my vow.'

CHAPTER FOURTEEN

Madame de Levoisier's

Sir Andrew MacKenzie stepped out of his club in Pall Mall, turned left and walked briskly towards St James's Street.

Above the roof tops of London, the night sky was powdered with stars, and the evening air felt unusually crisp and keen. Dressed appropriately for the rendezvous towards which he was now heading – black silk breeches and finest silk hose, waistcoat of pale watered silk trimmed with silver lace, and a coat of superfine cloth – there was an undoubted spring in his stride.

At the club he had just left, he had dined well; the food had been to his liking – not too fancy – the accompanying wine well chosen, and the conversation had been stimulating. He had particularly liked the tall, well-built Windham. His friends had nicknamed him 'Weathercock Windham' – but Sir Andrew was not sure why. Despite a dignified, graceful manner, William Windham was, Sir Andrew knew, one of the finest sportsmen of the time – very athletic and a pugilist not to be taken lightly. At Eton, later at University College, Oxford, he had been a contemporary of the very persuasive Charles James Fox, the great protagonist of reform, but subsequently, after re-election as Member of Parliament for Norwich, he had shared Edmund Burke's alarm at the developing French Revolution. Indeed, it had been as a result of Burke's urging that he had very recently agreed to take office under Prime Minister William Pitt.

He had become Secretary of State for War.

Perhaps even more importantly, for the first time ever the War Secretary had been given a seat in the Cabinet.

At dinner, therefore, in the seclusion of a private room at the club, the talk had been almost exclusively of the war with France. And Sir Andrew, in view of his comparatively recent experience of imprisonment at the hands of the Revolutionary French government, was flattered to find that his opinion was not only sought but attentively listened to by his dining companions.

Especially by another William – a protégé of Windham's – one, William Wickham, whose father was a professor of mathematics at Geneva University, and was also a close friend of the Foreign Secretary, Lord Grenville.

Wickham seemed to be particularly interested to know if Sir Andrew MacKenzie had any knowledge of royalist movements in that part of France, south of the Loire, and known as La Vendée. What was the strength of feeling against the Republican administration? How great was the support for the royalist cause?

'I gather that the peasants are incensed by the attempts of the Republicans to de-Christianize the community,' Sir Andrew volunteered, 'closure of churches, prohibiting the ringing of bells and denying the clergy the right to wear clerical garments, etc. And I must say, I don't blame 'em! After all, it's something they've grown up with all their lives, and they don't see why someone like Robespierre should tell them what they must, and what they must not do.'

The Secretary for War sagely nodded his fine, patrician head.

But Wickham was more positive. 'They deserve to be helped,' he averred. 'And before it's too late. While the Dauphin's still alive.'

'But do we know for *certain* that he *is* still alive?' asked a friend of Wickham's whose name Sir Andrew had momentarily forgotten.

Once again Windham nodded – with that air of omniscience appropriate to a newly appointed cabinet minister. 'Oh, yes. I think we can be sure of that,' he replied, inclining his head indulgently towards the questioner. 'My information is that having been separated from his mother last July, the boy was put in the care of a cobbler, named Simon, a friend of Marat . . .'

'Who let it be known, you may be sure,' interpolated Wickham, 'that the boy's death would in no wise be unwelcome to the "Comité de Sûreté Général". As a result,' he went on, 'the boy was treated with unbelievable brutality – kicks, cuffs, taunts and insults – to such an extent that by the time this cobbler-ruffian finally gave up his iniquitous post in January of this year, the spirit of this sensitive and lovingly nurtured royal child had been utterly destroyed.'

Warming to his subject, and urged on by expressions of horror from his listeners, Wickham continued: 'And having failed in his attempt to dispose of this unfortunate child by maltreatment, Robespierre is now trying to achieve a more positive result by total neglect. I understand the boy is now being denied even the barest necessities even of cleanliness and decency. As a result, he is covered with sores, and is at the mercy of vermin running freely in his filthy cell.'

Sir Andrew wondered how much of this was true. Totally committed adherents – whether royalists or republicans – tended to exaggerate when defending their cause. But he suspected that the well-educated, thirty-three-year-old Wickham with so many friends in high places and so many reliable contacts abroad, knew exactly what he was talking about. Indeed, rumour had it that he was on the point of being sent out to Switzerland on what was described as 'an exceedingly confidential mission' about which even the Foreign Office was kept in the dark. It was of the very greatest importance, it was said, that Pitt should know the real strength of the royalist movement in and around Mayenne and also in the Vendée, and his Secretary of State for War was using his friend, William Wickham, as an unofficial government spy on the Continent.

Turning now to Sir Andrew, Wickham enquired with the utmost casualness, 'During your unfortunate sojourn in captivity, Andrew, did you ever come in contact with a fellow by the name of Cadoudal?'

Sir Andrew shook his head. 'No, I can't recollect ever having heard the name. Cadoudal, did you say?'

Wickham nodded. 'Yes, Georges Cadoudal. Eldest of a large family of what we'd call "yeoman farmers", with land around Auray. Never met him, meself, but he could be quite an important character in the general scheme of things – if you know what I mean.' He flashed Sir Andrew an enigmatic smile. 'Very handsome, I understand,' he added, 'and a natural leader, as well.'

Again Sir Andrew shook his head. 'No, I can't say I've ever heard of the man.'

'No matter,' Wickham rejoined, airily. 'I just thought you might have come across him. He's been in and out of prison at Brest, I understand. Definitely anti-republican, and quite a thorn in the side of the Convention, if you follow me.'

Not to be outdone by his protégé, Secretary of State for War William Windham weighed in portentously with the information that 'he could be of considerable importance to us if the PM decides to help the émigrés.'

'I understand he's reluctant to become involved,' commented Flaherty, a club habitué and a friend of Sir Andrew for many years.

'Oh, indeed,' Windham informed. 'He shies away from it like a startled filly. Can't bring himself to take the plunge. Understandably so, really. He's never had much stomach for a fight. Having concluded that Treaty of Commerce with the French in '87, he's more reluctant than ever to go to war with them now.'

'*I* find it *very* hard to understand,' observed Wickham. 'To think that any of us can stand by and watch a country murder both its king and its queen, and then starve its little crown prince to death . . .'

'Ah, yes, that's all very well,' cautioned Windham, with the ponderous deliberation of a responsible minister, 'and you're probably too young to remember it, William, but in '75 it was thought that just four regiments would be enough to subdue our recalcitrant American colonies, and yet it lasted seven years, cost thousands of lives, and in the end we didn't subdue them. Instead, we got our fingers very badly burned – first at Saratoga and finally at Yorktown.'

'Aagh!' interposed Flaherty. 'Saratoga! 'Twas that singin' and drinkin' and womanizin' Johnny Burgoyne that lost us Saratoga. "Gentleman Johnny", they called him – but the man was more interested in findin' a receptive vagina for his rampant penis than ever he was in winnin' a battle!'

'The situation is entirely different,' insisted Wickham, irritated by Flaherty's lewd intervention. 'It's not the same at all. The Americans were doing no more than asserting their rights whereas these revolutionaries in France are chopping off heads just for the pleasure of the gore! I really think it's high time we did something to stop them.'

Around the table, all eyes were on the newly appointed Secretary of State for War. Very slowly, very deliberately, William Windham nodded his head.

'And what is more significant,' Wickham went on, encouraged by his chief's obvious approval, 'there are thousands of French exiles, including the flower of royal knighthood, "straining like greyhounds in the slips" and eager to return to their native land, to throw out the desecrators of religious objects, avenge the murdered priests, and after a victorious march on Paris, to rescue the boy-king from his persecutors and put him back on the throne where he rightfully belongs.'

William Wickham, 'ambassadeur extraordinaire' and unofficial spy for His Majesty's government, his eyes blazing, and beads of perspiration on his brow, sank back into his chair, watching the reactions of his companions.

He was pleased by what he saw. Every one around the table was signifying agreement and approval. Finally, after a pregnant pause, the Secretary of State for War concluded the topic of conversation by saying, 'I entirely agree with you, Wickham . . . the only difficulty lies in convincing the Prime Minister.'

That might be the problem exercising the thoughts of both the new Secretary of State for War and his political companion, William Wickham, but for Sir Andrew MacKenzie, walking briskly up St James's Street, there was a much more exciting prospect in his mind.

It was more than twenty years – twenty-two, to be exact – since he had lost his beloved wife while she and their two little daughters, Jeannie and Alethea, had been with him on a business trip to the West Indies. Having only just pulled through a difficult pregnancy with their second child, she had suddenly been struck down by a mystery illness from which she had never recovered. Shattered by this loss, Sir Andrew at first had no heart to go on, no will to live.

But then, as it so frequently does, time poured its soothing unguent on a broken spirit, and realizing that he was now solely responsible for two motherless children, one of them no more than a baby, he had picked himself up from the floor of self-pity and then resolutely set his face towards the upbringing of his bairns.

The thought of returning to Trevadne, the house overlooking the peaceful waters of the Helford river in Cornwall to which he had moved from his native Ross-shire on account of his wife's health, at first seemed impossible even to entertain. Trevadne was *her* creation, and hers alone. It had been little more than a romantic ruin when they had bought it; roof sagging, walls crumbling, and a garden like an African jungle. But *she* had transformed it; *she* had brought elegance and charm out of mouldering decay until every aspect, every corner of every room had become redolent with the fragrance of her personality. How could he ever live with such constant reminders of the woman he had loved – and lost?

But as time passed, the magic beauty of those words prompted by the twenty-third Psalm kept recurring in his mind – 'He leadeth me beside the waters of comfort; He restoreth my soul.'

They seemed to him like the directions on a signpost. He, with his two little daughters, had returned to Cornwall.

At first, the loneliness was almost unbearable. There were times when, riding around his estate, he would pause to allow his horse to drink at the tumbling stream beneath the tall trees at Polwheveral, and the strident, plaintive 'caar' of the rooks above seemed to be saying, 'She's gone. She's gone!' – and his desolation would finally brim over.

But then he had discovered Marianne Penberth. Her sorrow was as deep as his; her need even greater.

Her husband, returning from what he had promised her would be his last smuggling trip to Roscoff on account of the impending birth of their first child, had been wrecked on the Manacles. A few days later their son was born.

Sir Andrew had heard about the tragedy and had done what he could to console the widow. He had also helped her with the running of her husband's farm, Treworden, and had taken a fatherly interest in the boy as he grew up.

There had been times, too, when he had considered the possibility of marriage with the boy's mother, Marianne. She was a kindly soul, a farmer's daughter with all the domestic skills associated with a country upbringing, and he greatly enjoyed the homely warmth of her kitchen each time he dropped in for a talk with her. He did this quite often, especially when her son, Ashley, was sent away to a superior type of boarding school described as being 'for the sons of gentlemen'. He knew she would be feeling bereft, and an hour or so in her company certainly helped to dissolve the ache of his own loneliness.

But then he had encountered Michelle. Cast into prison on the flimsiest of pretexts, Michelle de Levoisier had, for a short while, shared with Sir Andrew MacKenzie and others the privations of imprisonment at the Château Fontanelle. She had committed no greater sin than to have been born to an aristocratic family. But in France in the year of Our Lord seventeen hundred and ninety-three – and at the whim or decree of Maximilien Robespierre – the life expectancy of an aristocrat could be measured in days only, or even hours.

For Madame Michelle de Levoisier, widowed at the early age of thirty-seven, her escape from the Château Fontanelle, and from the bloodthirsty grasp of Robespierre's Committee of Public Safety, had been a blessing for which her gratitude knew no bounds.

But the rescue had been carried out at a moment's notice, and Madame de Levoisier had escaped, like everyone else, with nothing more than the clothes she was wearing. First of all, therefore, Sir Andrew counted it his pleasure as well as his honourable duty to provide this extremely attractive lady with a wardrobe of clothes appropriate to her station. And it had not stopped there. At first he had very gladly welcomed her as his guest, for as long as she cared to stay, at Trevadne. But he could see that, to a Parisienne accustomed to the gay life of a metropolis, the quiet beauty of the Helford estuary and the simple pleasures of country life held little attraction. Madame de Levoisier pined for the vibrant life of a city – if not Paris, then at least the next best thing, London.

So, recognizing that a hot-house plant if exposed too long and too often to the outdoor elements – even though they be nothing worse than good, salt-encrusted Cornish air – that such a plant, despite struggling bravely to survive, will inevitably wither and die, Sir Andrew MacKenzie had set about finding a suitable residence in London for the woman of whom he had become disturbingly fond.

He crossed the broad thoroughfare of Piccadilly and began walking up Albemarle Street. About a third of the way along the street he paused and looked up. Through a chink in the curtain of a first-floor window a light streamed out. Madame de Levoisier was evidently at home. She had not gone to the theatre. He fervently hoped she was alone.

His hand was on the front door bell-pull when he paused once more. He was excited. He felt his heart thumping alarmingly. He must calm down – so he began walking along the street once more, turned right into Grafton Street, and then right again into Old Bond Street. Not only did he need time to calm down, he also needed time to think.

Throughout the long years since the death of his beloved Katrine he had lived the life of a celibate – for no other reason than that he could not bear to sully the memory of their idyllic love-life together. To have loved – and to have reached the stars – could never be repeated. It was enough for a lifetime – more than enough, he felt – more than is vouchsafed to most mortals indeed – and it would be a desecration of a divine gift to seek to renew it with another.

True, he had considered marriage with Marianne – and marriage, of course, meant bed – but although he fully admired and appreciated her homely qualities – and he most certainly enjoyed her company – he had never experienced the lure of her body. That she was comely enough he would not deny but he had never felt any desire – except perhaps very occasionally after a day's hunting – to feel the softness of her flesh in his hands. And such occasions, he recognized, sprang from raw sexual lust; something to do with the warmth of a mare's body coming up through the saddle.

But with Michelle it was different. Even in the dishevelled state to which all prisoners in the Château Fontanelle were eventually reduced, Michelle de Levoisier had exercised upon him a seemingly effortless allure. There could be no denying it. He lusted after her exceedingly. And in the ensuing months of captivity, and even more so thereafter, he burned to possess her body.

Now, as he turned back into Albemarle Street, some deep-seated instinct told him that the moment of supreme conquest was at hand.

Silently he communed with his beloved Katrine. He asked her forgiveness; he had loved her as he had never loved before or since; he would do nothing to destroy the uniqueness of the ecstatic moments they had shared; and ever since she had been snatched from him, he had known no other.

But now . . . he burned.

To his surprise – and relief – he received her indulgent smile of understanding. Even generous in life, she was even more so in the hereafter. He was free.

With a nostalgic backward glance in his thoughts, he stepped up to the front door, and rang.

Michelle de Levoisier was reclining on the chaise longue in her withdrawing room, reading a book, when he entered. The scene and the setting reminded him, as nothing else could, of Jacques Louis David's famous painting of 'Mme Recamier'. Her long, slender body was draped in folds of creamy, diaphanous chiffon so fine that it revealed just a hint of her shapely legs. Her feet, clearly visible beyond the folds of material, were without shoes.

Laying down her book on the table at her side, she stretched elegantly, like a cat awakening from sleep in front of the fire, and said, casually:

'You are later than I expected, m'sieur.'

'You were expecting me?'

'I thought you would come.'

'How did you know I was in town?'

She fixed him with a mock-accusing look from beneath long, dark eyelashes. 'My dear Andrew,' she purred, 'have you not yet realized that I know *everything* about you.'

'About me?' he retorted, flattered by the implication.

'Well, yes,' she pouted, '. . . and everyone else, of course.' She smiled, that engaging smile of hers which said so many things for which there are no words. But then, seeing the reaction it had encouraged on her visitor's face, she continued in a more matter-of-fact tone:

'And what has kept you, m'sieur?'

'Oh, just a rather tedious dinner at the club,' he replied, off-handedly. 'Well, not exactly tedious,' he corrected, '. . . except, of course, that it was keeping me from you . . . but they were talking . . . Wickham and Windham, that is . . . they were discussing the possibility of an invasion of your country by an army of émigrés and royalists.'

Madame de Levoisier's delicately fashioned, bow-shaped eyebrows lifted enquiringly. 'Oh, yes?' she questioned. 'And who are these Wickham and Windham?'

'Madame,' Sir Andrew chided, teasingly, 'I thought you said you knew everything.'

'Mais oui, of course I know everything,' she responded, '. . . everything, that is, about the proposed invasion.

Everyone is talking about it. It is no longer a secret. The only question is not "if", but "when". Everybody knows that.'

Sir Andrew nodded ruefully. 'That's the trouble with "the flower of royal knighthood" . . . they just can't keep their mouths shut!'

'Yes, yes,' Michelle de Levoisier dismissed, as though secrecy concerning military matters was of no consequence, 'but who are these Wickham and Windham, Andrew? You do not answer me.'

In shifting her position to get a better view of him, the folds of her gown fell away to expose a greater length of leg. Demurely she re-covered it – but not before the titillating view had quickened her visitor's pulse rate.

'Oh, Wickham and Windham,' he replied airily, 'they're . . . they're . . . well, they're politicians. At least, Windham is. Quite an important fellow, is Windham. Recently persuaded to take office under Pitt . . . Burke had something to do with it. You know Burke, of course . . .'

'Is he not your politician who is so much against our revolution in France?' she said prettily. 'Is he not the one who wrote the . . . er . . . the "Reflections" on the revolution?'

Sir Andrew nodded. He thought it time they changed the subject. In the presence of such a desirable woman, he found 'politics' a tedious digression.

He moved to the side of the chaise longue; sat down beside her; took her hand.

'You are absolutely right, madame . . . and to answer the rest of your question, Windham is now Secretary of State for War with a seat in the Cabinet, and Wickham is his friend who has very extensive contacts on the other side of the Channel.'

Madame de Levoisier elegantly inclined her head in amused acknowledgement of this information . . . and smiled.

Sir Andrew, still holding her hand, moved a little closer. 'But why do I waste time talking politics to such a pretty woman when I can think of so many other much more interesting things to talk about . . . and to do.'

Madame de Levoisier raised her eyebrows . . . but she did not resist when she felt her visitor's left hand stroke the back of her head . . . draw her towards him . . . brush her lips with his . . . at first a gentle, tender, exploratory kiss . . . culminating, as was inevitable from the very outset, in a deeply passionate embrace.

Drawing back at last, but still breathing hard, Sir Andrew buried his face in her curls, gently caressing her slender neck with his mouth. The power . . . the desire was rising, swelling within him. He wanted her now as he had never desired her before. Instinctively, his free hand felt for her thigh . . . the folds of her gown impeded him . . . got in the way. He could feel the warmth, the softness through the chiffon . . . but it was not the same as the flesh. Gently, surreptitiously he drew the material aside, slipped his hand beneath . . . waited for the expected protest. It did not come. He grew bolder . . . felt the garter of her stocking . . . bolder, bolder, higher up her leg, feeling the delicious sweetness of her silky thigh . . . higher . . . higher . . . higher. He thrust his lips against hers, parted them, and as his tongue met hers in an equally responsive surge of passion he bore her down against the circular, tasselled cushions.

Gently, but firmly she pushed him away. 'No, Andrew,' she murmured . . . but not reproachfully. 'Not now . . . and not here.'

Unable to control the urgency of his desire, he said, questingly, 'This time . . . sometime . . . never?'

She looked at him beneath her long dark lashes. Her lips formed the words 'sometime, maybe' . . . but her lovely grey-blue eyes said 'soon'.

CHAPTER FIFTEEN

There is a tide in the affairs of men . . .

Michelle de Levoisier, resplendent in an open robe of cream Pompadour silk, with flounced sleeves, laced ruffles and a long transparent apron of the finest black muslin, held court in a corner beside the Adam fireplace.

She had the expression – the indefinable look in her eyes – of a woman who, very recently, has experienced complete sexual satisfaction.

Beside her, in gold silk coat and matching waistcoat above black silk breeches, one arm resting casually along the back of her high-backed chair, stood Sir Andrew MacKenzie. Every now and then they exchanged glances which, to a discerning onlooker, would have indicated nothing if not the warm glow of a shared intimacy.

Around them, and similarly dressed in evening finery, stood a group of men who had come to pay their respects to one of the most attractive women in London.

Madame Michelle de Levoisier, widow of Anatole de Levoisier, formerly of l'École de Médecine, Paris, was holding one of her well-attended soirées. It seemed as though almost the whole émigré population in London had gravitated towards Madame de Levoisier's house in Albemarle Street that evening, but the hostess, herself, while receiving all her guests with impeccable charm, was interested primarily – apart from the man standing with his arm along the back of her chair – in the two men now threading their way towards her through the animated, gesticulating throng.

'Ahh! My dear Mr Windham,' she trilled, with uncharacteristic over-enthusiasm, 'how good of you to come. And to bring with you your most excellent friend, Mr Wickham.'

First, the Secretary of State for War took her gracefully extended hand and pressed it to his lips. He was followed immediately by his protégé, Wickham, who did exactly the same.

Many secrets – some concerning the State, others of no national importance whatsoever – have been allowed to fall to the pillow beneath a pretty woman's head. Much useful information, whether secret or not, is often passed on in a similar fashion. It is the common postage of politicians – and spies.

But Madame Michelle de Levoisier was no spy. She was a committed patriot. Although she had come to love England, particularly London, her heart had remained in the country of her birth. And France, under Robespierre, was tearing itself apart.

If there was anything that Madame de Levoisier could do to help her beloved country, then, with true patriotic fervour, she would do it.

And when she heard from Sir Andrew's passion-requited lips that an invasion of France was being actively considered in the highest quarters, she quickly made up her mind. She would further the project with any means at her disposal.

First thing next morning she had summoned a messenger-boy and despatched him with a note to the Secretary of State for War, 'une ancienne connaisance', seeking the pleasure of his company, together with his friend, Mr Wickham, even at such short notice, etcetera, etcetera.

Mr Wickham, when told, thought he recognized a covert opportunity to sample forbidden fruits. He was due to leave for Switzerland on an exceptionally confidential mission very shortly, and he would not be averse to taking with him an extramurally fragrant memory. For that reason alone he urged his chief to attend.

He received even greater encouragement to his hopes when, later in the evening, Madame de Levoisier invited him to accompany her to the privacy of an antechamber.

'Mr Wickham,' she began, seating herself in one of two matching Louis Quinze fauteuils and proffering the thirty-three-year-old diplomat the other, 'I am a Frenchwoman, as you know, and I have a great love for my country.'

Mr Wickham leaned forward in his chair, inclining his head in acknowledgement.

'The news that I receive from France is not good,' Michelle Levoisier went on. 'Indeed, monsieur, it gets worse and worse, almost by the hour.'

William Wickham remained silent, but nodded his head.

'More and more of my friends are being taken away and sent to the guillotine,' Madame de Levoisier continued, in genuine distress. 'Their only crime is that they were born to an aristocratic family.'

The young diplomat nodded once more – but this time more gravely.

Warming to her theme, Madame de Levoisier went on dramatically, 'The very, the very . . . how you say . . . the very flower of France is being cut down as though it were only a daisy in the field. And soon, monsieur . . . all too soon now, there will be no flower left to grow.'

'Madame,' Mr Wickham responded, readily submitting to the spell of her charm, 'I can assure you we are fully cognisant of the plight of your fellow countrymen.'

'But you do nothing for us!'

'Our hands are tied, madame.'

'Tied! But by whom are they tied?'

Mr Wickham glanced over his shoulder. There was no-one else in the room, and the door was closed. Nevertheless, it was in a tone of the utmost confidentiality that he apprised his charming listener that the stumbling block was none other than the Prime Minister, himself.

'But can you not persuade him? Monsieur, you have a very persuasive manner.'

Mr Wickham leaned even further forward . . . so that the full fragrance of Madame's perfume wafted up his

229

appreciative nostrils. 'That is precisely what we are endeavouring to do, madame.'

'Then why do you not succeed?'

'There are difficulties, madame.'

'But what difficulties?' Michelle de Levoisier persisted, 'There are thousands and thousands of Frenchmen in England, in Holland and in Germany who are willing to fight for the restoration of the "ancien regime" and for the little Dauphin who is being so badly treated by the Convention . . . so badly treated, in fact that I think any minute now he will die.'

Madame de Levoisier dabbed prettily at her eyes with a lace-trimmed handkerchief . . . just long enough, and just dramatically enough, to ensure her listener's sympathy.

With unusual temerity, Mr Wickham took the lady's hand. She did not withdraw it. Instead, she allowed her tear-filled eyes to wash over him, pleadingly.

'Oh, Mr Wickham,' she implored, 'do please do something for my suffering countrymen. You, who have so much influence not only with the Secretary of State for War but also, I am sure, with the Prime Minister himself. You are so powerful, Mr Wickham, there can only be very little that you cannot achieve.'

She lowered her eyes – but still she did not withdraw her hand. She had done her best; she could do no more. She waited.

With his free hand, Mr Wickham drew his chair a fraction closer, and in the most confidential manner prepared to deliver himself of information which he felt sure must endear him to his most delightful hostess.

'I should not really be telling you this, madame,' he began, immediately gratified by the rapt attention his words had engendered, 'but there is already a proposal that ships of the Royal Navy be permitted to escort – and indeed to convey – a substantial army of royalist sympathizers across the Channel for a landing somewhere on the west coast of France.'

'Ooh!' Madame de Levoisier exclaimed with the most

convincing simulated surprise and delight. 'Mr Wickham! But how marvellous! – si merveilleux, mon ami – and I suggest that it is all due to you, Mr Wickham, n'est ce pas?'

'Well,' the young diplomat replied deprecatingly, 'I suppose I did have a little something to do with it.'

Madame de Levoisier's eyes glowed. But then, quickly – perhaps a shade too quickly – her expression changed from one of admiration for the young diplomat sitting so confidentially beside her to an appearance of mounting alarm and despair.

'But why, Monsieur Wickham,' she entreated, 'is it only a proposal? Why is it not already a firmly agreed *plan*?'

Had it been physically possible for Mr Wickham to edge a little closer, he certainly would have done so. As it was, he had to content himself with lowering his voice and placing his mouth so that it almost touched Madame de Levoisier's delicately fashioned ear.

'Madame,' he whispered, 'it already *is* an agreed plan. The PM will give his approval – albeit very reluctantly – I am sure.'

Michelle de Levoisier delightedly clapped her slender-fingered hands together . . . but she did not remove her ear from Mr Wickham's informative lips. There was, she felt sure, more to come.

She was right. Continuing in an even more conspiratorial tone, Mr Wickham went on, 'Unless I am very much mistaken, madame, the Secretary of State for War, Mr Windham, whom it is my privilege to serve, will even now be in the most secret and confidential discussion with one of your guests.'

'One of *my* guests?' Madame retorted, with an appearance of genuine surprise. 'I cannot think that any of *my* friends could possibly be of interest to anyone so important and so influential as the Secretary of State for War!'

Mr Wickham smiled indulgently, and nodded. 'You know him well, I think. He is here this evening. I saw him when we came in.'

'Tell me, Mr Wickham. Who is of such great importance to your illustrious friend?'

Mr Wickham was enjoying the attentiveness of this most fascinating of women. He thought he would prolong his enjoyment a little longer.

'He is a fellow countryman of yours, madame.'

'But there are many French émigrés here this evening.'

'Yes, but this one is rather special. He has much power and influence in the western area of France – in Brittany to be precise.'

'Tell me who.'

'Can you not guess?'

Madame de Levoisier was growing tired of this cat and mouse charade. She had obtained the information she sought, and it was high time she rejoined those in the adjoining room.

'Mr Wickham,' she said, a note of command in her voice, 'I wish to know. Please tell me.'

In fairness it must be acknowledged that William Wickham, friend of Foreign Secretary, Lord Grenville, as well as confidant of the Secretary of State for War, was never one to overplay his hand – certainly not where a pretty woman was concerned. He leant forward again, brushed Madame de Levoisier's ear with his lips, and whispered:

'The Comte de Puisaye, madame.'

A look of delighted astonishment spread across Madame's features. 'Joseph de Puisaye, non! And what has the Comte de Puisaye to say to your Mister Windham, may I enquire?'

'It is not so much what he has to say to the Secretary for War, madame,' her informant confided, 'it is what he has already said to our Prime Minister, Mr Pitt. You see, madame, the Comte de Puisaye has come over as the representative of the royalists in Brittany and the Western Loire to try to persuade the English government to support an invasion of France – not only with words and sympathetic gestures but by ordering the Royal Navy to transport the invading army.'

It was enough. Madame de Levoisier had the information

she sought. She had neglected her guests for too long. She must return to them at once. Besides, something might be transpiring in her salon – some further titbit of émigré gossip – which she could not afford, as the most reliably informed hostess in London, to miss.

She rose from her chair, allowed Mr Wickham to press her outstretched hand to his lips – and then swept out of the room.

The billowing cloud of cigar smoke that enshrouded her as she returned to the salon she found quite nauseating. The smoking of foul-smelling tobacco leaves rolled into long, fat tubes was one of the disgusting habits of the English she considered most difficult to endure. She wished she could ban it completely from her soirées, but to do so, she realized, would almost certainly prevent some of the most interesting and influential men from attending – and this must never be allowed to happen. To be 'persona grata' at Madame de Levoisier's – for young bucks just down from Oxford as well as those who had already made their mark in the world – was definitely the 'ton', and Madame de Levoisier, herself, regarded this as her greatest achievement since being forced to flee her native land.

Threading her way through her guests – greeting this one with a welcoming smile, pausing to say a few words to that one as she walked – she observed the Secretary of State for War in deep conversation with her fellow-countryman, the Comte de Puisaye. She decided not to interrupt. Instead, she passed on to where Sir Andrew MacKenzie was listening intently to what a rather dashing dark-haired young man of some twenty-three years was saying.

'Andrew, mon cheri,' she intervened, 'you seem to be very considerably engaged. I do not think I know this young man. Be so good as to introduce him to me.'

'But of course, madame,' Sir Andrew responded. 'I would have introduced him much sooner, but I saw that you were otherwise engaged.' He flashed his hostess a knowing glance. Then he began the introduction. 'Allow me to have the honour of introducing, madame, Monsieur François de

Villecourt, lately from the Morbihan, an area of Brittany with which I think you are familiar.'

Madame de Levoisier extended her hand which the handsome young man took and, bowing low, pressed to his lips. 'Madame, c'est un grand plaisir,' he murmured.

'Monsieur de Villecourt is a friend of the Comte de Puisaye,' Sir Andrew continued. 'He is here on an important mission in connection with . . .'

'No, no, please,' the young man interrupted deprecatingly, 'I am only 'ere to do what I can to 'elp.'

'To help with what?' Madame de Levoisier interposed, and seeing the young man's obvious embarrassment, she proceeded encouragingly, 'To help, perhaps, with the invasion of France for which, in our hearts, we are all yearning?'

Again the young man looked embarrassed.

'Do not be afraid to speak of it, mon ami,' Madame assured. 'Everyone in London is talking about it. They even speak of it openly in Amsterdam, I believe. It is really no secret.'

Francois de Villecourt seemed relieved. 'And do you think the English government will agree to 'elp?' he asked.

Madame de Levoisier turned and glanced in the direction of the tall, well-built figure of Secretary of State for War Mr Windham, and the fashionably dressed Frenchman in the 'à l'enfant' perruque with whom he was in earnest conversation. 'You see,' she smiled, 'I think the Comte de Puisaye is even now doing his very best.'

'But will 'e succeed?' de Villecourt persisted. 'It is vital to our cause that 'e should.'

Madame de Levoisier shrugged her elegant shoulders. 'Je ne sais pas, monsieur. Time alone will reveal.' She turned her lovely grey-blue eyes once more upon the handsome, athletic figure of William Windham. Rumour had it that he was a practised pugilist and one of the finest sportsmen in the country. She could well believe the rumour. Despite his height and build, his movements were surprisingly graceful, his manner effortlessly dignified. He was a very considerable person.

Sir Andrew cleared his throat rather noisily. He thought Madame de Levoisier's eyes were lingering overlong on the figure of the Secretary of State for War.

'This young man has been telling me,' he announced, 'about his friend, Cadoudal.'

It caused Madame de Levoisier to switch her attention from William Windham to Francois de Villecourt. It was precisely what Sir Andrew intended.

'Cadoudal?' Madame enquired.

'Oui, madame,' Francois eagerly explained. ''E has been a friend for many years now. We were students together at the Vannes College, studying the law, you know, and at that time, like many others of our generation, we were in favour of the Revolution.'

'But then . . .' Madame de Levoisier prompted.

'But then,' this enthusiastic young man went on, 'about three years ago . . . in '91 I think it was . . . the college was closed because . . . because "ses professeurs ont refusé le serment." '

'Ah, oui.' Madame nodded, and turning to Sir Andrew, she interpreted, 'because the professors refused to give the sermon . . . the "sermon" required by the republican government declaring faithfulness to the revolutionary constitution. N'est ce pas?' she concluded, returning her appreciative gaze to de Villecourt.

'That is correct, madame. And when the notary for whom Georges was then working . . . that is my friend Georges Cadoudal you understand . . . when the notary who was also in favour of the Revolution at first . . . when 'e changed sides, both Georges and I changed sides as well.'

'And how is it that this friend of yours is so important to the success of any invasion?' Sir Andrew asked.

'Ah, mais c'est Les Chouans, monsieur!' de Villecourt explained, the surprise in his voice suggesting that Sir Andrew – and everyone else for that matter – ought to know.

'The Chouans?' Sir Andrew queried.

'Mais oui, m'sieur. Do you not know the Chouans?'

Sir Andrew shook his head. 'Should I?'

Madame de Levoisier laid a gentle hand on his sleeve. 'Of course not, Andrew. Why should you? You English gentlemen . . . I beg your pardon, I should say you gentlemen from Scotland . . . you never know what is going on beyond the shores of your country.'

'Oh, I don't know about that!' Sir Andrew protested. 'I have . . . or I *had*, I should say . . . a brother living in Brittany, and I was imprisoned over there, myself, for a time, as you well know . . .'

'Yes, yes,' Michelle de Levoisier soothed, 'but you do not know of the Chouans. Well, I will tell you . . . and Monsieur de Villecourt will correct me if I am wrong. The Chouans are peasants, mostly in Mayenne and around Fougères . . .'

'Under Jean Cottereau and 'is brothers in Mayenne,' put in François.

'. . . Oui, but also in Ille-et-Vilaine,' Madame continued . . .

'. . . de Boisguy in the forest of Fougères,' added de Villecourt, 'and Boulainvilliers in the forests of Paimpont and Montfort . . .'

'And in the Morbihan . . .' Mme de Levoisier went on.

'C'est de Silz. But it is Guillemot who leads in the country of Bignan and also around Locminé . . .' enlightened de Villecourt, proud of his extensive knowledge of the Chouan organization.

'But around d'Auray . . .' Madame concluded, giving the young man his cue, 'there is only one great leader and it is . . .'

'Cadoudal!' de Villecourt proudly announced. 'Georges Cadoudal of the Manoir de Kerleano in the environs d'Auray. My friend.' He turned enthusiastically towards Sir Andrew, saying, ''E is a great leader, monsieur. Even though 'e is of a family of "gros laboureurs" – 'ow you say – a family of yeomans, yes, 'e is the eldest of ten children and 'e is a born leader of men. Yes, monsieur, 'e is the very best of the Chouan leaders.'

'Clearly, you think a great deal of him,' Sir Andrew

commented, 'but how exactly could he help with an invasion – always assuming that our Prime Minister will agree to be party to it.'

'Because, m'sieur, wherever it is decided to land the army, Georges Cadoudal and his Chouans will be waiting. Together with the returning émigré army they will defeat the bloodthirsty republicans, the murderers of priests, the desecrators of sacred relics. And then . . . and then . . .' de Villecourt went on, his eyes blazing with fervour, 'they will march victoriously upon Paris and the Dauphin will be released from 'is foul imprisonment and elevated with glory to 'is rightful throne as King Louis the Seventeenth!'

'A noble ambition, no doubt,' Sir Andrew grunted, 'but . . .'

'*But* it all depends,' de Villecourt interposed, 'on 'ow successful the Comte Joseph de Puisaye is at persuading your Monsieur Windham and 'is Prime Minister to grant us the assistance of the Royal Navy. That, monsieur, is crucial to our success.'

He looked to Madame de Levousier for approval.

'Ye-es,' she agreed contemplatively, turning her head gracefully towards Mr Windham and viewing the Secretary of State for War through half-closed eyes, 'I think you are quite right, Monsieur de Villecourt. And perhaps,' she added dreamily, 'the time has come for us to apply "un peu de persuasion exceptionelle", yes?'

It was not without a pang of anxiety – not to say jealousy – that Sir Andrew MacKenzie watched her glide seductively in Mr Windham's direction.

CHAPTER SIXTEEN

Armand Lecroix

Citoyen Henri Bousillier sat behind his desk, running his
tongue laterally, and at lightning speed, between his fat,
sensual lips. Every now and again the tongue would dart
forward like the probing membrane of a viper.

Inwardly, Monsieur Bousillier seethed with venomous
anger. He had been thwarted.

Having allowed that healthy-looking hulk of a priest just
one night in which to take the virginity of the 'petite
anglaise', he had instructed the turnkey to bring her to his
room, confident that the prospect of good food and soft living
would induce her to accept his lewd designs, if not with
outright pleasure, at least with acquiescence.

That he had been so wrong in this assumption was what
now angered Monsieur Henri Bousillier.

Alone at last with the desirable 'anglaise', he had invited
her, in his seemingly most guileless manner, to help herself
to the bonbons which he had placed temptingly at the side
of his desk. To his mounting satisfaction the half-starved girl
had succumbed to the temptation, but when he had then
pulled her on to his knee and, as a preliminary to more
exciting adventures, he had run his hand up the skirt of her
home-made Carmelite habit – under which, of course, he
had correctly guessed that she would be wearing very little
else – he had been astonished to receive a vicious slap on
the side of his face.

Deeply affronted, Monsieur Bousillier had contemplated
using force. He was not accustomed to being denied. With
other prisoners on former occasions when he had felt con-

sumed by a rising need, he had experienced no difficulty. The sight of food, the prospect of a softer life, had been enough. But, he had to admit to himself, they had nearly all of them been either 'vieux bagage' or 'frigide'.

Now, M. Bousillier regarded himself as something of a connoisseur of women. The sinuous approach was his speciality. Let others do the forcing, if they must; he, Henri Jean-Marc Bousillier, was no rapist. Long experience had taught him that willing surrender, after extensive love-play in and around the seductive contours of the female body, almost always brought a deeper, more lasting sense of gratification. While enforcement might bring temporary relief to the overheated libido, it always brought with it an aftermath of 'tristesse'.

True to his vulpine nature, therefore, Citoyen Henri Bousillier had decided to play a waiting game. A brief sojourn in the dungeon beneath the west tower was usually enough to bring any wayward bitch to heel. Thenceforth, with a life of comparative luxury and comfort dangled before her, she would curl up in his lap and allow herself to be subjected to all manner of perverted indignities.

Monsieur Bousillier was in no desperate hurry. Far better a ripe, juicy plum than a sour, embittered aloe. He would bide his time . . .

To the summoned turnkey, Monsieur Bousillier angrily uttered just the one word: 'Cachot!' The man needed no further instruction. Roughly seizing Rose by the arm, he dragged her from the governor's room, and with a sardonic grin momentarily illuminating his atrabilious expression, he propelled her down a flight of slimy steps, unlocked a massive iron door, and flung her into the darkness of a putrid-smelling dungeon.

Having delivered his prisoner, the turnkey then left her to her fate, pulling the door after him with a reverberating clang, and turning the key in the lock.

Rose sank to her knees, buried her face in her hands – and wept.

Was this what her love for a Riding Officer – a 'King's

Man' – had brought her to? Was this to be her reward? There would be several in the Cornish village of St Keverne, she knew, who would regard it as nothing more than she deserved.

As she lay back in the damp, mouldy straw, exhausted by her weeping, she heard the unmistakable rustle of vermin. Despite having been brought up in the country, where rats abound in hedgerow and corn rick, Rose could not bear the sight of them. Mice were barely tolerable, but *rats* were an unmitigated abomination. She loathed them. The thought that she might now be forced to suffer their proximity, day and night – to be crawled over by them, bitten by them, even – was enough almost to derange a mind already stretched bow-string taut.

But what could she do? Was there no escape from these execrable surroundings – other than by surrender to the raw sexual demands of Monsieur Bousillier?

As her eyes gradually grew accustomed to the gloom, she saw that she had been thrown into an octagonal-shaped room without furniture or comfort of any kind. The only evidence that the outside world still existed came through a narrow slit at the extremity of an aperture in the wall, at about two and a half feet above the slime-ridden stone floor, and measuring something like two feet in height by about eighteen inches wide at the inside of the wall but tapering to no more than four inches in width at the outside.

Frantically, Rose searched this loophole. Might it not be made larger – even if only by dislodging a single stone – just enough to enable her to squeeze through to freedom? And what would she find outside if, by some miracle, she were able to escape? That the castle was surrounded by a moat was clear when the cart had rattled across the lowered drawbridge – but that would hold no terrors for her. Thanks to her father, Sampson Roskruge, she had become a strong swimmer, even as a child, so, if she could but ease out one of those stones at the far end of the aperture, she would be free.

But her hopes were immediately dashed when she found

that any attempt even to put one's face against the narrow opening – to see out, or just to inhale a few reviving draughts of sweet, untainted air – would be cruelly prevented by no fewer than three iron gratings, one on the inside, the second midway along the tapering aperture, and the third at the outer edge of the wall.

Once more Rose sank to her knees in despair. Would this nightmare *never* end!

Her feelings of utter desolation were temporarily interrupted by the sound of a key being inserted in the lock of the cell door. What now, she thought. Surely not that libidinous governor come, so soon, to offer her freedom in exchange for sexual favours!

Bolts were withdrawn, the key creaked noisily in the lock, and eventually the door was swung open.

But it was not the governor who entered. Instead, while the same surly turnkey held the door, Rose was relieved to see that it was only the same well-grown, shock-headed youth who, only the previous evening, had brought supper to herself and her fellow prisoner, Father Lemaître.

She regarded with dismay what the lad now offered on the rough platter. Even in the gloom she could see it was nothing more than bread and water.

'Is that all!' she asked, with distaste.

The youth merely shrugged, smiled apologetically, and shook his head.

'Est-ce que le plus rien?' she tried.

Yet again the shrug of incomprehensibility, the apologetic glance. Then the finger in the ear, the hand across the mouth, and a repetition of the hopeless shrug of incomprehension. At once Rose recognized that Père Lemaître had been right; the boy was both deaf and dumb. Simultaneously, it evoked in her a chord of sympathy. Someone else was also imprisoned – but in his case it was within the limitations of his own infirmities. Perhaps she had found a friend.

She smiled at him – as she had done the previous evening. Again, a look of astonishment spread across his intelligent young face. No one ever smiled at him, the deaf-mute – 'le sourd-muet'. Ridicule, kicks and clouts to the head were all he had ever received – for as far back as he could remember. Somebody's bastard – nobody's darling – he had been left to survive on such titbits as he could beg or pilfer, not only from the rich man's table but from anyone's table – even from the poorest. But the seed which had ultimately grown into this boy had been planted by a high-born, intelligent sire – and the intellect had been passed on to the offspring. Sadly, in the unsalubrious environs of a seaport, the mother had picked up a debilitating disease during pregnancy – and her child had been born without any sense of hearing.

Now, as Rose smiled at him, his face lit up like the flare of sparked tinder. He was trying hard to articulate – but the only sound coming out was a strangled 'Oo-oo-ooh'. Rose looked at him, encouragingly. He tried again – but it was no clearer. Perhaps he was trying to say 'tout', she wondered, – meaning, 'that's all'. But then, how could he; he had not even heard her original derisory comment – whether in English, or in her attempt at his own language.

Or had he, after all, understood? Was he, perhaps – with that extraordinary additional degree of comprehension granted to those deprived of one or more of the senses – able to interpret from a look or a gesture almost as much as those with normal facilities? Rose thought he well might; because he seemed to be trying to convey to her that although he must leave her now with just her bread and water – he glanced significantly over his shoulder towards the attendant gaoler – he would be back again soon with something a little more enticing.

Within half an hour he had returned. This time, without the gaoler. And when Rose indicated surprise that he was able to come and go so freely, he tapped the key in his hand, pointed upstairs and then gave a very realistic impersonation of a gaoler fast asleep.

From within the folds of his tattered smock he shyly produced a contrastingly brilliant white napkin, proudly unfolding it to reveal a large slice of cake. With a most comical grin of conspiracy he proffered it to Rose.

Her astonished delight produced an almost apoplectic response. The youth was doubled-up with embarrassed enjoyment. He was trying hard to say something – Rose doing her best to encourage him. But in the end he had to content himself with a comic demonstration of how someone who had become so practiced at pilfering in order to live could easily smuggle a piece of cake from a well-laden table. Finally, displaying an exceptional gift for mimicry, he was able to convey to Rose that the person from whom he had stolen it was none other than the governor himself, Monsieur Bousillier.

Rose rewarded this performance by delightedly clapping her hands.

Instinctively she asked, 'What is your name?' But the boy could only tilt his head to one side, like a dog trying to understand its master.

'Quel nom avez vous?' she tried, well aware of her own inadequacy; and yet again, 'Comment vous appellez vous?' – but receiving no sign of understanding, she moved across to the mildewed wall of the cell, and with the back of her thumb-nail she scratched the one word 'NOM?'

Suddenly his face lit up. Using the same method, he scratched the words 'ARMAND LECROIX'.

Rose wondered briefly how, with his almost insuperable affliction, he could have learnt to spell his own name. She supposed that someone, somewhere, had taught him to relate a few simple words to their meaning.

'Armand,' she mouthed, using her lips as definitively as she could. 'ARMAND LECROIX.' Immediately he responded with an appreciative fervour which, even in her own extremity, Rose found touchingly endearing.

And in that moment of recognized endeavour and mutual understanding, an enduring friendship was sealed.

He remained in the cell with Rose for as long as he dared, watching her every movement with a dog-like devotion as she devoured the cake, his intelligent features registering sympathetic pleasure at her every mouthful. At last, fearful that the turnkey must soon discover the theft of his keys, the youth reluctantly departed. But not before conveying his unspoken promise that before long he would return.

And when at length the already dim light finally faded into the darkness of night, and Rose, exhausted by her distress at her seemingly hopeless situation, lay down on the fetid straw amid the scurrying vermin, the only ray to sustain her in her feeling of utter dejection was this new-found friendship with Armand Lecroix.

Each day thereafter he contrived, somehow, to bring her something special – some delectable titbit from the governor's table which, it seemed, never lacked a variety of luxuries. Only when accompanied by a gaoler or turnkey was he unable to do so. At such times he would invariably be berated, jeered at, and frequently kicked by the callous official. But even then, while cowering beneath the painful blows of his tormentor, he managed to convey to Rose his urgent desire that she should not protest on his behalf. He would gladly endure – so long as he was allowed to be her servant, to bring her food.

As time went on he became more and more expert at understanding whatever Rose sought to communicate. Every day he would do his best to alleviate her depression – if possible, to make her laugh. He would make sure that her meagre ration of water was at least fresh from an underground spring instead of being drawn from the stagnant waters of the moat; and whenever he could – even at the risk of a severe thrashing – he would bring her a small quantity of the governor's wine in the hope of raising her spirits. He would change her straw more frequently than he should; he would bring her fruit from Rose knew not where; and with a facility almost beggaring description, he would delight in displaying his skill at rat-catching.

He would crouch, poised like a fox ready to spring, watching. Then, at the slightest movement within the straw bedding, he would pounce, bringing his fist down with the speed of lightning, before triumphantly holding aloft by its tail the inert body of a repulsive rat.

Armand Lecroix had never been happier. Never before had anyone been kind to him. Never before had anyone smiled at him. Never before had he laid eyes on such beauty.

Then one day he seemed unusually perturbed. He kept pointing upwards to the ceiling, violently shaking his head. Although there had by now developed between them a remarkable degree of understanding, Rose could not on this occasion fathom what it was he was trying to warn her against – and from the anxious expression on his face, that was undoubtedly what he was trying to do.

She very soon found out. As yet another dreary day was drawing to its close, Rose heard the heavy footsteps of the senior gaoler descending the steps of the tower stairway, jangling his keys. The door was flung open; the gaoler beckoned.

Following the heavy figure up the steps to the main entrance hall, Rose was then physically propelled towards the forbidding-looking door of the governor's office. What could this peremptory summons to 'the presence' mean? Could it possibly mean – oh! indescribable joy! – could it possibly mean freedom! . . . freedom to roam the fields once again, to sniff the precious scents of country air, to feel the warm embrace of a loved one's arms! Could it be *that* . . . *Was* such a thing really still possible? Or had the seemingly endless days and weeks of solitude, darkness and increasingly fearless vermin begun the inevitable process of deranging her mind?

Or did it portend another kind of freedom . . . the final release of death . . . death upon the scaffold . . . death by the bloodstained blade of the guillotine at Brest.

Citoyen Bousillier received her cordially. He sat behind his desk, fingertips gently tapping each other while his bulbous eyes devoured every curve of her young body. Speaking excruciatingly bad English, he enquired how his captive was enjoying her quarters, and upon being informed roundly that they were totally unfit for any level of human

245

habitation, Monsieur Bousillier lost no time in informing her, with a repulsively lecherous grin, that the remedy was in her own hands.

Having been apprised by his boot-licking toady of a junior at the Château Fontanelle that the young prisoner being transferred to the Château de Pontrechat 'for security reasons' appeared to be most desirably bedworthy, Monsieur Bousillier had laid his plans with care. He would leave her to rot in the dungeon for just long enouth to crave an improvement in her surroundings, no matter what the cost. Although he did not flatter himself that he was anything resembling an Adonis in looks – from whose blood might one day spring a scarlet anemone – like the boy Myron Pinnerton of St Keverne in Cornwall, nature had blessed him – or cursed him – with a 'phallus giganticus', as he was wont to boast, coupled with a near-insatiable itch to use it. He prided himself that women found such an accoutrement irresistible.

Rose, on the other hand, having divined from the moment of entry to the governor's room the price she would be required to pay for her freedom, was contemplating in her imagination the grotesqueness of his love-making. She wondered whether it would be worth the sacrifice.

Seemingly countless days and nights had gone by since she had thrown that heavy stone – that desperate cry for help – over the wall at the Château Fontanelle. Achingly, since then, there had been no response.

But what did she really expect – or even hope for? That Ashley would come for her, with a small army, perhaps, to storm the impregnability of the Château de Pontrechat? Had she not, in all conscience, been deluding herself with the belief – the hope – that he loved her so much that he would hazard his life and come for her?

The sad truth was, she concluded, that, yes, she must have been deluding herself.

She looked steadily at Monsieur Bousillier; imagined herself surrendering to his hot, slobbering kisses, to the feel of his hands probing her most intimate parts, and finally to the forceful entry of his rampant penis into her resisting body.

She recoiled in horror.

And yet . . . and yet . . . might not even that be preferable to the nightly attendance in her present cell of those horrible disease-ridden rats!

At that moment Monsieur Bousillier was irritated to see the door of his office being quietly opened to reveal the anxious face of Armand Lecroix peeping round it.

Seeing the look of thunderous annoyance boiling up within the governor, Rose feared for the very life of the youth.

'Ah, c'est le muet,' he snarled, making little effort to disguise his contempt for the boy. 'He has come to tell me my dinner is ready, y'know,' he explained, attempting an ingratiating smile at Rose. 'Poor boy. He is only a fool.' Then picking up a heavy paperweight from off his desk, he flung it at the youth, saying, 'Allez-vous en! Imbecile!'

But Armand was far too quick for him. He easily dodged the flying missile. He then left the room – but not before fixing Rose with his clear, childlike eyes, and violently shaking his head.

A wan smile spread across Rose's face. The youth was clearly doing his utmost to dissuade her from accepting what, instinctively, he knew would be Monsieur Bousillier's nefarious offer. Perhaps he would miss those sign-language conversations which they had been developing during the long, tedious days and at which they had both become so adept. Perhaps, Rose thought wistfully, he really cared about her.

But Armand did not have to undergo the trauma, day after wearisome day, night after restless night, in a damp dungeon cell, with little light and no sanitation, his nostrils constantly assailed by the smell of mouldering straw, his body violated by predacious vermin. True, he had to endure the taunts, the kicks and the cuffs; to be the punchbag and the whipping-boy of both prison staff and guarding soldiery; but at least he was free. He could come and go as he pleased, Rose had learnt, just as a dog is free to roam. But, sadly, he had nowhere else to go – nowhere, except a damp, pestiferous cell in a dungeon where a beautiful girl was kind to him.

Unknown to him, though, his concern for her, and his display of violent disapproval of the expected terms for her release from her life-sapping surroundings, had touched Rose deeply. The youth, who had probably witnessed it all before, was trying to warn her. In all likelihood, she guessed, the lecherous Monsieur Bousillier, having slaked his lust at her expense – or if she had not satisfied him in any respect – would send her back to the dungeon from which he would now be proposing to release her. Armand Lecroix was trying to make her aware of this. In doing so, he was putting heart back into her, re-awakening her determination to survive this appalling phase of her life, in the belief that, in the end, a richer experience would be hers.

She would procrastinate; she would dangle before M. Bousillier's eyes the desirable plum of her virtue – for just a little longer. In the meanwhile she would continue to live on hope; you never knew what might happen. Always, always was the dream that one day Ashley would come sailing up the Elorn river – just as she and he, and Zephanaiah Curnow, had sailed into the Baie de Morlaix on that former errand of rescue.

But how would he know where to find her? The message she had sent – if ever it reached him – had merely said 'Prison at Brest'. But there was another, much larger prison in the centre of Brest, or so she had heard. Might he not try to find her there. She would consult Armand; there was no one-else she could trust. And more than ever she was becoming convinced that the poor, unfortunate boy, so cruelly deprived of the normal faculties of hearing and speech, had been endowed with a compensating intelligence far above that of ordinary mortals.

Condemned to her dungeon cell once more for having rejected Monsieur Bousillier's conditional offer of release,

Rose, by means of the rapidly developing sign language between them, explained the situation to Armand.

To 'Le muet', it was simple. Nobody paid any attention to him. He could come and go from the château as he pleased, so long as he performed his daily tasks satisfactorily. At the same time, no one would readily get rid of him; after all, the bully is never fulfilled unless he has a 'cochon-bâtard' to kick!

This, Armand conveyed, was one of the few advantages of being a deprived human being – a nobody. 'Blessed are the Meek' – for shall they not inherit the earth? – and he, Armand Lecroix, would be able to maintain a constant watch upon the Elorn river. If he should spot a strange boat – and he knew all the usual shipping in and out of the port of Landerneau – he would somehow attract its attention . . . yes, even if he had to swim out to it, or run all the way upriver to the port.

Rose, he clearly implied in his inimical way, need have no worry. If an English lugger came up the Elorn river, then he, Armand Lecroix, would see it.

The days dragged drearily by. Every Friday evening, Rose was dragged up to the governor's room; every Friday evening, the invitation to whoredom was renewed. Every Friday evening, it was rejected. The monotony of daily life in her filth-ridden cell was such that this weekly performance was the only way she could reckon the passing of time.

On one such occasion, Monsieur Bousillier was unable to contain his desire. He burned exceedingly. Having peremptorily dismissed the turnkey, he pulled Rose onto his knee, planted his slavering mouth on hers, and once again slid his hand up the inside of her habit, stroking her thighs and groping for her most intimate anatomy. This time, it seemed, he would not be denied.

Despite her diminished strength, Rose was still just strong enough to administer such a stinging slap on the face that the startled governor recoiled sufficiently to allow Rose to slip from his grasp. Drooling with unrequited

249

desire, the governor stumbled after her, snatching at the thin girdle around her habit with one hand while with the other he tried to rip the whole garment from off her sinuous body.

But once again, and with the memory of Captain Loxley-Gregg flashing into her mind, she brought her knee up into her assailant's groin, wrenched her clothing from his hands, and fled – down the slippery stairway, back to her cell. She would *never* give in to this brute!

For the moment she felt reasonably safe. Such dignity as he still retained would not permit M. Bousillier to follow her to the dungeon. But for how much longer would her diminishing strength enable her to resist – even supposing that in her increasingly emaciated condition the governor would continue to desire her. And might it not really be simpler – far less exhausting, even – to yield to his demands. Undoubtedly it would improve her living conditions, provide her with better food, allow her to rebuild her strength for the day when Ashley would come.

And would it be such a terrible sacrifice – to have him crawling all over her, prostrating his repulsive body on hers, devouring her with his slobbering kisses – until the final, painful indignity as he forced himself into her.

Might it not be worth it – to end the living hell of her present circumstances, the degradation of her cell with its lack of sanitation, its fetid smell, its rats!

Once more she sank to her knees in utter despair; for the hundredth time, she buried her head in her hands. Yes, in the complete absence of any real hope that Ashley's heart still beat for her – perhaps it would be worth it.

In this renewed state of desolation, she hardly heard the bolts of her cell being quietly drawn back. The door opened, and Armand Lecroix tiptoed in.

His eyes were gleaming – clearly apparent even in the dim light. His mouth was moving with frenzied agitation. Unquestionably he had something of the utmost importance to tell her. But he could not speak. Rose could see the agony, the despair, the frustration that held him locked

250

within the chains of his crippling infirmity. She tried to encourage him – not to speak but to use his expressive hands, to demonstrate.

And then she suddenly realized that, with that remarkable facility for communication that had developed between them, he was trying to tell her what in all the world she most wanted to know – that an English lugger was even now coming up the Elorn river!

CHAPTER SEVENTEEN

Il revient!

High up in the west tower the clock tolled midnight.

In the Château de Pontrechat nothing stirred – nothing, that is, except the nightly forage of the rats in the castle dungeon, and the fretful tossing of Monsieur Bousillier in his four-poster bed.

The Château de Pontrechat was battened down for the night.

But Citizen Bousillier could not sleep. Not only were his testicles still smarting from their painful contact with Rose's well-directed knee, but he was feeling inordinately thwarted. The plum had slithered from his grasp. He had felt so sure that after such a long time in the pestilential filth of the dungeon cell, she would more than readily submit to his demands. He had been deliberately containing himself – savouring in advance the moment when he would have her within his physical strength, delighting in the silky smoothness of her hips, the tender contours of her young breasts, the yielding softness of her lips. And then . . . and then . . . his libido palpitatingly aroused . . . the ultimate plunge into the intoxicating chasm, the final release of pent-up passion.

Yes, he had been savouring the prospect for days and nights – especially nights. Yet, here he was, lying alone upon his feather mattress, gingerly massaging the tender area of his groin, and rueing yet another lost opportunity.

Where had he gone wrong? he wondered. Never before had any female prisoner, subjected to the ordurous stench and privations of the dungeon for more than a few days, felt able to decline his advances – even though he had to admit that never before had such an appetizing meal come within his grasp.

Was he losing his hitherto irresistible charm, he pondered; had that earthy, masculine ability to 'seduire' suddenly deserted him? He picked up the silver-backed hand mirror from the table beside his bed and consulted his reflection. The bulbous nose, the fleshy jowls, the yellowed teeth – all topped by the scarlet, floppy woollen night cap – stared back at him. He picked his nose reflectively; and then comprehensively, reverberatingly, broke wind.

He replaced the mirror and blew out the bedside candle. It could hardly be that she found him unattractive, he reflected, drawing on the conceit, implanted by a doting mother, which had sustained him throughout his life. No, it could not possibly be that; just a little bit of initial reluctance to yield her body to the power of his embrace – that was all. But he would have her tomorrow – and that was for certain, he resolved – even if he had to use force. He would not be denied.

Consoling himself with this all-fulfilling prospect, he farted once more, and then went to sleep.

Down in the dungeon cell, Rose knelt before the loop-hole grid, her eyes tightly closed in prayer. 'Dear God,' she murmured aloud, 'please let it be Ashley. Let him come safely up the river, and let Armand guide and direct him to a suitable anchorage.'

In between these imprecations she peered through the narrow slit forming the outlet of the loophole, straining her eyes in the hope that in the far distance and in the pale moonlight she might just catch sight of 'Heatherbelle II', and the man she yearned to see, rounding the bend of the Elorn river.

But she could see nothing . . . nothing but the surrounding castle wall, and the shimmer of the moon on the waters of the moat.

For an hour or more she remained in that same position, alternately praying and then staring into the night – while the rats made play around her feet.

All thought of sleep or even rest had vanished from her mind. She must be ready . . . ready, like those biblical Children of Israel anxiously awaiting their release from the bondage of the Pharoah . . . ready, with loins girded, shoes on feet, and staff in hand . . . ready, at that astonishing sign of the Lord's passover, to strike out for freedom and the promised land!

Oh, yes! she would be ready. But would there ever be, for her, a promised land − a land flowing with milk and honey? She hardly dared to hope.

Presently, she heard a key being inserted into the lock of her cell door. Stealthily the bolts were withdrawn. Heart in mouth she shuffled across the floor, scattering the rats as she went. Quietly − as quietly, that is, as the creaking, vibrating hinges would allow − the door was pushed open, no more than a fraction, and Armand Lecroix was eagerly beckoning to her. In that moment of unspeakable relief and joy she flung her arms around the youth, and kissed him.

To Armand, it was as the dew of paradise. Never before had anyone, ever, embraced him. For a long moment thereafter he stood, stupefied − transfixed − gazing at Rose as though he had just seen a heavenly vision. It was she who had to grasp his hand firmly, and give it a little shake, in order to bring him back to the realities of the moment.

Sensibly, as they crept out of the cell − that hell on earth that had been Rose's domain for what seemed like an eternity − Armand pulled the door closed after them and locked it, realizing, with that innate wisdom of the deprived which is sometimes confused with lunacy, that an open cell door would alert the duty gaoler sooner than was eventually inevitable. If they were to make their escape, the longer they could delay pursuit the better.

Motioning Rose to follow him, Armand scrambled up the slimy dungeon stairway, and then led the way to the main entrance hall from which access to the drawbridge was barred by a massive portcullis. Seeing Rose's dismay at the sight of this impenetrable barrier, Armand's face creased itself into a mischievous grin. Very slowly, like a conjuror producing a rabbit from a hat, Armand withdrew from a pocket in his smock yet another large key. Tapping the side of his nose with it, and scarcely able to contain his glee at the look of admiration on Rose's face, he pointed to a small side door close by the lowered teeth of the portcullis. Once again, with endearingly comic gestures, he mimed the manner in which he had extracted the key from a sleeping gaoler.

Inserting it in the lock he slowly turned the key, and pulled. With an ear-splitting screech, of which Armand himself was quite unaware, the heavy, iron-studded door swung open.

A few, lightning steps – and Rose was through the doorway, and the deliciously cool night air was caressing her cheeks. Oh heavenly freedom! . . . blissful sensation!

Again, Armand pulled the door closed behind him, and locked it. Again, a horrible screeching of hinges shattered the stillness of the night. But, to Rose, it mattered not. She had escaped at last from the degrading stench of that dungeon cell. For the first time in what seemed like a never-ending nightmare she could draw deep lungfuls of intoxicatingly clear, fresh air. Involuntarily, she flung her arms around Armand's neck and hugged him. Once more the youth was overcome with delighted embarrassment. He could not drag his eyes away from her face – poor, emaciated face that it had become. It mattered nothing to Armand what she looked like; it concerned him only that she had shown him affection. Unable to articulate in any recognizable form, he nevertheless felt a great surging desire to express his feeling of exaltation. Denied the great releasing agency of words, he could do no more than let out a high-pitched howl – more reminiscent of a dog ecstatically greeting its homecoming master rather than any human exclamation of joy.

Alas, poor Armand! Having no knowledge of sound, to him dogs howled silently, locks turned noiselessly, and doors swung on their hinges without so much as a whisper. But high up on the battlemented walk of the château wall the nightguard's peaceful doze was rudely interrupted. He grabbed his flintlock and ran to the parapet. The governor would certainly demand his head if ever there should be an escape from the Château de Pontrechat!

But nothing moved . . . nothing within the precincts of the castle. The well-kept lawn, surrounded by the inner buildings and the castle wall, lay like a velvet napkin swathed in the silver moonlight. Had he heard something . . . or had he, perhaps just been dreaming? At any rate, there was nothing untoward to be seen.

But then he distinctly heard a splash!

He hurried across to the outer parapet, the one over-looking the moat – and there, almost immediately below him, he saw two heads moving slowly through the water. They were making for the far bank of the moat and the perimeter wall of the castle.

Kneeling at the parapet, he raised his musket; took careful aim. But as he did so, the stock of the weapon momentarily grazed against a projection of the wall – only the merest of sounds. But it was enough to make Rose glance upwards. The long, thin barrel of the musket could clearly be made out, etched manacingly against the moonlit sky.

Instantly, she sank beneath the surface of the moat, forcibly dragging Armand down with her. Fractions of a second later the 'phfutt' and 'hiss' of a bullet burying itself in the water, only inches from Armand's head, confirmed that the soldier had fired.

Taking advantage of the inevitable time-lag between firing, reloading and then firing again, Rose struck out furiously, with Armand at her side, for the shadowed far bank of the moat. Then, judging the moment as best she could, and seeking to deny the guard a visible target to shoot at, she signalled Armand to take a deep breath, hold his nose, and sink beneath the surface yet again. In this position she encouraged the youth to swim alongside her until she felt the welcome assurance of soft mud beneath her feet and the slimy caress of pondweed around her legs.

Then, very gingerly, she allowed her head to come above the surface once more, motioning Armand to do the same.

256

Gasping for breath – but also with the deepest sigh of relief – she saw that they had attained the heavy shadow cast by the perimeter wall, and must therefore be invisible to the soldier scanning the moat from the castle parapet. Dripping with the slime of the moat, they scrambled up onto the grassy bank adjoining the high castle wall. This formidable barrier was now the only remaining obstacle between the hell of Pontrechat and the heavenly freedom of the outside world.

Would that world still contain the man she loved? Was it possible, as Armand had indicated, that Ashley Penberth was somewhere outside the walls of the Château de Pontrechat, waiting to take her back to England, back to her beloved Cornwall, back to the loving parents who had nurtured her since babyhood – but even before that, back into his own strong, protecting – and dare she hope – still loving arms?

Was it possible? Or was it only a dream – to dissolve once more into the bitter reality of that rat-infested dungeon?

But Armand was tugging at her sleeve. That at least was real. So, it seemed, was the high, formidable wall to which he was dragging her; the final obstacle to their freedom.

Unlike the Château Fontanelle, there were no conveniently placed trees with branches overhanging the wall around this bleak château. Fruitless, therefore, to sigh for the loss of the girdle-rope, long ago confiscated by the gaolers at the former prison, which had once encircled Rose's waist and which had proved so indispensable in scaling the wall around the Château Fontanelle on that never-to-be-forgotten escapade – now seemingly almost belonging to another world – when, together with Ashley, she had penetrated the defences of that castle.

But Armand – the deaf-mute, the apparent imbecile, the youth so frequently kicked and pilloried by those more fortunate than himself – was not without a high degree of resourcefulness. He had foreseen the problem of the high wall. Recognizing the difficulty in obtaining the key to the main gate, he, too, had thought of a rope. But where to find one within the precincts of the castle? In his 'kennel', and with little more than a meatless bone to satisfy his hunger, the so-called halfwit had pondered long and hard upon this problem. Then, at last, an idea had come to him. Unobserved by the aged and decrepit custodian, Armand Lecroix had entered the small chapel within the castle walls – no longer used as a place of worship, by precept of the Revolution – and had cut down one of the bell-ropes and concealed it beneath his tattered smock. That there were no tree branches or wall projections to attach it to had presented something of an additional problem, but while ranging the vicinity of the wall, he had found a half-buried block of masonry discarded at some time when the wall was being repaired.

Now, with an expression of truly impish delight, he pulled Rose as fast as she could run to the place where he had left the block, and then, after tying the bell-rope securely around it, he lifted it shoulder high. Summoning every ounce of his youthful strength, he catapulted the block over the top of the wall.

Before trying to climb up, he tested the rope to see if it would hold – and to Rose's horror she saw that it was snaking back over the top of the wall. Any moment now, she thought, and the block would topple back to the ground from where Armand had picked it up. But she had reckoned without those defensive projections, built into the top of castle walls to deter would-be assailants from trying to scale them from the outside. Between two such projections Armand's block had become securely wedged. The rope was holding.

With the agility of a startled gazelle, Armand scaled the wall and sat triumphantly astride the top, beckoning Rose to follow.

For the second time in her young life – but this time with the sounds of alerted guards and the lowering of the drawbridge shattering the peacefulness of the night – Rose clambered up the wall of a French château. As she reached the top, the clamour within the castle was increasing alarmingly, and the baying of hunting dogs being released from their compound became frighteningly clear. Armand was urging her to hurry.

Momentarily, a cloud had moved across the moon, throwing the far side of the wall into deep shadow. But clearly there was no time to lose. Without looking where she was going or what lay beneath her, Rose committed herself to the mercy of Providence – and jumped.

The way down seemed interminable; but just when she thought a broken leg or ankle would be the least she could expect, she felt herself caught by a pair of strong, welcoming arms.

She looked up into the face smiling down at her – and she would swear now that her heart stopped beating!

It was Ashley!

CHAPTER EIGHTEEN

Escape!

Armand Lecroix stood transfixed. Never before had he witnessed such joy, such overwhelming relief and happiness as was now taking place before his very eyes – there, in the silver moonlight, beneath the walls of that forbidding château.

Never before had he seen man and woman locked in such rapturous embrace. Never before had he observed a reunion of long-parted lovers!

At first he remained at a discreet distance, fascinated by what he saw. But then, as the realization of its import dawned through the veil of his innocence, he began to feel sick. And his sickness, he knew, had nothing whatever to do with the scraps of rancid meat and putrifying vegetables which he had filched for his supper. No . . . his feeling of sickness had no dietary origins; rather, it was as though some unseen hand was physically mangling his innards, twisting his guts – and with an emotional painfulness he had never before experienced . . . the pangs of jealousy, the agony of pubescent love.

It was with positive relief, therefore, that he felt beneath his feet the unmistakable, rumbling vibrations of the drawbridge being lowered – a welcome excuse to interrupt the passionate scene that was playing such havoc with his heart.

Through the mists enveloping her ecstatic reunion, Rose felt Armand almost roughly tapping her on the shoulder. Oblivious of the urgency, she turned to look at him . . . saw the anger and the agony in his eyes, understood instinctively

260

something of the pain which her love for Ashley must be causing him. Hitherto, Armand had been the very centre of her daily existence, her single ray of hope. In return, she knew how eagerly he had sought opportunities and excuses to visit her cell; how delighted he was to be able to bring her even the smallest delicacy smuggled from the governor's table. But now he must see all too clearly that her heart beat only for another. Could she ever explain to him that there were many kinds of love – that love itself can be an all-embracing emotion – that she could love Ashley Penberth to an unfathomable depth and yet still find room in her heart for Armand Lecroix as well? Could she make him understand that? She wondered; she hoped so; because she realized that her sympathy, her understanding and her affection for him which had grown up during these past terrible weeks had been the only ray of true sunshine in the whole of his sad life.

But, angry sounds from within the castle abruptly brought such musings to a halt. Upon the discovery of the escape, Monsieur Bousillier would undoubtedly have boiled over with frustrated rage. His most succulent plum had once more been dashed from his lips. Who, by all the Saints, had been such a blithering dunderhead as to let the 'petite anglaise' slip from his grasp? . . . and make no mistake, all hell would be let loose if the girl were not recaptured. The culprit would pay for his carelessness with his head.

Flight – immediate and unhampered by emotional out-pourings – was now the most urgent necessity.

Led by the agile Armand who ran with the lithe movements of a chamois, Rose, joyously feeling once again the warmth and reassurance of her hand in Ashley's, ran to the very limit of her capacity towards the forest which curtained the château on three sides. If they could but lose themselves among those tall fir trees they might yet escape the vengeance of the château guards.

Apart from that short, ecstatic embrace, there had been no time for Rose to express in words or, indeed, in further actions, the sheer delirium of her joy at seeing Ashley again.

Relief at being free from the awfulness of her imprison-ment had transcended, for the moment, any other, deeper emotions, and now that they were fleeing for their lives, all thoughts of romantic involvement must, for the time being at any rate, be subdued.

Firstly, they must seek the thick cover of the forest. Although a three-quarter moon was riding high in the night sky, the darkness beneath the spreading branches of the firs and spruces was almost complete, apart from the intermittent rides which traversed the forest and allowed oblique shafts of moonlight to penetrate the darkness. For all that, the pursuing château guards had already begun firing – more in hope than with any grounds for certainty; shooting at shadows, if for no other reason than to placate an irate prison governor deprived of his most treasured desire and thwarted in his salacious intent.

At last, when deep within the heavy shadows of the forest, the three fugitives felt sufficiently safe to pause for breath.

'Oh, Ashley!' Rose panted, grasping his hand and pressing it to her lips – caressing it, fondling it – 'How can I ever tell you just what this means to me . . .'

Ashley made no reply. Instead, impulsively he took her in his arms, pressed her to his powerful chest – ran his lips over her hair, her forehead, and then down to her mouth . . .

Armand, watching enviously, eventually turned on his heel and shuffled off, scuffing the pine needles disconsolately as he went. Aware of this, Ashley gently released Rose, saying, 'I might never have found you, had it not been for the help of that young man.'

Rose looked up, pricked by conscience. 'Armand, you mean. Why, yes, of course.'

She disengaged herself, and ran after the retreating figure. 'Armand!' she called softly, momentarily forgetting that he could not hear. Then, remembering, she took hold of his arm, turned him round to face her, and lifted the chin so unhappily buried in his chest. She drew him to her; kissed him, and enfolded him in her arms.

It was enough. Immediately, the gloom, the despair, the

dejection dissolved. The slow smile returned, and like a sudden burst of winter sunshine his face lightened and his eyes once more sparkled with their usual impish delight.

Rose drew him back to where Ashley had remained standing. In that extraordinary sign language which she had developed with Armand during the weary months of her incarceration, she formally introduced the two people who, at that moment, meant more to her than anyone else on earth.

For several seconds the youth regarded this intruder with suspicion. He had known for quite some time, of course, that someone – some man sailing an English lugger – would come and rescue the lovely prisoner who had been so kind to him. But he had imagined it would be someone older; her father, perhaps, or even some experienced fisherman, like the crusty old salts who seemed to take such delight in making fun of him whenever he had roamed the waterfront at Landerneau or at Brest. He had never expected to see a man so young and so strong as the one he had just seen putting his arms around the girl who haunted all his dreams. He kept looking suspiciously from Rose to Ashley, and then back again to Rose, with the hurt expression of a dog being scolded by its mistress for an uncomprehended misdemeanour.

Sensing the youth's understandable resentment, Ashley placed one hand on Armand's shoulder, waited until the youth felt able to look him straight in the eye, and then beamed the warmest smile of gratitude of which he was capable. Eventually, Armand signalled his acceptance of this token olive branch by grasping Ashley's extended hand in a mutually reassuring handshake.

Rose stood watching this little pantomime with an ache of affection rising in her heart. That these two – the handsome Cornishman, come to rescue her and take her back to the land and the people she loved, and this young Breton mute who, by his courage and his cheerful determination to overcome the appalling restraints of his disability, had given her a new insight into the meaning of endurance and human endeavour – that these two, standing there in the shadows cast by the moonlight, should both love her enough to risk their lives to save her she found intensely moving.

But, clearly, this was no time for sentimental reverie. Even now, the sounds of snapping twigs beneath heavy footfalls, of unintelligible commands being shouted to troops, and most ominous of all, the deep-throated baying of hounds on a scent, confirmed, as nothing else could, that the château soldiery were beating through the forest.

'Quick!' Ashley hissed in her ear. 'Back to the lugger! The boy knows the way.'

Before Rose could even try to transmit this command, Armand was dragging her after him, Ashley following, down through the trees to the small inlet below Guipavas where the lugger was anchored. The reckless speed at which Armand now ran suggested to Rose that either he was afraid of the skill and swiftness of those terrifying hounds, or that even now, with a rapidly ebbing tide, the boat might have gone aground.

Scarcely had they emerged from the forest than it became all too tragically clear that 'Heatherbelle II' was indeed stuck fast on the mud.

Held by her anchor, head to wind and receding tide, she sat like an elegant statuesque swan, unmoving and immobile in the pale, eerie moonlight.

It would be several hours at least before she could be refloated.

Cleverly suggesting the face of a clock, Armand began revolving one hand in a clockwise direction to indicate that they must now hide for eight hours until the tide came back up the river far enough for the lugger to carry them to safety. Again using his remarkable facility for mime, he explained most graphically how it had taken him longer than he had anticipated to extract the keys from the somnolent turnkey. At the very moment of success – his hand poised above the pocket wherein lay the bunch of keys – the snoozing gaoler would sleepily open one eye, yawn luxuriously, and then change his position in such a way that the magic pocket became inaccessible. Shrugging his shoulders, he comically expressed resignation to the whims of the Almighty and the ultimate acceptance of the inevitable.

Ever the optimist, he then beckoned both Rose and Ashley to follow him and weaving his way over the boulders bordering the tidal river, he led them to a narrow fissure in the low, overhanging cliff. Sidling through the aperture after him, Rose very quickly realized that they were in a sizeable cave from the roof of which long, icicle-like stalactites persistently dripped blobs of moisture onto the silted floor below.

Armand pressed her arm. Even in the semi-darkness she could see his eyes sparkling mischievously. Successfully he mimed a soldier searching, searching . . . but not finding. Obviously, the cave was well-known to him – a safe place to hide from authority, a bolt-hole for the hunted animal . . . and he was clearly delighted to offer it as a sanctuary to his friends. He suggested that they make themselves as comfortable as possible because they would have a long wait until the tide came in again.

Indicating a ledge at the back of the cave whereon, he suggested, Rose might sit without too much discomfort, Armand then began a sign-language conversation which clearly placed a question mark over his own future. At first, in the gloomy light of the cave Rose found it difficult to understand exactly what he was trying to convey, but when he moved into the shaft of light near the narrow entrance so that his mummery could be more easily followed, the message became clear. He could never return to the Château de Pontrechat. Monsieur Bousillier would certainly lose no time in . . . and Armand then gave a horribly realistic imitation of his head being severed by the blade of a guillotine.

Rose turned to Ashley who was standing just inside the cave entrance, listening intently for any evidence that they had been followed.

In a subdued voice, she said, 'If and when we get afloat, we shall have to take Armand with us. He wants to come, and we couldn't possibly leave him behind.'

To her great relief she heard Ashley say, 'No, no, of course not. He helped you to escape . . . we couldn't possibly go without him.'

'He did more than help me to escape,' Rose murmured, as though talking to herself. 'He kept me alive. Through all those long weeks and months – and it seemed more like years – Armand kept me from going out of my mind. He gave me hope.'

'Oh, we'll take him back with us, all right. You don't need to worry about that.'

'Back to England.'

'Back to Cornwall.'

'Oh, Ashley!' she breathed, scarcely able to control her emotion. 'You've no idea what the very sound of that means to me!'

'I can guess,' he grunted.

'And after that,' she went on, still thinking of Armand, 'what will there be for him then?'

'We'll deal with that when it arises,' he replied rather curtly. 'I'll find him something . . .' He paused momentarily remembering how dramatically things had changed since Rose was last in Cornwall. With a stab of conscience piercing his heart, he added gruffly, 'Something on the farm at Treworden, no doubt. He seems a strong, useful lad.'

'Something on the farm,' she purred nostalgically. 'What a wonderful thought! And is it still just the same,' she asked eagerly, 'the farm – at Treworden, I mean?'

'Very much the same,' he lied.

But she knew she had only half his attention. Hand on cutlass, he was listening acutely for the sound of any approaching footsteps. Nevertheless she persisted, repeating like a child. 'Treworden . . . Something on the farm . . . Cornwall. Oh, Ashley, after all this time . . . and in that filthy dungeon cell . . . can you imagine what it means to me to hear those words again . . . and to feel free at last!'

'Yes, I can imagine,' he said, tempering the earlier curtness of his tone. 'Yes, I can well imagine. But first of all, we've got to evade capture . . . and then get the lugger

266

afloat once more, otherwise, sooner or later they'll find us
. . . and then there'll be no going back to England or
Cornwall for any of us!'

She accepted the rebuke. She realised that for him it was
a matter of 'first things first' – but she wanted to ask him
so many questions . . . about her father and mother . . .
had they been terribly anxious about her . . . about his job
as a Riding Officer, and was he still causing havoc among
the contrabanders of St Keverne and other 'freetraders'
along the Lizard coast. That, and a thousand other questions
she wanted to ask him. But above all – above the sea, the
sky, and all the beauty of the Cornish countryside – what
she wanted to know most urgently was, Did he love her?
Because if the answer was 'No', then she had endured in
vain. Far better that she should have died among the rats
and the filth of that dungeon cell.

As so often in the recent past it was Armand who rescued
her from the dejection of her thoughts. He nudged her
arm, drawing attention to himself. Then, by means of his
comically descriptive sign language he indicated that his
tummy was rumbling and he was feeling hungry. Moreover,
he suggested that both she and her friend must be feeling
the same, and now that the immediate danger of recapture
had temporarily receded, he would leave the cave and find
something for them all to eat.

Immediately, Rose tried to dissuade him, remonstrated
with him; it would be far too dangerous, and the soldiers
would easily recognize him, even in the dark. They would
take him back to the Château de Pontrechat, and what they
would do to him there did not bear thinking about.

But Armand just laughed; he loved to see the concern in
her face, to know that she cared about him . . . even if it
was only just a little bit. In the shaft of moonlight filtering
through a crevice in the cave, Rose could see his eyes
sparkling with mischief. He was feeling full of bravado; she
could see the familiar signs. He would show this lovely
English lady just what he could do for her. He would really
surprise her.

267

With a gay toss of the head, he disappeared through the entrance of the cave.

Back at the Château de Pontrechat, Citoyen Bousillier was like a tiger denied. Having failed twice to slake his overwhelming lust upon the pretty little 'anglaise', he had, with great difficulty, contained himself until, as he deemed almost certain, she would come willingly to his bed in preference to the privations of a dungeon cell.

But now she had escaped! And it was all due to that imbecile boy who should have been knocked on the head at birth!

Citoyen Bousillier felt eaten up with a gnawing sense of deprivation. He burned within him. Even in his dreams he had been haunted by the thought of what lay beneath the folds of that tattered Carmelite habit. What did a nun – or a girl pretending to be a nun – wear beneath her habit? he wondered. The very ordinariness of such a top garment titillated the imagination about what might lie below. But on the single occasion when he had succeeded in running his hand up Rose's thigh, he had felt nothing! – excitingly *nothing* to bar the way to those sensuous female curves of the lower abdomen. It had increased his desire almost unbearably.

Monsieur Bousillier had been licking his fat, bulbous lips ever since; holding himself in check so that when the supreme moment of success arrived, the floodgates of his lust could be gloriously unleashed.

But now, those indescribable dunderheads had allowed the girl to escape. By heaven and Sainte Anne d'Auray! but he'd have their balls off! – stupid, incompetent gaolers! Par le mort-Dieu! but he would!

Or would he? An expression of fox-like cunning spread across the bloated features of the governor's face. Was it not more important to recapture that tasty morsel! Punish her for trying to escape; a few more days and nights in that verminous cell, and then . . . and then . . . A warm bath, perhaps, and the inviting comfort of clean bed-linen, a cosy fire, a beaker of mulled wine . . . several beakers of mulled wine, yes. After that . . . after that . . .

Citoyen Bousillier adjusted his position to ease the pressure at the crotch of his breeches, and then rang for his sergeant of the guard. First of all, he would pulverize the man with a vituperative outburst against his incompetence and crass ineptitude for allowing the prisoner to escape. Then he would offer a special reward of ten . . . no, on second thoughts, only five . . . louis d'or to the soldier who recaptured the 'petite anglaise' and returned her to him, unharmed.

*   *   *

As soon as Armand left the cave in search of food – something special to impress the lady, to make her fond of him, yes – grenouilles, moules, champignons, fruits de mer – Rose seized her opportunity. It was the first time she had been alone with Ashley since they had stood together in the forecourt of the Château Fontanelle, gazing at the seemingly impregnable fortress and wondering how on earth they would be able to get in. Then he had drawn her back into the deep shadow of an overhanging tree, taken her in his arms and, while the earth stood still, had kissed her with a depth of passion she had never known before.

Only with an agonized groan had he torn his lips from hers, saying, 'Oh, Rosie! What are we doing . . . why are we here?'

And then had come the words, imprinted on her mind in letters of shining gold – words which she swore she would remember for as long as she lived, 'Oh, Rosie! Why don't we just . . .'

He had never finished the sentence – but she knew, if she knew anything on this earth, just what those unspoken words were meant to convey. 'Why should they not run, there and then . . . run from the daunting task ahead of them . . . to be together, forever, in a bid for the happiness that beckoned. And the lugger was waiting for them, then – afloat, and alongside the quay.'

But it was she who had not let it happen; she who had

known, in her girlish wisdom, that he would never forgive himself if he ran away from a challenge of mercy. Oh, but how well she remembered the words she had uttered, 'It would haunt you for the rest of your life.'

And, oh! how she longed now to ask him whether she had been right. Had he ever regretted it; did he even remember it? That, and a thousand other questions were seething in her mind. But again, above all, did that kiss beneath the overhanging branches of the cedar tree in front of the Château Fontanelle, on that still, moonlit night, . . . did it mean anything to him, and did he still love her, as she had once thought he did?

Now, it seemed, was the moment – the awesome moment so fraught with the portents of destiny that she could hardly bring herself to face it – now was the moment when she could discover the truth.

Although he had seemed so overjoyed at that first moment of reunion, beneath the forbidding wall of the Château de Pontrechat – there, in the pale moonlight yet again – since then, even though the time had been short, he seemed to have cooled . . . become distant . . . it was hard to say exactly what it was. But her instinct told her there had been a subtle change. Was that first moment of ecstasy . . . when he had caught her as she slipped from the top of the wall, held her in his arms in such apparently delirious joy . . . was that really only *her* feeling for him? Was his own reaction merely one of relief – delight, even – that an extremely difficult task had been successfully accomplished? Was there really no love for her enshrined in his response?

She had to know. Whatever the truth, emotionally catastrophic or transcendentally joyous, she had to know. After all those nights and days in captivity, dreaming of this moment – she had to know.

Steeling herself to the shattering effect of disappointment – the awfulness of an unconvincing expression of love – she was about to ask the question when the sound of a shot, followed by a heart-rending groan, pierced the stillness of the cave.

270

'Armand!' she breathed, in horror. 'Dear God, let it not be Armand!'

She rushed to the cave entrance, and was about to peer out, when Ashley gripped her arm. 'No!' he commanded tersely. 'We can't have you shot as well.'

'But if it's Armand,' she blurted, 'I must go to him!'

She struggled to free herself from his grip. But he would not let her go. 'Not you!' he ordered. 'I'll be the one to do that.'

Keeping her firmly behind him, Ashley gingerly put his head around the edge of the boulder guarding the entrance to the cave. He peered into the semi-darkness. A hunched figure was staggering towards him, clutching his left shoulder. In the distance, a soldier stood watching, a curl of smoke rising from the barrel of his musket. It was obvious that the lurching figure was Armand, and that he was badly hurt. It was also obvious that the soldier was watching where he went, and that he meant to follow him.

Moving back inside the cave, Ashley responded to Rose's anxious enquiry with a nod of his head. 'Yes,' he said, quietly, 'it's Armand . . . and the lad's badly hurt.'

'How badly?' Rose asked, with a sharp intake of breath. 'How serious is it?'

'We shall very soon find out,' Ashley grunted, and scarcely had he spoken than the youth half-staggered, half-crawled through the entrance to the cave.

Rose received him into her arms. Together with Ashley, she carried Armand to the smooth ledge at the rear of the cave; laid him down gently; and while Rose examined the wound, Ashley returned to the mouth of the cave. From long experience of the countryside, he knew that a wounded animal will often lead the hunter to his lair.

He quietly drew his cutlass; stood ready.

* * *

Corporal Legrand pursed his lips. He felt comfortably sure

that the phantom figure he had just winged with his musket shot was one of the two accomplices escaping with the female he was after. He had but to allow his wounded quarry enough time to return to its hiding place . . . and then he would go in and capture the governor's 'poule'. He would march her back to the château, and rightfully claim the reward. He could almost hear the five louis d'or jingling in his pocket!

Reloading as he went, he stealthily made his way between the darkened trunks of the trees until he came to the rocky cliff bordering the river. He must not let the quarry know it was being followed. On the other hand he could not afford to dawdle. The sight of a wounded companion might flush the girl from her hiding place, and give her the chance to escape once more.

Clambering over the rockstrewn foreshore, Corporal Legrand was just in time to see the hunched figure stagger through the opening to the cave.

Cocking his reloaded musket, the corporal warily approached the cave entrance, at the same time loudly demanding that the fugitives give themselves up.

Nothing happened. He went a little closer; repeated the demand.

Again, nothing happened – no sound, no reappearance. Corporal Legrand went right up to the entrance; projected his bayonet-fixed musket through the aperture, once more demanding that the fugitives surrender.

Still no response; no sound other than an intermittent, half-stifled groan.

The corporal felt those precious louis d'or slipping through his fingers. He felt sure the girl was in there. There was no alternative; he must enter the cave and capture her, no matter what the risk.

Gingerly he moved forward. At first, the blackness inside was complete. But when his eyes became accustomed to the dark, he saw the figure of a youth lying on a ledge at the back of the cave. A young girl was cradling his head in her lap. No one else was visible. It was the girl he was after;

never mind about the youth. He could die where he lay, for all Corporal Legrand cared. He just wanted the girl – and the five louis d'or.

He took another step forward into the cave.

Ashley – standing in the deep shadow of the rock – was ready for him.

CHAPTER NINETEEN

Valete! et Salvete!

'Unless I'm very much mistaken,' Ashley panted, carrying the steadily weakening Armand in his arms, 'there's a cottage in a clearing not far from here where we may be able to get help.'

'How do you know that?' Rose asked, hurrying barefoot at his side.

'François showed it to me. It's not far from where we anchored the lugger.'

'Who is François?'

'He's the émigré Frenchman who came with me . . . knows the navigation into Brest – devilishly treacherous approach,' Ashley informed, struggling up a particularly steep incline thickly planted with spruce. 'Can't explain now . . . tell you the details later.'

Clearly, it was not the time for lengthy explanations, and although Rose was curious to know who this François was and how he had come into the picture, she wisely kept silent.

The long weeks and months of imprisonment and privation had rendered her an easy target for the spear-thrusts of emotion, and now, as she looked up at Ashley's profile, clean-cut against the shafts of moonlight filtering through the trees, her eyes filled with tears. Not only had he crossed the Channel to rescue her, risking life and limb in the treacherous waters of the Rade of Brest, but he was now showing a degree of tenderness and concern of which she had never believed him capable.

But it was not for her. It was for the injured Armand. He was carrying him as though he were a baby, and once again she was seeing a side of Ashley's nature she had never suspected. It was like the broken-down-cart incident of long ago; but it was different. Then his concern had been for her. Now it was for Armand . . . and it was hurtful.

'Can't I help in some way?' she asked at length, wishing to relieve him of at least some of the burden. 'Could we not carry him between us?'

'No, no,' he grunted. 'Better not move him unnecessarily. Might make him worse.'

'But he's heavy,' she persisted. 'He must be! Do let me help.'

He snorted. 'Not exactly a lightweight, I must admit. Not like a sack of corn you can swing over your shoulder.'

There was no warmth in his voice; no companionship of endeavour. He was evading her. She knew not why. He had given himself a difficult task to perform, she felt – and he would carry it through to the bitter end. But he was not the Ashley she had once known – or thought she had.

And then she chided herself. This was an emergency; it was no time for sentimentality. They still had a long way to go before they could feel free to indulge in romantic recollection.

In silence he continued to pick his way carefully between the trees, peering into the semi-darkness, while Rose, following closely behind, tried hard to minimize the painful pricking of pine needles in her bare feet.

Presently, they came to a convenient tree stump on which Ashley could rest for a moment to regain his breath.

'It should be somewhere about here,' he said at last, his shoulders heaving as he swallowed great lungfuls of the clean night air. 'But in this light, and with every damned tree looking exactly like another, it's the devil's own job to recognize anything.'

He shifted his position to achieve greater comfort, but he still cradled Armand gently in his arms.

'What exactly are we looking for?' Rose asked eventually. 'Is it a genuine cottage, or is it just a woodman's hut?'

'Something halfway between the two, I should imagine,'

275

Ashley replied. 'It's a "Chouan" cottage, so François says.'

'And what might that be?'

'The Chouans . . . they're disaffected peasants. They hate the present revolutionary regime, especially what's being done to their churches and their priests. They're a kind of peasant army, living in cottages or hovels, but ready to rise in revolt at a moment's notice, at the command of their leaders.'

'And how do you know all this?' Rose asked, genuinely impressed.

'François,' Ashley answered. 'He told me before we left, and also in the lugger on the way over.'

'And where is this François now?'

'At the cottage we're trying to find, I sincerely hope,' Ashley informed her. 'His job is to alert the Chouans in advance of the forthcoming invasion.'

'Invasion!' Rose queried. 'What . . .' then she checked herself. It was on the tip of her tongue to ask further questions. Again, she wanted to know about this man, François – how had Ashley met him, how was he connected with these 'Chouans', what was this talk of an invasion! – but she realized with increasing alarm that Armand was getting weaker by the moment, and further questioning would only impede their progress. The sooner they found this 'Chouan' hiding place, the better – although she wondered just what kind of assistance could be expected from such primitive folk. But, if nothing else, it would at least provide a refuge from the still pursuing soldiery from the Château de Pontrechat, and it would give her a chance to dress poor Armand's wound.

Besides, Ashley was now ready to move on.

So, curbing her curiosity for the time being, and taking Armand's hand in hers to give such encouragment as she could, she walked briskly beside Ashley through the densely planted wood.

At last they came to the clearing Ashley was seeking. In size no more than a couple of acres, it was enclosed by a low stone wall painstakingly built by successive occupiers over the years, Rose guessed, with stone carried from a nearby quarry, and in the centre of one wall a single opening – or gateway – was guarded by a long, slim tree trunk pivoting on a granite upright. This pole extended some distance beyond the post, to act as a counterpoise and thereby facilitate its lifting.

On the far side of the cultivated field could be seen a cottage – if such it could be called. In a flash of nostalgic memory, Rose could not help but compare it with some of the more primitive Cornish cottages which she knew so well. It was low, thatch-roofed, and its walls appeared to be of cob. But unlike Cornish cottages, even of the meanest kind, it had no windows – at least, none that were readily visible. True, there was a stable-type door which, when opened at the top half, would let in light during the day time, but now, in the darkness, it was tightly shut.

Approaching with caution, and with Ashley carrying Armand at her side, Rose knocked on the door. The top half opened a fraction – just enough for the inmate to see out without himself being seen.

'Pardon, monsieur,' Rose began urgently. 'C'est une crise serieuse . . . une urgence! Ouvrez, s'il vous plaît.'

Slowly, suspiciously, the door was opened wider – to reveal one of the strangest-looking creatures Rose had ever seen. Right up to his neck the man appeared to be dressed in goatskin, and his hair was so thick and so matted together that it was almost impossible to distinguish hair from goatskin. In the pale moonlight, all that could be seen was a pair of human eyes gleaming through the twisted strands of matted hair.

Even as the door was opened, a most over-powering smell of ordure greeted Rose's sensitive nostrils. Normally, such a foul stench would have made her quite ill, but having spent so long in the virtually airless dungeon of the Château de Pontrechat it seemed no more than a prolongation of her ordeal.

Stepping up to the half-opened door, Ashley indicated the stricken Armand, and then demanded, 'Est-ce-que Monsieur de Villecourt ici?'

Before the goatskin had time to reply, another figure appeared in the doorway, dressed in the aristocratic fashion of the day. 'Ah, it is my friend, Monsieur Penberth. I am so glad you find me, yes,' he greeted cheerfully. But then, seeing the crumpled figure in Ashley's arms, he exclaimed, 'Ah, parbleu! but what 'ave we 'ere!' and turning to the goatskinned figure stolidly holding the door, he said something to the peasant, unintelligible to Rose but which apparently satisfied the man that the visitors were in no way connected with the republican government. Only then was the lower half of the door swung open to allow Ashley and Rose to enter.

After very cursorily introducing François to Rose, Ashley then gently laid Armand down on a roughly constructed wooden bedstead bearing a straw-filled palliasse. At once Rose was kneeling beside the mute, holding his hand, soothing his brow.

Never before had she felt so helpless. The bullet had pierced the youth's chest, and even now he was having the greatest difficulty in breathing. 'Holy Virgin!' she entreated under her breath, 'but let the boy not suffer unto death in this foul-smelling hovel.'

When they entered at first, the room was lit only by a single pitch candle no larger than a man's little finger, but as Rose sought to minister to the rapidly sinking Armand she became aware that a second candle had been lit by a woman dressed similarly to the man. In fact, they looked so much alike that from their dress alone it was difficult to tell them apart. Surprisingly, however, it was the woman who carried a gun. She stood, staring down at the youth lying limply on the bed. She made no attempt to be of any assistance. The hard life she was forced to live, Rose concluded, had driven all sense of compassion from her.

Armand, gazing adoringly up at Rose, weakly indicated his desire for a drink and, searching the room for any evidence of a suppy of fresh water, Rose spotted in a dark corner an enormous cider cask. On a table beside it stood an earthenware jug. Cider would be better than nothing, but her unspoken request to the woman received no response whatever. However, not waiting to be asked, the man introduced as 'François' immediately stepped forward and without seeking the owner's approval, filled the jug from the cask and handed it to Rose. Gently she put it to Armand's lips.

For a while, the strong rough cider seemed to revive him, and he was able to smile his gratitude and even attempt to make a little joke about the helplessness of his condition. All the while, Rose continued tenderly to stroke his forehead and to convey to him in the wordless language they had developed between them that no matter what might be the outcome of the situation, she would never desert him.

But within her she felt an unsuppressible sense of foreboding. The youth clearly needed expert medical attention. But what chance was there in this hovel, isolated as it was in the midst of dense woodland, and with angry guardsmen eager to recapture the escaping fugitives – what chance could there possibly be of obtaining the services of a 'médecin'.

She glanced imploringly up at Ashley.

He, standing beside her and gazing sadly down at the now almost lifeless figure of Armand, was remembering how Madame de Levoisier had bravely agreed to extract, if she could, the bullet lodged in his thigh during the rescue from the Château Fontanelle. With exemplary courage – and armed only with a fearsome-looking marlin spike – she had gone to work. And she had succeeded. Even now he could remember his relief when, heavily cognac-drugged though he was, he heard the 'plop' of the bullet as it dropped into the sailcloth beneath his prostrate body. Ought he not now to be willing to try, at least, to do the same for Armand.

He knelt down beside Rose; gently lifted the ragged shirt which covered the top half of Armand's body. The rough, course material was already stuck fast with congealed blood to the skin immediately around the bullet hole.

'Water!' he snapped, half-turning his head. 'Apportez-moi de l'eau . . . un peu chaud. Vite!'

279

The demand was immediately confirmed and repeated by François who, quite inexplicably to Rose, addressed the Chouan as 'Beau-Nez'. The stocky, goatskin-clad peasant then relayed the request to his woman who reluctantly laid aside her gun and disappeared into what Rose concluded must do duty as a kitchen or wash-house.

While they waited, Ashley drumming his fingers impatiently on one knee, Rose glanced round the room. In one wall there was what appeared to be a window. But it was no ordinary window. Instead of the usual glass, the panes resembled the bottoms of bottles, broken off and held in position by heavy strips of lead which were so thick that they would do more to restrict the light than to admit it. In front of this window was a long wooden table bearing a few rudimentary cooking utensils. A rough-hewn bench ran along one side of it. Beyond the table, in the darkest corner of the room, stood the enormous cask of cider. Whatever else might be lacking in this humblest of hovels, there was evidently no shortage of alcoholic liquour.

In another corner of the room she could just discern a spinning-wheel, some primitive chairs, a carved chest, and a roughly made child's cradle.

Every Christmas, ever since she could remember, Rose had assisted in the creation and furnishing of a 'Nativity' tableau in her own village church of St Keverne, and now, in the mean surroundings of this hovel, illuminated only by the violet-coloured light of the pitch candles and with the sound as well as the smell of animals so close at hand, she was reminded of 'the stable at the inn' where the infant Jesus was born. And the image was conjured even more strongly by the sight of a small statuette of the Blessed Virgin Mary supported by a shelf above the wooden plaque bearing the inscription:

> 'Je suis la Mère de Dieu,
> Protectrice de ce lieu.'

Even in this simple dwelling, the Mother of God was not forgotten.

As soon as the Chouan wife reappeared bearing a crock

of warmed water, Ashley began soaking the rough cloth of Armand's shirt away from his chest and bathing the wound. The bullet had penetrated deeply, almost certainly puncturing a lung. Even were it advisable to do so, to extract the leaden ball from the youth's chest would require the skilled hands of a practised surgeon. To remove a bullet from the fleshy tissues of the thigh was one thing; it was within the competence of the unskilled, as Madame de Levoisier had so courageously demonstrated; to take it out from the delicate area of heart and lungs was quite another.

With a deep sigh of distress, Ashley looked at Rose. He sadly shook his head. She understood.

She was looking attentively at Armand. Already he was showing alarming signs of extreme shortness of breath. He was also weakly making signs with one hand – holding his nose, then pointing to the door through which he had been carried.

'He wants to be taken outside,' Rose said quickly. 'Out into the fresh air – away from the smell. He loves the fresh air.'

Once again Ashley picked the mute up in his arms; carried him out into the night.

Some distance from the hovel, beneath the towering pine trees and with the soft moonlight casting shadows on the peaty ground around her, Rose knelt down and received the limp body of Armand into her lap.

For a long time they remained quietly together in that position, Rose gently rocking to and fro while tenderly stroking Armand's cheek . . . until at last, and with an expression of complete calmness and contentment on his simple face, he smiled up at her once more . . . before the life slowly ebbed from his body.

Armand Lecroix, unwanted at birth, reviled and pilloried throughout his young life, had found in Rose . . . and in death . . . the sweetness and the love for which he had always longed.

* * *

They buried him reverently in a corner of the clearing around the Chouan dwelling. 'Beau-Nez', at François de Villecourt's request, supplied the spade. He also cut a rough wooden cross from a fallen pine tree.

And as they lowered the shrouded figure into the grave, Rose remembered the legend of le Folgoët – and how the imbecile, Salaün, in death had spoken to the world. She did not think any such legend would grow up around the mute, Armand Lecroix, but she made a solemn vow to herself that whatever might befall her in the years ahead, one day, somehow, she would return to lay a wreath on Armand's grave.

After they had completed the burial – and at Ashley's suggestion – François de Villecourt, 'Beau-Nez' and his family, and Ashley himself, withdrew to a respectful distance, leaving Rose alone at the side of the grave.

As she prayed, brushing away tears at the memory of Armand in life – of his cheerful optimism, of his willingness to take risks in order to supplement her uneatable dungeon food, and of his impish delight in arranging her eventual escape – she also rejoiced at the thought that he was now free at last from the hurts and the frustrations of his crushing disability; free from the restricting infirmities of earthly life; free of the crippling load that bound him in a world of silence and disappointment; free to laugh and to sing, and to express his feelings and his love.

Thus she could think of him – and through her sadness she could even find room to rejoice.

A light touch on her shoulder brought her back to reality. Ashley had rejoined her; was standing at her side.

'It's time to go,' he said quietly, his voice deep with sympathy and understanding. 'We can't afford to delay any longer. The tide'll be right, and we must take advantage of it to get away. We must hurry.'

He helped her to her feet, and taking her arm he led her away from the rough grave, back to where François and the Chouans were waiting.

In the shafting moonlight François bade farewell to 'Beau-Nez' and his woman, and after issuing last minute instructions to the goatskin-clad peasant – none of which were intelligible to Rose – he turned to Ashley, saying:

'And now, mon ami, we must find your lugger, set you and your charming lady on board, and then I shall bid you "bon voyage" back to your 'omeland. We shall meet again some day, I 'ope – after we 'ave driven these accursed republicans out of France and into the sea, yes!'

Ashley nodded vigorously. 'I sincerely hope we shall meet again,' he agreed, 'and once more I must thank you, François, for all your help.'

The gaily dressed Frenchman dismissed it with a wave of his hand. 'It was nothing, m'sieur. Nothing. Indeed, I am greatly indebted to *you* for providing me with the chance to get back into France. And now that I am back on French soil, nothing and no one shall dislodge me until we 'ave a glorious royalist victory and our boy-king is once more restored to 'is throne.'

'I sincerely hope that you are successful,' Ashley affirmed, 'and that . . .'

'Oh, we *shall* be successful,' François interposed. 'Always provided that your government agrees to help us.'

'Whether they will or not,' Ashley said, shaking his head doubtfully, 'it doesn't alter the fact that I shall always be grateful to you for navigating me through the Rade.'

François threw back his head and laughed. 'So you think you would have gone on the rocks of the Pointe de St Mathieu, ha!'

'I'd have avoided *them* all right,' Ashley grinned, 'but it was as we got closer to Brest that I might have been in trouble.'

'And now you have the problem of getting out again,' François reminded wickedly. 'But never fear; you will succeed. You English! Your food is terrible and your wine does not even exist, but you make wonderful sailors.' He sighed deeply. 'I only wish we 'ad a navy like yours,' he added with an expressive shrug, 'but perhaps your good Mister Pitt will allow us to borrow your navy – just for a little while, yes.'

Even in the half darkness, Rose could see his eyes twinkling mischievously.

'But we must not stand 'ere talking like this,' he went on. 'We must find your beautiful lugger, the " 'Etherbelle le seconde" yes, and then we must send you on your way back to England. Follow me.'

He set off at a brisk pace, threading his way confidently through the trees. Rose felt the excitement of the moment mounting within her. They were going HOME! In a few minutes, they would come to the edge of the river and there, gently swinging on her anchor, would be Ashley's lugger, 'Heatherbelle II'. Once aboard her, and then when they had negotiated the currents and the rocks of the treacherous Rade de Brest – they would be on their way HOME! Oh, heavenly thought! Glorious prospect! HOME!

For the moment, all the horrors and privations of the immediate past seemed to be slipping from her; all the disgusting food, the feeling of perpetual tiredness and under-nourishment were as nothing by comparison with the realization that at last she was going HOME! Unbelievable! But she found the strength to race along beside Ashley as, together, they followed François down to the River Elorn.

But as they emerged from the dense woodland and stepped out on to a grassy bank at the water's edge, she heard François exclaim exasperatedly, 'Ah, Mon Dieu! Mais non! Non! C'est impossible! C'est TERRIBLE!'

Ashley's head shot up; followed the direction of François' pointing arm.

The lugger had gone.

CHAPTER TWENTY

The die is cast

William Pitt, hands clasped behind immaculately tailored black silk tail-coat, stared unseeingly from a window overlooking Downing Street.

One foot was badly swollen and throbbing painfully; he knew exactly why.

Delicate from birth, educated by a private tutor to save him from the rigours of boarding school, he had been encouraged as a young man to take a glass of port each day to improve his health. He had got to like it; it had become a habit. And now he could not do without it. It helped him to relax.

And at the moment – as at nearly every moment of his comparatively young life – he had momentous matters on his mind.

Like this invasion of Western France, for instance. For so long he had resisted the urgings of those around him, especially those with strong royalist sympathies, to avenge the murder of the French king, but, almost in isolation, he had stood out against becoming embroiled in any conflict with France. But then France had declared war on England – and now there was this groundswell of opinion urging him to support a landing of émigrés on French soil to join forces with Chouans and Vendéeans who were, it was said, just waiting to rise again in defence of their priests and their churches and their child sovereign.

He had been against the idea at first – but then, at Windham's request, he had granted an interview to Comte Joseph de Puisaye who had been sent over by the Royalist faction in France to plead their case in England. He had promised to raise whole regiments of émigrés from Germany as well as from other parts of Europe. He had been very persuasive.

It might perhaps have been easier to resist de Puisaye's entreaties had he not, at the very end, drawn such a pathetic picture of the ten-year-old dauphin imprisoned by the Republicans and now being cruelly maltreated and starved, with a degree of callousness difficult for any civilized person to comprehend.

A knock on the door interrupted Pitt's musings, and his private secretary put his head round the door.

'The Secretary-at-War, Mr Windham, and the First Lord are below, sir. Shall I show them up.'

Pitt nodded. 'They're expected,' he said curtly.

For several more moments he remained staring out of the window, the shadow of his tall, erect figure casting a strangely elongated shape across the cabinet table.

Only when the door opened again to admit the well-built figure of William Windham, followed by the less athletic presence of the First Lord of the Admiralty, Lord Spencer, did the Prime Minister emerge from his reverie.

'Ah, come in, my dear Windham,' he welcomed, in a voice deprived of any personal warmth. 'Good of you to come so promptly. And you, too, George. Good of you to spare the time.' He motioned them to chairs on the opposite side of the table. 'Do please be seated,' he added rather formally.

He waited until both men were comfortably settled, his First Lord dressed similarly to himself but with black silk stockings instead of the white ones worn by the Prime Minister, while William Windham, fully living up to his reputation as 'the finest gentleman of his time', favoured the more colourful dress of the country squire, blue velvet jacket, embroidered waistcoat in dove and gold striped silk, with buff-coloured breeches in superfine cloth.

'You know why I sent for you, I presume,' the Prime Minister began.

Both visitors nodded.

'I felt I needed a brief discussion . . . unrecorded, of course . . .' he went on, 'before coming to a final decision.' He paused, regarding his Ministerial colleagues with that cold stare which inevitably seemed to distance them from him.

'It's about this Frenchman, de Puisaye,' he continued. 'A very persuasive fellow. He's almost convinced me that we should support his invasion proposals. He wants us to escort an army of something like twenty thousand émigrés and land them on the west coast of Brittany.'

'As you know, Prime Minister, I think we should assist,' Windham affirmed. 'My reports from Wickham in Switzerland are most encouraging.'

'In what way, particularly?' the First Lord asked.

'Tremendous enthusiasm in Geneva and in some of the main cities of Germany,' Windham informed.

The First Lord's eyebrows shot up. 'As far afield as that, eh?'

'Oh, yes,' Windham nodded. 'The "royals" are in exile all over Europe, and they're just burning to re-establish the "ancien régime".'

Pitt shook his head. 'That's what I don't like about it. There was much that was evil in their former system.'

'But it's really high time an end was brought to the atrocities over there,' Windham asserted strongly, 'and they're slowly killing that poor little boy . . .'

Pitt frowned deeply. Windham had touched him on a sensitive spot. He had no family of his own but he was absurdly fond of children; he loved romping with them; he couldn't bear to think of them being ill-treated.

For several moments he said nothing, head held erect, staring above the heads of his Ministers as if in a trance. Then, as though some trigger in his mental process had been pulled, he got to his feet and began pacing the dark green carpet of the cabinet room.

'And what is your opinion, George?' he suddenly shot at the First Lord. 'What do you advise?'

'The Royal Navy will respond in whatever manner is

required of it,' the First Lord replied unhelpfully, adding rather irritatingly, 'as, indeed, it always does.'

'Yes, yes, I'm sure it will,' Pitt snapped, with only thinly veiled asperity. He sat down again and began drumming the highly polished table with his fingers. 'I take it,' he said at length, looking severely first at one visitor then the other, 'that you have discussed the project and all its possible hazards very fully?'

'Oh, indeed, Prime Minister,' Windham assured with his usual breezy confidence, 'and I've kept in touch with de Puisaye and also d'Hervilly.'

'D'Hervilly?' Pitt queried. 'And what part will he play?'

'He'll command the troops until they land,' Windham informed. 'But then de Puisaye will take over as commander-in-chief – together with Sombreuil who'll join forces with him after the landing.'

Pitt frowned again. 'I don't care for the sound of that,' he said. 'Divided command. Spells trouble to me.'

Windham shrugged. 'Hardly our responsibility, I would aver, Prime Minister. Our task will be to get the army over there, and then let 'em get on with it, themselves.'

'And isn't there also the question of transportation of weaponry – arms and ammunition for the royalists waiting on French territory and ready to support the invasion?' Pitt queried. He felt out of his depth. He hated war.

'Oh, yes,' Windham confirmed, '. . . and English uniforms, as well.'

The Prime Minister looked up sharply. 'Why English uniforms?'

'Puisaye's special demand,' Windham observed. 'Apparently no Frenchman must return to France wearing a French uniform – to avoid being shot as a traitor, I suppose.'

'I don't like the use of our uniforms for that purpose,' Pitt frowned.

Windham merely shrugged. 'It's one of de Puisaye's requirements,' he said, 'and if we're going into this thing, we'd better let 'em have everything they want.

Otherwise, if anything goes wrong we'll be blamed.'

Pitt drew a deep breath. He had disliked the whole project from the outset, but now he seemed caught up in the tide. Relieved at the opportunity to change the subject slightly, he turned to the First Lord. 'And the ships you have detailed, George?'

'That's all arranged, Prime Minister. I've discussed the matter with the Sea Lords and we've agreed on the following: Three ships of the line, "Thunderer", "Robust" and "Standard", supported by six frigates, "Anson", "Artois", "Arethusa", "Concorde", "Galatea" and "Pomone", plus, of course, the fifty sail of transports to convey the two thousand, five hundred émigrés under de Puisaye's command.'

'And where is it proposed to put the troops ashore?'

The First Lord and the Secretary-at-War exchanged glances. Windham cleared his throat.

'We shall feint to go in on the north coast of Normandy,' he said, '. . . but in fact we shall make the landing at Quiberon. It's there that the Chouans will be waiting.'

Pitt nodded. He knew that, after himself, Windham was easily the most brilliant man in the cabinet. He was content to leave the arrangements in his hands.

'One final question,' he said, fixing the First Lord with a penetrating stare, 'but a vital one, I suggest. Who is to command?'

The First Lord shifted his position; settled himself more comfortably in his chair. He felt he was on familiar territory; he had prepared himself for just such a question.

'We've been considering this at some length,' he said importantly, 'and we've come to the conclusion that by far the best man for the task is John Warren.'

'Do I know him?' Pitt enquired.

'Almost certainly, Prime Minister,' Windham volunteered. 'He has an academic background – a graduate of Emmanuel, I seem to remember, and some years ago he was elected Member for Marlow . . .'

'But more important still,' interposed the First Lord, not

to be deprived of the chance to display his grasp of the situation, 'is the fact that John Warren has an intimate knowledge of the French coast, having served under Macbride in his frigate squadron off Brest, and only recently having been ordered to command a squadron detailed to search for French frigates playing havoc with our trade. In fact, he recently engaged the "Volontaire", near the Penmarch's, and . . .'

'Yes, yes, yes,' interrupted Pitt, 'I remember the success quite clearly.'

He drew a deep breath once more, rose from his chair and stalked to the window.

'That's settled then,' he said without turning to address his colleagues. 'Our part in the invasion goes ahead. Thank you for your attendance gentlemen – and now,' he added, swivelling round on one heel, 'I will bid you "Good-day!" '

A smile of satisfaction flickered across Windham's features, as he preceded the First Lord to the door.

The die was cast. The invasion of France would take place.

CHAPTER TWENTY-ONE

The Château de Plouvenez

'I'm sorry,' Rose wailed, 'but I can't go another step.' She sank to a smooth granite boulder and examined the soles of her feet. Though hardened by sixteen days of walking barefoot, painful blisters were now making further progress on foot impossible. She could not go on.

In those sixteen days they had covered the one hundred leagues from the bank of the Elorn river. It had been the only sensible thing to do, François had said. The lugger – Ashley's faithful 'Heatherbelle II' – had obviously been stolen. When they had anchored in the river Elorn below the Château de Pontrechat, both Ashley and François knew this was a risk – there are always unseen eyes watching the comings and goings up and down a tidal river, and in wartime, a foreign ship is a legitimate prize – but it was a risk that had to be taken. The lugger had to be left afloat on her anchor, ready to leave at the earliest opportunity. She could not be made any more secure, and at the same time fulfil her purpose of providing a swift evacuation for the fleeing fugitives.

There was nothing for it but to accept the fact that the lugger had been stolen. What then were the alternatives? To search for the boat and repossess her? But where to start looking? She could have gone either way – upstream to Landerneau or, more likely, downstream to be lost among the countless number of vessels in harbour at Brest. And in any case, as François pointed out, they were all three of them enemies of the Republic – Ashley and Rose because they were citizens of a country at war and therefore probably spies, and François because he was an émigré returning to his native land and, as such, a person most hated by the Convention. All three, if captured, would swiftly perish beneath the blade of Robespierre's guillotine.

So, their first task must be, at all costs, to avoid capture. Secondly, they must find some means by which Ashley and Rose could get back to England.

As usual, François declared that he had the answer. Before leaving London, he had received secret information, as a friend and confidant of those in the highest circles, that although all the talk was of an invasion somewhere along the Normandy coast to link up with Chouans' strongholds around Fougères and Mayenac, the landing was in fact going to be made at Quiberon. He, François de Villecourt, was to go ahead and arouse the Breton Chouans in the Montagnes Noires, around Gourin, and farther south in the woodlands around Rosporden and Hennebont. After that he would join up with his friend and great Chouan leader Georges Cadoudal at his family home, the Manoir de Kerleano near Auray.

This would be very good, François had exclaimed, because at Auray he would be very close to his own ancestral home the Château de Plouvenez which, if it had not already been burned to the ground by the revolutionaries, over-looked the approaches to Quiberon Bay. And there, he felt confident, he would be able to find accommodation at the castle of his 'grand-mère' for his new English friends.

'That's as maybe,' Rose had said doubtfully, 'but how far is that from here, how are we going to get there, and what assurance is there that when we do arrive without being captured, there will be some means available for Ashley and me to get back to our homeland?'

François had clapped his hands with delight. 'Ah, mamselle is rich,' he had laughed, ' "tout de richesses". She ask so many questions at once!'

'But all very sensible ones,' Ashley interpolated.

'Yes, yes, yes, very sensible as you say. And I will answer them one by one. Firstly, how far is it? Well, it depends.

I must visit the Chouans, you understand, and that will mean a little "detour" – but it will provide us with shelter if we need it – if you could call a Chouan 'ovel a "shelter",' he grimaced, holding his nose, 'but it could be better than sleeping out in the pouring rain, yes.'

After her recent experience of a Chouan hovel, Rose wondered.

'Secondly,' François continued, 'we shall travel by whatever means is available – sometime, we travel on a cart, yes; sometime we ride on a 'orse or a donkey – but most of all, I think we walk,' he concluded.

'How far?' Rose had repeated.

'Aw, er – maybe a 'undred leagues – maybe more, maybe less – but we will get there in the end.'

'And then what?'

'Then we wait for the most beautiful sight in the world, yes – the sight of the ships of your Royal Navy sailing into Quiberon Bay. It will mean salvation for us Frenchmen – and it will mean that two English fugitives from the wicked revolutionaries will be taken 'ome by a fast-sailing frigate, I suggest, to your beloved 'omeland.'

It had all sounded so straightforward. A mere hundred leagues or so, taken by easy stages – say seven or eight leagues a day – would take them not much more than a fortnight, Rose had reflected. And did that matter? Did anything matter – so long as she was with Ashley!

But he was still behaving strangely. Gone now was that feeling of companionship – of nearness to each other – which had prevailed so excitingly during their former relationship – especially during the rescue attempt from the Château Fontanelle – which had seemed to be moving inescapably towards a lasting relationship.

Now, he was distrait – close to her in physical presence yet somehow withdrawn. Perhaps it was because he needed to concentrate on the daunting task of getting them both back to Cornwall – to Treworden, to his mother and to Zeph Curnow – to St Keverne and to her loving parents at Thorn Cottage. Perhaps that was it. And what about the

MacKenzie family at Trevadne – that other daughter, the dark-haired vivacious one, with the voluptuous figure and inviting eyes – the one she had seen dancing with Ashley at the Lanteague Ball – whenever he wasn't dancing with the beautiful Alethea. What about her? Had she married that handsome, languid-looking dragoon officer who had turned up just in time to take all the credit after Ashley had fought so bravely with the wreckers at Porthleven – and who, Ashley had told her, had been at school with him?

She longed to ask – and yet his distant manner and the fact that they were on the run from hostile republicans, had prevented her from satisfying her curiosity. She would just have to wait. Perhaps when they reached their destination – whatever that might bring – she would feel able to ask him.

But, 'Not another step,' she now repeated, ruefully rubbing the soles of her blistered feet. 'We shall just have to stop here until my feet are less painful.'

'Poor mamselle,' François consoled, 'and you 'ave been going so bravely. What a shame. You shall rest 'ere and then in a little while you shall see the château where I was born – and that,' he went on with a wicked twinkle in his eye, 'is sure to make you feel so 'appy, yes.'

She was glad he thought she had gone 'bravely' – because she *had* tried. It had not been easy. Since leaving the banks of the Elorn river and the ugly shadows of imprisonment in the Château de Pontrechat, they had travelled to Landerneau on foot where they had entered the busy market town in broad daylight. Both Ashley and François were dressed in respectable clothing – Ashley in a sailing smock of brown canvas over an old pair of red cloth breeches and grey woollen stockings and short boots. François, more fashionable, in cinnamon coat, red waistcoat and yellow trousers, contrasted strangely with the rags covering Rose.

As they walked through the crowded market-street alongside the river – reminding Rose so poignantly of her earlier journey through the town seated beside the Jesuit priest, Père Lemaître – she was astonished to see François boldly walk up to a stall bearing various articles of feminine attire and proceed to select first a chemise, then a plain blue woollen dress, a checked apron, and a pair of grey woollen stockings and pay for them from what appeared to be a goodly supply of money. From then on, at a cobbler's stall, he told Rose to try on a pair of strong, but roughly made leather shoes. Unwisely, Rose had indicated a satisfactory fit – she genuinely thought so at the time – but it was a decision she regretted later; after the first few leagues her feet were so sore that she decided to do without shoes altogether.

At another stall, François bought enough food and fruit to last them for at least two days and then, realizing that their presence in the town was causing more interest than he deemed healthy, they set out along the road to Daoulas, guided by the tall spire of Dirinon church. Upon reaching the bank of the Daoulas river, Rose ordered the two men to take themselves off to a discreet distance while she, armed with the bundle of clothes bought for her at Landerneau, ran down to the water's edge and, with a cry of delight, threw off her rags and plunged into the water. All the recent traumas, the filth of the dungeon, the disgusting proximity of the vermin, the probing indecencies of Monsieur Bousillier seemed to slough from her as the chill water cascaded over her body. She gloried in the sensation of once again feeling cleansed. Although she had nothing with which to dry herself – her rags had been cast from her for ever – the steady breeze rippling over the soft contours of her naked body, and the pale sunshine on her back soon enabled her to cover herself with the newly acquired clothes. They did not fit, they were far removed from anything resembling current fashion – but they made her feel like a princess. She could now face whatever further privations might be ahead.

By the time she returned to her waiting companions, François had persuaded a Breton peasant returning from the market with his mule cart to give them a lift as far as Châteaulin, and from then onwards Rose was to experience the hospitality of the Chouans.

'Why are they called "Chouan"?' she had asked.

'Because they are named after the dashing Jean Cottereau,' she had been told.

'What is the connection between Chouan and Cottereau?'

'The word "Chouan" is a corruption of the word "Chat-huant" which means screech-owl. It is the call by which the Chouans recognize each other in the dark.' She had to be content with that.

They walked on, through the fading light into the forest of the Duke near Locronan, and once more a mean hovel lay before them.

Benjamin Filleuil, otherwise known as 'Le Chat' for the stealth of his movements, was dressed as had been 'Beau-Nez'. The very sight of his goatskin jacket and coarse white trousers brought back the painful memory of Armand's last hour. But 'Le Chat' was a little more civilized than had been 'Beau-Nez'. At least he was able to offer Rose a rough wooden bed to sleep on. If the food was limited in variety, it was at least plentiful in quantity – large earthenware bowls filled with a kind of soup made of goat's milk, coarse bread cut into small pieces and boiled chestnuts.

But yet again the smell of the hovel was overpowering. As in 'Beau-Nez's' hut, the wall dividing the living room and the animal byre was so thin that a part of it had been kicked in by the flying hoof of an animal, thus allowing the alkaline vapour of the excreta uninterrupted access to the living quarters.

But Rose felt so hungry that even this overpowering smell could not keep her from the appetizing bowl of food. She would need every ounce of nourishment to sustain her on the journey ahead.

And so they had travelled – from Landerneau to their present situation just south of the river Etel.

'I'm sorry,' Rose reiterated, 'but if you want me to go any further you'll have to carry me.'

And this is what they did. Between them Ashley and François carried her a short distance, and there facing them, its facade lit by the brilliant early morning sunshine, stood the Château de Plouvenez. 'Ah, pardieu!'

'C'est merveilleux, n'est pas? And it has not been burnt down by the rabble!'

They put Rose down and once again she sank to an elongated piece of granite, of which there seemed an abundance. Ashley rather thankfully also sank down beside her. But François was far too excited to rest.

'Now,' he said, as though issuing a battle command. 'You will both remain 'ere while I go to see my "grand-mère" at the château. But I do not leave you – I only go to prepare a place for you – not a heavenly place I'm afraid,' he laughed, 'but at least somewhere to lay your weary 'eads. I go – but then, in a little while, I come back.'

He hurried away in the direction of the château, leaving Rose and Ashley alone together for the first time since, many months ago, he had held her in his arms with such passionate fervour just before they had made their successful assault on the Château Fontanelle.

For them both, but for Ashley in particular, the moment of truth had arrived.

*　　*　　*

Rose got up from the stone and, despite the pain in the soles of her feet, she walked away and then stood with her back to him.

Try as she would, she could not hold back the tears. She did not want to break down in his presence – but she could not control her shaking shoulders.

When he had begun with 'There's something I've got to tell you, Rosie . . . something I ought to have told you sooner . . .' she knew then what was coming.

She had half expected it – had been half afraid of it – but when the words finally came 'And so I married Jeannie . . .' they burnt into her heart with the pain of a branding iron.

'And so I married Jeannie . . .'

Well, at least he had been honest with her. He could have kept it a dark secret until they returned to England. He could have done that — but he hadn't. He'd been honest with her and at the earliest convenient, if not the earliest possible, moment.

But did he love this Jeannie? She supposed he must — otherwise he would never have married her. But if he *did* love her, why had he come back to fetch the girl he could so easily have forgotten! Conscience, perhaps. Was that it? Nothing but a pricking conscience. No rest until he had assuaged that uncomfortable feeling that he had left her in the hands of the revolutionaries, to rot in a rat-infested dungeon. Was that it?

She was thankful that he had not come after her — tried to comfort her, tried to explain. That would have been *unbearable*.

She walked away yet further — sat down on a boulder, hugged herself — wrapped in the misery of this disclosure. The future which had once seemed so bright — the sun-streaked prospect which had sustained her through those long hours of darkness and solitude in dungeon filth — the very chalice of hope had been cruelly dashed from her lips.

How could she contemplate the future; there could be no future with *him*. Eventually, they would return to Cornwall, she supposed, where he would pick up the threads of his life with *her* — the wealthy, high-born MacKenzie girl — and what would there be left for the former barmaid of The Three Tuns Inn? A life lived out, pouring pints, until marriage to a lusty yokel carried her off to the hard grind of a kitchen stove and a granite sink — while Ashley lived in sumptuous splendour, dancing attendance on a squire's vivacious daughter, his conscience quieted by the knowledge that he had finally rescued the little barmaid with whom he had once dallied.

Was that really Ashley — the true Ashley? Would he lastingly be content with that life?

And was it entirely his fault?

Once again the memory of that rescue from the Château Fontanelle flashed into her mind. Had she not distinctly heard Ashley's voice saying, 'I'm going back for her'? And then Zeph's warning about the falling tide. Ashley's voice again, shouting this time, 'I can't *possibly* leave without Rose!' And then Sir Andrew's voice saying, 'Then we're as good as dead. Caught like rats in a trap.'

She remembered it all so clearly – every word. And those running footsteps – Ashley's! . . . coming back for her! And then that awful shot! Ohh!

Was it really his fault?

Might there not have been pressures – from Sir Andrew, perhaps, lacking an heir himself, wanting a son-in-law he knew and liked; from his mother, even – after all, it would make a good marriage for her son – and, by no means least, from Jeannie MacKenzie herself. Very attractive, very desirable, and used to getting her own way.

Rose remained seated, hugging her shoulders, staring at the peaty ground at her feet.

Although it hurt him to do so, wisely Ashley left her to herself. He could say no more. She must make up her own mind.

Presently, François returned. He had been joyfully re-united with his 'grand-mère', the Comtesse de Villecourt. There had been many changes, she told him, since last he had been at the Château de Plouvenez. Nearly all the servants had either left or been discharged – in these days of revolution-torn France you never knew who to trust. The sequestrators were everywhere; seals had been put on château after château; Ysabeau and Tallien were moving through the country, severing heads and denouncing to the Committee of Public Safety both the innocent as well as the guilty. No one was safe – not even the Mayor of Bordeaux, Monsieur Saige. Even he, with all his wealth and power could not escape the guillotine – and he had been but the first of the municipal authorities to be massacred.

But yes, she would be glad to find a place for her grandson's two English friends – as servants, of course, because as such they would be less likely to attract the attention of the local Commune, who were expected, any day, to come and make an inventory of the château. The

English couple could be lodged above the coach house in the quarters formerly occupied by one of the estate workers and his wife – until the 'invasion' took place, that is. They were married, of course, she had asked – and François, not wishing to jeopardize a favourable situation, had cheerfully said 'Yes'.

Ashley glanced at Rose, but said nothing. She, having rejoined him as soon as François had come back, turned on her heel and stared at the misty outline of Belle-Ile in the distance.

While François waited, wondering whether he had miscalculated their response, Rose suddenly swung round to face him, and looking Ashley squarely in the eyes, she said firmly, 'Yes, that's quite right.'

In those fleeting seconds, as she had stared at the island guarding the entrance to Quiberon Bay, the alternatives had flashed through her mind. To reject the offer would mean that she and Ashley would be forced either to continue to live rough or else – and little improvement on that – to seek shelter with one of the Chouan families in the nearby woods. She decided she had had more than enough of the Chouan existence to last her a lifetime.

So why not? – why not accept the offer? After all, what had she to lose?

'When can we start?' she asked.

*   *   *

That night, after being presented to the comtesse, who reminded Rose of a benign parrot with a small ball of wool beneath its beak, and after having had their duties outlined to them, Rose and Ashley climbed the coach-house stairs to their sparsely furnished bedroom.

After weeks of living rough, in woodlands and in the Chouan hovels, they were both so exhausted that at the sight of the plain wooden bedstead with its feather mattress and its long, bolster-like pillows, neither of them had the energy or the desire to undress. Without a word, they both flopped on

300

to the mattress and within minutes both were sound asleep.

Waking before Ashley next morning, Rose went to the window and looked out. Away to the south and in the distance, she could see the northern tip of Belle-Ile while further to the east, the long, thin strip of the Quiberon Peninsula snaked out into the sea.

On the bed, and still peacefully asleep, lay the man she loved. For the hundredth time she wondered what the future held for them. Was it now complicated beyond recall – now that he was married to Jeannie?

She decided she could not – would not – think about it. They lived in perilous times – they were aliens in a hostile country; if discovered, they would almost certainly be shot as spies or guillotined, without trial. Life was too short to think very deeply. Sufficient unto the day . . .

The second night was a repetition of the first – except that, waking in the early hours of the morning, she felt Ashley's arm fall loosely across her shoulders. She wasn't sure whether he was awake or not. Was this the first move, she wondered. Had he overcome his moral scruples? Did men ever entertain such scruples where women were concerned? From her experiences at the Three Tuns Inn and elsewhere, she thought not.

But she was still very tired – and she moved away. The long months of imprisonment and privation had sapped her vitality – her ardour. For the time being she wanted only sleep – even though, as she looked in the cracked mirror next morning, she noticed that the colour was returning to her cheeks.

It was the following night – the third night of their cohabitation in that plainly furnished servant's bedroom – that, naked, he climbed into the bed beside her and unashamedly drew her to him. Equally unashamedly, she responded by pulling her chemise over her head.

He was gentle with her at the outset, fondling her thighs, her hips and finally her breasts with the utmost tenderness, and caressing her body with his lips. Then, as his mouth found hers in a long, deeply passionate kiss, she felt herself descending, like a leaf in a whirlpool, down to the very depths of an abyss. She felt the force and strength of his manhood searching the cavern of her loins – and then – and then, in a mounting crescendo of breathtaking, palpitating excitement, she finally cried aloud with the pain and the ecstasy. She knew then that he had entered her – and that she was no longer a virgin.

As she lay in his arms in the afterglow – and with a fulfilled and wholly satisfied Ashley asleep on her shoulder – a sadness, a kind of 'tristesse', seemed to wash over her. She wondered why. Was it because she had lost her virginity? Surely not. She had never prized that very highly. Was it because he had made her an adulteress and himself an adulterer? She had felt no shame in the moment of surrender.

Nevertheless, when she arose in the morning and knew that his eyes were upon her, she quickly covered her nakedness. Why did she do that? she wondered. Was she sharing with the first woman the guilt that descended from that tree of knowledge?

But, fortunately, there was no time to linger over such thoughts – there was work to be done; for both of them.

Very easily they had each slipped into the tasks allotted to them. Ashley had found no difficulty in becoming a general handyman-cum-gardener, while Rose had become a maid of all work – helping the ancient family retainer to prepare the meals, washing the priceless china dishes bearing the de Villecourt crest, dusting, polishing and generally trying to maintain the elegance of a past but now rapidly fading glory of the Château de Plouvenez. She learnt how to pile high the comtesse's hair, after the fashion of her late-lamented queen; how to apply the rouge and brilliant polishes to her cheeks and how to lace her into her stiff-bodied gowns.

She even volunteered her skills as a seamstress, and it was while in search of a tailoress' dummy one evening, which the comtesse had informed her was stored in one of the attic rooms, that she made her momentous discovery.

Picking her way carefully from one rejected, dust-laden article of furniture to another she came upon a small pile of gilt-framed pictures. Idle curiosity caused her to turn them over, brushing away the layers of dust and cobwebs just enough to reveal the artist's subject. Some were landscapes; there were a few examples of still-life – and then she came upon a small stack of portraits.

Before she had even removed the obscuring layers of fluff and dust, she felt a premonition gripping her insides. She blew on the canvas – gently at first, then fiercely. She picked up the hem of her dress and rubbed frantically.

She was staring at the haughty, disdainful expression of a French aristocrat. Excitedly, she opened her locket, compared the two, staring from one to the other. The faces were identical!

Then she turned to the next portrait – equally dust-encrusted, equally exciting.

She had found the original portraits of which the miniatures in her locket were replicas.

She stared at them, her pulse racing. But who were they? Something to do with the Château de Plouvenez, some connection of . . . She sat back on her heels. 'But, of *course*!' she almost shouted. 'How could I have been so *stupid*! "L de V" – de Villecourt!'

She rushed downstairs, flung her arms around Ashley, who was cleaning the silver in the pantry, and cried, 'I've found them, Ashley! I've *found* them!'

'Found what, Rosie?' Ashley said, indulgently but without emotion. 'What is it that you've found?'

'My roots! My ancestors,' she gasped excitedly. 'Up there in the attic. I'm sure of it! I've just found these portraits – exactly the same as those in my locket!'

That night in bed, as she melted into his arms to be loved deeply, passionately, fulfillingly, a warm glow of an entirely non-sensual origin enriched the satiety of her body. For the first time ever, she knew where she came from. Tomorrow, she would find out, from the Comtesse de Villecourt, exactly who she was.

But in the morning when she arose, and went to the window, as she always did, she was suddenly arrested in mid-yawn.

'Ashley!' she called excitedly. 'Come here quickly! Look at this!'

He leaped out of bed, joined her at the window – and there, in all its majestic power and glory, was Admiral Warren's British Fleet, anchored in Quiberon Bay.

It was the 26th June 1795. The invasion of Brittany had begun.

CHAPTER TWENTY-TWO

Quiberon

They had stood together at the edge of the beach, Ashley and Rose, watching it all happen.

Having scrambled into their day clothes – and without disturbing the sleeping Comtesse de Villecourt – they had then run to the nearest vantage point, arriving just in time to see the first of the fifty sail of transports coming ashore.

Almost the unbelievable had then occurred.

From sandhills, from woodlands; from sea-girt hovels and from behind great granite dolmens they came – hundreds of them at first, then swelling into thousands – emerging like a sudden eruption of moles from the secrecy of their underground runs, and scampering down onto the beach.

First came the Chouans. As wild as Red Indians, they were; barefoot, and wearing only their goatskin jackets and soiled white breeches, their matted locks covered either by a dirty red woollen cap or a broad brimmed, coarse felt hat. Some were equipped with guns, but those without the luxury of such weapons carried a thick club of gnarled oak on his shoulder – an equally lethal weapon against an unsuspecting adversary caught in a Chouan ambush, Ashley thought.

Yelling with abandon, and shouting their distinguishing screech-owl war cry, 'CHAT-HUANT!', they swarmed onto the sands, embracing and bear-hugging the invading soldiers. Some were their own kith and kin; French prisoners from other theatres of war, dressed in English uniforms, and grateful only for the chance to return to their native land. It mattered not who they were nor where they came from; their purpose was the same; to deliver, first

305

Brittany and the Western Loire, and then the whole of France – eventually to deliver the entire country from the bondage of fear inspired by the merciless revolutionary government.

Then – and perhaps the most affecting sight of all – had come the unarmed peasants; hundreds of them, wave after wave; men, women and children, bringing not only their joy at the prospect of deliverance – young men as well as old could be seen weeping unashamedly as they greeted comrades – but bringing as well all manner of gifts; eggs, butter, bread, milk and wine, and refusing to accept as much as a sou or a penny piece in payment for them.

Tears had streamed down Rose's cheeks also – tears of joy at the sight of such simple, undemanding generosity; tears of deep emotional happiness stirred by the warmth of her new-found sense of oneness with the man she loved.

But her euphoria had been short-lived; for then the shooting had started. From the hills it had come; sporadic only and not in great volume – but it was enough for the Chouans. Ecstatic at the prospect of coming to grips once again with the blue-uniformed republican army, they swiftly grouped around their charismatic leader, Georges Cadoudal – 'Général George', as François had admiringly referred to his friend – and then swept into the hills, silencing the detachment of some two-hundred 'Blues' unwise enough to show themselves to the advance units of the invading army.

So well organized and so forceful had been the Chouan thrust that every enemy post was driven back and, threatened by a gunboat strategically placed to take them in the flank, the republicans had fled in total disorder. Within a matter of hours the Chouans were in possession of the nearby city of Vannes. The goatskinned, matted-haired peasant rebels were soon everywhere, spreading panic within the ramparts of the ancient Breton capital. Even François de Villecourt had felt constrained to admit to Rose and Ashley that, in all truth, the banishment of the princes and the ill-treatment of the priests was, to the Chouans, little more than a pretext for pillage. The law-abiding citizens of Vannes were soon to find that out.

But it was success – and success is the vintage to sustain the spirits of an invading army.

And in those first few days, success for the émigré troops was everywhere. A strategic advance by Général D'Hervilly at the northern end of the Quiberon Peninsula had provided Sir John Warren, in company with the Commander-in-Chief of the invading army, Général de Puisaye, with a contingent of La Châtre Régiment, 1300 Chouans and 250 British marines, to storm and occupy the Fort Sans Culottes some way further to the south.

This, François explained, was of the greatest importance because it would provide a very suitable and secure base for magazines of provisions and stores, a hospital for the sick and wounded – and, perhaps of equal importance, a place in which Georges Cadoudal could drill and discipline his unruly Chouans. Although numerous and very zealous, these peasant troops were not like regular soldiers; they could not be relied on for any distant expeditions; they had a habit, especially the married ones, of returning to their families when they felt so inclined. They needed training and discipline – and Georges Cadoudal, a natural leader if ever there was one, was the man to do it.

François' mention of a hospital had given Rose an idea. Already she and Ashley were dreaming of a moment when both could board one of the British ships returning with despatches to England. But that moment had not yet materialized. Despite being in constant touch with François, who found frequent opportunities to return to the comparative comfort of his 'grand-mère's' château, there had occurred no chance yet of contacting any officer of the British fleet anchored in the bay. Indeed, His Britannic Majesty's Royal Navy was fully occupied keeping a sharp lookout for a reprisal attack by Vice-Admiral Villaret-Joyeuse's fleet to which they had given a drubbing on the way over.

So Rose and Ashley had to await their opportunity.

In the meanwhile, if any help was needed at the hospital, Rose would be there to give it. In the meanwhile also, she would try to discover more details of her ancestry. But the comtesse was evasive. While agreeing that the possession of the locket clearly pointed to a relationship, she would go no further. She was old, she said, and her memory and her mind, sorely affected by the traumas of the Revolution which had sent so many of her friends to the guillotine, were no longer what they had once been. The two portraits up in the attic of which Rose possessed the replicas were of her late husband's parents or even grandparents, she thought. She could not remember. But what she did clearly recollect was her husband telling her that there had been some family schism arising from something to do with the revocation of the Edict of Nantes and the subsequent persecution of the Huguenots.

With that – for the time being – Rose had to be content. Descended from a family of French aristocrats, she felt sure – but in exactly what way, and how it was that her mother came to be shipwrecked off the Cornish coast, she would have to wait to discover. Perhaps she would never fathom the truth. And did it really matter – now that she knew that Ashley loved her? Was that not enough?

And he *did* love her. It *had* to be true – even though he had never actually said so. Men were like that. They could take you in their arms, fondle you with the utmost passion, enter your body and make the most expressive sounds of climactic ecstasy – and yet they seemed to find it quite impossible to say the three simple words, 'I love you!' At least, that was how it seemed to her. And yet he *did* love her – she was sure of it. The way he looked at her; the tenderness in his voice; the care he showed for her every day and the fact that he had sailed across the English Channel and rescued her from the lascivious clutches of Monsieur Bousillier *must* confirm it. He loved her.

But always there was the shadow of Jeannie.

*   *   *

They had run to the beach, Ashley and she, to watch the invasion taking place. It had been exciting. But that was just over four weeks ago.

Now they were running again; running towards a sandy beach. But it was not the same beach. It had the sea all around it; it seemed like the edge of the world.

And this time they were not alone. Everyone around them was running; men, women and children; running pell-mell, scattering clothes, shoes, hats . . . anything, even guns . . . anything that impeded them. They were running for their lives.

Some success had been achieved, it is true. The commander of the escorting British ships, Sir John Warren, had put to sea with 3,500 émigré troops, some in ships of war, the remainder in transports. They had carried with them also a large stock of arms, ammunition and uniforms for the Royalist insurgents known to be waiting for them on the shores of Brittany. Adding quality and 'élan' to the whole enterprise were eighty gentlemen volunteers drawn from the very best blood of France.

Six days later, Sir John was able to inform the First Lord of the Admiralty that he had taken Fort Sans Culottes at Penthièvre on the western side of the narrow strip of land joining Quiberon to the mainland, and although suffering from acute lack of sleep himself, having been up all night for the last three nights, and being forced to dictate his despatch to a confidential secretary aboard his frigate, 'La Pomone', being too tired himself to write, he was nevertheless tolerably well pleased with the success of the operation so far.

But success is a heady wine. Not for seasoned, dedicated officers like John Borlase Warren (intended originally for the church but eventually answering the call of the sea) but for returning émigré soldiers finding ample supplies of the best vintage wines in the recently captured magazines at Fort Sans Culottes. Drunkenness abounded; discipline went out through the portcullis.

And then had come what Pitt had feared – the jealousies and bickerings of a divided command.

'It is like this,' François attempted to explain, 'the Général, le Comte de Puisaye, 'e is very – 'ow you say –

'e is very enthusiastic, 'e is "sanguinaire" – bloodthirsty, yes, but the Général, le Comte d'Hervilly, 'e is an old soldier, you know. So, they put 'im, le Comte d'Hervilly, yes, they make 'im to command the troops – the English as well as the French, you understand, – until they land in France. But it is the Général de Puisaye who makes all the arrangements in England. It is 'e who persuade your Mister Pitt to 'elp us. So, naturally, 'e wants to be in command, you know. So they make 'im the Commander-in-Chief of all the armies, the French Royalists, the English troops, and also the Chouans *after* the landing 'as taken place, if you understand me . . .'

'Sounds like a recipe for disaster,' Ashley commented.

'Exactly! mon ami,' François asserted. 'That is just what it proved to be. D'Hervilly, 'e say 'e wants to command. The Comte de Puisaye, 'e say 'e was appointed by London, and 'e wants to attack while Général Hoche is still gathering 'is Republican troops. So, they decide to refer the matter to London – and you can just imagine how long that would take!'

'At least a week, I should think – even with a fast-sailing frigate,' Ashley observed. 'And knowing how long it takes governments to make up their mind,' he added.

François nodded sagely. 'Quite so, my friend. But in the meanwhile – and especially after your excellent Commodore Warren had 'elped us to take Fort Penthièvre where there was plenty of food and wine – D'Hervilly was in no hurry to move. And when, at last, 'e did decide to attack, it was Général Hoche and 'is Republican "Blues" that give 'im – how you say – "a bloody nose", yes, instead of the other way round. In other words, Général d'Hervilly, in spite of his elaborate movement with four detached columns, was badly beaten. And now we do not know what will 'appen,' François concluded gloomily.

They had been standing at a window in Fort Penthièvre staring out at the driving rain, listening to the howling of the wind of a late July storm. It was eerie.

Ever since the sixteenth day of the month, when Comte

d'Hervilly, at the head of five thousand men, including two hundred British marines, had attacked the right flank of Général Hoche's army, strongly placed on the heights of Sainte Barbe, and been soundly repulsed – Général d'Hervilly being wounded in the battle – ever since that defeat the rot had begun to set in.

Desertions among the enlisted prisoners of war, at first only a trickle, soon turned into a flood. Treachery was everywhere. No one knew who could be trusted. Thousands of local royalist inhabitants had taken refuge in the Fort which, it was felt, was virtually impregnable.

Now, everyone was waiting – waiting for something to happen, waiting for some decisive move by their leaders – waiting for the storm to abate.

Then, suddenly, there came a voice shouting, 'Vive la République!' – the hated cry of the revolutionaries. It was followed by another, and yet another . . . 'Vive la République!' Soon it became a chorus.

There were sounds of running feet. Someone said the guard had deserted; the way was open for the republican soldiers to swarm into the fort. The odious smell of treachery filled the air. Confusion everywhere. Some were for abject surrender; others, more stout-hearted, were determined to fight on to the end.

Briefly, Rose caught sight of the magnetic Georges Cadoudal speaking urgently to his friend, François de Villecourt. She could see why they called him the greatest Chouan of them all. Magnificent, country-bred physique, patrician head, clear eyes, short, curly hair.

''E says 'is Chouans will resist,' François reported. 'They will 'old up the advance of the "Blues" while we escape to the beaches. The British ships will rescue us – but we must 'urry! There is not much time before we are overrun.'

So, now they were running – the republican war-whoop, 'Vive la République!' ringing hideously in their ears – running for their lives, in pitch-darkness, buffeted by the wind, lashed by the pelting rain. Ashley and Rose together – helping a woman and her small boy over the uneven, rocky terrain; Ashley picking up the lad, carrying him over his shoulder, Rose with her arm around the frail waist of the mother, urging her forward.

The British ships would be waiting to rescue them, François had assured. But how were they to get close enough in-shore in this weather? Ashley wondered.

But still they ran.

Shivering in the whipping wind and driving rain, they waited on the beach at Port Haliguen. The Chouans and the troops under the young Comte de Sombreuil were fighting a skilful rearguard action, delaying the advance of Général Hoche's army. But they were all, troops and royalist sympathizers alike, being squeezed down to the southernmost tip of the peninsula. There was nothing beyond that but the sea – and the British ships.

As the first light of a murky dawn illuminated the broad expanse of Quiberon Bay, a cheer went up from the rapidly swelling group of drenched fugitives standing at the water's edge. Commodore Warren's ships had, despite the gale and darkness, worked their way into a position just off the south-east tip of the land. But, as Ashley had feared, the wind and the heavy swell had prevented them from getting close to the shore.

It was close enough, tho', for most of the fugitives to brave the pounding surf. Although the Comte de Sombreuil and his men were bravely resisting to the last, eventually to surrender to the republicans on what were thought to be honourable terms of capitulation, for the rest of the fugitives there was really no alternative but to strike out for the waiting ships. They were quite literally being driven into the sea.

Ashley had always been a strong swimmer, and it was fortunate that Rose's father had, at a very early age, taught her to swim in the clear but sometimes rough waters off the Cornish coast. The prospect ahead of them, therefore, held no great terrors – although it terrified the frail woman, if not her little boy who was too young to understand the danger. He was quite content to be in the hands of the big, strong man who was carrying him.

While Rose urged the woman to plunge into the waves, Ashley secured the little boy's arms around his neck, and then struck out for the nearest 'chasse marée' which was edging towards the shore. With one hand helping Rose to propel the mother through the surf, he guided them all towards the boat, relieved to see that a young seaman was already hanging over the gunwale, ready to haul exhausted swimmers aboard.

First, Ashley handed the boy into the massive arms of the sailor, who deposited the child safely on the deck, and then he and Rose, together, managed to hoist the near-drowned mother aboard as well.

After that, it was Rose's turn. By now, the stamina-sapping exertion of getting from shore to ship, and helping a near-exhausted woman, had become too much. In a moment of freezing horror, Ashley saw Rose's clutching fingers slither from the gunwale. The next minute she had disappeared beneath the swell. Frantically he dived for her . . . caught her as she was going down, hauled her to the surface. Her eyes were closed in a dead faint; the final effort had been too much. Another second . . . and he would have lost her forever. As it was, even in that short while, such was the power of the swell around them that they had drifted an alarming distance from the boat, and Ashley had to summon all his diminishing strength to regain the boat.

There, the strong hands of the sailor gripped Rose's arms, hauled her aboard, and tenderly swept the bedraggled strands of hair from her face. Ashley, climbing aboard unaided, was utterly astonished to hear the sailer exclaim in a familiar Cornish accent, 'Well, blister m' tripes! but if 'tedn Rosie!'

Hearing his voice filtering through the mists of returning consciousness, Rose was suddenly transported back in time to a summer's evening long ago. She was a child again, and she was returning to Thorn Cottage after having tea with her friend, Mellie, when she felt herself pinned against the hedgebank. A thick, familiar voice had purred in her ear, 'Hullo, Rosie. I got somethin' I wants to show ee . . . 'tis somethin' rather special, like' . . . and the accosting youth had hitched her dress on his rampant penis.

Now the voice was the same. And when at last she opened her eyes, she saw that it was Myron Pinnerton.

CHAPTER TWENTY-THREE

A Green and Pleasant Land

Having had his bottom as well as the procreative parts of his anatomy comprehensively tarred and feathered – he knew not exactly by whom but he had some very shrewd suspicions – and then having been fastened to the railings of the White Hart Inn to be pilloried by his schoolmates next morning, Myron Pinnerton had learnt his lesson. He no longer had any inclination to abuse little girls.

Instead – and as a direct result of his traumatic experience – he had run away from home and joined the Royal Navy. He had been rewarded for this quasi-patriotic action by falling in with Ruby Trevithick, the buxom lass who helped out of an evening at the Five Pilchards in Falmouth, the inn which was kept by Fanny Reynolds and her cheerful little husband, Mattie.

Now Ruby Trevithick was not, to use her own words, 'very pertikler' about the men she entertained – so long as they were big and strong. She was nearly always ready and willing, and she found Myron Pinnerton of special interest – extra-special interest, in fact, because Ruby Trevithick was always rather inclined towards *quantity* rather than quality. Big, for Ruby therefore, was quite definitely beautiful – and Myron Pinnerton filled the bill very adequately.

And this suited Myron as well. He now felt sure that whenever his ship was in Falmouth, Ruby would be waiting for him. The fact that she would also be waiting for others besides himself did not worry him overmuch. What he needed was extensive sexual exercise; to indulge himself to the very limit of his very considerable capacity. He required little else while in port. And Ruby Trevithick, good-hearted soul that she was, readily satisfied his voracious appetite – even though it left her feeling like a dishevelled gargany over-trodden by an outsize goosander.

But it did a world of good for Myron. It sent him back to his ship feeling refreshed, manly – and sure in the knowledge that his formidable anatomical equipment was really appreciated.

And he liked the navy. He did not mind long periods at sea . . . so long as he had Ruby, or her like, waiting to satisfy him on his return. After all, an indulgence after long contemplation is sometimes all the sweeter in eventual fulfilment. And the sea was in his blood; he had taken to it naturally.

So much so that when, after many years' absence from his home in St Keverne, he had set eyes again on the girl he had once so inexpertly tried to ravish in the field between Thorn Cottage and Trynance, he had risen to the exalted rank of bos'un in his ship, the 44-gun frigate HMS *Anson*.

It was in this capacity – one of no small pride to the former youth who had been pilloried by his younger school-mates – that he had greeted a bedraggled Rose with, ''Tis a right small world, i'nt it, Rosie,' as, throwing a blanket around her shoulders, he had helped her aboard his ship.

He had always liked Rose, even though he had constantly teased her at school – often the cloak for youthful infatua-tion – and now he looked at her more closely after she had dried her hair and settled into the welcome warmth of the blanket, he thought she was more beautiful than ever.

And although he still desired her – he had missed nothing of the way her wet clothes had clung to her shapely body as he hauled her from the sea – instinct told him that she would never yield to him like Ruby did – especially with this broad-shouldered companion of hers so closely in attendance.

Nevertheless, like a good Cornishman he felt a special bond of kinship with her, coming as she did from the same village. So, he would look after her while she was

316

in his ship – with the captain's permission, of course.

Having done all he could to rescue the royalist fugitives, Commodore Warren had, without opposition, taken possession of the nearby islands of Houat and Hoëdic, garrisoning the fort on the former and disembarking those fugitives, including Rose and Ashley, who wished to land.

After the turmoil, the treachery and the bloodshed of recent weeks, the peace and the plenty of the island of Houat was idyllic. And in the wake of the storm came the balm – warm sunshine and sou'westerly breezes tempered by the bastion of Belle-Ile.

After a day or two, the news went around the island that the Commodore had made arrangements for all those who wished to do so, especially old men, women and children, to return to the mainland; he had received what he believed to be satisfactory assurances that they would be allowed to reoccupy their homes, unmolested. He was more than glad to make this arrangement because he had brought with him from the tip of the Quiberon Peninsula, escaping from the advancing republican army, over one thousand and eight hundred souls, including 500 Chouans. They were eating too much of the food needed for his forces.

'I wish we could stay here for ever,' Ashley suddenly said, holding Rose's hand, and gazing up at the azure sky. 'I wish we never had to go back.'

They were lying at the edge of a small, sandy cove, watching the wavelets rhythmically lapping the rocks.

'It's remarkably like Cornwall, this – isn't it,' Rose observed, idly drawing with her finger in the sand.

'That's not the reason why I don't want to go back,' Ashley replied. 'It has nothing to do with the similarity or otherwise to our homeland.'

'I know it hasn't,' Rose said quietly. 'I know why you don't want to go back.'

They lay silent, side by side, each deeply preoccupied with intensely personal thoughts. 'Back' – or home – for Rose meant Thorn Cottage and the loving couple, Sampson and Amia Roskruge, who had rescued her from the pounding

317

waves of Godrevy Beach, twenty-five years ago, and brought her up as a Cornish country maid in the isolated, sea-girt village of St Keverne. It meant also The Three Tuns Inn, rebuilt after the fire it was true, but still only a small country tavern. Cheerful, good-hearted customers, imbibing their daily quota of intoxicating liquor, pulling her leg, making hopeful, licentious innuendoes, asking sly, thinly-veiled questions about, 'What be doin' wi' yersel' all this time, then Rose? Havin' a high ole time up at the "big house" wi' the gentry, eh?' It would be well-meaning, it would carry no malice, but it was not an exciting prospect for a girl who had ascended the heights – as well as the depths – of every emotion imaginable.

For Ashley, it would mean returning to Jeannie – to her bed, to her body, and to a love that had long since grown cold. Love? Had it been love – or had it really been no more than an irresistible stimulation of the physical senses?

He did not know. All he was sure of was that having climbed to the absolute pinnacle of sexual fulfilment with Rosie, the thought of having to make love to Jeannie was, if not actually repugnant, at least repellent.

On a sudden impulse, he rolled over and gathered Rose into his arms.

'Why *can't* we stay here for ever?' he groaned, burying his face in her curls. 'Would it be so impossible to live out the rest of our lives, together, on this idyllic small island – away from everything and everybody – castaways, not on a desert island, but in a green and pleasant land? Make an entirely fresh start – as man and wife – our marriage blessed, not by the dogmas of out-dated religion, but by the more realistic yet unseen hand of fate.'

He lifted his head; looked straight into her eyes – searchingly. 'Could we not?' he said, quietly.

For a long time Rose lay beside him, staring up at the sky. What a wonderful idea! Why should they not. Was this not what, for so long – during those endless hours of darkness and filth in the dungeon of the Château de Pontrechat – she had dreamed of. To be alone with Ashley; to be his

318

wife; to bear his children. Was this not really what she had lived for during the whole of her life; an idyllic end to a strange and chequered existence?

Should she not answer his plea with an emphatic 'Yes!' Surely they could find some way to make a living; they were both strong and healthy, and on this fruitful island there must be work to do.

But when she sat up, propping herself on one arm, the tears were streaming down her face. She slowly shook her head, the teardrops making mocking patterns in the sand.

'No,' she said softly, 'we could never be happy. In the end it would catch up with us. There would be too much guilt.'

CHAPTER TWENTY-FOUR

Homeward Bound

It was Myron Pinnerton who told them. He had clambered over the rocks separating the beach from the jetty, having spotted them as he came ashore in HMS *Anson*'s launch.

'Beg pardon, Rosie, . . . er . . . Miss Rosie, I should say,' he began, with exaggerated politeness, '. . . and excusin' I, sir,' he continued, glancing none too warmly at Ashley, who he remembered as the Riding Officer for the St Keverne district, 'but I thought ee might like to learn that the *Anson*'s sailin' tonight wi' the despatches, like. I thought ee might like to know.'

'Oh, thank you, Myron,' Rose answered, a sinking feeling suddenly developing in her stomach. 'Thank you for telling us.'

Myron hesitated; reluctant to leave; uncertain that the purport of his message had been fully understood. He put his hand to his mouth, coughed respectfully, and tried again. 'I was thinkin', how you an' the gentleman, Mr Penberth, might be wishin' to return home, like . . .'

How he's changed, Rose thought. From the rough-tongued, uncouth, loping youth of ten or more years ago, the navy had licked him into the shape of an upright, polite and seemingly efficient sailor. Was that the result of the well-known naval floggings? she wondered , . . . floggings for being the last man down from the yards, floggings for the merest whiff of disagreement or insubordination, floggings to within an inch of a man's life – and frequently beyond. Or was it the result of kindness? She was afraid it must be the former; kindness was not a quality for which the navy

320

was renowned. Silence, perhaps; but consideration and care, hardly. And yet there were some, they did say – and Cornwall's own Admiral Boscawen was among them – who had done much to minimize the harshness of a sailor's life.

'He'm a very hanzum gentleman, is Cap'n Durham,' Myron was saying, 'an' I do feel reasonable certin that if you was to have a word wi' un, Rosie . . . I mean, Mistress Rosie . . . if you was to have a word wi' the gentleman . . . Cap'n Durham, I mean . . .'

Again Rose thanked him. He looked so changed; so smart in his petticoat trousers, striped waistcoat and tarred straw hat; she could hardly believe the transformation. And yet the news he had brought her not only induced a churning sensation in her stomach, it also started a knell peeling in her mind. It meant the beginning of the end of a dream. They were going home.

There had been no difficulty. Ashley had sought, and been granted, an interview with Commodore Warren with whom he had quickly established a rapport. In the early days of his somewhat irregular naval service, John Borlase Warren had been employed on preventive duties along the east coast in the sloop 'Alderney', and when in the course of conversation he heard that Ashley was a former Riding Officer in the service of HM Customs, reminiscences soon began to flow.

A request was quickly transmitted to Captain Durham, and that very same evening, with Rose and Ashley on board, HMS *Anson* weighed anchor in Houat Road and set sail for Plymouth.

Captain Durham was politeness itself. He asked no questions, and having installed his two civilian passengers, whom he understandably took to be man and wife, in a small cabin aft of the mainmast, he then got on with making all speed with the despatches he had been ordered to deliver.

Coming on deck early next morning, with the sun already rising strongly in a clear, mid-summer sky, Rose and Ashley were greeted by a breathtaking sight. HMS *Anson*, under full sail and running proud before a brisk sou'westerly breeze, was passing – perilously close, it seemed – to the razor-sharp rocks of the Pointe du Raz. In the background lay the low outline of the rocky coast of Finisterre; in the foreground the shoal waters, feathered by the wind like swansdown blown from a dark blue carpet, masked the terror of the jagged rocks beneath the surface.

Rose shuddered involuntarily. 'Like the Manacles,' she said. And then pointing to a narrow strip of unruffled water between mainland and rocks, she added, 'And just look at that fishing lugger, working between the mainland and that terrifying group of rocks!'

She was forcing herself to make conversation. It was hard for both of them; both knew they were sailing inexorably towards separation. In another twenty-four hours or less they would have parted. It was like a massive stone bearing them to the ground, crushing them beneath its weight. Try as they would, they could not hold it up . . . could not escape the inevitable. Each bow wave surging away amid a shower of spray merely reminded them that, minute by minute, they were approaching their journey's end – and goodbye.

But she would not think about it, Rose kept telling herself. At all costs she would try to remain cheerful to the end. She wanted Ashley always to remember her as someone who had brought laughter and merriment into his life. She would not allow herself to be downcast. Whatever the future might hold for them, she would not allow these last hours together to be overshadowed by gloomy foreboding.

Ashley, following the direction of her pointing finger, remarked tonelessly, 'Yes, I can see it. Again, it's like the Manacles.' He was remembering how his father, according to hearsay, had tried to go through the Manacles while fleeing from the attentions of a revenue cruiser, long, long ago – and had been wrecked in the process. And for her part, Rose was remembering how her mother – again according to what she had been told – had been wrecked on those same fearsome Manacles rocks.

The silent recollections did nothing to cheer their spirits. But Ashley persisted, also anxious not to allow the gloom

322

to settle suffocatingly. 'And not unlike the Pointe de St Mathieu,' he said.

'And where's that?' Rose asked with forced brightness.

'Between Ushant and the mainland,' Ashley informed. 'We shall see it in a few moments, I expect. Over the star-board bow. Over there, look. I think I can just make it out.'

They fell silent again as HMS *Anson*, gently plunging and rearing to the rise and fall of the sea, ploughed her way towards the Chenal du Four between Le Conquet and the Isle de Beniguet.

'There it is, now,' Ashley pointed. 'You can see the church quite clearly. A useful landmark . . .'

Like St Keverne church spire, Rose thought.

'. . . for homecoming sailors,' Ashley added. 'François pointed it out when we came over. You keep it on your larboard beam when you start to go into Brest.'

The mention of François de Villecourt did not help. It was inadvertently made – but it still did not lighten the melancholy.

Shortly before HMS *Anson* left the Houat roadstead, bear-ing Commodore Warren's depressing despatch to the First Lord reporting the debacle at Fort Penthièvre and the sub-sequent evacuation of the mainland, news had come through that the rearguard under the young Comte de Sombreuil, fighting bravely to the last, and with François among them, had been granted terms of surrender.

No one knew exactly what those terms were – severe or lenient – but they feared the worst because Jean Lambert Tallien, commissioner for the Convention at Paris, paramour of the impeccably beautiful Madame de Fontenay, had been sent to Vannes to dispose of the troublesome captured royalists. Later it would emerge that he had decreed they should be shot – more than six hundred of them, including the Comte de Sombreuil and the Bishop of Dol, standing against a wall with their hands tied behind their backs. Some were massacred at Quiberon, some at Auray, the remainder at Vannes.

* * *

The Mail Coach from Plymouth was an hour late arriving at Falmouth. After a hot, dusty journey it rattled to a halt outside the Royal Hotel at half past five.

Climbing down from the outside seats, and brushing the dust from the new suit of clothes he had obtained in Plymouth – a customer reject of a high-collared brown cloth coat, cream-coloured waistcoat and buff breeches which although far from perfect, at least fitted tolerably well – Ashley was the first to alight. He then turned to assist Rose. She, too, had been able to acquire a new outfit – a riding habit of pompadour broadcloth – also a tailor's reject – a habit shirt of long lawn, and a pair of silver-buckled brown shoes.

As he lifted her down onto the cobbled forecourt, her cheeks prettily flushed from exposure to sun and fresh air, Ashley thought he had never seen her looking more lovely.

Immediately, one of the hotel porters was at his elbow. 'Carry your bags, sir?' he enquired eagerly, and was disappointed when Ashley indicated they had travelled without luggage.

It was the same at the hotel reception desk when Ashley, having requested a double room for the night, informed the identical, thick-headed porter that his services would not be required. The expression of surprise, puzzlement and vexation on the man's face – his eyebrows shot up into his wrinkled forehead with a look of bewildered disbelief – provided for Rose and Ashley almost the only moment of comedy in an evening over-shadowed by foreboding.

The room, containing a large four-poster and a marble-topped washstand, was uninspiring but at least adequate, and after a refreshing wash in delightfully cold water, they descended to the dining room.

Dinner, though plain, plentiful and wholesome, they could only pick at. Appetite, it seemed, had been left on the far side of the English Channel – in the servants' quarters of the Château de Plouvenez, and at the well-scrubbed kitchen table.

Conversation, too, was less than scintillating. It was brittle. It was as though they felt that, somehow, by keeping up a ceaseless flow of banalities they could hold back the tide of tomorrow; for tomorrow, as they were both poignantly aware, they must part – Rose to return to her loving parents at St Keverne, Ashley to his wife at Boscraddoc.

They finished dinner – and went straight up to bed.

Uppermost was the thought – the stark, ineradicable and off-recurring realization – that this must be their last night together. They discussed – oh, how often had they done so, up and down, round and round – the possibility that they might be able, no matter what the future held for them, to keep a 'lifeline' open between them. He would return to being a Riding Officer – how could he, in all honour, continue to accept Sir Andrew MacKenzie's bounty even though he might still be married, in name only, to his daughter. He would then come to St Keverne as often as he could. He would put up for the night at the Three Tuns Inn, as in the old days, and they could then be together.

Even to Rose, this bleak prospect – the waiting, the wondering, the never knowing if and when he was coming to her – the inevitable frustrations and insecurities of being his mistress – even that was better than losing him altogether.

That night, in the four-poster bed at the Royal Hotel in Falmouth their repeated love-making had the intensity of desperation. Each time it would be the last; each time they tried to raise it to the level of the stars. But there were no stars; there was no heaven. There was only apprehension.

At last, physically exhausted, and clasped in each other's arms as though afraid to let go, they fell asleep.

* * *

The sun was already streaming in through the bedroom window when Ashley awoke. It was late. He had overslept.

Turning over, to take Rose in his arms once more – for the very last time – he realized, with a sudden shock, that she was no longer there. He sat bolt upright. It was true; her place in the bed beside him was empty. Where once she had lain, warm, vibrant and alluringly desirable, there was now nothing but a pile of cold rumpled sheets. Nor was there any sign of her clothes, anywhere. She had gone.

Leaping off the bed, he crossed to the window; stared down into the courtyard below. No sign of her there; nothing but the normal morning activity of a busy sea-port hotel – guests departing, others arriving from a recently docked packet ship; a man with a shovel gathering steaming horse-droppings into his barrow.

But not a sign of Rose.

It was just like her, he reflected. She would wish to save him the embarrassment of 'goodbye'; it would be her choice to save each other from the agony of parting.

For a long time he stood by the window, staring down; he felt as though he had just been wrung through a mangle.

At first, he could not face the prospect of returning straightaway to Boscraddoc. He would do almost anything to put off the evil moment.

He paid his hotel bill, and then went down to the Packet Quay. He would immerse himself in the comings and goings, the hustle and bustle of the quayside. He stood, with one foot on a capstan, watching the crates of oranges being off-loaded, the sacks of potatoes and the bags of flour being carried on board. He drew comfort from the small groups of departing passengers and their attendant well-wishers, some maintaining an attitude of forced cheerfulness, others making no attempt to hide their tears. Clearly, there were those beside himself in the grip of distress. It brought him consolation. He was not alone.

He delayed for as long as he could, drawing courage from the throbbing life-blood of the busy port, composing his resolve – and every now and then castigating himself for his reluctance to face up to the task ahead.

Then, as though a spring had suddenly snapped within him, he set his face and his footsteps towards Boscraddoc.

He decided to go by the coastal path, along to Maenporth, and then up the smuggler's lane leading to Carlidnack and the smithy at Mawnan. Approaching the Red Lion Inn he slowed his pace. Should he go in for a 'stiffener'. 'Tub'

326

Richards, he who ran the smithy as well as the inn, and who had made the iron splint after Degory Logan had performed the skilful but excruciatingly painful operation on Ashley's leg after he had broken it at school – 'Tub' would certainly provide the warmest of welcomes, as well as a good strong measure of spirits to go with it.

It was tempting. It would bolster his courage – and he was feeling in need of that. He had been trying to compose his opening sentence upon greeting his wife. But what did a man say after being away so long? How did he tell his wife he no longer loved her – that he had fallen deeply, irrevocably in love with another woman? What was the language of rejection; how could one soften the blow?

A drop of brandy inside him would probably help. He slowed his pace still further as he came abreast of the familiar thatch-roofed inn.

And then he decided against it. It would merely put off the evil hour. Better to press on and get it over with.

He quickened his pace once more, striding resolutely ahead until he came to the long drive leading down to Boscraddoc. Nothing had changed. The solid, stone façade, with its two mullioned windows on each side of the front entrance, and its six similar windows above, was casting warm, lazy shadows up the drive as the sun began sinking in the western sky. It was in that bedroom, the one with the two windows to the left above the front door arch – the main bedroom in the house – that he had made such passionate love on the first night of his honeymoon. He remembered also how astonished he had been at the realization that Jeannie was not a virgin. And yet the memory stabbed at his heart. How could he now tell that beautiful, eager young bride that he had found a deeper love, a more fulfilling passion? How could he confess – as confess he must – that he never should have married her; that it was a mistake – an exciting passionate one – but a mistake, nevertheless?

He braced himself; set off down the drive.

The afternoon was now well-advanced, and the farm buildings to the right of the house were clothed in that stillness which descends on a farmyard at the end of the working day. The farm hands would be at their tea, gratefully relaxing after a hard day's labour. They would be going out again after tea to continue working in the fields until darkness sent them indoors again, but now it was time for tea and afterwards a short doze. Everything, in fact, seemed to be dozing, a hot summer's day was slipping down quietly into a warm, scented evening.

Ashley turned left at the bottom of the drive and made for the lych gate in the yew hedge which bordered and sheltered the terraced rose garden. He lifted the latch, pushed open the gate and went through into the neatly kept garden. He often used that way of entering the house, especially when returning on foot from shooting or from some farming activity; it was a convenient way round to the back door where he would take off his muddy boots before going indoors. As often as not, when passing the garden door and the windows overlooking the rose garden, he would see Jeannie reclining on the chaise longue with a book of her favourite poems in her hand. He would give her a cheery wave, go on round to the back door, divest himself of his country garments and then join her for tea in the drawing room.

As he now crossed the lawn, he noticed that the garden door was flung wide open. That was quite natural on a hot summer's day.

Once more he braced himself for the meeting with Jeannie. The moment had come. There was no going back. He must go through with it now.

He was about to enter through the garden doorway when he suddenly pulled up sharply – frozen to the spot.

On the carpet, near the chaise longue, a pair of black leather dragoon-type boots, obviously kicked off in a hurry, lay one on top of the other in an untidy heap. Beside them, in matching disarray, lay a pair of Jeannie's shoes.

Ashley took one tentative step closer – and then wished that he had not. On the sofa itself lay his wife, one exposed stockinged and gartered leg, crooked at the knee, was pointing ceilingwards; the other, horizontal and similarly

328

exposed, pointed towards the garden windows. In this cleft of erotic promise, and surrounded by a flurry of disarranged petticoat and underskirts, a pair of stockinged feet with breeches wrinkled and at half-mast around the wearer's ankles projected from the end of the chaise longue. Higher up, a pair of pink buttocks heaved with mounting fury.

Involuntarily – or was it at the devil's prompting – Ashley cleared his throat. For a fleeting moment, Jeannie, her face flushed and buried deep in a halo of dark curls, opened one climactic-glazed eye. She closed it again immediately, submerged by the sudden flood of sensual ecstasy.

But she had seen him.

Ashley hurriedly retreated, his heart pounding alarmingly. Despite his own infidelity – which he neither would nor could ever attempt to deny – it had nevertheless been a great shock to find his wife, 'in flagrante delicto', in the very act of copulation . . . and there was no doubt in his mind about the owner of those dragoon boots, those breeches, and those pink pulsating buttocks. Liggett-Fanshawe, the inveterate bully who might well have ended the young Penberth's life when he had hung him out of the high dormitory window at Lydford College and beaten his knuckles until the guiltless new boy could hold no longer. Now, the same Liggett-Fanshawe was taking his pleasure with his former victim's wife.

Ashley knew that he ought to feel utterly outraged; that he should now go straight into that drawing room, pull the prostrate, exhausted Liggett-Fanshawe to his feet and demand satisfaction from the scoundrel. He should use his own vastly superior strength to give the man the hiding of his life.

But he did nothing of the kind. Was there not a saying about people who lived in glass houses being well advised not to throw stones; was there not another proverb discouraging a man from looking a gift-horse in the mouth!

He slowly, thoughtfully, made his way down to the stable where he knew he would find his favourite mount, the cob Puncher, with whom he had shared so many lonely hours while riding the coast as one of His Majesty's Riding Officers in former years. The soft velvet of Puncher's nose, nuzzling his master's face in affectionate greeting, touched Ashley greatly. It soothed the pounding of his heart, calmed his nerves, clarified his thoughts.

After a while of patting and fondling an old friend, Ashley lifted a saddle from the saddle rack, threw it across Puncher's back, and to the accompaniment of whinnyings of delight he inserted a bridle and fastened the girth.

Then he swung up into the saddle. 'St Keverne, Puncher,' he commanded, as he had so often spoken to the horse in days gone by. 'St Keverne, laddie – and let's not be long about it. We'll take the coastal route, just like we used to in the old days – by Gweek and Manaccan, and then down to the coast at Porthallow and Porthoustock, remember?' He gathered up the reins, climbed into the saddle, and galloped off up the drive in a cloud of summer dust.

The Three Tuns Inn at St Keverne had been rebuilt since the fire, taller and straighter, and altogether more modern-looking, and Ashley no longer had to duck as he entered by the stable-yard door.

The bar was very much as he remembered it – except, of course, that it all looked newly decorated. The high-backed wooden settle had somehow survived the fire, and on it now sat the same old 'regulars', their blackened clay pipes still sprouting from their wizened faces.

Landlord Will Trenethy was the same, too; a little older perhaps; a bit more bent and shrunken, possibly – but still the same old nervous, haunted-looking Will Trenethy.

And when Ashley stalked into the bar, poor old Will looked as though he'd seen a ghost. His hand flew to his mouth, and with that well-remembered gesture, he nervously dabbed at his mouth with his fingertips.

Ashley recollected it all so clearly. Will had looked just like he did now, on the night of the fire when the inn had been burnt almost to the ground – the night when the 'gentlemen' of St Keverne and P'roustock had planned the biggest 'run' of contraband ever.

It was then he had first known Rosie.

As the Riding Officer of HM Customs, he had arrived at the inn unexpected, and at the most inconvenient moment possible. It was absolutely imperative that he should be got out of the way while the 'run' of brandy, 'baccy, silks and tea was successfully carried out. So, they had got the Riding Officer drunk – or very nearly so – and because her father, to whom she was devoted, was involved with the 'run', they had persuaded their comely young barmaid, Rosie Roskruge, to make sure that this tiresome King's Man was very much 'otherwise engaged' while the fleet of pack ponies went trotting into the night.

Will Trenethy was looking now just as he had then – almost paralyzed with nerves. Perhaps there was a 'run' on tonight, Ashley thought, suppressing a revealing smile. Will Trenethy would never believe that Ashley Penberth was no longer a Riding Officer, even though he had discarded the sky-blue coat and the naval-type cutlass he always used to wear. A suspicious landlord would think the high-collared brown cloth coat, the cream-coloured waistcoat and the buff breeches were just a clever disguise – to put them off their guard, and to catch them at it just the same.

But now, Will Trenethy had no Rosie – only a young lad to wash the pots and clean the floor of the bar. So, what in God's good name could he do – and altho' the rumour had flashed round the village, as rumours will, that 'Rosie is back!' he could never ask her to do again what she had done so successfully no more than a year or two back.

Or could he! If it were true that Rosie had indeed come home, might it not be worth a try. After all, he always knew that Rosie was rather 'pertikler fond' of the handsome Riding Officer, 'quite taken a shine to un', she had . . . so, might it not, in the desperate circumstances in which he found himself, might it not be worth a try.

Ever an optimist, albeit driven on by nerves and the ugly spectre of the gallows awaiting smugglers caught in the act, Will Trenethy decided to send his potboy down to Thorn Cottage, Rosenithon, with a very specially urgent message to an equally special young lady who, it was believed, had very recently returned from somewhere abroad.

And only just in time, Will reflected, when Ashley requested a room for the night – just exactly as he had done on that night of the fire.

Fearing, as previously, that a refusal might indicate guilt, Will dutifully showed Ashley up to the guest bedroom, the one with the immaculate view over Falmouth Bay.

'And send up some supper in due course, will you, Will,' he had requested, before slipping out of his new brown cloth coat, rolling up the sleeves of his cambric shirt and plunging his hands and face into cold water in the washstand.

It was as he was drying his face, looking out of the window, that he heard the back door slam, and a few seconds later saw Will's potboy scooting off in the direction of Rosenithon as though the hounds of hell were on his track. Smiling wryly to himself, Ashley murmured out loud, 'He's off to warn somebody. Perhaps there really *is* a "run" on tonight.'

He put his jacket on again and sat down at the table in the window to admire the view while at the same time trying to assemble his thoughts and plans into some kind of coherence.

So preoccupied was he with the problems that must inevitably lie ahead – divorce was an almost interminably protracted business as well as being ruinously expensive, while to live in sin was to invite the opprobrium of all decent society – problems that went round and round and round in his head, so much so that as he sat gazing at the beauty of the fading sunlit scene he lost all track of time.

He was just beginning to feel hungry, and wondering if his supper would soon be coming up, when there was a firmly struck knock on the door.

Casually he called 'Come in', while continuing to stare out of the window.

The door opened; there was a rustle of taffeta, and a lilting, almost cheeky voice said, 'Your supper, sir. Sorry its been so long a-coming.'

Ashley swung round, eyes blazing. The voice was unmistakable – unforgettable. 'Rosie!'

332

He took her in his arms, crushed her to him, speechless with joy.

For a long time they remained, clasped in each other's arms, savouring the magic of this unforeseen moment of reunion.

Then, at last, she drew away and looked into his eyes. She knew she must ask the question which had been filling her every moment since, very early that morning, she had slipped out of the hotel and made her way back to Rosenithon.

'What happened?' she asked simply.

He told her. He spared no detail.

She moved away to the window; stared out at the gathering darkness.

After a while, he joined her there; put his arm around her waist; drew her close.

'How did you know I was here?' he asked.

She turned; looked at him once more. A mischievous twinkle had crept into her eyes. So often in the past he had marvelled at the unquenchable effervescence of her spirit. Never had he known her to be truly down-hearted for very long. And now, even when she must be realizing how uncertain would be the future for them both, she could not let slip the chance of a teasing jest. She could never allow the gloom-clouds to gather oppressively.

'Will sent for me,' she said impishly. 'He'd heard I was home. He's really rather desperate,' she added, her eyes glowing with girlish mischief, 'because, you see, the "gentlemen" of P'roustock and St Keverne are about to make the biggest "run" they've ever attempted – and Will's quite convinced that you're still the Riding Officer.'

'Ye-es,' Ashley murmured. 'I thought he was very jumpy when I came in.'

'He was remembering that night, long ago, when another such "run" was about to be made . . .' Rose continued.

'And when the Riding Officer turned up at a *very* inconvenient moment,' Ashley observed darkly.

'And what happened then?' Rose prompted. She was smiling wickedly; looking quite ravishingly beautiful.

333

'I seem to remember,' he answered, 'that they – and especially the barmaid – got that same poor Riding Officer inordinately drunk.'

'You remember that, then?'

Ashley laughed. 'Oh yes, I remember that, all right.'

'And what then?'

'That same exceptionally pretty barmaid, wearing a dress which made a rustling noise whenever she moved, brought up my supper . . . into this very same room . . . except that it was different because . . .'

'And what was the colour of that dress?' Rose interrupted. 'D'you remember?'

'I remember it well,' he said. 'It was like the one you're wearing now.'

'It *was* the one I'm wearing now,' she declared.

He laughed again; took her in his arms; kissed her tenderly. He couldn't resist it. 'Quite like old times,' he murmured into her curls.

'And do you, by any chance, remember the rest of that scene,' she went on, taking hold of the lapels of his new brown cloth coat and gently easing the garment off his shoulders, 'on the night when The Three Tuns Inn got burnt to the ground?'

'Yes,' he replied, with mock deliberation, 'I remember that, too. It was the night when that Riding Officer fell deeply in love with the barmaid.'

Unresisting, he allowed her to propel him towards the bed – just as she had done on that special night, now seeming so far distant. First, she pulled back the coverlet; then she laid him down gently on the feather-filled mattress, removed his boots and stockings, and then his breeches – as on that former occasion.

He pretended to be drunk; pretended not to see her pull the dark blue taffeta-silk dress over her head and stand before him, most desirably, in her gartered stockings and short chemise. But, through half-closed eyes he enjoyed every moment.

'You do understand, Mr Penberth,' she said with

deliberately affected coquettishness, 'that I'm doing this for the landlord, Will Trenethy, and also to protect my beloved father . . .'

For answer, Ashley grasped her hand – pulled her down on to the bed. The time for play-acting was over.

As she melted into his arms beneath the coverlet, he fondled her with a tenderness passing belief – caressing her cheek, her brow, her nose and then her lips – exploring the contours of her warm, supple body with all the ardour of a first embrace.

Together, coupled at last in perfect harmony, they began the ascent of sublime sensual desire . . . slowly at first . . . and then with mounting frenzy . . . until at last they burst through the mists of complete erotic fulfilment, into the mystic wonder of the heavens and the stars.

Slowly . . . slowly . . . they descended from this realm of hitherto untasted ecstasy, the very elixir of the gods still seeming fresh upon their lips . . . down, down, slowly down . . . to the more abiding warmth of passionless love.

But he still clung to her; still gently caressed her curls, her cheeks, her lips.

The way ahead must inevitably be strewn with many difficulties, many emotional traumas – rivers to be forded, mountains to be climbed – but he had found her again.

And *this* time he would *never* let her go.

. THE END

A SELECTED LIST OF NOVELS
AVAILABLE FROM BANTAM BOOKS

THE PRICES SHOWN BELOW WERE CORRECT AT THE TIME OF GOING TO PRESS.
HOWEVER BANTAM BOOKS RESERVE THE RIGHT TO SHOW NEW RETAIL PRICES
ON COVERS WHICH MAY DIFFER FROM THOSE PREVIOUSLY ADVERTISED IN
THE TEXT OR ELSEWHERE.

☐	17383 9	PRIVILEGE	*Leona Blair*	£3.50
☐	17172 0	WILD SWAN	*Celeste De Blasis*	£3.95
☐	17252 2	SWAN'S CHANCE	*Celeste De Blasis*	£2.95
☐	17268 9	IMPULSE	*Barbara Harrison*	£3.50
☐	17208 5	PASSION'S PRICE	*Barbara Harrison*	£2.95
☐	17185 2	THIS CHERISHED DREAM	*Barbara Harrison*	£2.95
☐	17207 7	FACES	*Johanna Kingsley*	£2.95
☐	17151 8	SCENTS	*Johanna Kingsley*	£2.95
☐	17242 5	I'LL TAKE MANHATTAN	*Judith Krantz*	£3.95
☐	17174 7	MISTRAL'S DAUGHTER	*Judith Krantz*	£2.95
☐	17389 8	PRINCESS DAISY	*Judith Krantz*	£3.95
☐	17209 3	THE CLASS	*Erich Segal*	£2.95
☐	17192 5	THE ENCHANTRESS	*Han Suyin*	£2.95
☐	17150 X	TILL MORNING COMES	*Han Suyin*	£3.50
☐	17285 9	THE RIDING OFFICER	*Richard Stuart Wood*	£2.95

BANTAM BOOKS READERS' SERVICE, 61-63 Uxbridge Road, Ealing, London, W5 5SA.

Please send cheque or postal order, not cash. All cheques and postal orders must be in £ sterling
and made payable to Bantam Books Ltd.

Please allow cost of book(s) plus the following for postage and packing:

UK/Republic of Ireland Customers:
Orders in excess of £5; no charge.
Orders under £5; add 50p.

Overseas Customers:
All orders; add £1.50.

NAME (Block Letters): ....

ADDRESS ....

....